THE TRUTH ABOUT YOU

A NOVEL

MELISSA HILL

D1714675

Revised & updated print edition, 2023.
First published in the UK as 'The Truth About You'
by Hodder & Stoughton, 2010.

Copyright Little Blue Books, 2023

PREFACE

This book was written, produced and edited in the UK, where some spelling, grammar and word usage will vary from US English.

PROLOGUE

'The first thing that crossed my mind was that it had to be my doughnut delivery,' Ella began, 'or a delivery of some kind – it isn't unusual to find fresh stock on the doorstep so early in the morning.'

'What time was it, exactly?'

'Well, let me think ...' She paused for a moment. 'The milk is usually dropped off around five - a good two hours before I open up - and my usual half a dozen litres is tucked away to the left of the doorway. But the box was right on the front step, making it impossible for me to miss.'

'I see.'

'I was a bit annoyed to be honest, and thought I'd have to give the wholesaler a piece of my mind for not telling me they'd be delivering outside opening hours,' she continued, her tone measured. 'And then just as I was about to open the box, I heard ... well a kind of ... sound coming from it.'

'Sound?'

'A whine, I suppose. Very weak, like from a small animal or something. Of course straight away I thought, here we go, another wretched creature to add to the gang.'

'You thought that someone who knows you take in strays was leaving another for you?'

'Exactly. Everyone in this town knows that I can't say no.' She smiled a little. 'But then I thought, well at least this one was coming with a readymade name. So I reached inside, already deciding that if it was a cat, dog, hamster or whatever, that I would call it Doughnut.' She shook her head. 'But when I pulled back the folds and discovered exactly what I'd been landed with this time, I got the biggest shock of my life.'

Ella was quiet for a moment, as the impact of her words began to sink in.

'And what did you do then?'

'Well, I called the police of course ... Frank was here within a couple of minutes; the police station is within walking distance, but he took the car anyway. And I rang Jim Kelly too.'

'The local doctor.'

'Yes. An ambulance too, just in case, although the box looked well insulated and there were plenty of blankets. Still, I thought it best to be sure.'

'Sounds like you were pretty clear-headed about it.'

'Not at all,' she protested, sounding a little nervous. 'Truth be told I was in complete shock. It was only when the ambulance left and Doctor Kelly told us that vitals looked good and there were no signs of hypothermia that I managed to relax a little. As I said, I doubt the box was there that long – and we all agreed that whoever left it must have been acquainted with my routine.'

'No excuse though, is it? I mean, who would dump a newborn baby in a cardboard box on the side of the street in the freezing cold?'

'I know, and Frank suggested that maybe the mother was hiding nearby, keeping an eye out, waiting for me to show up. To be honest, I was so taken aback that I didn't think to look.'

'Right.'

'He reckoned that it was most likely a misunderstanding and that he'd have it all sorted out in no time. He said to me, "Ella, for what it's worth, I think leaving it outside your place was intentional because if there's one person who knows exactly what to do it's you. You're great with kids and sure aren't you always taking in strays? This place isn't nicknamed The Heartbreak Café for nothing." She shook her head sadly. 'And while I agreed with him, I just thought that this was a lot more than a miserable old mongrel – it was a poor, innocent little baby. And not only that, but this is a small town, a small community where people look out for each other.'

'I know what you mean.'

'So I had very little sympathy and as far as I was concerned, there's nothing – absolutely no reason in the world that could justify abandoning a poor defenseless baby on the street. But,' Ella added with a heavy sigh, 'I suppose it's all too easy to play judge and jury until you know the whole story ...'

1

----

*N*ina Hughes had never liked Lakeview and this time was certain she'd like it even less.

She sorely wished that her mother had picked another time to go traveling the world with her stepfather, especially when Nina really needed a shoulder to cry on – or more importantly, a place to stay. After all that had happened with Steve, she couldn't stay in Galway and run the risk of bumping into him; it was a small city after all.

She needed to get away and be somewhere she could clear her head. Even so, she couldn't believe that she'd been reduced to asking her father if she could stay with him.

But she'd had little choice. While normally she could just move back in with her mum for a while until she got herself sorted, her mother and Tony were currently traveling, and had rented their Dublin house out for the six months they'd be away. So instead, she'd decided to ask Patrick if she could come and stay in Lakeview. It would only be for a while; at least until she got her head together and figured out what she should do next.

Feeling like a silly teenager, and not at all like the mature, self-assured thirty-something old she was, Nina had phoned a few days before to ask if he could put her up.

'OK, Nina.' Her father had said in his usual calm, disinterested way, and she guessed that he hadn't changed much in the eight years or so since she'd had anything to do with him. Her mum used to force her on duty visits when she was younger, although in all honesty, Nina felt that Patrick didn't care one way or another whether or not he got to see his only daughter.

Her parents split up when she was a child, and Nina couldn't understand how they'd ever got together in the first place, as her quiet, stern father was the total opposite to her bright and bubbly mum. Probably because they'd both grown up in the same small town – although Lakeview was more of a village really.

And while Cathy her mother, had never admitted as much, Nina suspected that her conception hadn't exactly been planned, and that her parents' marriage was less of the romantic and more of the shotgun variety.

But that didn't bother her; her mum was now blissfully happy in Dublin with Tony (who was more of a father to Nina than Patrick had ever been) and while she'd endured the odd childhood weekend down in Lakeview, once she hit her mid-teens she'd put her foot down and stopped going altogether. If this bothered her father he'd never let on.

She wondered if he was still obsessed with collecting and fixing things. Patrick patiently taking apart and fixing TV sets, radios – anything electronic – was probably her most enduring memory of her childhood visits here.

'Your father is a kind and very generous man,' her mother would repeatedly tell her, determined never to say a bad word against him, which Nina suspected was mostly borne out of guilt for leaving him and taking away his daughter. 'Even after we separated, he never let me want for anything as far as you're concerned.'

Which Nina supposed was honorable given the fact that she knew Patrick had no interest in her whatsoever. She was always just this annoying kid who turned up now and again to mess up his pristine house and orderly way of life. And boy was her father orderly.

Back then, he used to rise at seven am on the dot (even at weekends), go out to the local newsagents, after which he'd read the morning paper over a breakfast of tea (with two sugars) and of fried eggs and bacon with toast. Nina recalled one time, in a childish attempt to please him, she'd overdone the toast and he'd gone ballistic. Not angry as such, just a quiet, barely controlled annoyance, which to a ten-year old was somehow even scarier. Nina had never again attempted to make him breakfast after that.

Now, as the bus approached the outskirts of Lakeview, she wondered if anything had changed. The popular tourist village – centered round a broad oxbow lake from which it took its name – was very pretty certainly. The lake, surrounded by low-hanging beech and willow trees, wound its way around the center and a small humpback stone bridge joined all sides of the township together.

But it was the cobbled streets and ornate lanterns on Main Street, as well as the beautiful one-hundred-year-old artisan cottages decorated with hanging floral baskets that were the true attraction here.

Because of its picturesque beauty, the village had long ago been designated heritage status by the Irish Tourist Board, so the chocolate-box look and feel of the place was intentionally well preserved.

As for changes Nina noted, well, there were certainly a lot more houses anyway; newer, more ostentatious ones on the outskirts, the kind that city types moving to the country built trying to prove to their friends that they were living the good life, when in reality most of them were probably desperate to escape back to Dublin. Humongous bedrooms, huge gardens and outdoor hot-tubs would never be enough to mask the dreary realities of small town living, at least not as far as she was concerned.

Nope, Lakeview was a temporary stop, an emergency stop almost, and as soon as she'd got her head together, she'd be out of here quick as you like.

She got off on Main Street at the bus stop nearest the lake, outside that café that had been there for donkeys' years, the Heartbreak Café, the locals used to jokingly refer to it – for whatever reason. She wondered if that older woman who collected all the stray animals still ran the place. Ella, wasn't it? What was it with this place and collecting things? Although that was unfair really, Ella had always been very nice to Nina, cottoning on to the fact that she was usually there against her will. Or perhaps she just sympathized with the fact that Nina's dad never really had much time for her.

Putting her backpack over her shoulders, she walked along the lake and headed out across the old stone bridge that led in the direction of her father's house.

She'd told him on the phone that she'd be there around six.

'That'll be dinnertime. Do you want me to make extra?' he asked.

Nina hesitated. 'What are you having?'

'Bacon and cabbage,' he told her and again, she couldn't help but shake her head in amazement. How could she forget? Pork chops on Mondays, steak on Tuesdays, and bacon and cabbage on Wednesdays... Patrick Hughes had cooked these same dishes without fail on the same days all that time ago, and now years later was still doing the same.

And once again Nina wondered what on earth she had let herself in for.

2

———

'Hello Nina,' Patrick said, somewhat distractedly when she reached the house a little after six. He stood back as she came through the doorway.

'Hi Dad, how are you?' She didn't attempt to hug or embrace him; theirs was not a hugging sort of relationship, but she did feel slightly put out by her father's almost casual indifference to her appearance after so long. There was no great welcome, or no sense of enthusiasm or interest in her visit.

OK, perhaps it had been her own choice not to visit for so long, but it still bothered her to think that her father had never once of his own accord tried to spend time with her either. She'd also hoped he might notice an improvement in her since the last time he'd seen her – she'd lost over a stone in weight and her previously short dark hair now reached well below her shoulders. But if Patrick noticed any changes in her, he didn't mention it.

'I'm fine, thanks. I was just having dinner. I made some for you, but it might be a bit cold now,' he told her and Nina immediately identified the root of his agitation. She'd told Patrick that she'd be here around six and it was now quarter past. She was late.

'The bus just dropped me off downtown; I thought I'd be earlier...' Then her voice trailed off as she wondered why she felt the need to explain herself like this. It wasn't as though she was ten years old anymore. 'I hope you went ahead and had yours; there was no need to wait for me and if it's cold, I can always stick it in the microwave.'

But she knew there was no question of her father waiting for her arrival before he ate his evening meal; as usual, he would eat without fail in front of the six o'clock news and a visit from the daughter he hadn't seen in years would hardly change that.

'I was just watching the news,' he said, confirming her suspicions.

She followed him into the living room, which hadn't changed a bit since the last time she was here, and dropped her bag on the sofa. Almost immediately, Patrick shot the backpack an agitated look.

'I made up your old room,' he said, which to Nina suggested that she should stow it away upstairs rather than mess up his nice tidy, living room.

'Thanks, I'll unpack after I've had dinner if that's OK – I'm a bit tired after the bus journey.' Again Nina hated the way she always felt so awkward and ill at ease around him.

'That's fine,' he said noncommittally as if she'd just told him she didn't want sugar in her tea. No offers to help her with her things or questions about the journey, just Patrick's typical disinterested response, before he sat down in his armchair to watch the TV.

Going into the kitchen (which also hadn't changed) Nina recalled exactly why she'd stopped visiting her father all that time ago. His constant lack of interest and almost downright indifference to her was frustrating, and actually quite hurtful. She was in a fix, her heart had been broken into a million pieces and like always her father just didn't want to know.

Couldn't he at least *pretend* to be curious as to why she'd turned up at his doorstep after all this time? Or was he so uninterested in her that he couldn't care less either way? He really was the complete opposite of her loving, kind-hearted mother, who Nina knew was beside herself with remorse for being so far away at such a difficult time.

OK, so she hadn't particularly expected Patrick to welcome her home with open arms and a box of Kleenex, but surely a simple enquiry about her well-being wasn't too much to ask?

Nina put the plate of food he'd prepared for her into the microwave, and while she waited for it to heat up, she looked around and marveled at her father's fastidiousness. Despite having prepared dinner, the kitchen was meticulous and there was no sign of food preparation anywhere. Pots, pans and cooking utensils were already rinsed out and neatly stacked in a pile ready to be washed, and there wasn't a drop of liquid or trace debris on any surface.

She recalled how her father had always cleaned and tidied as he went, instead of leaving piles of food packaging and vegetable peels on every surface like her mother did. At dinnertime, her mother's kitchen always looked like a bomb had hit it, the complete opposite of this calm, pristine space over which Patrick presided.

The microwave pinged and Nina reluctantly took her plate into the living room to join her father in front of the TV.

'This is lovely,' she commented, as she ate the boringly old-fashioned dish he was so fond of, although the bacon was quite nice.

But her father just gave a distracted nod in response. OK, so he was watching the news and probably didn't want to get involved in inane small talk until it was over, but couldn't the world's depressing problems wait for one day?

'Did you get the kitchen units changed since I was here last?' she piped up again, more out of politeness than anything else, as she knew well Patrick hadn't done a thing to the house in years.

'I'm not sure,' he replied, thinking seriously about it. 'When were you here last?'

'Eight years,' she said, intentionally ramming the point home, that as she hadn't been here in so long, the least he could have done was got the welcome wagons out.

But Patrick seemed oblivious. 'No,' he answered definitively, 'they haven't been changed since then.' With that, he picked up the remote control and rudely turned up the TV volume. End of conversation.

Right. So much for her opening gambits, Nina thought. Still, she was determined to make the effort, even if he wasn't. 'The garden looks well at this time of year with all the roses in full bloom, doesn't it?'

'Yes, it does.'

'I noticed on the bus that there are lots of new houses on the way in. I suppose the town is full of blow ins now,' she added jokingly, but her father obviously didn't get the joke or just wasn't interested, as again he just nodded impassively and continued watching TV.

Deflated and no longer hungry, Nina pushed the remainder of the food around on her plate. 'Um, Dad ... thanks for dinner, but I'm feeling a bit tired now. I think I might just go upstairs.'

Still Patrick didn't look away from the TV. 'OK Nina,' he said, as his daughter picked up her backpack and trundled upstairs to her old room, wondering already if she'd made yet another big mistake.

3

*R*uth Seymour turned to admire herself in the full-length mirror.

The incredible low backed silver Christian Dior dress she wore was perfect for tonight. She looked like a star and sparkled the way a diva should. Her long blonde hair cascaded past her shoulders in luxurious waves, her blue eyes sparkled, her full lips were glossy, and the dress she was wearing fit her size zero body like a glove.

Tonight was certainly not the night for basic black; she was not a backup singer, and definitely not just part of the scenery. She was Ruth Seymour, wildly successful star of the US TV series *Glamazons*, who was currently lighting up Hollywood like a supernova.

She turned around and looked at her assistant, Chloe, who was typing on her BlackBerry.

'So do I look OK?' she inquired, already knowing the answer, (she did pay Chloe after all) but still she needed the confidence boost.

'Oh, you look fabulous, truly!' Chloe exclaimed. 'What shoes are you wearing?'

Ruth smiled. The answer was a stupendous pair of silver, jeweled Manolo Blahniks that her stylist had just sent over. Thirteen hundred dollars and she got them for nothing because of who she was. Ruth preferred Louboutins, but apparently the designer refused to give freebies. Oh, well, it wasn't as though she couldn't afford to buy them, what with her agent now talking six figures per episode of *Glamazons*. And bought them, she had – several times over.

'Probably the Manolos,' she replied airily, catching the look of sheer envy on Chloe's face when she pulled them out of their dust-cover and put one on her elegantly petite foot. Imagine walking down the street in Lakeview wearing these? Their eyes would pop out of their heads with envy.

Well, perhaps she might just do that, Ruth thought, putting on the other shoe and making a mental note to pack them in her suitcase later. 'Remind me not to forget to bring these tomorrow, won't you?' she asked Chloe.

'Sure. Ready for champagne?' Her assistant twisted the cork on a bottle of Veuve Clicquot, which opened with a satisfactory 'pop' and Ruth grinned, deciding this was possibly her most favorite sound in the world.

'When was the last time you were home for a visit?' Chloe asked, handing her a glass.

Ruth took a sip of champagne. 'Oh, I don't know, a few years I guess,' she replied blithely. 'I've just been so busy and it's not exactly a quick trip so I haven't really had the time.' She moved in front of the mirror to again take in her appearance. 'What time does the car come?'

Chloe, wisely taking the change of subject as an indicator that the issue was closed for discussion, looked at her notes and told her boss that the car would arrive at seven.

Actually Ruth knew exactly when she was last back in Ireland. It had been five years and up until now, she'd avoided a return to her home country like the plague. It wasn't that she didn't yearn to see her family – she missed them terribly, and luckily they'd come to see her in LA a few times – it was everyone else that was the problem. She didn't want to be judged, was terrified of being pitied or worse, being called a failure. Not that she hadn't been close enough to drop in for a visit either; she never hesitated to travel to Paris or holiday on the

Riviera, but had never had any desire to go back to Ireland and the sleepy little backwater in which she grew up.

Until now.

Ruth smiled. Now, thanks to *Glamazons*, she was a huge success and it wasn't so hard to face your past when you were being celebrated. Ruth was currently at the top of her game. The first season of the TV show in which she starred – based around the glamorous and fashionable lifestyles of Malibu's elite – had been a huge ratings success across the country and they'd just finished shooting Season Two. There were murmurings of an Emmy nomination for her and one of her co-stars, and the show had just been commissioned for a further season, raising Ruth's stock even higher and further certifying her as a bona fide Hollywood star. The recent announcement was the reason for the party she was attending tonight, and she had just enough time to whoop it up before her flight to Dublin tomorrow.

The pilot of the show was just about to hit Irish TV screens, and she had been invited to be interviewed on *Late Tonight*, the country's most high profile and best-loved chat show. Ruth had been over the moon when she'd heard that; it was possibly the greatest honor she could ask for, and a definite two fingers to all those in her home country who had doubted her.

As shooting on the next season of *Glamazons* wasn't due to begin again until the autumn, she planned to spend the summer in Lakeview with her folks, making up for lost time and she thought happily, basking in her well-earned success.

Besides, she figured she'd earned a few months off. She'd been slogging hard for years to try and make it to this level and finally, *finally*, it was all coming together the way it was supposed to be.

Ruth had known from a very young age that she was destined for stardom. After all, she had always been attractive and her youthful prettiness had never left her, instead transforming her into a stunning woman. Even now at thirty years old, she didn't have to worry about Botox and some of the other procedures that her co-stars obsessed about. She had great genes and she knew it.

Plus, she'd always known she was a great actress and the past five years had been incredibly hard for her, so she was thrilled to know that people were finally recognizing her gift. Following early success in Ireland on a home-grown TV soap called *The Local*, everyone back home (including Ruth) had been convinced that the transition to Hollywood was a certainty.

However, upon landing in LA five years before she was immediately met as an outsider and had been stuck for the first few years in dreaded skincare commercials, as well as doing the odd, clichéd bit part as the nice, funny Irish girl in straight-to-DVD movies. She wrinkled her nose distastefully. Well, those days were over, Ruth knew it. Now the sky was the limit.

Finally, ready to leave and excited for the rest of the evening to begin, she felt completely relaxed when Chloe's BlackBerry buzzed to inform them that the car was downstairs.

Her assistant picked up her notes, Ruth's fur stole, and some other various 'things' just in case and shuttled Ruth out the door of her apartment and into the elevator.

Once outside, they were met with a swarm of paparazzi waiting in front of the building. The flashes from their cameras were blinding, but Ruth didn't care, she loved it, they wanted her! She smiled beatifically and had to restrain herself from waving even though every bone in her body wanted to wave like she was Miss America. Instead, she beamed and gave polite hellos, answered just a couple of questions, and accepted many congratulations as her doorman moved her through the crowd and into the waiting town car.

Hmm, Ruth thought, maybe it was time to start thinking about security or a bodyguard? She relished the idea and didn't understand how some stars could complain about the constant photographers following them around, it was *wonderful*! Besides, what was the point in being famous if you didn't enjoy the perks?

She settled back into the rich leather of the backseat of the car while Chloe sat next to her placing several advance phone calls to the people at the party who were waiting for her arrival.

As they neared the Beverly Hills Hotel, the driver inquired if he should take Ruth to a side entrance, to avoid the crowds and Chloe began to tell him that was a great idea, before Ruth quickly shushed her.

'Of course not, go straight to the front. After all, the fans wait for hours to get a glimpse of the cast.' She smiled, better to have everyone think she was doing a public service as opposed to feeding her ego. No one liked someone who was too into herself and Irish-born Ruth possibly understood that better than most.

The driver followed her command and pulled up in front of the hotel. Ruth looked out of her window at the swarm of people waiting for her to exit the car. Calling on her yoga-breathing exercises, she inhaled deeply.

Showtime …

Chloe handed her a mirror and she applied another coat of lip-gloss to freshen her look, before, again, looking at her assistant for affirmation.

'Perfect. You look absolutely *amazing*.' Chloe jumped out her side of the car, and a uniformed man stepped forward and opened the door on Ruth's side.

Flashbulbs exploded all around as Ruth unfolded one long, lean, graceful leg and extracted herself elegantly from the car. She started to glide up the red carpet slowly, posing for pictures, thanking cheering fans, basking in her glory. She planned on drawing out the fifty-foot walk to the door of the hotel as long as possible.

Out of the corner of her eye, she saw her co-star, Troy Valentine, who played her 'husband' on the show. He was looking particularly yummy tonight she thought, his black hair coiffed perfectly and his smile looked particularly white against his tan. Guess that's what living in a beach house will do for you Ruth thought, and wondered if maybe it was time to upgrade from her apartment in the Hollywood Hills.

Troy noticed her and nodded in her direction, as if to accompany her inside. She gave him a warm smile, but didn't pick up her pace; she would see him inside later. Best now to pay attention to the people who wouldn't be; namely the paparazzi and her adoring public.

. . .

INSIDE, the party was in full swing and the Cristal was flowing.

Ruth could barely move without having someone rush up to offer congratulations, and she truly felt like the belle of the ball. Bob, the producer of *Glamazons* was making a huge fuss of her; as were the network moguls and various others involved in the show. The confidence boost made her feel incredibly witty and beautiful and her charms were working to the max, or perhaps it was just the champagne?

Regardless, it was very interesting to find Troy Valentine so close at hand the entire night. Even though they'd both worked on *Glamazons* from the outset, Troy was already a well-established Hollywood actor, while she was the relative unknown, and although they had loads of chemistry onscreen she'd always felt a little overawed by his star power.

But thanks to her glamorous all-American portrayal of Mia Reynolds in the show, Ruth was now just as much of a draw, and as Troy leaned closer to whisper something in her ear, she figured he was beginning to understand that too.

'You look incredible tonight, you know that?' he said, his warm, velvety tones and the delicious scent of his aftershave sending shivers down her spine.

Troy, who typically had the most beautiful women in the world on his arm, tonight seemed to only have eyes for her and while she thought he was handsome, he didn't come across as the sharpest tool in the box.

Still, a little off screen flirtation couldn't hurt her standing; it wasn't as if either of them was married and more to the point, the tabloids would *love* it.

'Why thank you,' she said, gazing flirtatiously from beneath her eyelashes. Then she smiled at him and whispered something in return. 'Excuse me, but I'll be right back.' She headed towards the ladies room, briefly looking over her shoulder to make sure he was looking. He was.

Well, thank goodness I wore this dress, Ruth thought satisfactorily. She swung her hips ever so slightly; might as well give him something to look at.

Inside the ladies' room, she took a moment to freshen up and gather her thoughts. These last few days had been incredible, and she still couldn't believe how much ass-kissing was coming her way tonight. Feeling the love from Hollywood's most powerful was what she'd always dreamed of and now she had it.

She'd also had a lot of champagne and her head was spinning just a little, although it was probably a combination of alcohol and the intoxication of being so celebrated, she figured.

She was still pinching herself that the TV series had become such a ratings success and that according to the Hollywood press, she'd been a major part of that success. Her agent Erik had just copper-fastened an amazing second-series contract for her, and with the way things were going she wouldn't have to worry about money for a long time to come. There would be no more soul-destroying auditions, no more stereotyped walk-on parts and best of all, no more sniping and smart remarks from the Irish media. Hell, if this Emmy nomination happened there could even be a L'Oreal contract in the works so nobody back home could accuse her of being a failure now, could they?

Throughout her first few years in LA the media in Ireland had been relentless in their criticism, apparently only too delighted that Ruth Seymour hadn't managed to break through. While in the beginning Ruth had been reasonably confident, she still had no illusions about how hard she'd have to work and what she needed to do to make it in this town – although she honestly didn't envisage it would take so long. Her home country's criticism had been very hard to take and she just hoped that when she returned this time, things would be different.

So while she was looking forward to her return, she certainly wasn't looking forward to the ten-hour flight across the Atlantic, especially not after all this champagne.

Then again sod it, she thought; tonight certainly wasn't the night for being sensible and she could sleep as much as she wanted on the (first class) flight. Ruth knew better than most how fickle Hollywood could be, so best to soak up as much of the fantasy as possible while it lasted.

And speaking of fantasy ...

When she came back out Troy was leaning casually against the wall outside.

'Hello there,' he said in an unmistakably flirtatious tone.

'Hello yourself.'

'Man, I love that accent,' he gasped with a shake of his head and for a brief moment Ruth wasn't sure what he was referring to before it dawned on her. Damn it, alcohol often caused her to slip back into her Irish brogue, something she'd really rather didn't happen.

Still, if it worked for Troy...

She smiled. 'You never know, maybe next season the guys might write in an affair for you with someone Irish.'

'Me cheat on you with some piece of skirt? Not a chance.' He sidled closer and brushed an imaginary piece of lint from her shoulder. Ruth shivered. While the critics often described their on-screen performance as 'sizzling', in all the scenes they'd had together, she'd never really thought about Troy in that way. And whether it was the champagne or just the way he was looking at her, she was beginning to understand what they were talking about.

'I think you're mixing me up with Mia,' she teased. 'It wouldn't be cheating.'

'Yeah, it would,' Troy replied, gently pushing her into a shadowy corner by the pay phones. Ruth's breath caught in her throat as he inclined his head and kissed her hungrily on the lips.

He drew his head back and smiled softly. 'Much better when it's not for the cameras, huh?'

'You can say that again,' she agreed breathlessly, as he moved in for another kiss.

But he was right; this was nothing like kissing him on set – when usually they were surrounded by a dozen people or more – this was ... this was incredible.

He ran his hands gently across her body, faintly brushing her breasts through the thin material of her dress before moving them back down the small of her back and playing with the hem of her dress. His tongue was hot and eager as he explored her lips and her mouth and she pressed herself against him, her head swimming with a heady combination of alcohol and lust.

She couldn't believe that she was in the arms of Troy Valentine and he was kissing her, really kissing her!

'You are so beautiful Ruth – did I tell you I've wanted to do this since the first time I saw you?' He littered her neck with kisses and his lips eventually made their way to her cleavage, just stopping where the fabric began. As he went lower; she could feel his breath on her skin through the fabric and knew he was just as excited as she was.

Well, what took you so long then? she wanted to say, hardly able to believe how incredible this night was turning out to be. It was the ultimate Hollywood fairy-tale – so much better than she could possibly have dreamed and she really didn't want it to end.

Eventually, Troy moved his mouth away, and looked into her eyes. She could feel his chest rising and falling against her. 'Ruth, let's get the hell out of here.'

4

The morning light streamed in through the windows. Ruth tentatively opened her eyes, only to be hit with a major headache. Slowly moving her head off the pillow she turned to confirm what she now really hoped was just a dream. Oh hell ...

Her co-star was lying on his back next to her, and while he was still unmistakably handsome, the raw magnetism that was so much in evidence last night was no longer apparent. Troy moved in his sleep and began snoring heavily, and Ruth suspected that when he woke up his headache would be just as bad as hers.

She sat up slowly and looked around. Where on earth were they? Trying to recall the events of the previous evening, she vaguely remembered her and Troy deciding to leave the party separately, so as not to get anyone suspicious. They decided that they would go to the Chateau Marmont, not the most inconspicuous place for celebrities, but quite obviously, neither of them was thinking clearly.

Troy must have called ahead, or certainly someone did, because she didn't remember checking in, and hazily recalled the concierge meeting her upon arrival and ushering her to a room. This room.

Somehow Troy had made it here first, because he was already waiting with more Cristal.

Ugh, she groaned, her stomach turning at the thought of alcohol.

She looked at the floor to see her glorious silver dress lying in a heap on the ground beside the bed and her thirteen hundred dollar (albeit free) shoes were thrown haphazardly on opposite sides of the room. What the hell was she going to do? She couldn't leave in last night's clothes, not if the paparazzi had been tipped off and were waiting; she would have to get Chloe to bring her some.

All becoming too much to handle, she rested her head back on the pillows and closed her eyes.

More from last night began to come back, although really it was probably only a couple of hours since they'd settled down to sleep. Troy's playboy reputation sure was deserved and whatever about his brains, he certainly had star quality where it counted. He'd been pretty incredible, so much so she recalled –slightly embarrassed now – that it was a wonder security weren't called they were so loud. Or perhaps they were?

Either way, they *were* celebrities and the hotel was probably used to that kind of thing, Ruth reassured herself, feeling somewhat shamefaced.

Yet something was niggling at her, something at the very edge of her consciousness. But what? OK, so she didn't make a habit of sleeping around and certainly not with guys like Troy. But it had been a surreal and excitingly intoxicating night. It almost felt ... right.

Anyway, it wasn't as if –

Suddenly, the niggling feeling that had been bothering her came sharply into focus. And just like that, the pleasant reveries she'd been experiencing deserted her. Ruth started to breathe heavy, *oh ... oh no.*

She jumped out of the bed and started to survey the remains of the night before, clothes, champagne bottles, sheets, her purse, his phone ... and the condom.

Suddenly all the details came rushing back to her in Technicolor; the condom splitting ... the two of them pausing for a second, but then continuing on anyway ...

Oh, no ...

Ruth felt bile rising in her throat. She raced into the bathroom and stared in horror at herself in the mirror. The glossy goddess from last night was long gone. Her mascara was smeared on her face, her hair was dull and shag-tangled and she could feel sticky sweaty residue on her skin.

She leaned heavily on the bathroom's marble counter and turned on the water, splashing it on her face while she repeated a mantra to herself over and over.

This couldn't be happening ... it wasn't happening ... it *wouldn't* happen. Not now, not after last night, not with him. Not when everything was falling into place, when her life was exactly how she wanted it to be, when she was living the dream.

Ruth stifled a sob. She had to get out of here, and fast.

She crept back into the bedroom and helped herself to one of the rich, white, terrycloth robes the hotel provided. Troy was still sleeping heavily and careful not to wake him, she took her phone out of her purse, and made her way outside on to the balcony.

Chloe answered on the first ring. 'Chloe, it's Ruth, I need you to bring me some clothes to Chateau Marmont, as fast as possible, please.'

'Are you OK? I've been so worried, I never heard from you after the party and well, your flight is today and I ...' the concern in her assistant's voice was palpable. Ruth looked at her watch and wanted to cry; she was supposed to be on a plane to Dublin in a few hours.

Damn, damn, damn.

'I know, please just hurry, OK?'

'Sure, but what on earth are you doing in the Chateau Marmont?'

Ruth bit her lip. 'I kind of ... met someone.'

'Oh – anyone I know?' Chloe teased gently, and for some reason her playful tone made Ruth feel better – as if *real* Hollywood stars got up to this kind of thing all the time.

'Well ...Troy Valentine, actually,' she admitted wincing, yet at the same time she couldn't help but feel sort of ... proud.

As expected, Chloe was seriously impressed. 'You and *Troy Valentine*? Wow! Sounds like one hell of a night.'

Ruth forced a smile. It *would* have been, apart from ... 'It was but look, I really need to get out of here soon to make my flight, so if you could –'

'Got it. I'll be there soon, don't worry, you're all packed, we'll get you to the airport on time. And don't forget to slip in the Manolos.'

Ruth swallowed back tears, realizing she never wanted to see those damn shoes again.

5

*N*ina had spent her first night in Lakeview tossing and turning, thinking over all of her problems. She knew that the quiet of the countryside and the traveling that she did that day should have knocked her out, but instead she lay awake staring at the ceiling.

She was bothered by many things; to start with, the break-up with Steve. This time last month she had been as happy as she'd ever been, with no clue of what was to come and certainly no reason to suspect that anything was amiss.

How could I have been so stupid? she wondered bitterly. Still, no matter how much she loved him or how much he'd hurt her, she knew she'd made the right decision in ending the relationship. But as if breaking up with him wasn't bad enough, they'd worked together in the same company and Nina knew she couldn't bear having to face him every day – especially now – which was why she'd decided to pack up her entire life in Galway and come back East. As things stood, she had no relationship, no job, and a whole lot of other problems.

She rolled over in bed, wishing more than ever that her mother was here. Cathy would travel back in a shot if she realized the full extent of Nina's situation, she knew that, but this was supposed to be the trip of a lifetime for her and Tony and she didn't want to ruin it for her. Heaven knows her mother had sacrificed enough for her over the years, raising her by herself until meeting and falling in love with Tony when Nina was in her late teens. He was a wonderful man, kind, gentle and an absolute rock for Cathy – for them both really.

Nina sighed, thinking about how different Patrick – her real father – was. She wasn't sure why she'd thought he might have changed; change was anathema to a country man like Patrick. She wasn't sure if her father had ever even traveled outside the country, or even outside Lakeview. Although he must have to get all those bits and parts he needed for his TV repairs and suchlike.

Nope, they had nothing in common really, nothing except genetics. How long could she realistically stay here? Until she got her head together at least, Nina thought. That was the plan after all.

In the meantime, she needed to focus on trying to get to sleep. Deciding on the age-old solution of counting sheep, she was about to doze off when she heard a loud snore from across the hallway. Typical, she thought, that the only time her father chose to be involved in something she was doing was when she didn't want him to be.

Somewhere in the middle of all of her frustration, she drifted off, only to be woken a few hours later by Patrick knocking on her door, telling her to 'Rise and shine.'

Knowing it was seven a.m. and not enjoying the idea of having to spend another silent meal with Patrick so soon after last night, Nina decided to get out of bed, throw on some casual clothes and head down town for a coffee or something. Her father had always been a tea drinker and Nina knew he didn't even possess a jar of instant, let alone a cafetière.

She went downstairs to find Patrick in the kitchen, making his usual breakfast.

'Morning Dad,' she said, blearily.

Patrick turned around, as if he'd just remembered that she was in fact there. 'Oh, good morning, Nina. Would you like some breakfast?'

'No, thanks, it's a beautiful day so I thought I might go out for a walk, get some exercise maybe. I'll probably just grab something while I'm out.'

'Hmm,' he said, turning back to the frying pan.

She stood there for a second longer, trying to figure out if this reply was meant as some kind of acknowledgement. When she realized that it was in fact a dismissal, she turned on her heel and walked from the house. Goodness, she thought, how does anyone put up with him? Then almost immediately, she was met by a wave of compassion, remembering the fact that her father was a loner, and that her mother in fact had left him. She said a silent apology and vowed to not think about it.

She walked briskly, following the path along the side of the lake in the direction of the village, not really thinking about where she was headed, but allowing her feet to propel her naturally. She'd forgotten how familiar she was with Lakeview, regardless of the fact that she'd never done anything to endear herself to it, and had in fact, worked eagerly to distance herself. Yet somehow, she still had an innate sense of the place.

Following her feet to the end of the lakeside path, she reached the corner where Ella's Heartbreak Café was situated. It was a small two-storey building with an enviable position right at the edge of the lake and on the corner where Main Street began. Until she reached it, Nina was barely aware of the fact she had been walking, her mind was so intently focused, and before she knew it she was at the door and stepping through the entrance.

She was met by the familiar scent of the place, the combination of grease and the warm, fresh smell associated with baked goods. The interior hadn't changed much over the years – it was still the warm cozy room she remembered, with its parquet oak flooring, shelves full of dried flowers and old country-style knick-knacks, along with haphazard seating and mismatched tables, one of which was an antique Singer sewing table.

In front of the kitchen and serving area was a long granite countertop, where various solo customers nursed their coffees and pastries atop a row of stools. Alongside this was a glass display case filled with a selection of the most delicious-looking baked goods imaginable; muffins, doughnuts, carrot cake, brownies and cream puffs for the sweet-toothed, and pies, sausage rolls and Italian breads for the more savory-orientated. The chalkboard menu overhead listed a selection of breakfast choices ranging from yoghurt, muesli and bagels, to the Full Irish *heart attack* breakfast complete with locally produced black pudding.

If Nina wasn't hungry when she'd set out, a single whiff of Ella's famous home cooking now suddenly had her feeling ravenous. She looked around expectantly at the faces inside, wondering whom she would recognize, if anyone, after the changes through the years.

Her eyes scanned the room and then settled on the one person she would know anywhere, Ella, the owner. Nina observed her for a moment, rushing from table to table, cleaning surfaces, pouring coffee, saying a kind word to everyone she met. It was perhaps no accident that she'd ended up here; Ella was such a pleasant woman and a warm soul, that often as a teenager, Nina had felt more at home in this busy café than she did at her father's house.

Ella must have felt Nina watching her, because suddenly she looked up. Then the older woman studied her for a moment before recognition blossomed. She set down the pot of coffee she had been circulating with and rushed forward. Nina had barely moved a foot before Ella had embraced her in a warm bear-hug.

'Nina love, how wonderful to see you. I must admit I wasn't sure at first, you've grown up so much, but then I realized I would have known those green eyes anywhere!' she exclaimed. 'How long are you home? Is your mother with you? I haven't seen you both in ages.'

'No, it's just me – on a short visit,' Nina replied quickly, wondering why she felt the need to be evasive over how long she would be staying in Lakeview.

Ella looked at her and Nina glanced away, worried that she could read her mind and would guess all her secrets if she allowed her to look at her for too long. 'Are you feeling alright honey?' Ella asked. 'You look a bit pale and you've lost so much weight since the last time I've seen you – I hope you're not on some silly diet or something.'

'Of course not. Actually I'm really hungry.' Better to get Ella started on something other than her looks and her health, Nina thought, and sure enough, that did the trick.

'Of course you are. Take a seat there at the counter and I'll make you some breakfast. Then you can tell me all about what you've been up to since the last time you were here.'

Nina was oddly touched that Ella should be so interested in her life and happy to talk to her. It made a nice change from her father's non-existent welcome.

The two of them chatted on and off for a while, and Ella introduced Nina to the waitress, Alice, a friendly girl in her early twenties, with large blue eyes and freckles, whom Nina warmed to right away.

In between all the hustle and bustle, Ella wanted to know everything about what Nina had been doing for the last few years in Galway, where she'd been living, working or if she was seeing anyone. Nina was creatively editing the parts that she didn't feel like talking about, namely, everything that had happened after Steve arrived on the scene.

'And what brings you back to Lakeview?' Ella asked finally.

'Well, I just hadn't been back in so long and really, I ... I just felt that I wanted to see Patrick, I mean, Dad.' If that wasn't a lie, she didn't know what was. She had spoken so haltingly that she suspected Ella guessed there was something off, but the woman just nodded and poured more orange juice. 'So what has been happening around here?' she asked then, deciding to change the subject.

'Well, you know yourself, Lakeview is still Lakeview. Of course, as you've probably seen on your way in, it's a lot bigger than it was before and we have lots of city people who escape to the country only to spend all their time in the city,' she said and Nina smiled. Ella had echoed her own thoughts on the subject completely.

'And how are the kids?' If Nina remembered correctly, Ella was a widowed mother of three, but hadn't she fostered a couple of children over the years too? Along with every bedraggled cat/dog/rabbit that happened to cross her path. Kindhearted to the core, Ella Harris liked to look after people, which was why her little café had always been a hugely popular gathering place for the Lakeview locals. Here, there was no need to specify 'tall' or 'grande' as someone like Ella could guess a customer's preference almost on sight.

'Fine, fine – all keeping well thank goodness,' she replied, her face lighting up at the mention of her children. 'Dan my oldest helps out here from time to time, Carly works as a special needs assistant, and Lily's still at university,' she said, smiling fondly, 'I see them all from time to time, but they tend to do their own thing, you know yourself.'

'I can imagine,' Nina said, politely. She smiled; unsure what to say next, but soon found that she didn't have to, because right at that moment, the door of the café burst open and something like a tornado blew in.

An incredibly petite young woman with a shock of curly red hair tied up in one of those messy, yet incredibly fashionable 'half pony-tails' came inside. She had a very chic pair of Chanel sunglasses perched on the top of her head, and as she took a moment to look around; Nina could feel the energy pulsating off her.

'Ella, what a great morning it is!' she trilled. 'So, did you hear the news? Guess who's coming home this weekend? There is a big welcome home party and awards event being planned at Clancy's and I was just on my way over there to see the set up, but I had no break-fast so I said I'd pop in to grab a pastry and I ...' the redhead stopped mid-sentence and stared at Nina. 'Nina Hughes! Oh, my gosh! Speaking of homecomings ...' She lunged forward and pulled Nina into a tight embrace.

'Trish. Wow, I hardly recognized you. I wasn't sure if you still lived here actually.'

'Well, you would have known if you'd ever bothered phoning or maybe dropping an email,' Trish chided half-heartedly.

Nina winced. 'I know, I've been awful. I did mean to –'

'Not to worry. Sure, we're both as bad as each other. I was in Cork for a good while, but I'm back now, oh about ...two years now, isn't it Ella?' she said and the older woman nodded in affirmation.

'So tell me all. I want to know *everything* you have been doing since the last time I've seen you. It's been years. What have you been up to? How's Galway? How long are you here for? Are you staying with your dad? How is he, I haven't seen him in ages ...' Trish didn't take a breath.

'Wow, you really haven't changed a bit,' Nina laughed. 'Don't you ever come up for air?' Trish just grinned and Nina briefly recalled their shared history. The two were the same age and Trish had been one of the few friends Nina had as a child when she visited Lakeview. She couldn't remember when she had seen her last, but even then, the encounter wasn't in Lakeview, but in Galway. Trish had been up there for something – she couldn't remember what – but regardless, they had met up for dinner and a few drinks. It was a great night and a funny memory and right then, Nina couldn't understand why they hadn't stayed in touch.

'Nina just got in yesterday. She's staying with her father for a little while,' Ella replied, giving Trish the simplified version of what Nina had just told her. She turned to Nina. 'When Trish gets her breath back, she'll be able to tell you that she works for the *Lakeview News* now. If you can believe it, she is quite the interviewer when she allows her subjects to talk,' she added wryly, and Trish flushed a shade of red that just about matched her hair.

'Fantastic. So you did end up a writer after all,' Nina said, recalling how Trish used to love making up stories in her youth.

'Well, the local rag isn't exactly Pulitzer-winning stuff, but I enjoy it,' Trish told her. 'And even though we're not celeb-central around here, things are looking up,' she added excitedly.

When Nina and Ella both looked blank, she went on. 'Well, you're not going to believe this, but Ruth Seymour's coming home! The press release came in during the week.'

Of course, the actress. Nina had almost forgotten that she'd also known Ruth Seymour from her visits here.

'I've heard all about the show. Isn't it mad to think that we all played together years ago and now she's this huge Hollywood star?'

Trish wrinkled her nose. 'Hollywood Star or not – she puts her pants on the same way I do,' she giggled. 'That's if she remembers to wear any at all.'

'Trish!' Ella gasped, shocked, and Nina smiled. 'Although I read *heat* magazine too and I do think that Botox or not, she's a bit past the scraps of clothes she's been wearing lately.'

'What age *is* she?' Nina asked. 'She has to be at least thirty.'

'Twenty-five, according to the press release,' Trish confirmed with a chuckle. 'Does that mean we get to be twenty-five too? I do hope she realizes she is attracting a swarm of press to her hometown, and someone might pull her birth certificate,' she added her eyes sparkling mischievously.

'Now, now, don't be spiteful,' Ella warned. 'And don't you be stirring up trouble just because you have access to records for that project you are doing.'

Trish went on to explain to Nina how she was currently in the process of putting together a photographic history of Lakeview. 'I'm publishing it for charity, so I get access to all the town's records to compile it.'

'Sounds interesting,' Nina replied, thinking it was a very good idea indeed. The town was steeped in history, having been the site of a major republican rebellion a hundred years before. And seeing as it had changed immeasurably since even the last time she had seen it, it would be nice to have the changes down through the years documented.

'Anyway,' Trish continued. 'The town has arranged to give her a Lakeview Person of the Year award – I know; as if we have this *huge* pool to choose from,' she giggled, seeing Nina's amused look. 'There's going to be a huge party at Clancy's Hotel. You should come along. Everyone acts as if the queen is coming. Although I suppose it is very cool to think that someone from Lakeview, someone we *know*, is now so famous.'

'Will you get to interview her?'

'Yep, and I can't wait, for the sake of my career if nothing else,' Trish smiled. 'I would like to move on to one of the national papers eventually.'

'Of course,' Nina agreed, and no one better than Trish to do so. 'Well, when you do, do you think you can ask her a question for me?'

'Of course, what's that?'

'What it's like to spend her days on set making out with Troy Valentine?'

Trish threw her head back and laughed aloud. 'You must have been reading my mind! Well look, I'd better grab this pastry and get going. Oh, Nina it's brilliant to see you back. Having you home will be just like old times. You should come to the awards thing with me and we'll drink loads of champagne. I'll give you a call later to arrange the plans, OK?' she said, before breezing out the door.

'Sure,' Nina agreed, although Trish's words had ruined the light-heartedness of the moment and brought her screaming back to reality.

Ella was off serving customers, and deciding she'd already taken up enough of her time, Nina left some money on the counter and stood up to leave. Ella gave a friendly wave as she left, but once outside, the weight of all Nina's problems returned. It was nice to just feel normal and carefree for a moment with Trish and Ella she thought, sighing. And while she'd be happy to go to Ruth Seymour's official homecoming with her friend, there would be no champagne for her.

Nina couldn't well be partying it up and drinking bubbly in Clancy's hotel, not when she was twelve weeks pregnant.

6

_R_uth worried the entire way to Dublin. During the first flight from LA to New York she suffered through a hangover and a low level panic that pulsated in her stomach.

Now, as she walked through Kennedy airport, heading towards the gate for the connecting Aer Lingus flight to Dublin, she turned her cell phone back on and saw that she had voicemail waiting. She punched in her code and listened. When she heard the voice, her stomach clenched.

'Ruth, babe it's me, Troy. Hey, how did you get out of the hotel room so fast?' her co-star asked. 'You were gone before I woke up.' There was a pause; as if he was searching for something to say. 'Hey, just wanted to say that I had a great time last night and well ... I hope we're cool. We were both pretty smashed, I guess ... Anyway, I'd like to see you again. I know you'll be gone for a bit, but ... hey, maybe just call me when you get this?'

Oh, she thought to herself. What did all that mean? At first, it sounded like a message left by someone who really wanted to cover his ass, but then he'd asked to see her again. On a date, or just for more sex? She shook her head and wondered if he carried any of the same worries that she did right now. Unlikely, he was a man after all and a split condom wouldn't be an issue for him, wouldn't have potentially career-changing consequences.

She thought of her painstakingly maintained size zero body, pictured stretch marks developing on her toned stomach and winced. It couldn't happen, could it? Life really couldn't be that cruel.

She briefly remembered reading something about the age at which women were supposed to have a decline in fertility – age thirty she thought, so maybe for once, her age would work in her favor? Regardless that everyone in Hollywood believed she was twenty-five.

When Ruth reached her gate, she saw that the flight was already boarding. Good, she wouldn't have to wait around. She just wanted to try and put all this behind her, and while she wasn't as excited to be returning to Ireland now, she felt that the distance between her and that stupid mistake from last night was exactly what she needed, even if that distance was just miles.

Now, cruising at thirty thousand feet over the Atlantic, Ruth put the sleep mask over her eyes and tried to relax. But try as she might, she just couldn't get last night out of her mind. She briefly thought through her options. Ok, if (and it was a big 'if' at this point) she was pregnant, it could still be a secret. She would be in Ireland for the next few months; so she could always pop over to London to get it dealt with. No one would have to know.

But no, even though it was the obvious solution to what could potentially be a career-wrecking problem, Ruth found it difficult to even consider that. While she knew that she could not allow her glittering career to come falling down around her ankles, she would also not allow herself to do such a thing. There had to be another way. She would figure this out, in the same way she had always figured things out. She hadn't become a Hollywood star through lack of determination or know-how after all.

THE FLIGHT LANDED in Dublin early the following morning Irish-time. However, the fact that Ruth was still operating on Pacific Time immediately made her worry about the bags she knew had formed under her eyes. A good excuse as any to wear her sunglasses, despite the grey mist that was visible through the window.

To think that for years she had pictured this moment; her glorious homecoming, stepping off the plane to meet a swarm of Irish media, who all wanted to take her picture and shower her with compliments. She had always pictured herself looking ultra-glamorous but chic – the way Gwyneth always did when getting off a plane after ten hours.

Now, looking down at her wrinkled silk Dolce & Gabbana top over Seven for All Mankind jeans, she wondered how Gwyneth always looked so pristine and unrumpled. Maybe it had to do with the fact that she probably flew on a private jet, got actual sleep, because the aircraft had a bed, and was able to shower and change?

While Ruth didn't have the option to do any of those things, being hung-over for the majority of the flight probably didn't help either, and Gwyneth more than likely never flew anywhere without a team of stylists. Ruth immediately regretted not bringing Chloe on this trip, because not only did she miss the constant flattery that her assistant provided, but her organizational and PR skills too. She knew that upon arrival, she would be met by a driver, but it just wasn't the same.

The flight attendants were preparing the cabin to be opened and Ruth started to gather her things. She checked her makeup one more time in her compact, and made sure that the amount of lipstick she had on was acceptable. She also noted that tell-tale bags under her eyes were indeed present. Damn! Ruth put a stick of chewing gum in her mouth and chewed it intensely for a moment, trying to rid herself of the dreaded hangover breath. Ugh. Forget her triumphant home-coming, all Ruth wanted at that moment was to get to the nearest hotel room and sleep for days. But there would be little time for rest as the following afternoon she was due at the TV studios for her long-awaited appearance on the *Late Tonight* show.

Her brain was full of cobwebs, she shook her head and tried to regain that feeling of excitement that she'd had all week in the run-up to this, but found it was hard coming.

Eventually she exited the plane, but instead of descending the steps movie-star-like to a greeting swarm of media, she was instead shunted through a narrow passenger gangway tunnel with the rest of the hordes.

She exited the tunnel and made her way through to passport control. Looking around, she found that quite a lot had changed since the last time she had been here. The airport looked all shiny and modern, not too unlike LAX. Where were all the Guinness and Aran sweater shops? From what she could see they were even selling MAC here now. OK, so it had been a while since she was last here, and she knew Ireland had improved somewhat, but hell, was that a *caviar* bar?

She really hadn't expected this at all; this glossy, urbane first glimpse of her home country. She tried to alter the confused expression on her face and replace it with a carefree smile. After all, she reminded herself, no matter how sophisticated things seemed here now, people would still be excited by her visit, wouldn't they?

Best foot forward and all that...

Regardless of how miserable she was feeling, Ruth reminded herself that no one knew about what had happened last night, no one knew about her and Troy so really she'd be better off putting it to the back of her mind for now. It was her secret and she could deal with anything that she had to in her own time. So for the moment, why not soak up the platitudes and the magic of her big moment? She was allowed be happy today; she was returning home to Ireland as a huge success, would see her family soon, and would be appearing on the highest rating TV chat-show tomorrow night, so what was there to be glum about? Lifted by these thoughts, a wave of optimism flooded through her, and she straightened her shoulders as she approached the line for passport control.

She glanced tentatively around at the other travelers waiting in line, wondering if anyone recognized her and was vaguely disappointed to see that no one seemed to bat an eyelid at the glamorous woman in oversized sunglasses; they were all too interested in making it to the top of the queue. Didn't they realize that she was not only one of the hottest actresses around, but one of their own? Moving along, Ruth shivered, wondering if her homecoming would be the big fuss she'd hoped it would be. OK, so Irish people were famed for their down-to-earth attitude towards celebrities, but she was Ruth Seymour, for goodness sake!

Suddenly missing LA's star mania, she reached the booth and held out her passport for inspection. The name would no doubt mean nothing to this bored middle-aged immigration officer, who sure enough, waved her through without a second glance.

Having collected her baggage she went through to the arrivals area, and immediately spied the man who would be her driver. He was holding a small sign with the name 'R. Seymour' printed on it, and she approached him with a smile that could melt titanium.

'Hello there,' she cooed. 'I think you're waiting for me?'

The man smiled and gave her a brief once-over, and while she knew Chloe had arranged a respected Dublin chauffeur service to collect her, Ruth wondered just how often this guy got to meet stars of her caliber. Her ego gradually began to swell and she felt giddy at the thought of him regally leading her through the arrivals area.

But rather than greeting her profusely and offering to take her Louis Vuitton carrier, the man just consulted his clipboard and motioned for Ruth to follow him.

'I should let you know that there are a load of photographers outside – apparently they found out you would be arriving today somehow.'

Ruth smiled to herself. Well of course the press knew about her arrival, thanks to a 'leak' about her schedule. *Good job Chloe.*

'That's no problem, it's to be expected,' she sighed.

'Yes, well … there are a lot of them, and they seem *very* eager to talk to you,' the driver said, and immediately Ruth felt the hairs on the back of her neck stand up.

The Irish press were clambering to see her. *Yes!* For most of her life Ruth had been dreaming of this moment, and through every crappy commercial, every embarrassing *gombeen* bit-part she'd been reduced to, she'd known this was her destiny. Now it was happening, it was really happening and Ruth felt more exhilarated than she'd ever been in her life.

Forget LA and what had happened last night; it was a blip, a tiny blot on an otherwise perfect week. Now, today this was her shot, her opportunity. And she was going to soak up every last minute of it.

'Anyway,' he continued. 'When we go through, just stay close to me and I'll make sure you get into the car safely.'

'Of course, thank you for your concern.'

She duly followed the driver through the pair of automatic doors to where the limo was parked. At least Ruth assumed it was towards the limo because once the doors opened, she couldn't see anything but a wall of blinding white light. Hundreds of camera flashes exploded in unison, and a throng of people surged towards her. Whoa, this was one hell of a welcome!

Ruth looked up and assumed her best superstar smile, courtesy of her six hundred dollars an hour orthodontist.

'Ruth, is it true you spent last night with Troy Valentine?' she heard one of them say, and all of a sudden her smile froze.

Her initial elation immediately turned to full blown panic as she was met with the yells and questions of a hundred people, yet all of the voices were asking the same question. 'Ruth, can you confirm that you left Chateau Marmont yesterday morning after spending the night with your co-star? Ruth, did you and Troy sleep together? Ruth, can you confirm this picture is you? Ruth, can you comment on what happened last night? Ruth, how long have you and Troy been sleeping together? Ruth, have you been having a secret relationship with Troy? Does your assistant always turn up with clean clothes the day after? Is Troy the reason for your recent success?'

Oh, my word ... Ruth screamed internally, her feet still immobile, until the driver caught her arm and began to carefully guide her forward through a crowd that was getting more demanding and chaotic by the second. They all know, she thought horrified, they all know what happened! And what was all that about a picture?

She thanked heaven that she'd had the good sense to keep her sunglasses on so she could hide her eyes, because at that moment she knew she must resemble a deer caught in the headlights. While she was of course used to media interest, she had never before met press that demanded answers; had never met photographers that seemed intent on embarrassing her; no one had been this vicious to her before. This is certainly not how she imagined her homecoming.

Guided by the driver, she tried to push her own way through the crowd; she needed to get out of here and safely into that car, she needed to talk to Chloe ... to her agent and –

Suddenly, a photographer pushed his way right into her line of sight, and stopped in front of her. Ruth stepped back quickly, sending her sunglasses flying in the process. As she tried to catch them, the guy snapped a picture. 'Ruth, how does it feel to be Hollywood's newest good-time girl?'

A fresh wave of horror overtook her, followed closely by shame. Hollywood's newest good-time girl? Is that how people were thinking of her here – in her own country! It hadn't even been twenty-four hours since she'd been lauded as Hollywood's newest golden girl...

Finally, she reached the waiting car and as the driver held open the door, she tried to get past a new crush of bodies that threatened to separate her from salvation. In doing so, she elbowed someone who was way too close and had shoved an 8 x 10 glossy photograph under her nose. Eyes widening, Ruth grabbed it and dove into the interior of the Mercedes.

The driver shut the door with a bang. Ruth let out a sigh and rested her head against the back of the seat. Tears began to fill in her eyes, but she was scared to show emotion, afraid that the people outside the car could see in. What if the tinting on the windows didn't work the way it was supposed to?

Outside the car, the throng of people continued to pound on the windows, and ask their relentless questions. Ruth realized she was dangerously close to a full-blown panic attack and thought she was going to lose it.

'Can we please go?' she said to the driver.

'I'm trying my best to get away love, but I don't want to hit anyone.'

Finally, airport security got involved and helped navigate the mobbed car away from the curb. Ruth let a single tear escape and was trying to slow down her breathing when she realized she was clutching something in her hand. It was the picture she'd grabbed.

Breathing deeply, she gave herself time to examine it. It looked like footage taken from a security camera and while the image was a little grainy, you could see it was of a man and a woman pictured beside a couple of public phones.

The woman was pressed up against the wall and had one leg wrapped around the man with the hem of the dress pushed up almost to her hip. They were in the throes of a very passionate kiss and looked like they didn't care who saw them.

Oh, no ...

No matter that at the time it had felt like one of the most romantic moments of her life, from this perspective, and for anyone who didn't know the details, it could be considered lewd and even trashy, especially with the poor picture quality.

Still, despite the grainy pixels affect there was no mistaking that the woman in the picture was her.

Ruth, how does it feel to be Hollywood's newest good-time girl? Is Troy the reason for your recent success?

Ruth wanted to die.

7

_N_ ina studied her appearance in the bedroom mirror. She didn't feel any different, and was having a hard time believing that she was in fact different – except for the test that had come up positive, and the recent scan she'd had back in Galway that very much confirmed that yes, she was indeed pregnant.

She stood sideways to look at her profile. Nope, definitely no bump yet. As her build was small, she worried that the slightest change would be noticeable, but still nothing. Thank goodness, she thought to herself. When she did start showing, she had no idea what she was going to tell people, least of all her mother.

Suddenly, as if on cue, Nina's mobile phone began ringing from inside her handbag, and when she checked the display she saw it was Cathy.

'Hi!' she answered, thrilled to be able to hear her mother's voice.

'Hey sweetheart, how are you doing?'

The line sounded broken-up so Nina moved to the window of the bedroom in the hope of improving the reception.

But it seemed the problem was on Cathy's end. 'I'm in Vietnam, calling from some crazy excuse for a phone box. Our mobiles won't work here. I'll keep pumping money in for as long as I can, but I might not be on for long –'

'Well then stop yapping about it and tell me how you're getting on? Is it brilliant? How was Kuala Lumpur? Where are you headed next? And how's Tony?'

The questions came thick and fast as Nina realized how much she truly missed her mum and how she wished she could be here beside her. She'd like nothing better than to be able to discuss all this with her, discuss the pregnancy and what she should do about it. But there was no way she would ruin her mother's trip of a lifetime by revealing any of it.

'He's great, everything's great, but more to the point, how are you? Has Steve been in touch, or have you guys already kissed and made up?'

Nina smiled sadly. There wasn't a hope in hell of that happening.

'No, Mum, it's really finished. But I'm fine about it so try not to worry.'

'Seriously? Honey, tell me the truth, and don't think you have to spare my feelings just 'cos I'm here. You know I'd come home in a second if you needed me and –'

'Mum, don't be silly,' Nina interjected, forcing a laugh that she hoped sounded genuine. 'I'm a big girl now and I'm fine.'

'But what about work? It must be tough having to face one another every day.'

She didn't have the courage to confess to her mother that she'd left both the job and Galway, or reveal her current living circumstances, as Cathy would know immediately that her daughter wouldn't have gone within a hair's breadth of Lakeview unless she was forced to. And she didn't want to tell her mother she was staying with Patrick unless it was absolutely necessary; Cathy would almost certainly be on the next flight back. 'No, it's fine, I've already organized something else,' she said, evasively. *Please don't ask for details,* she prayed silently.

'Really? That's great – at least I think it is, although I suppose that means that things really are over with you two then.'

'Yes, but listen, stop wasting your call credit on me; tell me all about what you two have been up to.'

'Well ...' and as Nina listened to her mother recount tales of jungle treks and Asian scenery, she was relieved that Cathy seemed content with her explanation and hadn't tried to press her about her circumstances.

Maybe it was silly not to tell her – not least about being in Lakeview, but about ... everything, but Nina truly believed that she was doing the right thing. She owed that much at least to Cathy, who had sacrificed everything for her growing up. Anyway, she'd know about it in good time she mused, as mother and daughter said their goodbyes; everyone would know about it in good time. As it was, her pregnancy was still her little secret and no one (other than the doctor of course) knew about it.

Her stomach twisted at the thought of her ex. Despite being madly in love, she never really knew him at all, did she? She'd been so sure they would get married one day, live happily ever after and have a lovely little family. And although becoming pregnant was an accident, Nina hadn't been too upset about it initially; she figured it would just speed up the natural course of things somewhat. However, she couldn't have known, could never have anticipated that their relationship was based entirely on lies. Should she have known? No, she thought, shaking her head; it wasn't her fault that she'd trusted him, and wasn't her character flaw, but his.

She banished Steve from her brain then; she didn't want to think about him, or his lies.

She lay back down on the bed and absently patted her stomach. She really was a million miles away from the state of maternal bliss most soon-to-be-mums tended to experience, she thought sadly. Still, despite its parents' mistakes, this was a brand new life and she would never dream of having an abortion. Even in the aftermath of their break-up, she'd never considered such a thing for even one second. No, there were definitely other options available; all Nina had to do was find one that suited everyone best. That's why she was here, in Lakeview after all, to help clear her head, gather her thoughts and figure out her life.

Reluctantly, she pushed herself up off the bed. Gosh, she was tired! She could easily go back to sleep for a couple more hours without a problem, but of course Patrick had again knocked on her door at seven a.m. Frustrating, considering he then proceeded to hog the only bathroom, leaving her to twiddle her thumbs while she waited for it to be free.

Finally, she heard the bathroom door open and her father make his way downstairs. She was just about to head for the door, when suddenly she broke into a cold sweat, followed by an immediate wave of nausea. Propelling herself out of the room, she barely made it to the bathroom in time before emptying her stomach of last night's dinner.

Nina held on to the side of the bowl as another wave came and she gagged pitifully, tears forming at the corner of her eyes from the strain. Then suddenly, her face flushed, not just from the strain, but embarrassment. In her rush, she hadn't closed the bathroom door, and now Patrick was standing in the doorway observing her.

'Um, I was just going to ask if you wanted an egg this morning. There are only two left.'

Nina gritted her teeth, as the mere mention of food was enough to send her off again.

'No, you carry on and have them yourself,' she said, knowing that he usually had two fried eggs himself, and she didn't want to leave him short.

'Grand. Um, bit of a stomach ache?' he asked awkwardly, and despite herself Nina smiled. He'd just witnessed something akin to *The Exorcist* and all he could say was 'bit of a stomach ache?'

'Apparently,' she said, standing up and wiping her mouth. Stomach ache, no – morning sickness, yes, she thought to herself. Such a thing however, would hardly dawn on Patrick, so she didn't have to worry. 'I must have eaten something funny last night.'

'Right,' Patrick said, still standing there, looking at her. Nina couldn't believe it. Why couldn't he just go away or at least offer to help in some way?

'Is there any chance you could maybe get me a glass of water?' she urged and Patrick duly headed downstairs. Moments later he returned with the water and she noticed that at least he'd had the courtesy to put ice in it.

Handing her the glass, Patrick looked awkwardly around the bathroom. 'Anything else?' he asked stiltedly.

Nina shook her head, and happy to be released from his duties, Patrick complied.

She washed her hands, cursing herself for leaving the door open. Her father wasn't stupid and if this happened again he was liable to get suspicious, so she'd have to make sure to do it more quietly or get out of the house in the morning. Both ideas troubled her; she hated having to sneak around, wished she had her own space and didn't have to worry about someone suspecting something.

But for the moment, she had little other choice.

8

*H*aving composed herself, Nina once again refused Patrick's offer of breakfast and went outside for some fresh air. She was still a little peaky so the short walk down town should help somewhat.

But some twenty minutes later, she felt more stirrings, this time not of nausea, but of hunger, and once again she headed for Ella's café.

The cozy little room was so much more welcoming than Patrick's, plus it had the added bonus of providing her with some normal conversation.

When she walked in this morning, Trish was already at the counter, looking over a section of newspaper. Her friend had the same fashionably messy ponytail in place and appeared to be deep in thought.

'Hiya Trish,' Nina said, pleased to see her. She took a seat on a stool close by.

'Oh, hey Nina,' Looking up from the paper, Trish smiled and removed the pen she'd been chewing on from her mouth.

'Am I interrupting something?'

'Oh no, just flicking through the gossip pages. I know it's complete rubbish, but I can't help myself.'

Nina smiled. It was funny the way people always had to defend their interest in celeb gossip, especially when it was often the first section they went to.

'Anything interesting?'

Trish looked up. 'Well now that you ask ...' she purred mischievously. She pushed forward the page, upon which was emblazoned a half-page photograph of a decidedly frazzled-looking Ruth Seymour. 'Look at this awful picture of our old friend arriving at Dublin airport in the early hours of this morning.'

'No ...' Despite herself, Nina was captivated. Trish was right; it was a *dreadful* picture. Ruth was pushing through photographers, her sunglasses dangled halfway off her head and strands of her blonde hair were caught in her mouth. The normally beautifully groomed actress looked almost haggard, and the shot was so close-up, dark circles around her eyes were clearly visible.

'So much for our leading lady,' Trish groaned as if disappointed. '*Bag* lady is a more accurate description, if you ask me.'

Coffee pot in hand, Ella leaned over the counter for a better look. 'Ah Trish, be fair,' she said. 'The girl just got off an overnight flight. I'm sure you wouldn't look so hot.' Smiling at Nina, she reached beneath the counter and put a fresh cup of coffee in front of her, joined soon after by a slice of toasted, thickly buttered soda bread – exactly what Nina needed to settle her stomach.

'I don't think that it's that simple,' Trish grimaced, pointing to the accompanying story which suggested that Ruth had spent much of the Aer Lingus flight green – not through patriotism, but from her drunken romp the night before. Accounts from people who were supposedly 'in the know' in Hollywood outlined the fact that a very intoxicated Ruth and Troy Valentine had practically had sex in public at the Beverly Hills Hotel, before taking their liaison to Chateau Marmont, where the noise they made kept up other hotel patrons for the better part of the night. A second picture accompanied the story; a grainy shot of a couple in the throes of passion in what looked to be a hotel lobby. 'Apparently our Ruth is quite the screamer.'

Ella *tsked*, 'Stop that Trish, it's probably all rubbish anyway.

Besides, keep your voice down, some of her relations are sitting over there.'

Trish giggled guiltily. 'Anyway, she's supposedly been holed up at the Four Seasons since this morning, afraid to show her face, I'd say. She's doing the *Late* show tonight and then she and the family are heading back here tomorrow. You still on for the party tomorrow night?' she asked Nina.

'Oh yes, looking forward to it.'

'Good, it'll be fun to have a girl's night out again. Unless of course your fella's around, in which case he's welcome to come too.'

'Oh, I'm not seeing anyone at the moment,' Nina replied uncomfortably.

'Really? Sorry, aren't you still with that guy, what was his name? Steve, wasn't it?'

Nina had forgotten that Trish had met Steve briefly that time she'd met up with her in Galway.

'No, that ended a while back.'

'Oh. OK.' Luckily Trish wasn't too interested in the specifics. 'Great, well that means it's just you and me then.'

'No one on the scene for you either then?'

Trish's eyes twinkled. 'Well, actually there is, but he won't be around tomorrow night. He has something else on.'

'That's great Trish. I can't wait to meet him.'

'I'm sure you will, if you're around long enough. How long are you going to be here for anyway?'

'Not sure yet, just for a while, we'll see.'

'Is your dad OK? You're not here because he's sick or anything?'

'No, he's fine, completely healthy,' she said. Despite his *heart attack* breakfasts, Nina thought wryly.

Trish was silent; she obviously wanted some kind of explanation, so Nina gave her one. 'It's just because ... well with living so far away and all, it's important to spend time with your parents, isn't it?'

Trish nodded, and while Nina wasn't sure how good a cover story it was, it would have to do. Thankfully at that moment her friend was distracted by two women entering the café. One was carrying a young baby and the other was holding two small boys by the hand. Noticing their entry, Trish turned back to the newspaper.

'Friends of yours?' Nina asked, noticing her sudden change of mood. The women had taken a table at the further end of the room, one that had enough space around it to accommodate them and all their paraphernalia. Each had a baby changing bag, an oversized handbag as well as some kind of sack containing lots of toys. Another was carrying a type of chair contraption that she was now trying to attach to a baby seat. It seemed an awful lot of gear to be carrying just to go out for coffee. Hmm, Nina thought, figuring all that stuff was likely expensive too; she had a lot to learn.

'Oh no, just a couple of the newcomers from Dublin, dreadful 'mumzilla' types, you know yourself.'

Nina smiled at the description, wondering if Trish would classify her in the future as one of those 'dreadful 'mumzilla' types'.

In the meantime, Ella had gone over to greet them. 'Emer, Deirdre. How are you both? And all the lovely little ones?'

As the commotion grew ever louder, Trish turned to Nina and rolled her eyes, 'I'd better get to work. See you tomorrow?'

Nina took this as a clear indication that her friend must not like kids very much, to not even want to be in the same room as them. As her friend stood to go, noisily clicking her high heels on the floor of the café, one of the women looked up and noticed her.

'Hey, Trish, how are you?' she said in a very warm tone for someone who'd been dismissed as 'just a newcomer'.

'Hi Emer, fine thanks, nice to see you,' Trish replied in a way that was a million miles away from her usual chatty self.

'Have you time for a coffee? I'm not sure if you know Deirdre and –'

'Sorry, can't, I'm on a deadline,' Trish tapped her watch. 'But maybe Nina might like to?' She motioned to Nina, who smiled at the women, even though she was mortified. Why had she put her in a position like that?

'Yes, well, maybe next time,' the woman said, turning her attention back to her baby.

'Sure. Have a lovely breakfast. Anyway, better get going, bye!' Like a flash Trish was gone.

The woman called Emer looked up and smiled kindly at Nina. 'Join us for a coffee?'

'Oh, I don't want to impose ...'

'Not at all, please do,' she insisted and Nina reluctantly assented, not sure what to expect, given that Trish had given this woman a definite brush-off.

'So are you new in town?' Emer asked when introductions had been made.

'Not exactly. My father lives here, and I'm staying with him for a while.'

'Oh, right. Who's that? Maybe we know him; our families only moved here last year, but it's such a small place you sort of get to know everyone, don't you Deirdre?' she said and the other woman rolled her eyes.

'The joys of small-town living!' she joked.

'Patrick Hughes,' Nina told them and was she imagining it, or did the two women exchange a surreptitious look?

'Oh yes, that's the TV repair guy, isn't it?' Emer replied. 'I've heard of him, but don't think we've ever met, and hope we don't have to.' Seeing Nina's expression, she added hastily, 'I mean the plasma that Dave bought cost a packet, so I sincerely hope it doesn't need mending any time soon!'

The three of them laughed and Nina was immediately put at ease; for a second there, she'd worried that Patrick had done something to offend one of them, or that his 'odd' reputation had preceded him. But apparently not.

The kids were noisy and full of fun, and while the table quickly became messy and slightly chaotic, it was a nice atmosphere to be involved in. Emer and Deirdre seemed like nice women and their children were enjoyable to be around. She couldn't understand her friend's quick departure upon the women's entrance. Some people just didn't like being around children, of course, but wasn't her friend's reaction a little extreme? Oh, well, she thought, not everyone was going to mesh, but she did worry what Trish would think if she learned about her own situation.

Thinking about this, in the other mums' company, she felt for the first time ever a slight twinge of excitement and allowed herself to enjoy it. Although, listening to their conversation did worry her somewhat. Babies sounded *very* expensive, what with nappies, clothes and buggies, and she couldn't believe some of the numbers they were throwing out. Maybe she should think about getting a job while she was here.

'Well, goodness, look at the time, I'd better get Amy home for her nap,' Emer said after a while. Her little girl Amy was indeed rubbing her eyes and looking sleepy. 'Nina, it really was lovely chatting with you, and no doubt we'll see you around.'

'Lovely talking to you too,' Nina said, pleased she had made some new friends and soon after, Deirdre and Emer left the café pretty much the same way that they'd arrived, in a whirlwind of kids, toys and noise.

Nina settled back in at the counter, happy thus far with her morning and in no real hurry to go home. 'Would you like another cup of coffee, love?' Ella offered, on her way into the kitchen with another order.

'I'd love one, but since I'm here propping up your counter all morning, I should probably get it myself.' Nina laughed.

'Well, feel free,' Ella said, smiling. 'The place is a bit mad at the moment.' She paused as she watched Nina deftly negotiate the coffee-maker. 'Actually, I was wondering ...'

'What?'

'Well, I'm not sure how long you're staying, but I could do with an extra pair of hands round here for the summer months. My usual baker, Colm, do you remember him? He's off on a career break for a few months, traveling around the world. This place gets crazy with the tourists and everything. I normally get one of the school-leavers, but what do you think? Only part-time mind, but would you fancy it?'

'I'd love to,' Nina said, liking the idea. A part-time job at the café would be a godsend. As well as giving her something to do and keeping her out of Patrick's way, it would also give her a couple of quid towards some baby things, should she need them.

'Fantastic. Well then, grab an apron and like that Donald Trump fella says, "you're hired".'

9

*J*ess Armstrong was having enormous difficulty trying to decide between the Fendi and the Prada. The former was pebbled brown leather and gold hardware; the latter squishy calfskin embellished with tiny lavender flowers.

If she were buying the handbag for herself it wouldn't be an issue, but trying to pick one that was special enough as a gift while also being practical to suit Emer's day-to-day lifestyle was a real challenge. The elegant Fendi was the obvious choice of course, but the Prada was so pretty and had way more of a wow factor, didn't it?

And Jess really wanted her best friend to be wowed by her birthday present – she deserved it.

Ten months ago Emer had given birth to her first child, little Amy, but had found the initial transition to motherhood difficult and Jess had been really worried about her. The two had been friends for many years, and when Emer in the early days admitted to Jess she was struggling, she tried her utmost to help in every way she could; a shoulder to cry on, someone to talk to, but mostly just to be there as much as possible for her friend during such a difficult period. Thankfully, Emer had come through the worst though, and these days, was taking to family life like the proverbial duck to water.

So this and the fact that her friend's thirty-fifth birthday was this weekend was reason enough for Jess to want to spoil her with something extra special. They weren't usually so extravagant in their gifts to one another and she knew Emer would be blown away by such a lavish present. Which was exactly the point.

'I just can't decide,' she said to the Brown Thomas store assistant, who confused her even further by suggesting a temptingly beautiful petrol blue patent Alexander McQueen.

Jess resisted the urge to chew on a strand of honey blonde hair – an awful childhood habit that she could never quite break – as she wondered if patent might actually be a good idea for a new mum; it would be more practical for baby stains, wouldn't it? Yet, at the same time she couldn't picture Emer wandering around Lakeview with a bright blue space-aged style McQueen, she'd definitely get some weird looks from the locals.

Less than an hour's drive from Dublin on the motorway, Lakeview was very much your quintessential Irish small town, locally owned pubs and shops and a gorgeous café along one short street, surrounded by pretty older houses, and lavish, sprawling newer ones further out – all centered round the large oxbow lake.

Emer and her husband had moved there on the advice of their other mutual friends Deirdre and Kevin, who had already relocated there – the houses in Lakeview were larger and cheaper than what was available in Dublin; and the quieter pace of life was perfect for growing families. Jess loved visiting her friends down there and harbored the odd hope that she and Brian might one day follow the other couples in setting up home in the area, but at the same time her hubby was a Dub through and through, and she knew he'd miss the cut and thrust of city life. In truth, Jess would probably miss it too. It was lovely to visit a sleepy place like Lakeview for a couple of hours and enjoy the laid-back way of things, but after a while the quieter pace of life might very well be grating.

Eventually deciding on the lavender Prada (to hell with practicality) Jess left the store and headed out into the late afternoon sunshine towards St Stephen's Green shopping center where her car was parked. It was a beautifully sunny May day, and for once she got to make proper use of her Ray Bans instead of just perching them on the top of her head like she usually did. Grafton Street was especially buzzy on days like this; the street performers and late-evening shoppers were out in force and she smiled as she sauntered along, jauntily swinging the striped Brown Thomas carrier bag.

On her way, she couldn't resist nipping into a nearby toy store to pick up a cute teddy bear for little Amy. Well, her niece deserved a treat too, didn't she? Not that Amy was *really* her niece, but she was the closest thing Jess was going to get to one, as she herself was an only child.

And Emer was as good as any sister. They'd known one another for what seemed like forever, but in reality was only about fifteen years, when they'd met on the first day of college. Having both graduated with marketing degrees, they'd taken up work at the same Dublin-based drinks distribution company, and while Emer had in the meantime given up the job, moved to Lakeview and started a family, Jess was still working with the same company. Well, in theory at least, as the small Irish firm had since been taken over and rebranded under the massive international Piccolo label. The company was responsible for the majority of Irish premium brand alcoholic beverages, and Jess's recently promoted role to marketing manager for Ireland was to ensure that their key brands remained fresh and desirable to the drinking public both here and internationally. And speaking of which ... as she passed by a popular tourist pub, Jess was gratified to see that the majority of customers sitting outdoors were enjoying the sunshine over longneck bottles of Piccolo's current brand leader.

If only her latest campaign could so easily convince Brian, she thought fondly. Her hubby just couldn't be persuaded to switch from his lifetime favorite, Guinness, to Piccolo's equivalent Porters, much to his wife's chagrin. She'd tried hundreds of times throughout their seven-year marriage to persuade him of Porters' merits, but he just couldn't be turned. His doggedness (or contrariness as Jess called it) was something that amused their friends no end, and something that frustrated her in equal measures, but as it was just about the only thing he did that annoyed her she could certainly live with it. Jess shook her head in silent amazement. Seven years now. It was hard to believe she and Brian had been married that long, especially when it still felt almost like only seven months. He was a great friend, confidant and her absolute soul mate, and she didn't know what she would do without him. Although she had no choice but to do without him this week at least, as he was away with work in Singapore and wouldn't be back until Sunday night.

Well, she'd have plenty to occupy her until then. Having been out every single night this week at work-related parties and events, tonight would be a rare night in, and Jess planned to go home and have a good long soak in the bath, which should help recharge the batteries. Tomorrow afternoon she'd pop down to Lakeview for a visit and give Emer and Amy their presents.

She wondered idly if Emer's husband Dave would be taking her out for dinner tonight. Probably not; finding a babysitter would undoubtedly be difficult, and anyway, Jess suspected the still-new parents might find it a wrench to leave their precious baby daughter with anyone. Still, she wondered now if she should forgo her quiet night in tonight and at least offer to look after Amy just in case the two of them would like some time on their own. She could be down there by seven, barring heavy traffic, and still allowing enough time to pop back home to her own place to pick up an overnight bag.

Yes, that's what she'd do, Jess thought, checking the time on her mobile phone before dialing her friend's home number. It was just after five-thirty; Emer was sure to be home, but she hoped the ringing wouldn't interrupt poor Amy's nap or something. For this reason, she was nearly always wary of phoning Emer's house or mobile without warning as she could only imagine how frustrating it must be for new mums trying to get a young baby settled.

'You'd swear you had experience with this kind of thing,' Brian often teased her, making fun of her concerns, when they both knew that Jess hadn't the foggiest idea about babies or what was involved in raising them.

'It doesn't take a genius to work out that noise wakes people – tiny or otherwise,' she'd retorted tartly.

Now, as she waited for Emer to answer the phone, she seriously hoped that this wasn't a bad time and that her friend wouldn't be cursing her from a height when she picked up.

'Hello?' Emer said, somewhat tiredly and Jess winced.

'Oops, sorry – I hope I haven't woken her up?'

'What? Oh, hi Jess, how are you? No, you haven't woken Amy up, she's here beside me.'

'Oh, great, I'm nearly always holding my breath about phoning at the wrong time, just in case. So how is she? And how are you? Looking forward to tomorrow?'

'Tomorrow ...'

Jess smiled. 'Come on – stop trying to fool me by pretending it's no big deal. Every birthday is a big deal Emer, especially when this time you'll be getting a card that says Mummy on it.'

'I know, that *will* be weird.'

'Well, I don't want to keep you as I'm sure you're up to your eyes, but I just wondered if you and Dave wanted a night out on your own tonight, or tomorrow night even? I'd be happy to watch Amy. Brian's away this weekend so I could come down and stay over?'

'Oh ...'

Jess raised an eyebrow, wondering why her friend sounded so taken aback by this. Or wait no, was it more like ... uncomfortable? Thinking about it now, maybe it was stupid of her to offer and perhaps Emer wouldn't in a million years dream of leaving her baby daughter with someone of limited experience, and no real idea about what was involved? But Jess was certain it would be a piece of cake; Amy was a little darling and thanks to Brian's extended family, she wasn't completely clueless when it came to changing nappies and suchlike. But whatever her reasons, Emer definitely didn't sound enthusiastic at the prospect.

'Thanks for the offer Jess, that's really nice of you, but it's fine. We don't really fancy going out.'

'Are you sure? No need to worry; I'm positive I could handle her and –'

'It's nothing like that, honestly, it's just that ... well, we'd really rather just have a quiet night in – no fuss you know?'

'OK ... well as long as you're sure. And don't ever be afraid to ask either; you know I'd only be too delighted to give you guys a break.'

'I know that, thanks Jess.'

'So will you be around tomorrow? I was going to pop down with your birthday present.'

'Oh, you really shouldn't have. But yes, we'll be at home all day, although around lunchtime would probably be best.'

'No problem. Hopefully the nice weather will hold. It's great at the moment, isn't it? Must be brilliant for you and Amy to be able to spend time out in the garden.'

'We're really enjoying it, yes.'

Unlike her and Brian's postage stamp in Booterstown, Emer and Dave's house had the benefit of a huge back garden with plenty of space for Amy when she got to running-around age. One of the major benefits of moving to the countryside, Jess supposed.

'Well, hopefully we'll get a chance to grab a few rays tomorrow. I'll bring a bottle of bubbly, and maybe I can persuade you into having a sneaky glass over lunch – just for your birthday.' As far as she knew Emer was still off alcohol, her friend having decided well before her pregnancy that it was no longer appropriate for her to be behaving like the town wino. A casualty of their profession, Jess knew, (although some people might call it a perk) but she knew where her friend was coming from. Working for a drinks company inevitably led to lots and lots of alcohol-related and themed social events and gatherings over the years, and while Emer had since got off that particular merry-go-round, Jess was still very much in full, ahem ... flow.

Emer laughed. 'We'll see how it goes.'

'Great. Well, enjoy your quiet night in, and I'll see you tomorrow. Give Amy a kiss for me, won't you?'

'Will do, Jess. See you then.'

. . .

THE FOLLOWING DAY Jess got in her Mercedes SLK and reached Lakeview around lunchtime, having phoned Emer on the way to ask if she needed her to bring anything.

'Thanks a million, but no,' her friend replied, sounding a bit groggy and Jess deduced that the baby must have been keeping her up the previous night.

Well, hopefully her new handbag would give her a boost, she thought, looking forward to seeing her friend's face when she opened the specially-wrapped gift box. Emer was always admiring Jess's own faithful Jimmy Choo and now that the Kellerman's were a one-income household, she suspected that Emer didn't have a whole lot of money to spend on herself. Another reason Jess felt she deserved something a little bit special.

'Oh dear, bad night with Amy?' she said sympathetically to Emer upon arrival, catching sight of her friend's grey and rather haggard appearance as they went through to the kitchen. Actually, she looked pretty much like she used to after one of their many nights out on the town.

'No, she was fine,' Emer said, waving away Jess's concern. 'Dave had to go out for the afternoon, but he says to say hi.'

'Oh, sorry I missed him. Well, anyway – before I forget, happy birthday!'

'What's this?' Emer looked mystified by the large Brown Thomas gift box Jess handed to her. 'Don't say that's for me.'

'Of course it's for you,' Jess said, grinning.

'Jess, I –'

'Oh go on and just open the darned thing. And don't say anything else until you do.'

'Well ...' Emer untied the soft black ribbon and slowly lifted back the folds of tissue paper. And when she finally revealed the magnificent leather bag, she froze, and her face flushed in appreciation ... or discomfort, Jess couldn't be sure.

'Do you like it?' she asked, worried now that she'd chosen the wrong option. Maybe this was too 'over the top' and the Fendi would have been much more Emer's style? 'Perhaps the color is a bit tricky, but –'

'It's amazing. Wow Jess, I don't know what to say ...'

'You don't need to say anything. I know it's a bit unexpected, but I really wanted to get you something nice this time, something special I suppose after everything you've been through this year.'

'I just can't believe it. I'm astonished, never in a million years did I expect something like ... or that you would ...'

'Well, of course you didn't expect it; it wouldn't be a surprise then, would it?' Jess smiled, pleased that her gift seemed to be having the desired effect, although she really hoped it hadn't made Emer uncomfortable or anything – or worse, made her worry that she had to return the favor. 'Look, this is just a once off, something to celebrate you becoming a mum, and your birthday of course, but also just for being a great friend for all these years, you know?'

Emer was shaking her head. 'I just can't believe it. And Prada! Jess, this really must have cost you a fortune.'

'It's nothing really. I got a surprise bonus last month so it's really no big deal.' That wasn't strictly true, but if it made Emer feel better then ...

'No big deal? Wow, looks like I got out of the game too soon. That promotion obviously has you rolling in it.' And did Jess imagine it, or was there a slight tinge of ... resentment in her tone? No, surely not, Emer was the one who'd decided to bow out of the workplace in order to move to Lakeview and concentrate on family life, and she knew better than anyone how hard Jess worked.

'Well not quite, but unlike you, I suppose I don't really have anyone else to spend it on, but oh, speaking of which ...' Jess reached again into the bag and took out the small teddy bear. 'This is for Amy.'

'Thank you – again. I'm sure she'll love it.' But although her friend sounded normal enough, Jess still thought she noticed something on the edge of her tone.

Oh, she was probably just imagining it, she thought, shaking off the feeling. Maybe Emer was just wrong-footed by her extravagance

with the handbag and still a little taken aback to respond as enthusiastically as Jess had hoped?

'Where is Amy anyway?' she asked.

'Out on the decking in her bouncer – and still asleep, I hope. Will
a sandwich be OK for you for lunch? I didn't have to time to prepare
much –'

'A sandwich is perfect and don't go to any fuss, anything at all will
be fine. Actually, do you want me to sort out something while you go
and check on her?' Jess didn't want Emer to feel as though she needed
to wait on her hand and foot, especially when she'd obviously had
such a hard night.

'No, it's fine, I've got some made up. Orange juice OK too?'

'Perfect.' Somehow for reasons Jess still couldn't identify, the vibe
didn't seem right for champagne.

'You know you could have told me to get lost today if you wanted
to,' she said to Emer when they were seated outside at the patio table,
Amy sleeping peacefully alongside them.

'Get lost?'

'Well, if you weren't up to having visitors.' Jess couldn't think of
any other reason why the atmosphere between her and Emer seemed
so strained. It couldn't be about the bag could it? Had she got that
really wrong and made her friend uncomfortable rather than
delighted?

'Not at all, it's fine,' her friend said, but her tone definitely didn't
make Jess feel any happier.

'Right. Well cheers then,' she said, holding her glass of orange
juice aloft. 'Happy Birthday.'

'Thanks Jess, and thanks so much again for the beautiful handbag. I'm floored by it.'

'As I said, you deserve it.' Jess smiled. 'I don't know what the hell
you'll *wear* it with, but –'

Just then Emer's doorbell rang, and her friend jumped up to
answer it. 'I wonder who that is?' she said, frowning. 'I'm not
expecting anyone ...'

A few seconds later, she returned with a woman Jess didn't recognize, but who was carrying a baby that looked a little bit older than Amy.

'Jess this is Grainne, one of the neighbors.'

Jess stood up to greet her. 'Really nice to meet you. And who's this gorgeous little fellow?' she cooed, smiling at the little boy the woman held in her arms.

'This is Ross. And great to meet you too,' Grainne said before turning again to Emer. 'Listen, I'm sorry to interrupt, but amid last night's craziness, I think Ross might have left his toy here. It's a little black and white thing that looks like it might have been a dog at one stage, except for the two chewed off paws?'

'Oh, right. I don't think I've seen it,' Emer replied, but there was no mistaking the deep red flush that appeared on her face and traveled all the way down her neck.

Jess was perplexed. What on earth was up with Emer today? Anyone would think that she was embarrassed about having her here. What was going on? And what did Grainne mean by last night's craziness?

'Not to worry. Maybe one of the other kids picked it up. I can only blame myself for not being um ... observant enough to keep an eye on it. And the O'Connors weren't much better. I blame Emer for force-feeding us all that booze, or should I say force-drinking,' she added winking at Jess. 'Great barbeque though,' she added to Emer, who didn't seem to know where to look. 'I met Jill Carney earlier and she's as bad as I am – none of us are able for late nights anymore. Oh, and happy birthday again.'

Now it was Jess's turn to feel wrong-footed. Late nights? Didn't Emer tell her when she offered to babysit last night that she and Dave were having a quiet night in? But instead it seemed they'd hosted a big birthday barbeque. Not that it was any of Jess's business what they did or didn't do, but why lie about it?

'I'll keep an eye out,' Emer was saying now, as she walked Grainne back through to the front door, while Jess remained in the garden, perplexed. She tried to get a handle on this for a second. Not only had Emer refused her offer to babysit, but she'd also lied outright about a party and decided not to invite her, while knowing well that Brian was away and she was at a loose end. And then to top it all off, today she'd been sniffy about Jess's earnings and had questioned her generosity.

'So a late night last night then?' she said evenly, when Emer came back outside.

'Yeah. It was one of those unexpected things, you know.'

'So you and Dave didn't get your quiet night in after all?'

'No. Look Jess, I would have invited you, but ...'

There was a heavy silence, and right then Jess understood that something major had shifted in their friendship.

'Well it's just ... it was more of a kid's thing really, so I didn't think ...'

Immediately Jess felt wounded. So she needed children to gain a pass to her friend's life these days?

'Look, I just thought it would be easier if you didn't ... I mean ...' The sentence trailed off, but Jess didn't really need to hear the rest.

Her heart sank. Best friends or not, clearly Emer felt it was preferable to cut her out of certain aspects of her life and keep her at arm's length – simply because she wasn't a member of that exclusive club, that lately most of her friends seemed to have joined.

The mummy club.

ack in Dublin, Jess worried over what had happened at Emer's. She felt hurt and betrayed that her so-called best friend would lie in order to keep her away from her Happy Families party.

So now that Emer had a child and Jess didn't, it was easier to just cut her out of her life? Why? What difference did it make, and why should it make a difference at all?

It certainly made no sense to Jess anyway, and she couldn't believe that Emer seriously felt the need to purposely leave her out of the celebrations. And to think she even offered to babysit.

Earlier that day, Emer had tried her best to smooth things over when her neighbor left, by being overly chatty and offering to share the bottle of champagne she'd been so reluctant about before.

'Oh, go on then, you've twisted my arm,' she'd said, cheerily, as if nothing at all had happened.

'No, it's fine, maybe you should just keep it for your next party,' Jess murmured, before eventually making her excuses and leaving.

While she'd tried her utmost not to betray her feelings about the situation, it was difficult. On the one hand, she felt a bit silly for being so upset about it, but on the other there was no question that she had been deceived. By someone who was supposed to be her best friend, the person with whom she'd shared pretty much everything with over the last fifteen years. Well, clearly Emer wasn't interested in sharing her new life with her, Jess mused unhappily, not while she remained childfree in any case.

And that wasn't on the cards, not yet anyway. She and Brian would like to have children someday of course, but the time wasn't quite right. Granted, they'd been married for seven years and together for over ten, but somehow the idea had never really occurred to them. Their careers probably had a lot to do with it; Brian was away so much with the executive travel agency he managed, and Jess had been working her way up the corporate ladder at Piccolo.

Thinking about it now as she moved through their Dublin townhouse, she wasn't quite sure why they'd never thought seriously about going down that route; goodness knows enough of their immediate circle had done it. Emer and Dave, Deirdre and Kevin, and many of the other couples they socialized with.

Or used to.

Jess knew Brian would be an amazing dad and she hoped she'd be a good mother, as she adored babies and liked spending time with children; Emer's little Amy being a case in point. Yet, she'd never really pictured herself as a mother, for some reason feeling that there was plenty of time for that and when the time came, she'd know about it. After all, there was a time in every woman's life when she just knew, wasn't there? Although perhaps this line of thinking was fine when you're twenty-four but not so much when you're thirty-five.

It was strange, but still Jess associated settling down and starting a family as something older, more mature people did, and didn't feel she and Brian were quite at that stage yet. Her maternal instinct hadn't yet kicked in, and because of this, babies still didn't really feature in their plans.

Why not? Was there some other subconscious reason that she hadn't considered?

She went to the bedroom and stripped off her clothes, changing into a pair of pajama pants and an old t-shirt and tying her fair hair into a ponytail.

She looked around the bedroom she shared with her husband, realizing that the normal sense of calm that she got from this tranquil place with its bright interior and luxurious fabrics was not apparent today. She tried to see it through Emer's eyes, suspecting that her friend might note the room for its beauty, but would possibly deem it lacking because the floor wasn't strewn with toys.

Then a sudden bubble of defensiveness rose up inside her. Why should she be feeling undermined by this? She had a fabulous career, a wonderful husband who loved her, and an all-round great life. She was happy with her own choices, happy with her life as it was. At least, she was until this weekend.

She wanted desperately to talk to Brian about what had happened, and on any other day would have phoned him immediately, but at that moment he was thirty-thousand feet above sea-level on his way back from Singapore. He'd be home later and they could talk about it then.

Jess sighed, wishing she didn't have to wait. She needed to talk to someone, needed to share what had happened and reassure herself that she wasn't just imagining things; that her friendship with Emer really was in jeopardy.

In the open wardrobe, her eyes rested on a DVF dress that her friend Deirdre had admired last time she'd worn it. Of course, Deirdre! No better woman to talk to about this, and who being both a friend of hers and Emer's would be able to shine a light on it. She too lived in Lakeview, and was also a mum to two small toddlers, something which as far as Jess could recall had never had any negative bearing on their relationship.

Feeling slightly heartened at the thought of being able to discuss her worries with a sympathetic third party, Jess reached for the bedside phone, and dialed Deirdre's number.

The phone rang seven times, and Jess was beginning to think that her friend wasn't home when finally, on the eighth ring, Deirdre picked up.

'Hello?' she gasped, and Jess noted how frazzled she sounded.

'Deirdre, hey it's Jess.'

'Oh, hello there!' she replied and as Jess heard the genuine warmth in her voice, she began to feel more at ease.

'How are you? Just thought I'd phone and say –'

'Boys, I said NO! Hold on Jess, it's World War Three here.' Deirdre didn't wait for Jess to respond; instead she placed the phone down on whatever surface must have been closest and went off to scold one of the boys for doing something ... with a frog apparently. OK, Jess thought with a smile, whatever that was about, she really didn't want to know. Finally, all seemed quiet again and Jess waited for her friend to get back on the line.

'I'm sorry Jess,' Deirdre groaned. 'Both boys are in a mood and I'm being referee all day.'

'No worries,' Jess said, easily. 'I can imagine.' Although she couldn't, not really.

'So how are you?'

'Well ...' Jess wasn't quite sure how to broach the subject without feeling like an idiot. 'I'm having a bit of a crisis actually.'

'Crisis – you?' Deirdre said with a faint laugh as if the very idea were preposterous. 'Ah, let me guess, you can't get those new season Choos in your size?'

While she might have been joking (and almost certainly was), Jess's heart sank afresh at the idea that her friend would think her so shallow that the only crisis she could possibly have was a wardrobe one. It wasn't as though Jess was some bimbo airhead with nothing to do but shop all day. She was a professional businesswoman with an important job and a full team under her remit.

But realizing that she was liable to be touchy just now, she resisted the urge to remind Deirdre so. 'Ah, no nothing like that,' she chuckled. 'No, this is actually about Emer.'

'Oh?'

'Well, I called down to Lakeview earlier with her birthday present and –'

'Ah blast it – I forgot her birthday was today. I wouldn't mind, but we were only talking about it a few days ago and ... sorry go on,' Deirdre said, the rest of her sentence trailing off.

Jess duly filled Deirdre in on her afternoon with Emer, from the offer and subsequent refusal to babysit, Emer's outright lie about her plans, to the arrival of her neighbor and the truth coming out.

Deirdre listened silently at first as she took in the story, and hearing herself recount it, Jess felt surer than ever that she had been hard done by.

'So you see, it's not so much that I'm upset she didn't invite me, more that she felt the need to lie about it,' she said in conclusion. 'Although I suppose I am a bit miffed about that too, especially when she knew I was at a loose end.'

'I know what you mean,' her friend replied, and Jess immediately started to feel better; sensing she had an advocate.

'So what do you think?' she urged. 'Am I right in being totally cheesed off? Not to mention pretty hurt.'

There was silence on the other end of the line. 'Well ... you see, this is a bit of a tricky situation. I understand you being mad, but I have to admit I kind of understand Emer's side of it too.'

'Really?' Jess said, sitting up straight in bed. Emer's side? 'What do you mean?' Then something Deirdre had said hit her. '*I wouldn't mind, but we were only talking about it a few days ago ...*'

'Wait a minute, were you there last night? Did you go to the party too?'

'No I wasn't there,' Deirdre said, quickly, and Jess started to relax again, happier in the knowledge that she wasn't the only one who had been excluded. 'I mean ... we were invited, but we didn't go in the end. Dougie had a bit of a throat infection during the week, so I thought it was better not to, just in case he infected any other children.'

Jess blinked. 'Oh, so I guess I am the pariah then. None of you want me around because I don't have any kids of my own.'

'No. Of course, not,' Deirdre soothed. 'Look, it's just ... well, I think Emer thought that it wouldn't be your thing, or Brian's if he came along too. I mean, why would you two want to be around the lot of us and our kids?'

'Yes, but 'the lot of you' are my friends. At least before you all moved to the country and started playing happy families.' She was trying her utmost not to sound bitter or insensitive, but she couldn't help it. Clearly *they* weren't worried about being insensitive towards her.

Deirdre sighed into the phone, 'Look Jess, we are still your friends, but you can imagine how it is ...'

'Well, I honestly can't, so why don't you tell me?' Jess had no idea why she was being so petulant with Deirdre, this wasn't her fault, although her friend seemed to be only perpetuating her earlier theory about how breeders and non-breeders shouldn't mix.

'Look Jess, think about it – I suppose it's about the interest level really. Emer and Dave's would have been full of kids' toys, nappies and screaming children and if I didn't have kids it wouldn't sound remotely like fun to me. It's like last week when she and I were in Dublin shopping and were laughing about how these days we spend most of our time in kid's stores and ...' Deirdre cut herself off, too late, realizing her slip.

But Jess picked up on it immediately and felt a fresh wave of betrayal. 'You and Emer were here in Dublin ...?'

Deirdre sounded chastened. 'We were going to ask if you wanted to meet up, but –'

'Hey, don't worry about it," she said, quickly, but again this hurt. There was a time when she and the girls did everything together – in fact, Jess had originally introduced Deirdre and Emer to one another, but since they'd moved to Lakeview it seemed the two women had paired off and left her behind. Now, even when they did come back for a visit or a shopping trip they couldn't be bothered including her.

'Honestly, we just didn't think you'd be interested. And we know how much you love the whole trying on shoes and personal shopper stuff ...' Her sentence trailed off as if to suggest that this kind of thing would be way too tiresome. 'Of course, we had the kids with us too, and when you're not used to it, it can be a bit manic so ...'

Listening to her friend's words, Jess wondered when exactly the friendship had become 'we' and 'you'. But of course she knew when, and more importantly why. She was being ostracized because, unlike

Deirdre and Emer, she hadn't utilized her ovaries, and wasn't part of the cozy little club they now shared.

Yet, she'd never neglected her friends and wouldn't dream of leaving them out of her plans, and whenever she and Brian had a party she always invited everyone, regardless of their family circumstances.

Oh, my goodness, she thought, remembering something, the girls and their husbands hadn't come to any of her and Brian's dinner parties recently; did they feel they were past a childless couple's petty little interests?

'So I guess this is why you and Emer don't come and visit us anymore either,' she said, quietly.

'What? No, we always try to come if we can, and if we can't, it's only because we can't find a babysitter. Come on, Jess, please don't be like this.'

'I'm sorry … I just don't understand why …' By now, Jess felt wrong-footed and upset, and worried she would end up saying something she regretted, she issued a quick apology to Deirdre and told her she would call her later.

The reality of what was happening with her friendship with the girls was making her vulnerable and uneasy, and feeling unaccountably lonely, Jess lay back on the bed and closed her eyes, trying not to fret about it.

Hours later, she sat up and blinked through the early evening darkness. A noise from downstairs had woken her up. Brian was home.

'Jess honey, are you here?' She heard his footsteps on the stairs.

'In here.'

The bedroom door opened and her husband entered and Jess couldn't resist a smile. Although obviously tired from the flight, he still looked handsome as always. He was tall, well over six-foot, with dark hair and deep brown eyes. And tired or not, those sharp eyes missed nothing.

'Hi gorgeous,' he began, but then frowned when he saw her sad face and mussed-up hair. 'Hey, what's wrong? Are you not feeling well?'

'No, I'm fine,' she lied, not wanting to ruin his homecoming. She stood up and went to embrace him. 'How was Singapore?'

Seeing her expression, he cocked his head to the side. 'Doesn't look like fine to me. What's happened?'

His concern merely served to bring on a fresh wave of dismay, and through fits and starts, Jess once again unleashed the story of everything that had happened. Brian listened patiently, allowing her to get it all out.

'I just can't believe it. And now that I think of it, it's been happening for a while too. Brian, I never thought we'd be outcasts just because we don't have kids. I mean, soon they won't want to talk to us at all, won't want us around them in case we ... infect them with our shallowness!'

Brian seemed to be trying to keep a straight face. 'Always so melodramatic,' he teased. . 'Look, you need to try and look at this from a practical point of view, instead of letting that crazy imagination of yours go off on wild tangents as usual.'

Jess looked at him. He was always teasing her about her supposedly vivid imagination and yes, perhaps she did have a tendency to overreach sometimes, but such a trait wasn't always a bad thing, not to mention pretty much essential in her line of work. Anyway, in this case her imagination *wasn't* running away with her. Her friends were ostracizing her, plain and simple, and things would only get worse surely?

Brian was smiling as if reading her mind. 'Don't even go there. OK, so what Emer did with the party was a bit foolish, but she probably didn't mean any harm by it, and I'm sure you'll all make up in the end.' He chuckled as he leaned down and nuzzled her neck. 'I'm sure it's all just a silly misunderstanding.'

But Jess wasn't so easily convinced. 'How could I misunderstand being purposely lied to about a party? And being deliberately left out of their shopping trip while they probably had a great time poking fun at me and my stupid little shoe fetishes,' she added, remembering

Deirdre's comments earlier. 'They think my life is silly and pointless, and now they're alienating me, and Brian, it can only be because we don't have kids.'

Brian sighed. 'Well, have you even considered that it might be less about alienating you, and more about them not wanting to wreck your head? Kids can be painful after all.'

Jess looked at him. She hadn't really thought it might be a case of the girls trying to save her from noise or hassle. And it wasn't as if she ever minded that kind of thing anyway; she enjoyed being around their children.

'Do you really think that's all it is?'

'Of course. What else could it be?'

'Well, what I already said – about us not being able to join in.'

'If that is the case, then more fool them,' Brian grinned. 'Honestly, Jess, I really do think you're blowing all of this out of proportion. So Emer left you out of her mommy party – what do you care?'

But Jess did care, that was the crux of the problem. She cared deeply about her friendship and she was very worried that this was only the beginning.

'Anyway, try and think about the benefits of *not* having kids,' Brian went on chuckling. 'You and I have so much freedom just as a couple, whereas the likes of Deirdre and Kevin can't even go out to McDonald's for a milkshake without bringing in the National Guard.' Brian kissed her and smiled. 'Plus, you still have an incredibly sexy body minus stretch marks and C-section scars,' he added tickling her, and Jess gradually began to feel a weight lift.

He was right; they could do whatever they wanted, hop on last-minute flights to Paris or New York, take off on round-the-world cruises at the drop of a hat, and quaff champagne at glamorous parties without a care in the world.

Not that she and Brian did do many of those things, but the important thing was that they *could* ...

Feeling much better, she put her arms around her husband and kissed him, and when they pulled apart he looked at her. 'Look, sounds to me like you've had a weird weekend, so I think you need to get over it by going out somewhere nice tonight with your lovely hubby.' His eyes twinkled. 'And the only thing you need to think about is what cocktail you should order.'

Jess smiled, she did like the idea of going out with Brian later and forgetting all about what had happened. Trust him to put it all into perspective and help remind her of just how fabulous a life she led. She had a fantastic job, gorgeous house, beautiful clothes, and a loving husband. Truly, she was very fortunate and she shouldn't allow an incident like that get the better of her.

Brian was right; her imagination had run away with her, this probably was just a silly misunderstanding, and she and the girls would no doubt get over it.

'Come on then,' he said, holding out his hand to help her off the bed. 'Let's go and get a couple of margaritas.'

And much later that night, as she and her husband shared more than just 'a couple' of margaritas and spent much of their time laughing and chatting like they always did, Jess wondered what on earth she had been worrying about.

Her life was wonderful and she had everything to be grateful for. So why on earth waste time stressing about what she didn't have?

11

Ruth paced the floors of her suite at the Four Seasons. While she'd tried her utmost to get some rest in order to get over the jetlag (and the hangover), proper sleep was impossible.

Which wasn't good considering her big TV interview was coming up in a couple of hours and she wanted to look her absolute best.

Ruth kneaded her forehead and took another look at the newspapers she'd had sent up to her room; she couldn't believe what the Irish press were saying about her, and still couldn't quite comprehend how the news had traveled so fast. More to the point, how on earth had news of her and Troy reached the media at all, let alone so quickly?

After the debacle at Dublin airport in the early hours of the morning, she'd immediately got Chloe on the phone, whereupon her assistant had blearily explained that a security guard at the Beverly Hills Hotel had leaked the CCTV footage from the lobby. Then, following press investigations, the remainder of the story had been backed up by an unnamed source at the Chateau Marmont.

'An unnamed source? What kind of operation is the hotel running that they're so willing to leak personal information about their guests?' Ruth demanded.

'Well, I kinda get the impression the source *was* a guest,' Chloe said sheepishly. 'Someone who was peeved about not getting any sleep?'

Ruth was mortified that her sex life was the subject of such public discussion and even more embarrassed that such discussions had followed her all the way across the Atlantic.

'Ruth Scream-more shows Tinseltown how to party!' announced one of the more restrained headlines, and while it was bad enough for her to take, Ruth couldn't even begin to imagine what her parents were making of all this.

The Seymours were traveling up from Lakeview this evening to catch a few minutes with Ruth at the hotel before the PR people whisked them all away to the TV studio. As was customary for guests of the show, the family was given complimentary audience tickets and would be in studio while she was being interviewed.

Ruth had been looking forward to the bit where the TV cameras turned to the delighted parents in the audience while the show's host asked them just how proud they were of their offspring's achievements. Now she wasn't so sure if that was such a good idea.

Casting the papers aside, she decided to bite the bullet and call home to let them know that she'd arrived in Dublin safely and was up and about. It was a call that she was especially nervous about now, given the circumstances.

For weeks she'd been looking forward to making the call announcing her arrival from the plush hotel, but now she was less than excited, especially if they'd read all those horrible headlines. So much for returning in a blaze of glory; now it seemed she'd be cowering beneath a cloud of shame.

Sadly, Ruth thought that she could somehow deal with other people saying bad things about her (she'd been doing it for years after all) but the one thing she'd find hard would be the idea that her parents were ashamed of her. As it was, it had been hard enough trying to prove to them for all these years that she wasn't wasting her time.

Sitting back on the comfy bed, she turned the newspapers face down so she wouldn't have to look at them and dialed her parents' number. Typically, her mother answered on the first ring.

'Mum? Hi, it's me.' Ruth's mouth went dry as she waited for Breda Seymour's reply.

'Oh hello, love, you've arrived safely then?' Thank goodness, Ruth thought to herself, realizing that her mother's tone seemed normal so perhaps they hadn't seen the papers.

'Yes, the flight got in about five this morning, and I've just been catching up on some sleep. How are you all? I can't wait to see you. You and Dad still OK to come up for the show tonight?'

'Of course, looking forward to it. Will we be able to see you beforehand?'

'Yes, absolutely. I'll be here at The Four Seasons until five; I think they're sending a car to bring us to the studio so we should have plenty of time for a chat.'

'Great, we're really looking forward to seeing you, love.'

Ruth felt elated; they were looking forward to seeing her, which must mean that they hadn't seen the headlines.

'Um love, just so you're prepared ... I tried as long as I could to keep the papers away from your father, and I thought I might be able to until this whole mess passed over, but well, he turned on the television and they were talking about the TV appearance and how you'd be putting the record straight on the scandal. Needless to say, he fished out the papers I'd put in the bin.'

The blood drained from her face, and she shook her head, trying to shake away the thought of her father reading those lurid headlines ... seeing that awful picture ... everything. She should have guessed that her mother would have tried to cover for her and equally guessed that her father would have found out in the end. Ollie was wonderful, but he'd always been very strict, always demanding Ruth behave like a lady. When she was a teenager, he used to be waiting up for her to get home every time she went out, and always interrogated, at length, any of the guys she went out with. Well almost all of them, she thought sadly.

Then as a teenager, when she was offered the part in the TV soap, he'd taken it upon himself to ensure that filming didn't interfere with her schooling, or that she never went out to parties with the older cast members.

Ollie had believed, perhaps even more than Ruth herself that she was destined to be a star and he wasn't going to let anything ruin that for her.

Ironic then Ruth thought, that after taking so many years to finally achieve her dream, she'd gone ahead and ruined it herself.

12

'Our next guest has been on the radar since her first appearance as a lovesick teenager on *The Local*. And now after a long hard slog, Hollywood has finally recognized her talent and she stars in one of the biggest TV hits Stateside. Tonight, she's back in Dublin to talk about her new hit show *Glamazons*, and we're delighted to welcome the very talented Ms Ruth Seymour!'

Ruth waved at the audience as she walked on to the set of the *Late Tonight* studio. Her smile was dazzling and thanks to the professional make-up artist the station had arranged back at the hotel, she knew she looked every inch the Hollywood star.

She walked gracefully across the set and extended her hand to the show's host, former DJ Eamonn Kennedy, who much to her disappointment was standing in for the show's regular host who apparently had broken his leg earlier that week. While the older interviewer was famous for his soft-touch questioning and sycophantic approach, the same couldn't be said of Kennedy who, from what little Ruth knew of him, was a man who had made a name for himself by being controversial. Tonight though, he seemed just warm and welcoming as he took Ruth's hand, and kissed her on both cheeks before offering her a seat.

Smoothing down her Catherine Malandrino jade-colored satin

dress, which she knew set off her bouncy, bright blonde locks, Ruth crossed her long legs in such a way so as to show off the tell-tale crimson soles of her elegant (and self-bought) Christian Louboutins.

'So, Ruth, welcome back. It's wonderful to have you home. Although after all this time in LA, do you even still consider the *'oul sod* your home?'

'Of course I do, Eamonn,' she smiled. 'Ireland will always be my home. I'm delighted to be back and over the moon to be here.'

'Tell us about *Glamazons*. As you know the series hasn't appeared on Irish screens just yet, but they're really raving about it in the States.'

Ruth beamed. Yes, *this* was exactly how it was supposed to be, lots of praise and talk about the show, her amazing achievements and the triumphant return of one of Ireland's success stories.

'Well, I'm very fortunate to be involved with the project. *Glamazons* is a great show, the US ratings have been just amazing, and we're all really looking forward to filming the next season.'

'Yes, and such a great cast too.'

OK, this was potentially tricky, she thought, but trying her utmost to remain professional, she made sure to keep her winning smile in place. 'Absolutely, we have a very talented cast and everyone is a pleasure to work with.'

Eamonn's eyes sparkled in such a way, that it was too late; Ruth knew she'd walked right into a trap. 'Hmm, I'd imagine some of your co-stars are more pleasurable to work with than others,' he joked and the audience laughed.

Out of the corner of her eye, Ruth saw on the monitor that the cameras had moved in for a close-up of her face, and she tried her utmost not to betray her reaction.

'Well, of course everyone has their own individual strengths, but what we all have to remember is that we act as a team and everyone plays an equal part in our success.'

Eamonn smiled. 'Yes, that's all important, but I think what I'm referring to here is your "teaming up" with Troy Valentine, who plays your husband on the show. You two looked, hmm ... awfully comfortable at a party in Hollywood the other night. Is this a case of true life imitating art?' he joked and the audience clapped, as if in agreement.

Ruth's smile was plastered on.

'Yes Troy and I have worked together for a while and are of course good friends –'

'Good friends? I wish I had more "good friends" like you, Ruth,' he said boorishly and Ruth wanted to die. So the shock-jock hadn't changed his stripes after all, despite the fact that this was supposed to be a family show.

'Now really, you should know better than to believe the rubbish that the tabloids are printing, we all know how ridiculous –'

'Are you telling us that nothing happened?' Eamonn interrupted. 'After all, what about this?' To Ruth's horror, that horrible security still flashed up on the monitor and onward to the TV screens of the nation. 'This doesn't look like tabloid rubbish to me.'

Damn that photo! Ruth's heart was in her stomach and despite herself she felt her top lip start to tremble.

'Now Eamonn, I'm really not going to dignify any of that with an answer.' High level, Ruth reminded herself, keep it high level.

Eamonn was like a cat ready to pounce. 'Hmm, sounds like some-body has a secret.' The audience cheered loudly and Ruth could feel her face flush. Despite going over the questions pre-show he clearly wasn't going to stick to the script.

'I'm sorry, but I'm here to talk about the show not my personal life.' The smile was starting to slip from her face and she felt as if she'd been sabotaged. 'I'm here to talk about my show and to spend the summer with my family.' She was hoping to remind him that her family was in fact in the audience in the hope he'd have the decency to lay off.

But incredibly this seemed to make him even more determined.

'Yes, yes, of course you are. And speaking of which, what does your family think about this, about your fame? Or perhaps I should say your infamy? Are your parents proud of your success?' Every word was laced with acid and Eamonn looked like he was really enjoying this 'interview'. 'Mr & Mrs Seymour, can you tell us how you feel about your daughter stepping out with one of Hollywood's most notorious playboys?'

The cameras duly panned to the audience, and to her parents' anxious faces, and it was nothing, *nothing* like Ruth had imagined. And whatever about trying to humiliate her on live TV, he had no right to do this to her parents.

A calm faced Breda spoke to the camera. 'We've always been proud of Ruth in everything she does.'

Ruth's bottom lip started to throb at the sight of her kind, ordinary mother standing up for her and trying to defend the indefensible, while Ollie sat stony-faced alongside her.

She looked off set, to where the production team stood, scrambling to find a sympathetic face, to find someone, anyone who could help her. Once again, she missed Chloe; her assistant would have swept her from this situation in a heartbeat, promising legal action in their wake.

However, Chloe wasn't there and Ruth had to do something before this horrible talk show host did something worse, like ask what positions they did it in or if Troy was well endowed.

'You know Eamonn, I've been a fan of this show since I was a little girl and I've always admired its presenters,' Ruth spat as she stood up. To try to save face she added, 'But you've gone too far dragging my parents into this and you really should be ashamed of yourself.' She felt her pulse racing as she ran off camera.

Embarrassed and close to tears, she rushed off the set, past all the cameras, producers and handlers. And as she raced to the bathroom for some privacy, she realized how ironic it was, her telling Eamonn he should be ashamed of himself.

Because if anyone should be ashamed, Ruth decided, it was her.

13

The doorbell rang and Nina rushed to answer it, feeling like a teenager all over again for not wanting her father to get there first in case he would do or say something weird to embarrass her in front of her friends.

However, she was too late. Trish was standing in the middle of the living room; trying her utmost to make small talk with Patrick.

'So I bet you are just loving having Nina back?' she heard her say.

'I suppose so,' Patrick replied, with his typical lack of enthusiasm. 'It's a bit of an adjustment, having her things all over the place.'

Nina felt hurt; the way he was talking you'd swear she was a teenager scattering things around left right and center. As it was, there was nothing that belonged to her downstairs, and what little she'd brought with her was neatly put away in her bedroom. And it was a bit rich of him to complain about her things when he was the one who clogged up the place with his half-mended electronics!

From Trish's carefully composed expression, Nina guessed she was thinking the same thing and she decided to change to subject.

'Hi Trish, thanks for calling for me. Are you ready to go?'

'Oh, hey Nina, yeah, I was actually just telling your father about my charity book and all that's going on tonight. I was wondering if he'd like to come along to Ruth Seymour's party ...' She smiled at Patrick.

'Well, I'm not really sure it would be your kind of thing, Dad,' Nina interrupted. She smoothed down the hem of her floral summer dress, deliberately avoiding his gaze.

'No, no, not so much,' Patrick replied with a blank face.

'Are you sure? Because –'

'Honestly, Trish, we'd better get going,' Nina interjected hurriedly grabbing her arm and shuttling her to the door. The last thing she wanted was Patrick dragging out of them all night. 'See you later Dad, don't wait up!' she added lightly, knowing there wasn't a snowball's chance in hell of this happening in any case. Most of the time she was lucky if he even remembered she was there.

Once they were outside, Trish eyed Nina skeptically, 'Hmm, not exactly the behavior of a daughter who's been missing her father – could you have got me out the door any faster?'

'Ah, come on, did you really think he'd want to go to a local do?' Nina replied, trying to deflect the question. 'Anyway, speaking of running out the door, why did you leave the café in such a rush yesterday morning?' Nina was still confused by Trish's speedy exit following Emer and Deirdre's appearance.

'What?' Trish looked bemused. 'I was late for work and had a bit of a headache coming on too, so I just couldn't face those screaming kids, that's all.'

'Oh.' Nina didn't remember any of the kids crying when they entered, but decided to let it go. 'Well tonight should be good fun, shouldn't it?'

Trish raised an eyebrow. 'Unless Ruth runs out on us the way she did on the *Late Tonight* interview last night.'

Nina grimaced; she had seen the horrible interview and while she felt sorry for Ruth and particularly her parents, she felt that it was Eamonn Kennedy who came away looking the worst of it.

'Wasn't it just awful?' she said. 'I thought your man Kennedy was a terrible weasel putting her parents on the spot like that. John Monroe would never have done anything like that. Eamonn's a nasty so-and-so and I'd say she's sorry she ever agreed to go on.'

'Yes, but her walking off like that didn't help either. If anything, it gave the scandal even more legs.' She was referring to one of the tabloid Sunday papers which today carried an 'interview' with one of Ruth's ex-boyfriends. 'Ten years later and he can supposedly still remember every last detail?' Trish shook her head. 'I'm ashamed of my own profession sometimes.'

'Yeah, but you don't go in for that kind of thing, do you?' Nina said, hoping this was the case, although somehow she couldn't see the *Lakeview News* being a hotbed of kiss'n tells.

'Nah, of course not. Although I'm sure those kind of stories must be marginally more interesting than 'Local man steals Crème Egg',' she said wryly.

'I hope poor Ruth is holding up OK though,' Nina ventured. 'Granted, I didn't know her that well back when we were teenagers, but I don't envy anyone having to put up with that kind of smut.'

'I suppose she should have thought of that before she decided to get smashed and have it off with her co-star, shouldn't she?' Trish wasn't so sympathetic. 'Someone like her really should know better, especially at this stage in the game.'

'I get what you're saying, but don't we all have things we'd rather not be public knowledge and if it is true, that Ruth had a drunken one night stand, it's still her own business, isn't it?'

Trish gave her a sideways look and Nina worried that she might have said too much, but then her friend grinned. 'OK, OK, I hear you – sorry Mum.'

Nina gulped and tried to compose her expression. Did she really sound like a nagging mother? Although it was no doubt a throwaway remark, Trish wouldn't have had a clue of the irony.

They soon arrived at Clancy's hotel, and made their way through to the ballroom where the party was being held.

Nina scanned the crowd, realizing that there were many faces she recognized and many she did not, but of course, Lakeview had changed considerably since she was young.

Trish was working the crowd as they made their way to the bar and Nina found herself being introduced to loads of people and many names that she knew she wouldn't remember. They sidled up to the drinks table, upon which sat trays of wine and champagne. Trish looked at Nina, 'Champagne I think, don't you?'

'Um yes, I suppose so,' Nina mumbled automatically. Blast it, how would she get by not drinking under Trish's watchful gaze? The young waiter handed them each a champagne flute. Nina took hers and Trish offered up a toast. 'To homecomings!'

'Yes, to homecomings,' she said, and the two women clinked glasses.

Nina was just about to take a small sip of her drink, (a sip couldn't hurt, could it?), when a man walked up beside them. Seeing him approach, Trish smiled broadly.

'Dave, how are things?' she said to the tall, rather attractive man. Very well built, he had dark eyes, closely cropped chestnut hair and an air about him that suggested he was important in some way. 'Nina, this is Dave Kellerman,' she said, introducing them and Nina looked at him, wondering if she knew him from previous visits; the last name certainly rang a bell. But then again, he would surely have mentioned this, and he didn't. 'This is my friend Nina Hughes. She just recently moved back to Lakeview.'

'For a little while,' Nina added quickly, although she still wasn't sure why she'd felt the need to specify.

'Moved back?' Dave queried with a smile. 'So you're not a blow-in like me, then.' He went on to explain how he'd moved from Dublin a couple of years ago to work for the local brewery.

'We're sponsoring this little soirée, actually, although of course the local brew wouldn't do for a Hollywood star so we had to call on the rivals,' he said, indicating the champagne tray. 'Nearly killed us,' he added amiably and Nina decided that she liked this guy with his easy smile and chatty manner. She looked around the ballroom at the various decorations that had been put up for the occasion. The white and red roses gracing the tables were quite pretty and while she was sure the decor would be nowhere near as elaborate as what Ruth would be used to in LA, it was impressive just the same.

'So, the guest of honor must be on the way,' Dave said, as some commotion looked to be happening out front. 'Did you hear about her and that guy?'

'Well of course, who hasn't?' Trish laughed, but then met Nina's disapproving gaze. 'But at the same time, who cares, she's an adult isn't she? Besides, people who live in glass houses shouldn't throw stones – you know, bad karma and all that.'

Then all conversation in the room stopped as at that moment, Ruth made her entrance. She was wearing a strapless white dress with a scarlet sash around the middle and bright ruby red stilettos. Her glossy hair was pulled back into a loose, romantic knot, and she had a smile on her face and looked every inch the star.

The room erupted in applause and Ruth made her way through the crowd, shaking hands and posing for pictures.

'Doesn't she look beautiful?' Trish said enviously and Nina had to agree that yes, there was indeed something ethereal, almost fragile about Ruth's beauty, and there was no doubt that she was pure star quality.

A few minutes later the official ceremony began and Ruth was invited onstage by the local MC to accept her award, a piece of Waterford Crystal. Although she looked delighted with her reception and gave a lovely acceptance speech, Nina noticed the shadows under the actress's eyes, and the beaming smile she wore seemed tense.

Nina's heart went out to her. She couldn't imagine having to live under that sort of scrutiny. While she knew she'd made her fair share of mistakes (and was actually living with one right now), she could deal with them in private and never had to experience having her secrets spilled across the gossip pages for all to see. How could anyone deal with that sort of embarrassment?

The official part of the ceremony completed, Ruth descended the stage and eventually began to circulate through the crowd. As the actress neared closer, Trish grabbed Nina's arm and thrust the two of them forward.

'Ruth, Ruth, hello, do you remember us?' Trish asked, smiling wildly. Ruth turned their way and Nina could tell she was on sensory overload at the moment, but still she remained the true professional.

'Oh yes, yes of course! We went to school together ...?' As they were about the same age, it was no doubt a guess on Ruth's part, but she handled it beautifully.

'That's right,' Trish grinned. 'It's so wonderful to see you!' To Ruth's obvious surprise, Trish threw her arms around her and welcomed her with a big hug. Nina could see the poor girl's eyes racing back and forth as she tried to take in everything, the distinct look of a caged animal.

'I'm not sure if you remember Nina Hughes?' Trish offered as the two women turned to face her.

'I was only ever here on occasion,' Nina offered shyly, extending her hand.

'Oh, but of course. You used to come and visit your dad, right?'

'That's right.' She felt stupidly pleased that this ultra-glamorous woman had in fact remembered her.

'Well it's wonderful to be home,' Ruth went on. 'Although, it's changed a lot, hasn't it? I can't believe it's the same Lakeview.'

'I know, I haven't been back in years, so I couldn't believe it either.'

'Did you see all those new houses on the way in? For a minute there, I thought I was back in Beverly Hills,' she laughed, and Nina was struck by how normal she seemed. Sure, her outfit probably cost more than she herself had in her bank account, but she couldn't help thinking that Ruth wasn't all that different from her really; she just happened to live her life on a much grander stage.

She tried to recall what she knew of Ruth from their childhood. Incredibly pretty, she had always been the center of attention, and drama and action tended to follow her from one place to the next. She'd been one of the most popular girls around and was the type of person who drew people to her, with a natural charisma that most people didn't have. No wonder she'd ended up a star, Nina thought. Although in truth, everyone was surprised at how long it had taken.

'So, boring old Lakeview must be a big change from LA?' Trish asked then.

'Oh, my goodness, yes,' Ruth sighed, and very briefly, Nina saw a break in the façade, but just as quickly, it was back. 'I mean, it's all glorious, the weather, the shops, the restaurants and all that ... but you know, it's nice to get away for a while too, escape from the hustle and bustle.'

There was no missing the emphasis she placed on the word escape.

'Oh, I can only imagine, especially now,' Trish laughed. 'What with all this business with you and Troy, eh?' she added jokingly, and Nina shot a daggers look at Trish, unable to believe her friend's lack of tact.

Ruth's smile was gone in a flash, and too late; tears were forming in her eyes. She blinked hard as if trying to hold them back, but there was no denying she was under serious strain.

'Are you OK?' Nina asked her gently, and Ruth bit her lip and ever so faintly shook her head. She looked as if she wasn't sure which was worse, breaking down in front of a couple of strangers or losing it in front of the entire town.

Nina decided to act fast. 'Trish, is there a backroom around here?' she asked.

'What?' Trish hadn't noticed anything amiss. 'If you mean the Ladies –'

'No, I meant somewhere private,' she cocked a surreptitious head towards a slowly crumbling Ruth.

'Ah Ruth, I'm sorry for upsetting you; I didn't mean ... I just thought it would be a bit of a joke, you know, we've all shagged people that –'

'For goodness sake, Trish,' Nina groaned. 'Is there a hallway, or a back kitchen or something?' Ruth was now seriously close to losing it.

'Oh, uh, over here,' Trish led the way, suddenly realizing that they needed to get Ruth out of there; and the last thing she needed was to start crying in front of all the great and good of Lakeview. Nina watched as they passed by locals and Ruth's admirers, and she noticed that the actress did a great job of keeping her head down while she rifled through her trendy evening bag, pretending to look for something. Trish ushered them down a hallway and turned the corner, out of sight of prying eyes. Hearing noises from behind, Nina looked to the left and spotted a door, which she hoped was unlocked.

Her prayers were answered and holding the door open for Trish and Ruth, she waved them both inside. Trish switched on an overhead light and the three of them looked around the small space, which was littered with cleaning supplies.

'Ah, kind of reminds me of when we used to sneak into the janitor's closet at school for a smoke, doesn't it Ruth?' Trish offered, and despite herself Ruth smiled. 'Hey look, that was a really stupid thing to say back there. I mean, I just forgot really –'

'What she's trying to say is she left her manners at home,' Nina scolded good-naturedly.

'It's just been a tough couple of days,' Ruth ventured, her tone weary.

'I can imagine. I mean, the hangover alone must have been horrible, let alone having to deal with your knickers, or lack thereof, being splashed –'

'Bloody hell Trish,' Nina's mouth dropped open and she nudged her in the arm. 'Will you please shut up?' Now tears were spilling down Ruth's cheeks. 'Ah no sweetheart, don't cry,' she soothed. 'You'll ruin your lovely makeup.'

'I'm ... so ... sorry,' Ruth gulped. 'I'm just so stressed out, the last few days have been absolutely dreadful, all the questions ... accusations and cameras following me around. They're all treating me like some kind of common tart and I'm not. They have no right, no *right* to say such dreadful things about me!' She was getting more and more animated by the second and Nina knew that they had to try and calm her down, after all, you never knew who might be watching or listening outside the door for that matter.

'Shh, shh, I know, I know, it's all very unfair,' Nina soothed, but Trish was too busy listening to the fresh, 'straight from the horse's mouth' gossip that was coming out of Ruth to worry about calming her.

'It's just so hard, I mean, I'm a *public figure*, a *celebrity* for crying out loud, I *deserve* to be treated with some sort of *respect*.'

Ah, so there's the diva, Nina thought. She grabbed her purse and fished out a tissue. 'Look Ruth, this will all blow over in the next few days. I'm sure Britney Spears or Paris Hilton will do something outrageous soon and this will all be forgotten about in no time,' she said encouragingly.

'Yeah, after all, no one pays much attention to what happens in Ireland,' Trish offered.

Ruth looked at the two women and Nina could see she was somewhat torn between the idea of being old news, *and* the fact that for the summer she would be geographically somewhere that no one paid attention to. She wondered then if Ruth actually got a kick out of being in the lion's den that was Hollywood with paparazzi following her everywhere. She was reminded briefly of her earlier thoughts about drama following Ruth everywhere, and now she wondered if the woman didn't actually feed off it, as opposed to actively try and avoid it.

Ruth sniffled into the hanky. 'Thank you for being so nice to me,' she said, looking at Nina.

'Not a problem,' she replied with a smile.

'Yeah, not a problem,' Trish added, completely oblivious that she'd caused much of the strife in the first place. 'I heard you were staying on here for the summer, is that true?'

Ruth nodded. 'That's the plan anyway. Shooting doesn't start back until October, so I've got a bit of time on my hands.'

Nina guessed that the notion of spending the summer in Lakeview basking in the glory of her Hollywood success had sounded a lot better in theory. Instead the poor thing had been thrown to the wolves.

'Do you think you're OK to go back out there?' she asked.

'I guess so.' Ruth took a deep breath and Nina helped her up from the stool she was sitting on. 'Trish, why don't you pop out and make sure the coast is clear.'

'Of course.' Trish did as she was bid, leaving Nina and Ruth in the closet.

'Does my makeup look all right?' Ruth asked self-consciously.

'Absolutely – you look amazing.'

Ruth stared blankly at the door ahead of her and Nina wondered what she was thinking. Yes, she was beautiful, and had been blessed with fame and fortune, but was she really happy? She wondered when was the last time the girl had the opportunity to go out and be herself or behave like a normal person. LA was renowned for being fake and cutthroat, and from what she could tell Ruth had fought for a very long time for her success. She couldn't be sure, but she got the impression that Ruth wasn't particularly used to people being nice to her, and was genuinely grateful and hugely surprised by the intervention.

Nina considered how Ruth's situation compared to her own. Nope, she wasn't a celebrity, but when she examined her life she was reminded of why she herself was in Lakeview right now, she had got herself in trouble and she didn't have any other place to go. Strange that she and Ruth had both ended up in Lakeview at the same time after a long absence; Ruth in an unexpected state of self-imposed isolation and Nina in a state of self-imposed limbo.

There was a knock on the door and Trish informed the two women that it was clear to come out. Nina was about to turn the doorknob when Ruth grabbed her hand and squeezed it.

'Honestly, I mean it; thank you for being so kind,' the actress said gently. 'It's honestly the first time I felt like I've had a friend in ages.'

Nina smiled and squeezed back, thinking that the two of them had a lot more in common than they'd thought.

14

*D*espite herself, Jess just couldn't stop thinking about what had happened with Emer and her conversation with Deirdre.

Brian had spent a lot of time over the weekend entertaining her and trying to keep her mind off things, but still she couldn't help but worry about the problems that had surfaced between her and her friends.

Now in the office, staring at her computer screen, she couldn't focus on the projects at hand, namely the marketing strategy behind the launch of Piccolo's brand new energy drink. Her deadline hovered, days away, but for some reason, all she could think about was babies.

It wasn't a 'biological clock' response either; more like Jess was concentrating so hard on the idea of a baby in an effort to try and jumpstart the damned clock.

There was no doubt that what had happened at the weekend, and the discovery of her friends purposeful alienation of her was bringing a lot of things to the fore – namely children or more to the point, the lack of them.

She pushed away the material in front of her, unable to concentrate. She couldn't deny how troubled she was. She was thirty-five years old and had pretty much taken it for granted that someday she would be a mother. Someday.

But when? When was the right time? All along she'd just assumed that she'd know when it was time; that suddenly a light would go on or something. She sighed, wondering if there was something wrong with her, if she was one of those women who had some sort of psychological aversion to children. But no, of course that wasn't it, she loved babies, had enjoyed playing with dolls as a child, and remembered pleading at length with her parents for a brother or a sister, a ready-made playmate for her as an only child.

She grabbed her computer keyboard and pulled it closer. Bringing up Google, she started surfing the web, clicking on to Mamas & Papas and other various baby-related sites in the hope that she would get the warm and fuzzies from looking at all the paraphernalia, but nope, nothing.

Feeling deflated she checked her email and saw a message from Net-a-Porter advertising a Betsey Johnson sale. Immediately, her attention perked up and she rushed to click on it.

And something dawned on her. Betsey Johnson? Wasn't she a little past polka-dots and flouncy skirts? But that was partly the problem, wasn't it? She realized now; she was thirty-five, but still felt only *twenty*-five.

And whatever about being past wearing younger clothes, she realized, her heart quickening, wasn't she also fast approaching being past optimum fertility age? Clicking on to a medical site, she began pulling up information on pregnancy, recalling how panicky Emer had been in the early days about not immediately falling pregnant. 'Maybe I've left it too late,' her friend used to worry, and at the time Jess had brushed her comments aside, as Emer could be a worrier at the best of times.

But now the more she read, the more concerned Jess became. At thirty-five, it seemed she was more liable to have a 'high risk' pregnancy, and the chances of her not getting pregnant *at all* were higher than she'd originally thought. Her fertility had been declining since she was at least thirty, and the amount of alcohol she'd been knocking back for the last couple of decades or so probably wouldn't have helped either ...

Jess's brow furrowed. What if she'd been spending so much time concentrating on her career, traveling around the world and enjoying life that her chance to have a baby had passed her by?

Feeling very worried now, she reached out to pick up the phone. Ticking biological clock or not, she was just about ready to call Brian and demand he meet her at home to knock her up, when suddenly the phone rang.

'Jess Armstrong,' she answered distractedly.

'Jess? Hi, it's Emer, is this a good time?'

She felt her pulse pick up a little. Why was Emer calling her at work? She never did that; especially when she knew first-hand how crazy things often were here at the office, and for the last few years they'd only communicated in the evenings at home when they had time to chat.

'Of course, how are you?' she said easily, careful not to betray her surprise.

'Are you sure? Because when you picked up the phone there you sounded a bit stressed.'

What could Jess say? *I just had this mad notion to rush home and get impregnated?* 'No, no, it's just been a bit of a crazy morning, but nothing I can't handle.' She *hoped*.

Emer was silent for a bit before she spoke again. 'Well um ... I just wanted to call and apologize for what happened at the weekend. It was bad of me to exclude you, I know that, but it wasn't my intention to hurt you; I honestly just thought it wouldn't be your scene.'

Ah, so she's been talking to Deirdre, Jess realized immediately. But never one to hold a grudge, her voice lightened and she smiled. 'Hey, no need to apologize. I don't mind admitting that I was a bit taken aback at the time, but look, it's all forgotten about now and I understand.'

'No, no, it still wasn't right and I really am sorry. I talked to Deirdre and well, we both agree that maybe we've been a bit too caught up in baby stuff lately. We should do something together, just the three of us, you know, maybe a girlie night out or something.'

'Emer, honestly; there's no need.' Now Jess was mortified that Emer and Deirdre were feeling obligated into spending time with her out of guilt.

'But there is. You and I haven't really been out together since Amy was born, and I know Deirdre would jump at the chance to get dressed up and go clubbing.'

Again Jess couldn't help but wonder if they thought clubbing was what *she* did all the time; again, a twenty-five year old trapped in a thirty-five-year old body.

'Maybe just dinner somewhere would be nice? Not sure that I'm really able for clubbing these days,' she joked.

'OK, well how about Deirdre and I come up to Dublin the weekend after next – it's really the soonest that I could arrange it, especially if I stay overnight and –'

'Don't be silly, I can come to Lakeview. After all, it's much easier for me to stay overnight there than for you two to trek all the way up here. If Deirdre's up for it, should we try and do it at the weekend?'

'Oh,' Emer replied, sounding a bit miffed, and Jess worried if in her haste to dismiss the girls coming to Dublin, she'd somehow offended her, rather than make things easier, as was her intention. What was going on with her and Emer these days that she felt like she was walking on eggshells around her?

'Well, you can come here if you'd like, but I just thought it might be easier to arrange a babysitter?' she explained quickly.

'I suppose,' Emer agreed. 'Friday night would be best, I think – not sure if himself has to work late or not, but if so, I'll get the girl down the street. I'll check with Deirdre and if she's on for it, then great.'

'Brilliant, let me know and if you're both good to go, then I'll drive down on Friday night. Is there anywhere nice in Lakeview we could go? I saw a nice Italian place I liked the look of last time I was there.'

'Yeah, Casa Rosa. It's only cheap and cheerful though – will that be OK for you?'

'Of course.' Again Jess wondered if her friends really did think she did nothing but eat haute cuisine, quaff champagne and buy shoes.

But as their conversation continued, catching up about other goings-on and news about mutual friends, Emer's tone seemed to soften a little and Jess felt relieved that the earlier awkwardness seemed to have passed. And after a good chat over cheap wine and nice food this weekend, surely everything would be just like old times again?

LATER IN THE week as she was getting ready for work, Jess watched Brian pack for his latest business trip. He was catching a flight to London and would be gone for most of the week including the weekend. If she hadn't made plans with the girls, she would have been spending another weekend alone, Jess reflected glumly.

However, that was neither here nor there, because she was heading to Lakeview on Friday afternoon and would spend the night at Emer's. She studied her handsome husband as he collected his things.

Although he knew she was upset about the girls excluding her, she hadn't yet confided her recent worries about her fertility and definitely didn't want to admit that the other day she'd been on the verge of ringing him for a quickie! Thinking about it now, there would have been little point anyway, as she was still taking the birth control pill.

Jess wondered what he'd say if she sprang such an idea on him, particularly after the drama with her friends as of late. She knew he was a logical thinker and would no doubt again try to tell her that her imagination was running away with her, and likely suggest that the notion was rooted in fear of the distance growing between her and her friends.

However, as she'd recently learned, they both needed to remind themselves that she wasn't getting any younger, and really if they waited any longer, there was a chance she might not be able to fall pregnant at all.

She pushed all these thoughts aside when Brian came up behind her and put his arms around her.

'You're looking particularly gorgeous today,' he said nibbling her ear. 'Is that presentation happening this morning?'

Jess nodded. 'Thanks – kind of important to look fresh and energetic when you're presenting an energy drink, isn't it?'

'You know, I'm tempted to skip this damn trip and stay home with you instead. I hate leaving you again so soon after Singapore.'

She turned around and kissed him. He really was the most amazing man, she thought, and would no doubt be a spectacular father. She studied his face for a moment.

'What are you looking so serious about?' he asked softly.

'Oh, nothing, I'm just thinking about how much I'll miss you.'

'Me too. Anyway, at least it's only a few days this time. Besides, you're going out with the girls at the weekend and after a few glasses of wine, the three of ye will have forgotten all about your husbands,' he teased.

Jess laughed. 'Too right.'

'Well, as long as they don't spend the night boring you to tears with baby-talk you should be fine,' he added, and Jess was glad he wasn't able to read her mind.

Because she was now beginning to wonder if baby-talk would bore her that much after all.

15

---

*T*he following Friday afternoon, Jess left work early to beat the traffic and arrived in Lakeview around six o'clock.

When Emer answered the door, she smiled broadly and pulled Jess into a tight embrace. None of the earlier drama was mentioned, and Jess realized for sure that she'd worried for nothing and everything was back to normal.

'Is Dave here?' she asked, going through to the living room.

'No, he ended up having a late meeting today, but will be back later to let the babysitter go early. Poor thing has been working twice as hard since Amy was born, but I try not to complain too much, after all, he's not only pulling the weight of two, but three now.' She laughed. 'The babysitter arrived just before you and we were trying to get Amy down. I'll just pop back up to make sure she's OK and then we'll have a glass of wine while we wait for Deirdre, OK?'

'Of course,' Jess agreed and while Emer was upstairs she wandered over to the fireplace and studied the pictures on the mantelpiece. She remembered her friend's old place back in Dublin which had been littered with various snaps of Emer and Dave together on nights out, their travels and the wedding. Now, except for a small one of the big day, it looked like all those pictures had been tidied away and replaced with baby pictures – Amy as a newborn, with her first tooth and various other milestones. Jess wondered if this was what she and Brian would do if they had a child; replace all the memories they made before the baby, with memories the baby would make for them?

Emer returned to the living room with a bottle of wine and two glasses. 'Jess, I'm so glad we were all able to do this on such short notice. You're a gem by the way, for coming all the way down here for us.'

'Not a problem at all. Glad to do it and much easier for me to stay overnight.'

'Brian away again?' her friend queried and Jess thought she heard a slight edge in her tone.

'Yes, all the traveling is driving him mad lately, but then again … it's what he does.' She laughed lightly.

Emer nodded and sat back on the sofa, clearly relishing the first glass of wine she'd had in ages. Jess was pleased to see her friend relax, and she could sense last week's tension literally melt away as they got comfortable discussing what they'd been up to in the meantime. They chatted easily about going's-on at Piccolo; Emer asking loads of questions about the latest campaign and seemed genuinely interested in all that was going on in Jess's life.

It felt so normal, back to the way it had always been, and Jess chastised herself internally over her silliness in believing there was a gap growing between them.

Deirdre arrived about forty minutes later, dressed up to the nines and full of beans. As all three women were wearing heels, they decided to call a cab to drive them the short distance from Emer's house on the edge of Lakeview down to Main Street, where the restaurant was located.

When they arrived, the friendly owner of Casa Rosa led them to a cozy corner table before bringing them a large carafe of white wine.

The conversation remained lively and Emer and Deirdre asked Jess endless questions about how things were in Dublin, what restaurants she and Brian had been frequenting, and where their next holiday would be.

'Well, we're thinking maybe Borneo. Brian loves Malaysia and we've been pretty much everywhere else,' she joked. 'There's a beautiful resort way out in the jungle, a sort of hideaway retreat Brian says.'

'Sounds like heaven,' Deirdre gushed. 'The retreat part especially. What I wouldn't give to be able to hide away like that and have my every whim catered for.'

'It does sound amazing,' Emer agreed. 'But yes,' she added, smiling at Deirdre, 'I think our days of that kind of thing are over with. From now on we can only look forward to the jungles we've made for ourselves!'

'Yes, but let's not talk about the kids tonight,' Deirdre said pointedly and Jess cringed. The last thing she wanted was the girls to feel that discussing the kids was off limits in front of her.

'Are you planning to go away yourselves this year?' she asked quickly, as if Deirdre hadn't spoken. 'Somewhere like Disneyland would be great for the boys, wouldn't it?'

'Great if we could afford it,' her friend replied, and immediately Jess felt guilty for banging on about her and Brian's comparatively ostentatious plans. With her husband usually arranging their trips in-house it was sometimes easy to forget how much these things actually cost.

'I know, I find it hard to believe myself how tight things are now that only one of us is working,' Emer added glumly.

'Do you think you'll go back?' Jess asked.

'To work? You must be joking. No, I know I'd find it really hard to be away from Amy now and would just hate for someone else to raise her.'

'I agree. A few extra quid would be nice, but when it comes down to it, the boys matter more than money.'

As she couldn't particularly contribute to this line of conversation, Jess found herself growing quiet as the two women continued to chat about motherhood and its associated challenges. She couldn't believe some of the concerns they had; not least because her own problems seemed so much more trivial and silly by comparison. Worrying about positive influences in a child's life and making sure that they had a happy upbringing seemed a lot more important than the contemplation Brian and Jess gave to which hotspot in Dublin to frequent.

Now listening to Emer and Deirdre's conversation made her conscious again that her life seemed rather petty and superficial, and that everything she'd talked about when they first arrived now paled in comparison to the subject matter that was on the table.

Jess drank back the wine and tried to shake off the feeling of melancholy that was settling upon her. She tried to assume a more placid expression as the last thing she needed was either of them trying to read her thoughts and thinking that this night out was a bad idea.

She certainly didn't want them to reconsider inviting her places as she really needed her friends. She felt a trickle of fear thinking back to before when Brian was packing for his business trip. If she wasn't out with Emer and Deirdre tonight, what would she be doing right now? Probably, working late at the office, or at home alone ordering takeout and watching TV.

Then a conflicting voice rose inside her. That wasn't completely true, she mused, recalling recent nights when she'd gone out with colleagues from work when Brian was away. Still, most of the girls from work were single and by and large younger than her, and she didn't share the same kind of bond with them as she did with Emer and Deirdre. Her colleagues were simply acquaintances; people to have a laugh with, rather than real friends.

The women she was sitting with now were her real friends and Jess worried that if Brian continued his traveling, and her and the girls' lives continued to diverge, there was a very good chance she would be spending a lot more time on her own in the future.

She would quite literally be left behind.

Trying to tune out that scary thought, she tried to concentrate on what was being said around the table. Listening to what they were discussing, she tried to think ahead for intelligent questions to ask about children, knowing she didn't have a very broad knowledge of the subject.

Finally, Deirdre stopped and said, 'Oh hell, Jess, sorry – you must be bored out of your mind listening to us prattling on.'

'No, no, not at all; it's actually good to know this stuff,' she insisted and saw Emer's gaze shift to Deirdre's, as if a silent message was being passed between the two women. Chances were they figured she was trying to overcompensate so she tried to rescue the matter. 'After all, it's one of those things that I'm going to have to learn about sooner rather than later.'

Emer raised an eyebrow. 'Really? What do you mean?'

Jess blushed. 'Oh, well, it's just that Brian and I were talking ... and we decided that maybe it's time.' She wasn't sure where that had come from – maybe she had decided it was time, but Brian didn't know anything about it, did he?

And come to think of it, *had* she actually decided anything?

Her friends once again exchanged a look; this time a much more appreciative one and Deirdre clapped her hands in delight. 'Oh, wow! Does that mean you're trying?'

'Um, well yes ... we are starting to ... consider the possibility of that,' Jess stuttered. She was sure they'd pick up on her uncertainty, but from the excitement emanating around the table it was almost like she'd stood up in the middle of the restaurant and announced, 'I have decided to procreate!'

'Oh, my goodness, that's so exciting!' Emer exclaimed. 'I'm so happy for you. Now, I presume you're off the pill, but have you started tracking the days it's best to conceive on, because that's really crucial you know, especially in the early days.'

'Ah ...' Jess's eyes grew wide, but she found she didn't really need to answer, as the girls continued their outpourings of maternal wisdom.

'Oh, and you have to buy *What to Expect When You're Expecting*,' Deirdre assured her. 'It's not just for when you are pregnant, but for before you get pregnant too, things to eat or not to eat, when you're at your most fertile ...'

Jess couldn't believe it. Suddenly, she was being included, really included and all because she'd mentioned that she and Brian might sometime soon be trying to have a baby? She was in the mummy club, just like that!

Maybe this was the answer; maybe she wouldn't lose her friendships with Deirdre and Emer after all. If she had a baby, she would be back on the same ground with these women and everything would be ok.

Jess felt elated and the rest of the evening was just like old times – the three friends chatting and laughing about all the things they had in common. Well, maybe not exactly like old times she admitted, when they got on to the subject of baby names that she and Brian liked.

But since she'd told the girls about her momentous decision to have a baby, Jess figured that now might be a good time to talk to Brian.

---

16

*I*t was Saturday morning and Ruth was feeling good. She'd slept soundly every night this week and wasn't sure if it was because up to now she'd been running on empty, her days fueled by stress, worry and caffeine, or simply because she was back in the semi-protective cocoon of Lakeview.

Since her return to her childhood home, her parents had been treating her like a queen, and thankfully there was no mention of the craziness of the last week, or the embarrassment of the *Late Tonight* interview. In fact, it was almost as if her hometown was immune to happenings in the outside world, or at least that's how it made Ruth feel.

The homecoming reception and Person of the Year Award had been everything she'd dreamed of, everything she'd hoped for, apart from that temporary meltdown in the utility closet. Still, the party had been a huge success and while most of the people there had probably seen the tabloid coverage, and most definitely had seen her disastrous interview, somehow they were all too decent and too polite to make mention of either.

She laughed softly to herself; that would never have happened at an LA party. There, everyone was quick to cast people as pariahs, whores, or even wackos quicker than anywhere else in the world. She supposed the mere fact that her hometown had welcomed her back without questions and scrutiny spoke volumes about the character of the people, and she was grateful for the fact that they'd managed to overlook her temporary lapse of judgement.

Nice to have old friends looking out for her too, she thought, smiling as she thought about mad Trish, who hadn't changed a bit. In truth, Ruth had been so bamboozled by the crowds she hadn't recognized her at first, but once the girl opened her mouth it was all too clear. She had a vague recollection of Nina Hughes from her teenage years, really just some fleeting memories of her visiting occasionally to see her father, that rather odd man from across town, Patrick, wasn't it? Nevertheless, Ruth decided that she already liked Nina, notwithstanding her kindness and cool head in helping her through her meltdown in the hotel closet.

Both Trish and Nina had invited her to meet for coffee this morning at the Heartbreak Café. Amazing that the place was still there; it had been around for as long as Ruth could remember. The owner Ella was a nice old soul and unlike some of the other business owners in the town, had never minded Ruth and her friends spending hour after hour there when they were teenagers, often buying nothing but a single glass of cola between the lot of them.

It had always been a warm and welcoming place and despite herself, she found she was looking forward to meeting the girls there today and couldn't remember the last time she'd just hung out with real people, real friends. Sure, she'd been out with fellow actors or her agent at restaurants and clubs, but being honest it was usually in the name of business or networking.

Ruth paused for a moment and examined her life. Truthfully, in Hollywood she actually had very few genuine friends, and while most of the time people pretended otherwise, pretty much everyone in LA had a façade.

Including herself.

She'd spoken to Chloe on the telephone since, and while the story of Troy and Ruth had been a big entertainment story on the day, the gossip columnists, frustrated by the lack of reaction from both her or

Troy, had got bored and quickly moved on to hounding someone else. Ruth was in two minds about this; on the one hand, she was thrilled Hollywood had ceased calling her the town slag, but on the other, as her manager Erik had pointed out, the publicity (embarrassing or otherwise) was good for her profile.

Still Ruth welcomed the opportunity to escape from fake people and pretension, at least for a while, so today she was going to join Nina and Trish for coffee. Once back in LA, she would have plenty of time to keep up appearances, but right now, she was going to enjoy just being herself.

She got out of bed and riffled through the clothes her mother had very kindly unpacked and hung up in the wardrobe. OK, so her mum was no Chloe, but really she hadn't let Ruth lift a finger all week. Another good reason to stay around for a while.

Going into the en-suite bathroom, she showered and dried before starting to apply her makeup. Going through her cosmetics bag, she stopped short, catching sight of the pink and white box Chloe had given her 'just in case'.

Damn, she thought, as the full extent of last week's actions came flooding back. She'd been so obsessed with the news stories that she'd practically forgotten about ... that.

Ruth pushed the pregnancy test to the back of the bag, underneath the pile of face lotions and hand creams.

Out of sight, out of mind ...

17

*L*ater that morning, she stepped over a couple of cats lazing on the step out front and pushed open the door of the Heartbreak Café.

She was immediately met with a brief silence, the locals evidently stunned wordless by the excitement of her patronage. For a brief moment, Ruth wondered if the papers had uncovered something else, perhaps another embarrassing slip-up, but soon a chorus of 'hellos' and 'good mornings' helped her let her guard down a bit. She smiled her best Hollywood smile and waved regally as she looked around for the girls.

'Ruth, over here!' Trish called from a window table overlooking the lake, at which she and Nina were sitting. Relieved, Ruth turned in their direction and sashayed over.

'Hey there,' she said cheerfully, taking a seat beside them.

'Great you could make it,' Nina said. 'I love your shoes by the way,' she added, glancing wistfully under the table at Ruth's purple suede Rupert Sanderson heels, which she wore with a light pink Lanvin shirt-dress.

'Are you on your way somewhere else?' Trish asked and Ruth immediately felt foolish and overdressed compared to the girls who were just wearing jeans and casual tops.

'No, but I guess I'm not used to dressing down ...'

'You look lovely,' Nina smiled.

'Doesn't she just?' Ella cried, waltzing over to the table with a pot of coffee. 'Love, I didn't get a chance to talk to you the other night, but can I just tell you how proud I was of you, that you put that stupid toad in his place last week.'

Ruth reddened. 'I'm not sure who was putting who in their place ...' she said, not wanting to be reminded of the TV interview.

'Not at all, he deserved his comeuppance and you gave it to him. No better woman too,' she said proudly and Ruth looked at her, touched.

'Thanks Ella.'

'So what can I get you? I know those LA types don't eat a bean and by the look of you you've gone down that road too,' she said with a glance at Ruth's size zero frame. 'But I'll wager you won't be able to resist my soda bread. You never could when you were younger,' she added and Ruth wondered how she was going to break it to Ella that she no longer touched carbs.

'Oh, I've already had breakfast actually, so just a coffee would be fine thanks.'

'Soda bread it is then and I'll cut it good and thick too,' the older woman said, as if Ruth hadn't spoken.

'So what do you have planned while you're here?' Trish inquired when Ella left.

'I'm really not sure. I don't usually have this much downtime and of course, I don't really know too many people around here, besides my family and you two.'

'Well, now that all the hubbub about your homecoming is over with, I'd like to organize a time with you for an interview – for the *Lakeview News*?'

'Of course.' Ruth quite looked forward to doing an interview that she knew would be hugely flattering and most importantly, would be read by everyone in this town. The local paper had always been a staple in the Seymour household and she was sure nothing had changed.

'And I wonder if you might be interested in helping out with a project I've just started working on. I've already asked Nina and she's game.'

'What kind of project?' Ruth knew better than to commit to something before she knew the facts.

'Well, I'm compiling a photographic history of Lakeview, and publishing it for charity,' Trish said, excitedly, and Ruth smiled graciously, unwilling to betray her hesitation. Sifting through old photographs of her sleepy hometown didn't particularly sound like her cup of tea, however worthy the cause might be. Still she supposed it would be an interesting way to pass some of her time.

'It would be great if we could incorporate you into the book too, into the present day bits as our most famous local resident.'

'Sure, sounds like fun.'

'We're going to check out the library archives tomorrow if you feel like joining us?' Nina asked.

'Count me in,' she replied, smiling. 'So what else do you like to do around here?'

Trish sat forward. 'Well, as you know, the place has really improved since you left, we've got some great new restaurants and pubs, but really for any great level of excitement or indeed shopping, you have to go to Dublin.'

'I see,' Ruth was beginning to wonder if spending the summer here would be such a good idea after all.

'Bit different from LA, I'd imagine?' Nina laughed. 'Don't worry; I know how you feel being away from the big city. I miss the hustle and bustle of Galway as well, although I know that too is a million miles from Hollywood.'

Ruth shook her head, 'Yes, I guess I'll have to get used to that. LA is such a different world and I'm always so busy and have so much going on and well ... everything seems so quiet and slow here.'

'Well, Lakeview has its charms too,' Trish said, a little defensively.

'Oh, of course, I didn't mean ...' The last thing Ruth wanted to do was alienate her new friends, especially when they'd already been so good to her.

'So tell me about the two of you, are you married, do you have boyfriends? What have you both been up to?' she asked, hoping to break the ice.

Both Trish and Nina filled her in on everything they'd been doing for the last few years. Nina spoke briefly about wanting to swap Galway for a quieter life after a recent break-up and Trish gave some details about some guy she'd just started seeing.

'What about you and yummy Troy?' she asked, clearly looking for the scoop.

Trying not to forget that her old friend was in fact a reporter, Ruth wasn't sure how much she should divulge. 'Oh, he and I aren't really a couple or anything. It was really just a one-time thing.'

'A delicious one-time thing, I'll bet!'

Ruth laughed, the first time she'd done that in days. 'It wasn't ... bad,' she said coyly. 'Although, I really wish the whole world didn't have to know about it.'

'Did he really make you scream the place down?' Trish said, eyes bulging, and Nina nudged her.

'Sorry, Ruth,' she said, smiling kindly at her. 'Personally, I really don't understand the big deal. I mean, you're both single, so who cares? It's not as if you're married or anything,' she added with a shrug. 'So how come it's front page news?'

Ruth resisted the urge to remind Nina that she and Troy were wildly famous, incredibly attractive celebrities, which made *everyone* care. But she supposed they wouldn't understand.

'So no one special in your life, then?' Trish persisted.

'No, honestly I've been so busy the past few years; there hasn't been a lot of time to date.'

'Never found anyone to replace Charlie then?'

Ruth's face burned. 'What?'

'Ah, I'm only joking,' Trish went on, 'I know we're talking ancient history there, but to be honest, I only remembered it because he just walked in.'

Ruth felt her heart drop into her stomach. Charlie ... here?

Trying her utmost to be discreet, she slowly turned around to face the door of the café. Her mouth fell open slightly; Trish hadn't been lying, Charlie Mellon was indeed standing there like a ghost from her past. And although it had been five long years, still she would have recognized him anywhere. He had the same tousled blond hair and ruddy complexion, the same broad shoulders and huge hands. He was speaking to someone by the entrance, shaking hands and nodding. Ruth watched him for a moment, remembering the last time she saw him.

She'd wondered if he might be at the welcome home party the other night, and had wondered what she might say or do if he was. But just as quickly she'd reminded herself that Charlie Mellon had probably left this town long ago. She'd never quite been able to bring herself to ask her mother about him and as Breda had never mentioned anything she'd just assumed ...

Suddenly, it was as if Charlie felt her eyes on him, because he stopped what he was saying and turned to look in her direction.

Ruth met his level gaze and felt her pulse race; she had no idea what her next move should be.

'Charlie, how's it going?' Trish said, waving.

But he made no move towards their table, nor did he wave in acknowledgement at the greeting.

Trish was unperturbed. 'Typical, rushing around the place as usual. He took over his dad's place a few years ago,' she informed Ruth. 'Transformed it into a huge place.'

She must have been talking about his father's car dealership, Ruth mused. He'd always talked about taking it to the next level. Clearly he'd done exactly that.

In the meantime, Charlie had finished talking to his companion so deciding to bite the bullet, she got up out of her seat. 'I suppose I'd better say hello,' she murmured to the other two.

Turning towards the door, she placed one foot in front of the other, suddenly very aware of just how great the distance was between the two of them. In reality it was probably only twenty-five feet, but it felt like several miles. She was also acutely aware of the eyes that followed her; after all it was public knowledge what had happened between them all those years ago.

Charlie however, did not make a move towards her and as Ruth neared, she tried to summon up a smile. Still, knowing him, he would see right through it, know just how nervous she was at this moment. As it was, she could see he was appraising her, taking in her appearance.

'Hello Charlie,' she said, standing in front of him.

He didn't answer immediately, instead he just studied her intently, and Ruth's face was beginning to flush with embarrassment when finally he opened his mouth, 'Well, if it isn't Hollywood Ruth ...' Although it sounded like a joke, there was an edge to his tone.

Ruth tried laughing it off, but her insides felt like jelly. 'Oh Charlie, of course it's just Ruth,' she joked, plastering on the smile that always wowed the cameras at premieres, and completely disguised her churning insides. 'Great to see you, it's been a long time, hasn't it?'

'Yes, it has been a long time.'

'So how are things with you? I hear you're doing well.'

'Well you know, I'm no star, but I'm doing well enough for someone who was stuck in Lakeview.'

The coldness of his words cut her to the bone, and while on some level Ruth knew that perhaps she deserved it; on another she wasn't letting him away with such a put-down.

'I'm glad to hear it,' she said, shifting her weight from one foot to the other. 'I always knew you'd be a huge success.' When he didn't reply, she smiled through her embarrassment, unsure what to say next. 'Well, I'll be in town for a little while so maybe we can get together for a coffee or something? I'd love to hear about all the goings-on.'

At this Charlie eyes darkened. He leaned in, getting close enough for her to smell the scent of his aftershave and without ceremony, took her by the elbow and guided her from the café.

'Charlie ... what?' Ruth gasped as he led her out the door. 'What's going on?'

Once outside, he spun on his heel and the hitherto lazy cats quickly scattered. 'I knew I was going to run into you at some point,' he said drolly.

'But, what ... what's all this about –?

'Spare me the small talk, princess. I have no desire to be part of all this, no intention of being pulled into some Hollywood-paparazzi-crap simply because it suits you. I'll deal with your presence in my town this summer, but other than that, I will not give you another thought. You have been out of my life for the past five years and I plan to keep it that way.'

Ruth was shocked at such directness. 'Charlie, I ...'

'Before you start, I don't care about you anymore, but I will not have my life disrupted while you are here because you happen to be a shameless drama queen OK? So let's get the rules straight right now. I don't want to have coffee with you; I don't want to have dinner with you – anything. I don't want to be involved with you or the lapdogs that follow you around.'

His words stung her and she puffed out her chest in indignation. 'How dare you insult me Charlie Mellon? You have no right to talk to me in such a manner.'

He laughed out loud and right then, Ruth felt relieved; clearly he was only joking around, messing with her head a little.

But what he said next didn't sound humorous at all. 'Please,' he said, shaking his head. 'Next time you do righteous indignation; try not to make it sound so rehearsed. I guess you're not that great an actress after all.' Then, before Ruth could respond, he patted her cheek in a patronizing manner, and walked off leaving her standing there alone. The irony wasn't lost on her. At their last meeting, Ruth had made Charlie look like a fool.

Now five years on, it was her turn.

his would have to be the marketing campaign of Jess's life. She was going to have to sell this idea like no other, make it sound like the ultimate must-have.

And Jess could do it, she was sure of it; after all, wasn't selling an idea her absolute specialty?

She paced the floor of the living room, listening intently for the front door to open, signaling Brian's return from London. She'd set the table, picked up a nice lamb moussaka from a nearby deli, and had a bottle of his favorite Pinot Grigio in the cooler. She'd also picked up something very nice from La Perla to wear beneath her figure-hugging Issa dress in the hope that all would go well and things could get moving immediately.

It was nine-thirty in the evening, and Brian had called about half an hour ago from the taxi on his way from the airport. He should be here any moment and while Jess always looked forward to her husband's return, this time was different. This time, she was ...well if truth be told, a little nervous.

Then right on cue, she heard the front door open and her heart began to race.

'Hey sweetheart,' Brian greeted happily, but stopped short as he caught sight of the wine and the carefully laid dining table. Surprise registered on his face, and Jess tried to ignore the way the side of his mouth twitched, something that usually happened when he was amused.

'What's all this?' he said, casting an eye over Jess's attire and her blonde hair worn loose around her face. 'I was expecting you to be in your comfy pajamas by now.'

Jess smiled. 'Well, I missed you and wanted to surprise you.'

Placing his overnight bag down, he loosened his tie and moved across the room towards her. 'What's the special occasion?' he asked, taking her into his arms. 'I didn't forget our anniversary or something, did I?'

Jess laughed. 'You know that's months away. There's no occasion really,' she said, her heart thumping so loud she was sure he could hear it. 'I was back early today so I just thought it would be nice to do something special.'

'You're right, it *is* nice. And what a wonderful surprise, thank you,' he said, kissing her softly.

'So how was London?' Jess asked, when they were seated at the table. She poured them each a glass of Pinot Grigio, making extra sure his was well filled. Tonight, she wanted her husband to be as relaxed as possible.

'Ah not too bad, you know yourself. Actually, I'd rather not talk about work – I've had it up to here with all the goings on.' He took a sip from his glass and smiled appreciatively as Jess put the steaming dinner plate in front of him. 'How was your weekend? Did you have a good time with the girls?'

'It was good fun.'

'Everything back to normal, then – no more baby talk?'

Jess gulped. 'Well, now that you mention that ...'

'What, they were banging on about it again?' He rolled his eyes.

'Kind of, but ... well to be honest honey, all of that stuff kind of got me thinking a little.'

'Oh – about what?'

'Well, about us, and our own ... situation.'

Brian's fork stopped halfway to his mouth. 'Our own "situation"?'

'Yes, you know regarding that ... department.' So much for her big pitch, Jess thought. As it was, she could barely get the words out.

'Wait a minute,' Brian said, looking at her. 'Are we talking about us having children?'

She nodded, her eyes shining. 'I was just thinking that maybe, you know, it's time.'

He was silent as he stared at her. 'This is about the girls again, isn't it?' he said evenly.

Jess stared down at the tablecloth; the relaxing mood that she'd worked so carefully to cultivate was well and truly broken. 'What? No, this has nothing to do with them.'

'Ah Jess, come on, you've never been a good liar.'

'Well, it isn't about my friends. It's about us, and if you ask me, it's something I really feel we should be thinking about. '

A smile played at the corners of his mouth. 'Really. So this big welcome home dinner has nothing to do with the fact that you were out with Emer and Deirdre at the weekend, and all of a sudden you want to have a baby?'

'It's not all of a sudden – I've been thinking about this for a while actually.'

'For a while? Strange that you hadn't mentioned it before that thing with Emer. And do you honestly think that you having a baby will help mend the problems with your friendship?'

How did he do that? Jess thought. How did he hit the nail right on the head?

'Honestly, Jess, you should know better than to let this bother you; those two are like a pair of 'oul biddies since they moved down to the countryside.'

'No, the girls have nothing to do with this Brian, honestly. This is about us. This is about *me*. We're ... well, I'm getting old.' She decided there was no choice but to call in the big guns and go all out with the dramatics.

'Old?' Brian chuckled. 'You cannot be serious.'

'I am serious. I'm thirty-five and while we're sitting here talking about it, my eggs are drying up. I looked it up on the internet, it's a fact.' Saying the words out loud was actually harder than reading them on screen and despite herself, she felt scared.

'Ah love, this has got to be the stupidest thing I've ever heard ...'

Jess's heart began to thump; this really wasn't how she'd planned tonight at all. She'd hoped for a calm, reasonable discussion about having a baby. She certainly didn't think Brian would be so against it; didn't men usually just go along with their wives on this kind of decision? 'Look we always said we would have a baby someday, didn't we?' she pointed out. 'But there's no denying that whatever you say, I am getting older, and soon it might be too late.'

Brian's tone softened. 'Sweetheart, of course we should think about having a baby sometime, but don't give me all this "old" business. Women have babies well into their forties these days.'

'Well, I don't want to be an older mum,' Jess said dejectedly, standing up and going into the kitchen. Brian followed her, but she stood and faced the window, away from him. 'A few more years and I might have to follow my kid around in a walker.'

Brian stood back, shaking his head. Then he sighed, and put his arms around her. 'Look, I know we always said we'd have children someday and I'm still committed to that idea. But can't you admit that maybe some of this – even a teeny tiny bit of it might have been brought on by you feeling left out of Emer and Deirdre's mummy club?'

'No.'

He sighed. 'Okay, if you can't admit that, fine, I'll go along with it. But regardless, don't you think that a decision like this, a huge, momentous life-changing decision like having a baby deserves a little more talk and planning?'

'Of course, but –'

'Wait, let me finish. Don't you think that maybe we should discuss the practicalities, look at our finances, see if we still have things we want to do before we commit to such a huge change?'

'But our finances are fine,' Jess argued. 'And we can continue to do whatever we want; the only difference is we'll have a little one to tag along.'

Brian nuzzled Jess's neck, 'Love, you do realize a baby isn't an accessory, don't you?'

Immediately she pushed her husband away. 'Don't patronize me, Brian.'

'I'm only teasing, but you really should hear yourself,' he said, pulling her back to him, but again she wriggled away. 'Can you see that I'm really serious about this?'

'OK, duly noted,' he said. 'But come on, let's not rush into anything before we're sure it's right for us. Yes of course we can start talking about it, but we also need to make sure that it's something we really want. Truthfully, I suggest you should let some of this rubbish with the girls blow over before you even start considering it seriously. Just because you're feeling a bit left out of their lives now isn't a good enough reason for us to embark on starting a family. That kind of clouded judgment won't do anyone any good, especially when you're talking about a decision as big as this. Come on, you of all people should know that it isn't something to take lightly.'

'I do, but ...' Jess sighed. Of course Brian was going to be all methodical and logical about it, wasn't he? Still, he did agree to consider it, and that was something, wasn't it? And seeing as the idea had (however muddily) been pitched, maybe now it was just about speeding up the selling process.

'So what do you think?' he asked in conclusion.

'You promise we can talk about it?'

'Of course, but we aren't going to jump into this blindly.'

Not exactly the answer she wanted, considering she'd already told the girls they were trying, but it was close. 'OK then, let's talk about it.'

'You mean now?'

'Why not?'

He ran a hand through his hair. 'Ah, come on, Jess, I've just got home after a long hard week and another flight. I don't have the energy, emotional or otherwise, to even think about something like this just now.'

'Tomorrow then?'

Brian sighed heavily. 'I have a long day tomorrow too, but fine OK, tomorrow.'

'My clock is ticking, remember?' she said, half-jokingly.

'So is mine and every second we spend here talking about your biological clock is one second closer to when I need to get up in the morning.'

'Alright, alright,' she decided to let the subject drop for now.

'So, is that new?' Brian asked, smiling at the raspberry colored lace peeking out at the V of her dress.

'It is, actually,' she said, smiling back at him.

He encircled her in his arms and bent his head to kiss her. 'Well then, let's try and make those seconds count.'

So be it, Jess thought, as she kissed her husband. She'd laid the groundwork and with a little more prodding, Brian would be on board.

Because while he might have won the battle tonight, he definitely wouldn't win the war.

19

On Monday morning, Nina met Trish outside Lakeview public library where they planned to search through old newspapers for relevant articles and photographs for the charity book. They had phoned Ruth and asked her to join them, but couldn't contact her and neither one of them had seen her since they'd met up at the café.

'What's the story with those two?' Nina had asked that day when Ruth and Charlie went outside. It was obvious there was some kind of history between them, but Nina hadn't known Ruth well enough back then to know who she was or wasn't seeing.

Trish was unperturbed. 'I suppose they're just catching up. It's impossible to talk to Ruth these days without people gawping at you so I'd imagine he wanted to talk to her in peace. Didn't you see them all staring when she was with us?'

Nina hadn't in fact noticed anything untoward, but then again, she'd been sitting beside the actress and facing the other direction. While she had no idea what was said, she figured it couldn't have been terribly positive considering that Ruth never returned to their table.

'They were engaged you know,' Trish told her, referring to Ruth and Charlie.

'Really?'

'Yeah, well, kind of, I heard he proposed, but ... Actually, I can't remember the exact gist of it, but it was around the time Ruth really made it big on *The Local*. Obviously they broke up when she moved to LA.'

'Right. That must have been tough.' Nina wondered if this was partly the reason Ruth had taken so long to return home. A broken heart, perhaps? 'I wonder why he didn't go with her?'

'Charlie Mellon in Hollywood? You must be joking. The same man can't stand going to Dublin, so he'd hardly be cut out for La-La Land.'

'I see.' Sounded like Ruth had, had to make a choice; a glittering acting career or life as a Lakeview housewife. Knowing what little of the girl she did, she suspected it wasn't a difficult one. Yet she wondered if Ruth had privately ever had any regrets?

Since then Nina had tried calling Ruth and had spoken to her briefly about coming to the library, yet she seemed intent on keeping to herself for the moment. Which was why she and Trish were on their own this morning.

Going into the library, they were escorted to a room out back by the friendly head librarian. 'I'm not sure if there's much here to help you, Trish,' the woman, who was called Martha, said, 'but if there's anything I can do don't hesitate to ask. I think this book is a brilliant idea and it's about time someone other than Madame Seymour did something to put Lakeview on the map.' She sniffed, her tone leaving them in no doubt as to her opinion of the local celebrity and Nina figured it was probably a stroke of good luck that Ruth had decided not to accompany them today.

When Martha left, Trish plopped down her large leather bag and started perusing the shelves. 'What do you think we should look for?' she asked.

Nina grimaced. 'I was hoping you would know, this is your project, after all.'

'Yeah, well, truth be told, I have no idea.'

Nina grabbed a volume containing newspaper clippings off the wall. 'This is impressive. I suppose I didn't think that Lakeview had any history that was worthwhile enough to merit an entire room.'

Trish smiled at her tone. 'Oh, aren't you the sarcastic one, Lakeview happens to have a splendid history, rich and colorful and ...' Trish faltered.

'Exactly,' Nina said, laughing. 'You know as much about this town's history as I do.'

'Well, I *will* know the history,' Trish said haughtily and Nina raised an eyebrow. 'Just as soon as I finish this book,' she added giggling. 'Seriously though, I suppose I'm looking for stuff that's interesting, a bit quirky maybe? Something that'll surprise people.'

Typical, Nina thought, smiling; she should have known that Trish's instructions would be clear as mud. Interesting and quirky weren't exactly words that jumped out at you when you thought of this place.

Several hours later, she stood up to stretch, feeling dusty and yellowed, a little bit like this room. And there was no denying her hunger. These days she couldn't stop eating, a side-effect of not being able to keep breakfast down, she supposed. Trish, on the other hand was still eagerly reading each and every piece of newspaper and examining every picture with the intense scrutiny of a pit-bull.

'I'm hungry,' Nina said, checking her watch. It was almost lunchtime; they'd already been here for three hours.

'Just a little while longer ...' answered Trish distractedly.

Nina rolled her eyes and ran her hand over the spines of the scrapbooks on the shelves. She had to admit, it had been a mildly interesting morning. She'd come across several mentions of her mother among the stacks – pictures and articles from when Cathy was in school or various community events she had been involved in. She had to give her mother credit; she'd been quite the popular one.

On the other hand, she'd only come across evidence of her father a couple of times, once in a class photo of his high school graduation and a second mention in the wedding announcements. It didn't surprise her; clearly in those days Patrick had been just as anti-social and invisible as he was now. It made her further question why her mother had ever got involved with such a wallflower, such an *outcast*, when clearly she could have had her pick of any of the men in town. Her mother was a stunner, and while she could see from the photo that Patrick had been reasonably handsome in his youth, she couldn't figure out how this was enough to catch her mother's eye.

Right now, though, Nina was bored and eager to get out of this little room. She felt her stomach growling and traced a subconscious circle around her abdomen. She was wearing a loose top today, as looking at her profile in the mirror this morning she was sure she'd seen the beginnings of a bump.

Trying to put the thought out of her head, she chattered meaning-lessly with Trish.

'So what about this guy you're seeing,' she asked her, 'what's he like?'

Her friend smiled. 'He's great.'

'Is he local? How long have you been seeing each other?'

Trish shrugged. 'A few months, nothing to get overly excited about.'

But Nina could tell by her demeanor that, despite her protests, she was actually very excited by him indeed. She smiled.

'So, what does he do?'

'He runs a company, is very busy and has a lot on his plate.' Nina looked at her, intrigued by her short, rather cryptic answers. It was as if Trish, who was normally so talkative, was purposely avoiding giving her a straight answer about this particular subject. 'Look, I think we're finished here for a while,' she said, snapping shut the book she was examining. 'Let's go out and grab a bite. Heaven knows you've been complaining enough about being hungry, you'd think that you've hollow legs or are eating for two!'

Trish turned her back and Nina blanched, relieved that her friend had missed the flush creeping up her neck.

They grabbed a sandwich at the supermarket deli, and afterwards, Trish decided to head home to work on what she'd collated so far.

Nina returned to her house, feeling drained of her energy after the short walk home. Opening the front door, she was met with the smells of her father cooking his own lunch.

She walked into the kitchen, and he greeted her with an absent nod.

'Did you have a nice morning, Dad?' Nina asked, making a vain attempt at conversation with the man she shared half of her genes with.

'Yes, thank you, Nina.'

'Did you do anything interesting?'

His eyes turned to her, almost as if he'd just realized that she was talking to him. 'I found the problem in Mrs Murphy's set. It was easy in the end, don't know why I didn't figure it out before.' He pointed to a TV set in the living room, its innards scattered all over the dining room table. Nina didn't know what was more disturbing, the mess in the room, or the words that had just come out of Patrick's mouth – more than she had heard him say since she arrived.

'Great, sounds ... interesting.' She paused for a moment, not quite sure what else to say, then it dawned on her. 'Well, I spent the morning at the library, going through old newspapers looking for photos for Trish's book. I found a lot of pictures and articles with you and Mum in them.'

Patrick looked up, and finally Nina felt that she had his full attention. 'Pictures?'

'Yes, while I was looking through the archives with Trish, I thought I'd told you about that. Well, she's putting together this book for charity, a photographic history of Lakeview.'

Patrick looked blankly at her, as if she'd just told him Trish was planning to fly to the moon.

'Well, the stuff I looked at was interesting; some from when Mum was in school and some other events. I saw your wedding announcement, and an old class photo of you,' she added smiling kindly.

Patrick looked somewhat troubled and Nina wondered if the mention of her mother was making him uncomfortable. She felt bad then, but there was a side of her that wanted to continue this conversation as it was the first thing in ages that had caught her father's attention. 'She seemed to have a lot going on when she was young, didn't she?' she added, wondering if he might be tempted to confess some interesting titbit about how they met or how they came to be married.

But once again, Patrick simply nodded disinterestedly and offered nothing, turning his attention back to making lunch. Nina waited for a bit, wondering if he would say anything else. When he didn't, she shrugged her shoulders and made one last attempt at communication. 'Well, I've already eaten so I'm going to head up to the room and read for a while. Let me know if you need anything.'

'OK, Nina.'

As she turned to climb the stairs, she looked behind her one last time, and as she did, she could have sworn that her father's brow was creased. But was it through concentration – or concern?

Nina didn't know.

20

'*O*h, isn't this the most gorgeous little thing? I so want to have a little girl!' Deirdre exclaimed, holding up a small pink babygro with little roses sprinkled over the length of it.

Emer smiled. 'I know. I got one just like that as a present before Amy was born. That's the beauty of knowing in advance what we were having.'

Jess looked at the small piece of clothing, wondering if this was some sort of test from her friends. If it was she definitely wanted to pass it. 'It *is* so cute! I can't wait to get cracking on buying all these,' she said with gusto. She had to admit, all the baby accessories, cute clothes, toys and gadgets did seem awfully fun. It was almost like going back to the days of her own childhood, and all the pretty little things she used to have.

Emer smiled and Deirdre looked delighted.

Jess still couldn't believe the change in her friends since she had announced her intention to get pregnant. Since then, they'd been inviting her on all their outings; be it coffee in Lakeview or on shopping trips in Dublin and this weekend Emer had asked her to stay over for the night as Dave had a work thing. Jess was only too eager to agree, as once again, Brian would be away. Today they'd spent the morning strolling around Lakeview, and popping in and out of anywhere that caught their interest.

There was no doubt that the brand new camaraderie she now shared with the girls was worth the baby bombardment. Only problem was they still thought she and Brian were trying in earnest for a child of their own.

Since their initial conversation about it, Jess had become more and more convinced that they needed to think seriously about their future, but so far Brian was still having none of it.

'Ah Jess, come on,' he'd complained when, recently she'd raised the subject of going off the pill. 'I thought you said we'd talk about this first.'

'Brian, I've read all about it. It can take up to a year for the drug to fully leave my system, which means I could be thirty-six before we even start.'

'Well, I think that's no harm, seeing as you'd get pregnant tomorrow if you thought it'd make your friends happy,' he chuckled, still completely unable to take her concerns seriously. 'Love, I know you better than you think and I honestly believe that this is just another one of your nutty fixations.' He then went on to remind Jess about a recent incident whereby she'd fallen in love with a shockingly expensive Chanel handbag, and had obsessed about it for weeks afterwards before finally giving in and buying it. 'And how many times have you used it since?' he challenged, forcing Jess to admit that yes, once she'd got the darned thing home the thrill had very quickly worn off.

'This isn't the same as a stupid handbag Brian,' she grunted, annoyed that yet again she was being painted as shallow and idiotic.

He kissed the top of her head. 'I know that hon, and maybe it's a poor comparison, but I'm just trying to make you understand that a decision like this needs time.'

The difficulty, Jess pointed out, was that they were fast running out of time. But was it really that, she wondered now as she saw Emer smile beatifically at her little daughter, or was it like Brian said, that she no longer wanted her life to be viewed as silly and pointless by her best friends.

'Did you find out what you were having when you were pregnant?' she asked Deirdre now, preferring to keep them talking, as when they directed such questions at her she became uncomfortable and perplexed. Especially when sometimes they carried on like she was already pregnant, asking her about what she and Brian were thinking about this or that, and what they planned to do when the baby was born. Because let's face it, Brian wasn't thinking anything other than how vexed the subject made him.

She cringed thinking about what he'd say if he was a fly on the wall at one of these outings.

Deirdre beamed. 'Not for Dougie, but we knew about Dylan. Do you think you and Brian will want to know?'

'Not sure really, is there a rule about that?' Jess felt herself flush.

'No, just your own preference,' Emer said. 'We did because I really wanted the nursery all set for Amy, all pink and pretty and girlie and I knew I wouldn't have the energy to do it afterwards. Anyway, Dave is useless at DIY and all that so I decided better to know in advance and just get it done.'

'I see,' Jess said.

'Anyway, let's get going,' her friend went on. 'I'm starving – Amy had me up at five this morning and I haven't eaten since then. Will we head to the café?'

'Great. I'll just pay for this first.' Deirdre went to pay for some Transformers contraption she'd picked out for the boys and soon after, the three women and their children headed further down the main street to the Heartbreak Café.

'Hello there,' a young and friendly looking woman greeted them upon arrival.

'Oh, hello Nina,' Emer replied. 'How are you?'

'Great, great. You're in luck; your usual table is free this morning. Do you need a hand with anything?' she asked and Jess noticed she seemed especially amenable to their entire entourage, given that the room was pretty small and the buggies and carriers would take up lots of space.

'Not at all, we're grand thanks. Oh, by the way, this is Jess.'

'Hello. I'm Nina,' she said, holding out her hand, and with her bright green eyes and open smile, Jess automatically felt she was a person you would feel at ease around.

'Jess Armstrong. Nice to meet you.'

'Jess is a friend of ours from Dublin,' Deirdre supplied. 'She still lives there, but who knows, maybe we can recruit her to Lakeview someday, eh Emer?'

Jess just smiled and laughed, knowing full well what Brian would have to say about that.

'Are you working here all the time now, Nina?' Emer asked.

Nina looked down at her shirt, which had the café logo over the left breast. 'You could say that. I thought myself that it would only be a few hours a week, but Colm – you know the bakery manager?' she said and Emer nodded. 'Well he'll be away over the summer, so I told Ella I'd cover for her whenever she needs me. Anyway, how are you all? Busy morning?'

'Sort of. We were just going around the shops, looking at baby clothes.' Deirdre told her.

Nina twirled her dark ponytail. 'Oh, who's having a baby?'

'Jess is,' Emer said and Jess's head snapped up.

'Congratulations!' Nina enthused, her gaze immediately shifting to Jess's stomach.

'No, well actually I'm not pregnant. Yet, I mean, um ...' Jess spluttered, to Nina's obvious confusion.

'What she means is that she's not pregnant *yet*, but she and her husband have decided it's time,' Deirdre answered more diplomatically.

Jess smiled, pleased that someone was able to explain on her behalf. 'Soon, hopefully.'

'Oh, that's ... great,' Nina nodded, looking unsure of what to say next. 'Well, good luck with it.'

Jess squirmed with mortification. 'Thanks very much,' she said, taking a seat beside the others at the table, while Nina waited to take their orders.

'So, how are things with you? Have you grown tired of us yet?' Emer asked her, before filling Jess in on how Nina was just here visiting her father for the summer.

'Oh, I've been keeping busy. As well as being here, I've also been helping out Trish with the charity book.'

'The photography thing? When is that coming out?'

Jess was amazed at how Deirdre and Emer had slotted so easily into small town life. To think that once upon a time the group of them had shared everything, and now here her friends were chatting away about all these people Jess had never even heard of.

Nina rolled her eyes indulgently. 'With Trish, who knows? It's slow going at the moment, but she's getting there. I think she's planning on knocking on doors soon, asking some of the older people if they have any interesting stories from way back when.'

'I haven't seen her for a while,' Emer commented. 'That piece she did for the paper about Ruth Seymour's homecoming party was really good though. Have you seen her around by the way? I thought she was supposed to be in town for a while, but I haven't heard much about her since that party. Which I missed anyway because I couldn't get a babysitter,' she added glumly.

'Ruth Seymour, you mean the actress?' Jess asked surprised.

'Yes, didn't I tell you she was from Lakeview? Well, there you have it, not such a backwater now is it?' her friend said triumphantly, and Jess blanched, horrified that this nice waitress would think she was slagging off her hometown.

'I never said anything like that,' she said quickly.

'Oh, I'm only teasing,' Emer grinned, before adding. 'Jess is a real city girl. You know, has a stroke if she's not close to all her little shoe shops and cocktail bars.'

'I'd like to think there's a little more to me than that,' Jess said testily before she could stop herself, and Emer and Deirdre looked at her, surprised.

'Yes, well she's very sweet and more down to earth than you'd think,' Nina said quickly, evidently sensing some tension. 'Under a lot of strain it seems, but very nice. I knew her when we were younger and Trish and I have met up with her once or twice, but for the most part, I think she just wants to relax and spend time with her parents. And who could blame her, after all that mania? Anyway, what can I get you?' She smiled at the children. 'I'm sure you lot would love a lollipop to start with, what do you think?'

Jess looked at Nina for a moment. She seemed lovely; incredibly warm and sincere.

'Do you have children yourself?' she asked her.

'Oh, no,' she replied quickly, and Jess thought somewhat uncomfortably, but at that moment, someone at another table signaled for her attention. 'Oops, give me a second, I'll be right back.'

'She seems really nice,' Jess said when Nina moved away.

Emer looked up from her menu. 'She is and she's a gem, really sweet. Now her friend Trish, the one she was just talking about? Totally different story, isn't she Deirdre?'

'Bit of a grouch, yes,' Deirdre agreed and Jess looked up expectantly; it sounded like they were going to have a good old-fashioned gossip, just like they used to, but then Emer changed the subject again. 'Oh, by the way, I forgot to ask you, what age was Dylan when he first started walking?'

'Thirteen months, why?'

'Well, I think Amy might be on her way to trumping that,' she said, smiling proudly.

This was another thing Jess had noticed lately, this huge passive-aggressive competitiveness between the two women as to their baby's developmental progress. There was a lot of talk about how, at ten months, Amy already had seven new teeth, whereas Dylan only had five at the same age etc. Did it really matter? Jess wondered.

It was one more thing that she failed to understand about all this, the complete change of outlook. She allowed herself to zone out for a moment, wondering if she would be like that if she had a baby. Would she talk non-stop about teething, crawling and vaccinations, and try to undermine other mums with her child's progress, or end up feeling insecure if hers was behind? And if it was all such a big race when they were babies, what on earth would it be like when they got older and there were academic and sporting achievements to measure up to?

Despite herself, Jess shuddered and gazed across the room at Nina, who was making her way with a tray full of pastries. She saw how the girl chatted away to the other patrons of the café, and wished for a moment that Nina would come this way and talk to them, because if she was being honest, she was once again running out of things to say to the other two.

She decided that maybe it wouldn't be so bad when she actually was pregnant; then she wouldn't have to pretend about all of this, and could genuinely be excited about a real event, something that was actually going to happen. She would have a due date and Emer and Deirdre would have great fun making plans with her, she could discuss all the different stages of pregnancy with them and it would be *real*. As opposed to now shopping in baby stores with them for something that was nothing more than an unfertilized egg. If Jess was pregnant, then she would be so much more into it all.

Which brought her right back to her original conundrum; how was she going to get Brian to see her side of things, how was she going to convince him she was truly ready to be a mother?

Unintentionally she sighed out loud and Emer looked at her. 'Sorry, Jess, are we boring you again?'

'Oh, no, no, not at all, I was just thinking about the time,' she said quickly. 'You see, I told Brian I would be back around lunchtime; one of his colleagues has invited us to a garden party this evening and I need to go back and get ready.'

'A garden party, you lucky thing,' Deirdre smiled enviously. 'It seems like ages since I've got all dressed up for a night out on the town with my husband.'

Emer snorted. 'All dressed up? I would take just a night out *with* my husband!'

'What are you wearing Jess?' Deirdre asked.

'Oh, I'll just pick something out of my wardrobe.' Jess didn't feel comfortable telling them that she'd bought a beautiful Tory Burch ochre-colored silk sheath especially for the occasion.

'Well, I'm sure you'll have lots to choose from,' Emer said shortly, and again she noticed a disapproving edge to her friend's tone, as if having a designer wardrobe was yet another example of Jess's trivial priorities.

When had this happened? Jess wondered. When had the things in life she'd enjoyed, things like nice clothes and staying in good hotels change from being rewards of her hard work, to symbols of her superficiality?

Eventually, she got up from the table and hugged both of her friends goodbye. 'Talk soon, and you guys should bring the kids up to see us sometime,' she said, even though she knew there wasn't much of a chance of that happening.

'Will do. Good luck with everything,' Deirdre said, 'and who knows, tonight could be the night.'

Jess looked at her blankly. 'Tonight?'

'That it happens of course,' her friend laughed and Jess smiled tightly.

'Oh, yes, absolutely. Fingers crossed.'

21

_B_ack in Dublin, she pulled to a stop in front of the townhouse. She scanned the street for Brian's car, but it looked like he wasn't home from his golf outing yet.

She went inside the house and started up the stairs towards the bedroom.

Opening her wardrobe, she flicked through the various dresses she owned until she found the one she was going to wear this evening.

It really was beautiful; and OK, so it had cost an arm and a leg, but she would have it forever. Well, she would if she stayed a size ten forever and if she _did_ end up getting pregnant chances were that might not happen.

Emer had put on a lot of weight with Amy and had since lost most of it, although she guessed the last thing on her friend's mind these days was worrying about fitting into designer labels. But perhaps that was why she'd seemed so sniffy during their conversation earlier? If so, Jess couldn't truly understand why. If she had a little angel like Amy, fancy labels and keeping up appearances would no doubt fade into insignificance.

Hanging the dress outside the wardrobe, she got undressed and padded barefoot into the en-suite. A few minutes later, she got out of the shower and wrapped a towel around her, listening for signs of her husband's arrival. Nope, still nothing – he must be running late.

Jess sat down in front of the vanity unit to start on her makeup. Opening the drawer where she kept her everyday cosmetics, something immediately jumped out at her; her birth control pills.

She hadn't yet taken it today, had she? She opened the little blue case up and sure enough, the pill marked 'Saturday' was still in its protective plastic. She popped it out and was about to put it in her mouth when something made her pause.

She froze and pulled her hand back, looking at the little tablet. If she was so sure she wanted to get pregnant, why was she continuing to take these pills? *Because Brian's not on board yet*, the little voice answered. Still, as she'd pointed out to him before, it could take up to a year for her body to get back to normal, and ready for conception.

Jess studied her reflection in the mirror, realizing that she couldn't wait that long. A whole year before they could even begin? No, there was no point in waiting until Brian gave the go ahead; that would delay things even further. As it was he was so easy-going he would probably come round soon, so she might as well get the ball rolling now.

Jess dropped the case back into the drawer and hid it beneath a pile of Lancôme creams and eye shadows.

Maybe, just maybe the answer would present itself, and nature would work it all out.

22

*R*uth paced back and forth in the bathroom of her parents' house. She thought that her heart was going to jump out of her chest it was pounding so hard. Frankly, she wouldn't be surprised if she had a heart attack and died right there and then, the way her luck was going lately. She couldn't believe just how horrible everything was at the moment. For someone who'd always believed she'd been born under a lucky star and that fate had directed her up to this point, it certainly had been a long few weeks of bad luck. Or was it bad karma?

She sat down on the corner of the bed and placed her head in her hands. How much longer, damn it? She looked at her watch, amazed. Was it really possible that only a minute had passed?

Ruth groaned. The *thing* sat on top of the en-suite washbasin, beckoning her, taunting her.

It was now well over a month since that ill-fated encounter with Troy and the day of reckoning had arrived. She knew she shouldn't have been so surprised when her period didn't start last week like it was supposed to, but she was. She was not only surprised; but completely frantic that the morning after pill might not have worked.

But by day three of 'the missed period' she knew she could no longer put off the inevitable. That morning, she'd fished out the pregnancy test that Chloe had given her, read the directions and peed on the stick. Which was why she was sitting here like an idiot, waiting for some little piece of white plastic to decide her fate.

She checked her watch again; two minutes had passed.

Ruth stood up and started to pace again. To say that her trip home had so far not gone as planned was an understatement. Right from the beginning, from that upsetting arrival at the airport to that horrible TV interview, to hiding in a closet at her own goddamn party! Then, as if that wasn't enough, there was that mortifying confrontation with Charlie outside the café. At this stage, Ruth didn't know whether she should just pack up and head straight back to Los Angeles.

Still, however mortifying being in Lakeview was, at least she wasn't alone here. Her parents had been wonderful and the locals (especially Trish and Nina) had gone out of their way to be kind, well Nina had at least, Ruth still wasn't sure about Trish.

At Trish's pleading, she'd met with her for the interview for the paper, and while the questions seemed innocuous enough, Ruth hadn't known what to expect from the finished article. Who knew what way her words could be twisted? She'd been careful not to mention anything about Troy or their 'relationship' and had tried her best to come across as the 'local girl done good', speaking at length about her Beverly Hills home and glamorous LA lifestyle.

It was due to appear in the paper today, but Ruth didn't have the stomach to go out and get it, especially if it turned out to be yet another hatchet job. She tried her utmost to make it all sound fairy-tale-like, conscious of the fact that Charlie Mellon would undoubtedly read it.

Thinking again about Charlie, Ruth's stomach twisted at what had happened when she'd bumped into him. She really hadn't expected him to still be so bitter. Granted, what she'd done had been pretty hurtful, but she was sure he'd be over that by now. It was five years ago after all. Yet Charlie had never been one to take rejection easily, and given the circumstances ...

Ruth thought back to how it had been when they were together.

She'd known him for as long as she could remember, and their families lived on the same road. They'd attended the same school and had always got on reasonably well, albeit they moved in very different circles. Ruth ran with the popular gang while Charlie was quieter, more studious.

Late in their teens, he'd disappeared to Dublin for a few years to attend university, but after graduation, came back with a view to taking over his dad's business. When Ruth bumped into him one day, she couldn't believe that this was the same guy who used to heckle her as a child. The skinny, silly adolescent who'd left four years earlier had come back a full-on man.

Their romance started slowly, they'd flirted casually whenever they ran into one another, which oddly enough, happened quite a lot.

Then one night, Charlie gave her a lift home, even though her house was only walking distance from the village center. She'd known that something was going to happen and in truth, couldn't wait. At that point, she was so ready for Charlie to kiss her that before they traveled the short distance to her house she asked him to pull down a side street. Her dad usually kept an eye out for her to return so she didn't want an audience. He stopped the car and looked at her and saying nothing, Ruth used her now-classic 'come hither' expression. Charlie immediately leaned across the center console and pulled her close, his lips gentle, warm, and tender. Ruth kissed him back with a fervent passion, and quickly began pulling his shirt from the waistband of his pants.

Charlie stopped. 'No, no, not like this,' he said in a low growl.

'What? What are you talking about?' Ruth was persistent, continuing to kiss his neck, his mouth, his ears until finally, he grabbed both sides of her face.

'No, I don't want to ruin this,' he said. 'I think you and I might have something here – something good, and I want to give it a chance. If there is an 'us', I want to give it time to develop, and if it does happen, I want it to be special.'

She remembered worrying that she had been too pushy, coming on to him like that, but her worries had been unfounded, because

Charlie's next move was to ask her out on an official date. His sweet, almost old-fashioned approach was surprising, and merely served to make Ruth want him all the more. Hell, they'd been together for months before they finally slept together.

She remembered that first time, how he had told her he loved her, how tender and sweet he had been. It was like something from a movie, and she recalled at the time how she'd felt she was in fact playing a part. Charlie knew all about her dreams of an acting career, knew how much she wanted to move on from the TV soap, how she ached to go right to the top.

Then one night, after filming on the soap had wrapped for the day, Charlie had come up to Dublin and arranged a special night out for them. He'd booked a room in the Shelbourne hotel, they had dinner, dancing, and champagne and when later that night they went back to their room, there was one more surprise. A diamond engagement ring.

Ruth froze, the ring signifying all the things she didn't want. If she married Charlie, she would end up stuck in Lakeview, in Ireland. There would be no Hollywood, no glamour, no film premieres. She was born to be a star, not an Irish jobbing actor and just the wife of a small-town local boy.

However much she cared about that local boy.

When Charlie got down on one knee, Ruth cut him off; not wanting to hear what she knew he was going to say.

'Don't do this, you know I don't want this.'

He stared at her, hurt and confused, and she remembered telling herself that she was an idiot, that she loved Charlie and would never find anyone better than him. Still for both their sakes, she had to do it, had to make sure he didn't get the words out.

It was too late anyway; Charlie fled the room and didn't return and Ruth wondered if he ever really took her seriously when she told him she would be a star. Did he think, like the rest of the Irish acting world, that she was deluding herself, that Hollywood was only a pipe dream? If so, why on earth would he stop that dream in its tracks by proposing? There was no question of him going along with her to LA;

he had all his responsibilities in Lakeview, and she'd always thought there was this unspoken agreement that their time together would inevitably come to an end.

That night in Dublin was the last time she had seen him, and a week later Ruth bought a plane ticket to LA and decided to never look back.

Out of sight, out of mind.

Glancing at her watch again, she noted that almost five minutes had passed. Right, that stick should surely be done by now.

She walked tentatively into the bathroom, peeking around the corner first as if the test had suddenly grown teeth and would snap at her if she got too close. When she was about two feet away, she closed her eyes and covered the remaining space by rote. Ruth placed her hands on the cool ceramic and took a deep breath, hoping to try and calm herself. She repeated her yoga mantra over and over in her head. Positive or negative, life would go on ... positive or negative ...

Slowly she opened her eyes, and stared at her reflection in the mirror. Finally, she allowed her gaze move to the surface of the counter and the white plastic stick that lay on top of it. Focusing in on the display window, she sucked in her breath.

There was a tiny pink cross.

She was pregnant.

23

*M*inutes later, Ruth grabbed a towel and wiped her mouth. So much for her yoga chant. Almost as soon as she'd seen the positive sign and realized its significance, her stomach had recoiled and she'd lost her breakfast. Thankfully, she'd been in close enough proximity to the toilet.

She grabbed the test and wrapped it in a plastic bag, before burying it deep at the back of her wardrobe; she couldn't run the risk of her mother finding it. Then, collapsing on to her bed, she crawled under the covers and felt the tears come.

How the hell had she got herself into this mess?

She'd give anything to go back and do that stupid party all over again. If she could turn back time, she would have refused the champagne and the compliments, would have kept her wits about her, would never have fallen for Troy's romantic claptrap.

Troy.

Ruth groaned, thinking of the upcoming *Glamazons* shoot when she'd have no choice but to see him again. Thinking about the series brought everything sharply into focus. Oh, no, she couldn't have this baby, her career would be over, her body would be ruined, everything that she had worked for flushed down the toilet, all because of one stupid drunken night!

How had she been such an idiot? How was she going to tell Troy, or the producers ...?

Then again, Ruth thought quickly, maybe Troy didn't even have to know, nobody might have to know.

No, she had to tell him, there was no way that she could get through this without him knowing what had happened. Regardless of the fact that she owed him nothing and they weren't a couple, weren't even dating, she still knew that telling him would be the right thing to do.

Then they would be in it together, and who knew, maybe the show's writers might be able to work it into the plot, and come up with an even better storyline as a result? Actually Ruth thought, her mind racing, it could be the making of them. Not of her and Troy as a couple, surely there was no question of that, but imagine the publicity!

She grabbed her cellphone and scrolled through her contacts. When she came to his name she paused for a moment, thinking of that night, the way he felt, the things he said to her. Her hands subconsciously moved to her stomach. Wow, to think that they'd created a life that night.

Then Ruth shook her head; she couldn't think about that just now, couldn't waste time wondering about it. It was the implications that mattered at the moment.

She pressed a button on her phone and waited for their call to be connected across thousands of miles. It rang four or five times and she was sure it was about to go to voicemail when:

'Hello ...?' Troy said groggily, and at the sound of his voice, Ruth felt her stomach twist involuntarily. Then she checked the time. Uh-oh, she'd forgotten it was the middle of the night in LA

'Troy?'

'Yeah, who is it?'

'Um ... did I wake you?'

A low groan. 'Yeah ... who is this?'

'It's Ruth. I'm so sorry – I can call you back ...'

'No, it's fine, I'm awake.'

'Look, it's grand, it wasn't that important, and I suppose it can wait –'

'Wow, your accent is *really* strong!'

Ruth too realized that her Irish accent had come out in full force. Nerves, she supposed. 'Well, after a few weeks here, I suppose it does come back a bit.'

'So hey, how are you babes? Did you get my message from before? That morning – you just took off.'

She realized he was talking about the last time they saw each other. 'I got your message, thanks and yes, I'm sorry about that.'

'Why?'

She frowned. 'You mean, why am I sorry, or why did I run off?'

There was a laugh on the other end. 'Maybe both. I would have really liked to kiss you good morning.'

Was he flirting with her? 'Oh.'

'So what's up Ruth? Why are you calling now? Did you miss me? Just had to hear the sound of my voice, huh?'

Ruth had almost forgotten about the size of the guy's ego, but of course it was almost in direct proportion to ... Shocked by her own train of thought, she shook the idea out of her head.

'Well, I'm calling for a reason actually,'

'I knew it. You do miss me. So when are you coming back?'

'No. I mean ... well, I'm actually not sure.'

'You want me to catch a plane over there to you, babe? Finish what we started?'

Ruth felt annoyed, wishing he would just shut up for a minute so she could get this out.

'Troy, please, I need to talk to you. This is serious.'

It seemed he finally got the message. 'Hey, are you ok?'

'Yes, yes, I'm fine. Well, actually, I'm not fine, I'm sort of shocked and really confused and well ...'

'What is it? Whatever it is, I'll help you get through it.'

Ruth raised an eyebrow, liking the way he said that. Maybe she would actually be able to count on his support? Maybe his notorious playboy image was just that – an image, and by the flirty way he was talking to her, maybe there might be a future for them?

'Really? It's good to hear that Troy, because ... you see, well actually ... it's just that ... I'm pregnant.'

For a long moment, there was complete silence on the other end of the line.

'What the hell?' he spluttered eventually, his velvet tone turning to venomous. 'What's that supposed to mean?'

Ruth's heart raced. 'It means ... that I'm pregnant Troy, I just took a test.'

'And you're telling *me* because ...?'

It was as if he'd slapped her. She wasn't sure exactly what kind of a response she'd been expecting from him, but it certainly wasn't this. 'Why do you think?'

'Ah, come on Ruth. You're not thinking it could be mine?'

Her eyes widened. '*Thinking* ... Troy, we had sex about a zillion times that night and remember that whole problem with the condom? I realize the night is probably a little fuzzy round the edges – for both of us – but surely you remember that much?'

'Yeah, but who's to say it happened that night?'

Ruth froze. He'd basically implied she was a whore, suggesting the same thing that the papers have been saying about her.

That might have been easier to take if there was any truth in it, but the thing was that he was the one who was constantly hooking up with his co-stars, while she on the other hand, hadn't dated anyone seriously in years.

'What are you trying to say to me, Troy?' she replied, ice in her tone.

'Well, you know, I read the papers too and ...' he trailed off and she sensed him shrug.

As if this sort of stuff should be just par for the course for her.

'Wow ...' she began hoarsely. 'To think that I looked up to you, respected you even ... And not that it matters, but just so you know you're actually the first man I've gone to bed with in years.'

'I guess that explains the screaming, huh?' he chuckled and Ruth tried to figure out which was worse, that she'd actually slept with this idiot, or that such a man could be the father of her unborn child.

'How dare you, Troy?' she croaked. 'How dare you make me feel this small?'

On the other end, she heard him exhale and then his voice softened. 'Look, I'm sorry, I shouldn't be making light of this.'

'Damn right you shouldn't.'

'It's just that ... well to be frank, this isn't the first time a girl has laid this kind of stuff on me.'

'Oh, well I guess that explains your insensitivity perfectly then,' she cried. 'How stupid of me to think that I deserved a little respect. This might not be the first time someone has told you something like this, but believe me, it's most definitely the first time I've had to tell anyone!' Now she felt like punching someone, she was so angry.

'Ruth, hey I'm sorry I overreacted, maybe I was an asshole.'

'*Maybe*?'

'OK, OK. Anyways, so you're knocked up. You're sure?'

'Yes I'm sure, I'm not an idiot, you know.' Although Ruth couldn't be sure if that last part were true.

'OK then, you need to get back here fast, so we can get this taken care of. There's a clinic I know that will do it and we can trust them that it won't leak.'

As he continued to talk, Ruth felt herself automatically zoning out. There he was rattling on about an abortion clinic that would keep everything under wraps, get it taken care of. He just *assumed* that she was going to have an abortion and never even asked how she was doing, how she was coping with it all. What's more, he never even considered that she might actually *want* to have the baby. Instead, he'd just determined what was in his best interests and opted for that; regardless of her opinion.

'So, I can get my assistant to make you an appointment for, say, end of this week? You'd better get booked on a flight back to LA right away. I'm serious, the sooner this is taken care of, the better 'cause we don't need any further speculation.'

Ruth was quiet. Speculation? He was talking about the press

again. And yes, of course they would be on something like this like a shot, and once again she would be all over the papers, her name mud. She could see the headlines already; no doubt she would be dubbed as the fledgling actress who was trying to make an even bigger name for herself by getting knocked up by the great Troy Valentine.

Oh hell...

Maybe Troy was right. Maybe it was better for everyone that they got this 'situation' dealt with quickly. Over and done with. As it was, the time away from LA had helped her survive the recent negative publicity, and she could go back in September with her head held high and an amazing second series to work on. The fling with Troy would be mostly forgotten and she could move on to the next stage of her career, bruised certainly, but maybe not as battered as she'd be if she didn't take his advice.

They both had their careers, and they weren't married, weren't even together so it wasn't as if she could raise a baby with her co-star, much less even contemplate raising one on her own ...

Could she?

Ruth thought about it. She'd always figured she'd have kids one day – someday.

Someday when she was famous enough and rich enough. She pictured dressing her kids in cute little designer outfits and pushing a stroller along Rodeo Drive. She'd always cooed over babies, although she hadn't had much of an opportunity recently. She pictured tiny hands and tiny feet and the kisses that she'd cover her baby in, and was brought up short by the vision.

No, she thought, shaking her head. This wasn't a baby. Troy was right; this was a mistake, merely the product of too much champagne and a definitive lack of judgement.

Wasn't it?

'Ruth? Ruth, sweetheart, are you still there? You don't have to be afraid, you know. Really, it's not a problem – you'll be in and out before you know it and this will all be behind us. Just a simple proce-dure.' Troy spoke with the knowledge of someone who'd almost certainly been down this road before.

'A simple procedure.' Ruth felt as if she was in a trance.

'Yes, there's nothing to worry about – there'll be no scars or anything. Honestly, it'll be just like it never happened.'

'Like it never happened.' Ruth paused for a moment and looked down at her stomach. Then she took a deep breath. 'Troy, what makes you think that I would even consider something like this?'

'What ... what are you talking about?'

'You never even *asked* me what I wanted, you just assumed that I would –'

'Well of course I assumed. Jeez Ruth, no one in Hollywood would do anything else in a situation like this.'

'You never asked me my opinion on this subject. You were just ready to get your assistant to make an appointment at some clinic. It almost sounds like you don't even have to look up the number; like you already have it on speed dial.'

'Ruth, what the hell are you talking about? Of course you are getting this dealt with. Are you out of your mind? Do you want both of our careers to be over?'

'Is that all you're worried about? Your stupid career? This is a baby we're talking about – a life!'

'It's a goddamn mistake, that's what it is!'

Ruth shook her head, and tears blurred her vision. 'Don't say that. It's not like that. Anyway, I believe in —'

'You can believe in the freakin' tooth fairy for all I care. This can't happen.'

'Well, it is going to happen Troy. I'm not getting rid of this baby,' she announced determinedly. Whatever about anything else, at least she knew that much.

'Well sweetheart, good luck with that. But you won't get a cent from me. And good luck with trying to get sympathy from Bob and the producers too. Can't you see you're making a huge mistake here, Ruth? Your career's going down the pan with this!'

'Yeah, well, I'll think about that when I need to.' With luck she wouldn't have to think about it for a while yet. And who knows, maybe the second series would be even bigger and the producers would have no choice but to be supportive. Either way, she couldn't even contemplate past anything other than what she'd just decided.

'And don't think you can drag me down with you either. I've been around long enough not to let some two-bit tramp rain on my parade.'

This was the parting shot from Hollywood's favorite heartthrob before he hung up.

Ruth pushed her phone to the side and stared at the wall, still in shock. Shock from all that had been said, but mostly from the unexpected conclusion she'd arrived at. In spite of Troy's reaction, in spite of all the upheaval this would surely cause, she'd made her decision; she was going to have their baby.

And she still didn't know how to feel about that.

24

'*Y*ou're in Lakeview?' Cathy's shock was evident, as Nina had known it would be. 'What are you doing there?'

As the weeks went by it had become harder to remain evasive about her location, and so she had no choice but to confess to her mother where she was staying. Luckily, and so Cathy wouldn't start worrying, she'd come up with a great cover story.

'Well, remember Trish? We met up recently and she told me she was doing this charity book on Lakeview and that she could really use a hand. And because I had nothing else on ...'

'Nothing else on? What about work?'

'I told you I had to leave the company, Mum. With the way things ended, I didn't want to stay there and have to see Steve every day ...'

'Well, maybe I can understand that, but why leave Galway too? Seems a bit drastic ...'

'I don't know – I just needed some time away – a fresh start I suppose.'

'I see.' Cathy sighed, rightly suspecting that there was a lot more going on than meets the eye. 'But I didn't think you and Trish were still in touch.'

'Ah, we are. She came up to see me in Galway a few times and we've always got on well ... and anyway Mum, I thought the change of scenery would do me good.'

'And you're staying with Patrick?' The surprise was evident in her tone and Nina knew that she was amazed by this, considering that her daughter had come up with every excuse under the sun not to spend time with her father over the years.

'Yes, he's been great letting me stay with him.'

'Really?' Her mother's tone suggested she didn't believe a word of it. 'And how is he?'

'Oh, well, you know Dad, he keeps himself to himself.'

'I see.'

'But he's been very good, making me dinner and breakfast and all that. But truthfully, I try and keep out of his way as much as I can.'

'Is he still fixing TVs and all that?'

'Yep.'

There was a smile in Cathy's voice. 'I'd imagine that's a lot of fun, all those parts laid out everywhere.'

'It's not too bad. But I tend not to stay around the house too much. I see Trish quite a bit and of course I've got the café job –'

'Job? You have a *job* in Lakeview too?' she said and Nina winced. She hadn't planned on mentioning that; it would give away that she'd been here for some time.

'Just a couple of mornings in Ella's – you know the Heartbreak Café?'

'Of course.'

'Well, actually, it kind of happened by accident. I was in there one day and she was telling me about how busy she gets over the summer so I sort of offered to help out.'

'Very kind of you to help out so many of Lakeview's finest. Nina, is there something you're not telling me?' Cathy was shrewd as ever.

'Of course not, why?'

'Well, it just seems odd to me that's all. There you are, working and living in Lakeview of all places. A place you really seemed to hate when you were growing up.'

'Well, I feel a bit guilty about that too. I mean, Patrick is my dad and I haven't spent all that much time with him. I mean, of course Tony has been brilliant, but ... and speaking of which, how is he?' Nina decided to use the mention of her stepfather as an excuse to change the subject. 'How's the travels going? Where are you headed next?'

'We're in Hong Kong now, about to start a week-long tour of China.'

'It sounds amazing Mum; you must be loving every second.'

'Well of course we are, but it just seems so long since I've seen you honey. And I miss you. I miss being around for you when you're going through so much ...'

'Mum, please don't worry about me; I'm absolutely fine. Yes, it was tough in the aftermath, but being honest, coming to Lakeview was the best possible thing for me. I have friends here now and it's good fun.'

'Well, as long as you're sure, but you know I'd come home in a second if you needed me.'

'There's no need, honestly. Of course I miss you loads too, but I'm really fine.'

Nina smiled into the phone and she wrapped the phone cord around her wrist. She smiled, still unable to believe Patrick still had a phone with a cord.

'So has Lakeview changed much? Is it still the same as you remember?'

'It is different, bigger I think. But people have been great, really friendly.'

'Well, that's good. Does Ella still have all those sad rescue cases roaming around the place?'

Nina smiled, thinking of her boss's latest rescue case – a one-eyed dog called Claus she'd picked up from the local shelter, which slept out back and was worthy competition to the cats for the café's left-overs. 'Yes, but don't worry, she's very protective of her 'Good Food' award so it's all very hygienic.'

'Well that's more than I can say for this place. Honestly, Nina, you should see some of the stuff they eat here. Deep-fried crickets and everything! I'll tell you, Tony nearly lost his life!'

Nina laughed. Her stepdad was a die-hard meat and spuds Irishman so she could only imagine his reaction to the local Asian cuisine.

'So I'm sure you're meeting lots of people at the café. Anyone interesting?'

'Interesting? You mean, like a man? Oh, come on Mum, I'm just over one guy and have no interest in meeting another.'

'Of course you don't,' Cathy replied. 'But who have you met, really?'

'Well, Ella is great of course, and Trish and ... oh, I'm sure you know Ruth ... Seymour, the actress? She's back for the summer.'

'*The* Ruth Seymour? Of course I'd almost forgotten she was from Lakeview. So you're friends with her now too?'

'Well, we've met up for coffee a couple of times, I'm not saying we're best friends or anything,' Nina insisted. 'But working on Trish's book is good fun. We've been going through the archives at the library and found a lot of great stuff – some of it about you actually.'

'Really, like what?'

'Just old newspaper articles about various school events and such-like. You were quite the social butterfly, Mum.'

'I suppose so, back in my younger days,' Cathy said and Nina heard a smile in her voice. Actually, her mother was *still* the social butterfly.

'I didn't see much about Patrick though.'

'Well, you know he's always liked to do his own thing.'

'I know, and don't get me wrong, but I still can't understand how you two ever got together. It looked like you could have had the pick of the lads in Lakeview.'

'Ah, Nina stop.'

'No really; I mean he's such a loner now, I can't help wondering if he was like that when he was younger. And you and he are just so different; I really hope I didn't get his weird genes.'

'Look, as I've said before, your father is who he is and he played a very special role in my life. He gave me you after all. OK, so he might not be typical, but he has his own charm and he's done the best by me

– by us. And now he's obviously been kind enough to give you a place to live. Really, you shouldn't be so hard on him.'

Nina sighed heavily, feeling guilty and unkind for her criticism, after all Patrick was allowing her to stay here without asking questions, he let her do her own thing and didn't ask for any rent.

'I know, I'm sorry. It's just well you know how he can be.'

'Still having cabbage on Wednesdays?' Cathy joked. 'I know how much you used to love that.'

Nina laughed. 'Yes, but like you say, he has been good to me.'

'Exactly. So how long are you planning on staying there?'

'I'm not sure really. It was a kind of a spur of the moment thing, but I suppose I'm sort of ... settled here now.'

'Well that's good to know. I worry about you a lot you know. And really, I'm kicking myself that I'm not there for you at such a tough time. Have you heard anything from Steve?'

'No Mum and I really don't want to. That's definitely over and done with.'

'You're sure?'

'Definitely.' Suddenly, Nina found herself eager to get off the phone. 'Anyway, I'm going to have to run, have a fantastic time in China and give my love to Tony, OK? We'll talk again soon.'

'OK honey, be good.'

Nina put the handset back in the receiver and stared at the ceiling.

That had gone reasonably well, hadn't it? Cathy didn't seem unduly suspicious about her whereabouts, which was great, as she'd been so sure her mother would guess something. Not that she could have guessed this of course. Nina subconsciously ran a hand over her stomach.

She almost jumped out of her skin when her mobile phone rang again. Picking it up, she saw it was an unfamiliar number, but she decided to answer it anyway.

'Hello.'

'Hello Nina? Hi, it's Ruth here.'

'Oh, hi, how are you?'

'OK I guess,' she said, not sounding OK at all. 'Look my mum passed on your messages and ... well I'm sorry about not getting back to you guys sooner, but –'

'Not at all, I'm sure you have a lot going on.'

'You could say that.' She sounded flustered, Nina thought. Trish had insisted that her *Lakeview News* interview with Ruth would be balanced and pretty complimentary, but maybe there'd been another horrible story in the papers in the meantime? 'Actually, I was wondering if maybe you wanted to meet up for lunch or something?'

'Today?'

'Well, yes, if you don't have anything else on.'

Nina didn't. Ella didn't need her at the café and Trish was working flat out on the upcoming edition of the newspaper so she was at a loose end. 'That would be lovely. Do you want to meet at the café?'

'Well is there any chance you could come here to my place? My parents are out at the moment,' she added hastily. 'And I was just thinking that I really don't feel like putting on makeup and getting dressed up.'

Yes, Nina could only imagine the pressure of having to look a million dollars every time you put your nose outside the door.

'Sounds perfect, can I bring anything?'

'Well, now that you say it, could you pop to the shops and maybe pick up a salad or something?' she asked and Nina got the impression that she was used to having minions at her beck and call. But she didn't mind, as long as the other girl didn't make a habit of it.

'Why don't I pop into the café and get Ella to rustle us up a salad roll or something?'

'That would be fantastic,' Ruth said, sounding relieved, but also Nina noted, a little frazzled. 'Nothing with wheat, though, you know how it is. And nothing with butter, eggs, or meat ...oh and no tomatoes either; they give me breakouts.'

'OK.' Nina wondered what options she actually had left. Soda bread and lettuce?

'Oh, sod it; actually, maybe I need a carb blowout,' she said with a sigh.

'Ruth, are you OK? You sound a bit ... stressed.'

'What? No, no, I'm fine. I just didn't want you to think I was ignoring your calls or anything. You and Trish have been so nice to me and –'

'No need to worry about that,' Nina reassured her. 'Tell you what, I'm just going to get changed, pick us up something nice, and I should be with you sometime after one o'clock OK?'

'Great, see you then.'

Getting off the phone once more, Nina went into the bathroom to freshen up. As she was getting ready, she studied her changing body shape in the mirror. Hmm, her boobs were definitely bigger, as was her stomach. She grimaced, placing her hands gently on either side and turned to look at her profile. Yep, over four months in she was now very definitely starting to show.

She felt a sense of awe as she thought about the baby growing inside her. Would it be a girl or a boy? What color eyes would it have and would it have dark hair like hers or dusty blond like Steve's? Then Nina shook her head, preventing herself from thinking about such things. What did it matter who it looked like? What mattered was what the hell she was going to do about it.

She slipped on a white form fitting t-shirt with the intention of placing a bulky sweater over it to hide her growing frame. Then she realized that she'd left the sweater back in her bedroom. She padded barefoot back out to the hallway and almost collided with Patrick at the top of the stairs.

'Oh!' Nina stopped in her tracks and locked eyes with her father.

'I was just wondering if ...' His words trailed off as his gaze trailed to her mid-section, settling on the small bump highlighted by the tight-fitting T-shirt. Nina instinctively lowered the towels and clothes that she had been carrying.

'Yes?' she prompted, hoping that he was just embarrassed about seeing her still half-dressed. His eyes wouldn't meet hers; they were shifting back and forth as he stood there, dumbstruck.

Nina felt her face becoming hot, and before he could say anything, she moved away and down towards her room, closing the door behind her. She threw the towels on the bed, and rushed to put on the sweater. Damn! Could her father possibly put it all into place? Had he spotted that she was pregnant? Or maybe she just looked bloated like she'd eaten too much for breakfast?

She rose to look again in the mirror. No, she definitely looked pregnant, there was no way anyone could pass that off as too much food.

Then again, what of it? What business was it of his? She wasn't asking him to raise it and she wasn't sixteen either. She was thirty years old and only living here temporarily. There was no reason for Patrick to care one way or the other; he knew that she'd been living with her boyfriend, so why would he care?

Still, she didn't want Patrick to know, didn't want anyone to know in case word would get back to her mother. And the last thing Nina wanted was to have to deal with other people's emotions; it was hard enough dealing with it all herself. Not to mention that she hadn't even begun dealing with ... the consequences.

The last conversation she wanted was one with her father, where she had to explain she was pregnant by a man who was no longer her boyfriend, and who had no intention of marrying her nor helping her raise the baby.

Still, Nina knew that regardless of how odd Patrick may be, he wasn't an idiot. If he did suspect something, it was only a matter of time before he'd ask what the hell was going on. Not to mention that sooner or later she'd need to tell him the truth.

Or would he ask? Nina didn't know. Patrick could be so strange sometimes that he might not have noticed a thing, or even if he had, might not make mention of it in any case.

And for once in her life, Nina was somewhat glad that her father wasn't quite like anyone else.

he doorbell of her parents' house rang and Ruth went to answer it, expecting to see Nina. She'd phoned her on the spur of the moment really; needing to talk to someone after Troy's wholehearted and very hurtful rejection of her.

Of course she had no intention of confiding in Nina about her newly discovered state – it was way too early for that – but she'd spent so much time cooped up in this house lately that she needed something to take her mind off her problems. And in truth, she felt guilty about avoiding Nina's messages this last while; she was a lovely person, easy to be around and had this nice sort of calming effect on Ruth – sort of like Chloe, but better.

But when Ruth answered the door, she was met by none other than Charlie Mellon.

'Charlie?' she gasped, confused. What was *he* doing here?

'May I come in?' he asked somberly.

'Sure.' Ruth stood back to let him pass and he stood in the hallway looking around. 'The place hasn't changed much,' he commented lightly. Then he glanced towards the kitchen. 'Are the folks home?'

'No, they went to Dublin for the day.'

'I thought as much when I didn't see the car outside. You didn't go with them?'

She smiled tightly. 'I'm trying my best to keep a low profile these days.'

'Ah. Know what you mean. I guess that explains why I haven't seen you around town lately.'

'I would have thought you'd be glad about that, seeing as apparently my presence here offends you so much,' she said, clearly recalling their last meeting.

'Well, actually, that's what I wanted to talk to you about. I wanted to apologize for my behavior in the café that time.'

Ruth couldn't hide her surprise. 'Apologize? Why?'

'Because I know I shouldn't have been so rude to you.'

She raised an eyebrow. 'Well, I won't argue with that. But why the sudden change of heart?'

Charlie sighed. 'Look, any chance I could have a cup of coffee while I'm here?' he said, eyes twinkling in the slightly roguish way that had always made him irresistible.

'Depends on whether or not you deserve one.' Ruth wasn't going to make things that easy for him.

'OK, OK. I admit it; I was an ass for talking to you the way I did. You didn't deserve it.'

'Agreed and I'm still trying to figure out where this turnaround is coming from.'

He held up a newspaper she hadn't noticed he was carrying. 'I read the interview in the *Lakeview News* this morning and to be honest, I didn't realize that you'd had it so tough in Hollywood.'

'Tough?' Eyes wide, Ruth reached for the paper. What the hell had Trish been saying about her?

She flicked through the pages until she found the two-page spread, including (an admittedly fabulous photograph) of her taken down by the lake. Ruth was impressed; she hadn't expected the local photographer to be that good. But the headline wasn't so good.

Our Ruth Overcomes Hollywood Casting Couch Hell To Finally Make It To The Top.

Damn! Ruth had mentioned very briefly how she'd had to work

hard to break away from the *Oirish* stereotype, but it had been nothing like the 'hell' the headline suggested! Carrying the open newspaper through to the kitchen, her eyes scanned through the interview. It was for the most part flattering, and while Trish had mercifully glossed over the Troy Valentine and *Late Tonight* incidents, she did imply that Ruth enjoyed and embraced the party-girl tag, pointing out that she'd always been an attention seeker while growing up.

'I think it's pretty good.' Charlie commented, but there was mirth in his voice. 'Particularly the bit about you being a 'go-getter' and 'always destined for bigger things.'

'Translate; too-big-for-her-boots stuck-up cow,' Ruth said acerbically.

'Come on, I think all in all Trish did a good job. And she's a journalist, so of course she's going to bring her own ... slant to things,' he chuckled, choosing his words carefully.

'Does she still have a crush on you then?' Ruth asked drolly.

'Come on Ruth; it's been a long time since our school days.'

She looked at him. 'That's not an answer.'

'What more of an answer do you want? Anyway, let's not change the subject. As I said, I was unfair to you before and I wanted to make up for it. Coffee?' He was making himself at home, opening the kitchen cupboard doors like he did it every day. Which of course he practically did back when they were together.

She pointed to the edge of the counter. 'They've got a cafetière now.'

He paused for a moment and then shook his head from side to side, the beginnings of a smile on his face. 'You really are used to being waited on hand and foot, aren't you? You expect me to make us both coffees too?'

'Oh, cripes, sorry.' Ruth truly hadn't intended on him making the coffee; she wasn't that bad a hostess, but her mind was still preoccupied with not only the interview, but what she'd learned that morning. 'I'll do it.'

'Good. After coming all the way up here to apologize, the least a guy could expect is a decent cup of coffee. Seeing as he clearly isn't going to get a pardon.'

'What?' Ruth said distractedly.

'Ruth what is wrong with you? I know I acted like an ass that day, but don't tell me you're still going to hold a grudge?'

Ruth bit her lip; she really didn't know what he wanted from her. 'OK, fine, then, you're forgiven,' she said haughtily.

Charlie's eyebrows shot up. 'Well, thank you so much for accepting *my* apology.' He said each word pointedly as if bringing it to her attention that she'd never apologized for her behavior in the past.

It worked. 'Look, I'm sorry too – sorry for what I did ...back then. I know I should have handled it better, and shouldn't have ... run out like that.'

'I think that could just about be described as an understatement.'

She didn't need to deal with this right now, with these thoughts, feelings from her past ... Goodness knows she had enough on her mind at the moment without throwing all this older stuff into the mix.

She plopped down in a nearby chair and sighed. 'Look, I realize what I did was wrong, especially with how we were, but it was all such a long time ago. I mean, really, would you have actually wanted to marry *me*?' She was surprised how she'd made that sound, almost as though she herself believed she wasn't worthy.

He blinked. 'I don't think I would have asked if I didn't.'

'Well, for what it's worth, I really am truly sorry for causing all of that. I know it was horrible at the time, and yes, perhaps I don't blame you for saying you didn't want anything more to do with me. But really, you wouldn't have wanted my life, the way it is now.'

'The way it is now ... what does that mean?'

Ruth had no idea why she had phrased it that way. After all, she was living the dream life wasn't she? The result of all those years of hard work?

She shook her head. 'Ah, don't mind me; I'm just a little stressed out lately, all that media stuff, you know.'

'I can imagine.'

Despite his earlier teasing, Charlie took over making the coffee.

As he stood up, suddenly Ruth was aware of how much smaller the room felt with him in it. She couldn't deny he looked great and had really kept himself in good shape over the years. She started to wonder if he still looked just as good with his clothes off, but then caught herself, realizing she shouldn't be thinking like that, especially now. She put her head in her hands and massaged her temples.

'Hey, are you all right?' She noticed the change in his voice and she looked up as he placed a couple of coffee mugs on the table between them. The concern on his face was so real and familiar that guilt flooded through her. She felt terrible that she had been the one to cause this lovely man so much pain. I truly am a rotten person, she thought, before bursting into tears.

'I'm sorry, but it's just so horrible; everything is horrible," she sniffed, as Charlie stared at her, bewildered. "I've just made so many mistakes Charlie ... I made them with you ... made them with my career ... with everything. Why can't I just make good choices, *sensible* choices?'

He moved his chair closer to hers and put a comforting hand on her arm. 'Hey, come on, don't cry, it's OK. All right, so it might not have looked like it before, but honestly, I've long forgiven you for what happened, and the choice you made.' He paused and she looked at him.

'It's not just that though,' she sobbed. 'I've been messing things up my whole life. I messed it up with you, and now have probably messed up my career, everything!' She was crying openly now. 'I can't trust myself to do anything without making mistakes.'

'Well, I'm not sure what you're talking about, but maybe they aren't mistakes at all. Maybe it's just that the path to the place you're supposed to be is longer?'

Ruth smiled a little and wiped her eyes. 'That's like something you'd hear in LA.'

'Well, maybe I would have been cut out for the place after all,' he grinned, but his eyes were sad, and she saw a flicker of something in them that brought back a memory; it was the way he used to look at her. She didn't know what to say. 'But for the record Ruth, I would have welcomed any path my life took, so long as it was with you.'

'What?' she whispered, feeling something flutter in her stomach.

He shrugged. 'I knew you wanted to be a star and had bigger ideas and dreams than just Lakeview. I would have gone anywhere you wanted Ruth, but you never gave me the chance.'

'Charlie ...'

'I would have done anything. Then, when I heard you were coming home, I must admit that I tried to make myself feel angry. I wanted to hate you,' he laughed shortly. 'And believe me I've tried to do that for a long time, but Ruth, I also wanted to see you.'

'You did? But you were so furious ...'

'Of course I was furious, the last time I saw you, you left me holding an engagement ring. But after you left, I realized that I'd just have to move on with my life. There was a side of me that was kind of hoping you'd get in touch and maybe ask me to come over there and see you, but then the years went by and nothing happened.'

Ruth had no idea – no clue that he'd felt that way. She'd always believed that he was content to stay in Lakeview, that he'd intended for them to settle down and spend the rest of their lives there as a regular couple. Never for a second did she think Charlie would have come with her to LA. Would it have been different if he had, she couldn't help wonder now?

Charlie was still talking. 'So before you arrived, while I had prepared myself for bumping into you sometime, I hadn't prepared myself for all that stuff in the newspapers, pictures of you with that ... guy.' At the mention of Troy, Ruth felt her heart harden – for more reasons than one.

'I didn't want to look at them, because I had my own memories of you ...'

There was a very long and heavy silence for a while, but then, and Ruth wasn't sure how it happened, suddenly his mouth was on hers and he was kissing her with an intensity that made her heart feel like it was going to stop.

He cupped her face tightly in his hands, and instinctively she threw her arms around his neck. She was amazed at how familiar he felt, how easily the old feelings came rushing back; it was incredible. It almost felt like discovering exactly what had been missing from her life. Maybe he was right; maybe the path to where she was supposed to be just took longer, and had many detours. Maybe she and Charlie were supposed to be together and they could really make it work this time.

Then something tapped at the back of Ruth's brain, and she quickly pulled away.

'I'm sorry,' she gasped, standing back and putting a hand to her mouth.

Charlie stared at her, his expression unfathomable.

'It's just that ...this is a really bad time for ... this.'

He was staring at the floor. 'I understand.'

'No – you don't.' She stepped forward, reaching for him, but he stood up.

'I think I do.' His tone was cold. 'You're sorry for what happened before, but it was a long time ago and you've moved on. I get it.'

'No Charlie, you really don't,' Ruth said, tears brimming in her eyes again. She had to tell him; needed to tell someone. Never mind that the circumstances were crazy, and that given what had just happened, he was possibly the last person in the world who'd be able to sympathize. 'Remember those mistakes I was talking about earlier?' She took a deep breath as he met her gaze. 'Well, I actually left out the mother of them all ...'

26

'You're pregnant?' he gasped in disbelief when she'd finished telling him the whole sorry story.

Ruth felt like crying. Her life was going to go down in The Guinness Book of World Records as 'Worst Life Ever.'

'I just found out this morning,' she told him gently.

'You mean before I got here?'

'Yes.'

'Unbelievable! So who's the ... father?' It was the obvious question, but he looked as though he was steeling himself to ask it. Ruth's eyes were downcast, her expression guilty. 'Him? The Valentine guy, seriously?' He ran his hands through his hair.

'It was an accident – obviously,' Ruth defended. 'It wasn't supposed to happen.'

'Well, I should hope not, otherwise you must have to do some crazy things to make it in Hollywood these days.' Then seeing her hurt expression, his tone softened. 'Ruth, it's starting to feel like everything is an accident with you.'

'You and me both,' she said, her bottom lip trembling.

'And you just found out this morning,' he repeated. 'Yet you let me kiss you, and you kissed me back ...' She knew by his tone that he found it disturbing and he was right; it was awful.

'I know, but for a minute there, I sort of … forgot.'

Charlie was dubious. 'You just "forgot" you were pregnant?'

'Yes! Look, I didn't expect to see you, let alone find that I still …' She shook her head, not wanting to go down that road. There was no point. 'Charlie, I've had a really bad morning, first I find this out, then I tell Troy and he tells me to stuff it and –'

'He told you to what?' Charlie's eyes narrowed.

Ruth explained how the conversation with the father of her baby had not gone well. 'I'm still not sure why I even told him, but I really felt it would be the right thing to do.'

'It was the right thing to do, but maybe not so soon. You should have given yourself time to think about it first.'

He was right, of course, but that was Charlie, always the sensible one.

'So he immediately assumed I would have an abortion, which made me so mad, so I told him to go to hell that I was going to have it anyway – even though I hadn't actually decided anything at that stage.'

'And are you?' he asked. 'Going to have the baby, I mean.'

Ruth sighed. 'It's not ideal, especially with the business I'm in …'

'I can imagine.' His eyes moved to her midriff and she knew he was trying to imagine what pregnancy would do to her body. Ruth had tried to imagine that too, but couldn't. And the truth was that despite what she'd said to Troy, she still wasn't one hundred percent sure how to deal with this. OK, so she could perhaps sacrifice a few months of her career to have the baby if needs be – but what about afterwards? She couldn't realistically continue her acting career as a single mum with a baby in tow, could she? 'And what does he think about you keeping it?' Charlie asked then.

'He wasn't happy about it, but there's not a whole lot he can do about it.'

'But he's going to support you surely?' Such things were clear in Charlie Mellon's straight-as-a-die world.

Ruth shook her head. 'He told me I wouldn't get a dime. Not that I want anything from the stupid ass, but …'

Charlie looked horrified. He stood up and started to pace back and forth, which made her feel uneasy. Still, it was sort of a relief to have someone to talk to about this, someone who was able to discuss the matter and take it seriously. But she couldn't help wondering how different things would be if it had been Charlie's and not Troy's baby she was carrying.

'You know Ruth, you were always good with surprises.'

She looked at him, ashamed. 'Look, I know I shouldn't have let you kiss me and I certainly shouldn't have kissed you back. That was crazy.'

'That much we can agree on.'

'And with all that's happened lately, I'm sure you probably think I'm some kind of slut or something,' she said, herself feeling somewhat cheap and common at that moment. 'But for what it's worth, I'd like you to know that up until that night with Troy, which I agree was a mistake and it wouldn't have happened if we hadn't had so much champagne ...' she said, realizing she was babbling. 'My point being that, up until that night, I hadn't slept with anyone in a long time. As a matter of fact, I'm probably the least slutty woman in Hollywood. This was all just one big mistake.'

'But one that will steadily progress all the same.'

She nodded defiantly. 'Yes, and I'm just going to have to live with it.'

Charlie stopped pacing and sat back down on the chair next to her. 'I just don't know what to do here Ruth, I can't say I've ever been in this situation before.'

'What situation? You don't owe me anything – you can get up and walk out that door the same way you walked in.'

'You're right, I could and truthfully, when you first told me about this, I almost did. But –' He shook his head. 'He really told you he wanted nothing to do with it?'

'Yes, he did.'

'You're not lying.'

She looked at him, stung. 'Charlie, I may be a lot of things, but I have never been a liar.'

'No, no, I know that; it's just I ...' his voice trailed off. 'I just don't know what my next move should be. I still care about you Ruth; I can't deny that. And before this I was wondering if we might be able to put the past behind us and maybe ...'

Ruth put her head down, and found she couldn't even summon tears, she was all cried out. The way Charlie was putting it; it felt like she was damaged goods.

'You know, there was a time when I thought we would have kids together,' he said softly.

She looked at him. 'Really?'

'Yes.'

Ruth put her head in her hands. 'Oh, this is all such a mess. I don't know what to do, if I'm making the right decision ... what it'll do to my career ...'

Charlie took her hand. 'I don't think now is the time to be second guessing yourself, regardless of your career or what I'm telling you. Honestly, I think you might have spoken from the heart when you were on the phone with ... him.'

Ruth hadn't considered that, that maybe this time she had made the right decision. She had made so many bad ones of late, she didn't know if she was even capable of a good one.

'Charlie, I'm really sorry ... for everything.'

He nodded and patted her hand. 'I suppose I should go.'

'That's probably best.'

He stood up and placed a light kiss on her cheek. 'Regardless of what you might be thinking right now, I know you will be a fantastic mother.'

She smiled sadly. 'I'm glad one of us does. Any child of mine will probably have hooves.'

Charlie chuckled. 'Possibly, but it's also going to have a very special person for a mum, so it won't be all bad. Bye Ruth.'

'Bye.'

Ruth stayed motionless on the chair as she watched him leave the room. Once he was gone it felt as if all of the air had been sucked out of it.

Could she really do this? she thought, staring at her midriff. No one wanted her, Troy didn't want her and after what he'd learned just now, Charlie certainly wouldn't either. She patted her belly. It would just be her and her baby. Whatever happened, she would just have to live with it.

Suddenly, Hollywood felt a million miles away. It was as if over the course of a few short hours her priorities had suddenly shifted, and she felt almost like a completely different person. The things that had been so important up to now, things that held so much glitter and excitement seemed to have faded.

And Ruth didn't have the faintest idea what to expect next.

27

*N*ina never made it to Ruth's house in the end. As she was on her way into town, Ruth called and explained that she wasn't feeling well and needed to lie down for a while, and could they do it some other time?

Nina thought she sounded upset, like she'd been crying, but when she'd enquired as to whether she was OK; Ruth assured her she was fine.

It was no business of Nina's and she didn't want to push it, but again she wondered if there had been another newspaper rumor or suchlike. She didn't know how Ruth put up with such intrusions and knew she would go insane if she had to live a life like that. As it was she found it hard enough putting up with this morning's intrusion by her dad. Not that it could be called that really; but there was no doubt that he'd had some kind of reaction to her appearance. And such reactions were rare from her father, particularly when growing up she used to go out of her way to try and get his attention.

She was so busy pondering this thought while walking down Main Street that she almost collided with the person going in the other direction.

'Whoa, slow down there,' the person joked and Nina looked up to find that it was Dave, the guy she and Trish had met at Ruth's home-coming party a few weeks before.

'Oh ... hi. Sorry about that, I was miles away.'

'You sure were.' Nina couldn't help notice how his eyes crinkled at the corners when he smiled, which he was doing now. 'Nina isn't it? I see you're still here then.'

'Still here?'

'Yes. I thought you said you were only planning on visiting your father for a little while.'

'That's right.' She shrugged. 'I suppose the time just sort of slips away before you know it. Anyway, I'm enjoying spending time here, and I got a job ... at Ella's.' Nina wasn't sure why she was giving him so much information, particularly as she barely even knew him, but there was something about Dave that made her want to keep talking to him.

Which was crazy considering.

'At the café? I didn't know that.'

And what would it matter if you did? Nina wondered. 'Just part-time, whenever Ella needs me.'

'I know where to go if I fancy a doughnut then,' he grinned and Nina colored, sure he was flirting with her.

'Yes, certainly,' she mumbled, unsure how to feel.

'Well, I'd better get going. I was just on my way back to the office,' he told her and Nina recalled how he'd mentioned something before about being involved with the local brewery. 'See you around Nina.' With that, he flashed a smile that immediately made her insides feel weak.

Or was that the baby making his or her protests?

'Sure, bye now.' Shaking her head, Nina continued across town and back towards her father's house. What was she *doing*, having those kind of thoughts about some guy she'd only met once or twice? There was no denying that Dave was extremely good-looking and seemed very nice, but at the end of the day didn't she have enough to be going on with at the moment, rather than making eyes at one of the locals? Anyway, after Steve, she'd had more than enough of men and their carry-on ...

Approaching the house, she hoped against hope that Patrick had since gone out and that she wouldn't have to face trying to avoid him for the rest of the day – or worse actually have to face him.

She climbed the steps and put a tentative hand on the door handle, willing it to be locked. If it was locked, Patrick wouldn't be here. Her fingers tightened on it and she twisted it, hoping she would find resistance, but it started to turn, which meant that he was still home. Oh, well ...

Nina didn't know why she'd thought any different; it wasn't as if Patrick actually went anywhere – other than out to collect more of those TV relics.

Stepping inside, she went straight into the living room to find her father sitting there alone, staring at her. Immediately she felt uneasy – it was almost as if he'd been waiting for her.

She tried to sound casual. 'Hey Dad, what's up? Nothing to work on today?'

Patrick said nothing for a while, until finally his eyes locked on hers, something that was hugely disconcerting, as typically her father had trouble meeting anyone's gaze. When he spoke, his voice was quiet. 'Do you have something to tell me, Nina?' he asked evenly.

Her heart began to pound. 'What? What do you mean?'

Patrick started to fidget; it was clear that he was finding it just as uncomfortable as she was. 'Are you having a baby?' he asked then, and Nina wasn't sure if it was the directness of the question or the tone behind it that shocked her. He sounded furious.

'What ... what do you mean?' Nina wasn't sure why, but all of a sudden she was terrified. She didn't think she'd ever seen her father so calm and controlled, especially when he was always so restless and fidgety. It was hugely disconcerting.

'You're the same as your mother.'

'What?' Her mind raced - the mention of her mother was the last thing she expected. And what the hell was that supposed to mean?

'I don't know what you –'

'You're having a baby,' he stated flatly, all the while kneading his fists in what Nina realized was barely controlled fury. But why was he so angry? What business was it of his? OK, so she might be living under his roof, but it wasn't as if she expected anything from him ...

'Dad, I –'

'This is not good,' he muttered, almost under his breath. 'Not good.'

The cold, almost callous way he was talking about it put Nina on the defensive.

'What business is it of yours?' she challenged, tears springing to her eyes, but she made an internal vow that she would not allow him to see her cry.

'It's a big mistake, a big mistake. Just like your mother,' he continued and all of a sudden Nina realized what he was saying. The mistake he was referring to ... was it hers, or actually *her*? Was she herself the mistake that Patrick and Cathy had made way back when?

If so, it certainly explained a hell of lot with regard to how they'd ended up together. Back in those days, an accidental pregnancy would have generated huge pressure on the parents to make things right by marrying. Which explained why her lovely, fun-loving mum had got stuck with a man who was almost her complete opposite.

Yes, that had to be it, Nina thought, and although the realization was troubling, she decided it wasn't all that much of a surprise. It made sense. But why hadn't Cathy said anything? Shotgun marriages were two-a-penny in those days and it wasn't as though her mother had remained stuck in the loveless marriage. Nina would have understood, of course she would and there was certainly no reason for anyone to feel ashamed.

Still, whether she was technically illegitimate or not, Nina was still Patrick's daughter and perhaps she owed him an explanation.

'You're right, it is a mistake and honestly, I'm still not sure what to do about it.' She decided to try and appeal to his better nature. 'I was going to tell you, but I needed some time ... to think about it. And Mum doesn't know yet so please don't tell her.' This was highly unlikely as to the best of her knowledge, her parents were barely in contact and it wasn't as if he would be able to track Cathy down in the wilds of China. Still, she wanted to be sure.

'This is why you're here.' It was a statement more than a question, as if it was something he'd been puzzling over.

'In Lakeview? Yes. The baby's father and I ... well, we split up. He's not going to have anything to do with it.'

'Well, you can't keep it here,' he said coldly, as if he hadn't even heard her admission.

'I wasn't planning to,' Nina said, wounded by his callousness. 'As I said, I needed some time to think about this, and I had nowhere else to go. It's not due for a fair few months yet so don't worry, I'll make sure I'm long gone by then.'

Patrick nodded. 'That's good.' And with that, he stood up and walked out of the room, leaving Nina feeling like something he'd just cleaned off the bottom of his shoe.

Outraged, she followed him out into the hallway.

'That's good? Is that all you have to say?' she cried, hurt by his indifference to her feelings. Is this how he'd treated her mother, like some kind of worthless tramp? 'I'm your daughter, for Christ sake, and I'm going through a tough time at the moment. OK, so maybe I should have told you from the start, but this is hard Dad, can't you see that?'

Patrick just stood there fidgeting. 'You shouldn't take the Lord's name in vain,' he replied finally and Nina's mouth dropped open. After everything she'd just said ... that was all he was worried about? And when did he get so pious all of a sudden?

By now tears were streaming down her cheeks. 'Wow, now I completely understand why Mum left you – you're nothing but a heartless bastard!' she cried.

At this Patrick's head snapped up, almost as if she'd slapped him and Nina immediately felt guilty. She didn't mean to say that; hadn't meant to be so mean, so nasty. Although his expression was impassive, his face flushed and it was clear that she had hurt him.

She tried her best to take it back. 'Dad ... I'm sorry, I shouldn't have said that... I didn't mean it.' She stretched out her hands, not sure if she wanted to embrace him, or just entreat him not to walk away.

But Patrick wouldn't look at her. He just stood there blankly, the side of his mouth twitching, and Nina sorely wished she could read his thoughts. 'Dad? Really, I'm sorry, I didn't mean any of those things.'

Little by little his face lost its color. 'This isn't right Nina. You'll see.'

'What ...?' She stared at him perplexed. Was he so bound by religion that he couldn't see past the morals and try and understand what his daughter was going through? Or try to understand how difficult and confusing this was for her? Some of her earlier anger simmered beneath the surface and she fought hard against lashing out again. No, she would not do that, she would not give him the satisfaction.

'Fine,' she said finally. 'Don't worry yourself about any of this. I won't be here much longer. As soon as I can, I'll get out of your hair and take my problems with me.' She placed a protective hand over her stomach, oddly guilty about referring out loud to it as a 'problem'.

Patrick looked at her with an expression so unreadable it was confounding. It was like he was a million miles away ... as if he'd suddenly forgotten what they were talking about.

'Well?' she asked, throwing up her hands in exasperation. 'Is that all? Am I free to go back upstairs now?'

'Of course you are, Nina.'

'Fine. And just to let you know that as soon as Mum gets back, I'm out of here.'

'Yes, that's a good idea,' he said, all agreeable now.

Nina turned on her heel, annoyed and now feeling almost trapped by this house. She pounded up the stairs to her room and collapsed on to the bed, still shaken by the encounter.

She crawled under the covers, not bothering to take off her clothes and found herself crying again. Damn hormones, she thought, always crying at the drop of a hat. Although this time there was of course more to it.

She reached for her mobile phone on the bedside locker and automatically dialed her mother's number.

It went straight to voicemail. 'Hi Mum, it's me, Nina,' she said, trying to control her sniffles so it wouldn't sound like she'd been crying. 'I know we spoke this morning and you're probably on the road now, but ...' Then she paused, wondering what she was trying to achieve. The last thing she should do was make a huge fuss and have her mother worrying about her. Yet, at a time like this, it was incredibly difficult not having Cathy to talk to. All throughout Nina's life, her mother was always her first port of call, but really this wasn't the time. She took a deep breath. 'Anyway, I just wanted to say hi and I hope you and Tony are having a really good time. Talk soon.' She hung up the phone and stared at it for another moment, almost willing it to ring, willing her mother to have already listened to her message and to call her back. But the phone stayed silent.

She lay back down on the pillow and closed her eyes. What had Patrick meant when he said that she was just like her mother? Was he still so angry with Cathy for leaving him that he believed her to be a bad person? Nina couldn't understand most of what he said at the best of times, never mind the riddles he'd come out with just now.

She clasped her eyes shut. Regardless of what he had said, she wished she could take back her own biting comments, she had told them just out of spite and that wasn't like her. Still, it was notable that Patrick had displayed some kind of emotion about that, when he usually behaved as if he cared about nothing.

But he had obviously cared about her mother.

Nina decided not to ponder it; the main thing was she knew she had to get out of here as soon as possible.

She laughed bitterly; realizing yet again that she'd been forced out on her backside by the actions of a heartless male. Thinking of Steve she felt her heart harden. She wondered where he was right now, what he was doing.

Mostly, she loathed the fact that her baby would have any of his genes. She wanted to scream, at someone, anyone. She thought about picking up the phone and calling Steve to bawl him out again, but fear got the best of her. If anyone else happened to answer his phone, it would be just too much for her, and she didn't think she could take any more emotional outbursts today.

She curled up in bed and tried to calm her thoughts. It was a pity because all in all, things had been looking up in Lakeview; she had some friends, a job and developed a somewhat civil relationship with her father. But now that relationship was back to the tense place it had been before.

She didn't want to live here, but still, she had nowhere else to go.

Recalling Patrick's religious reference, Nina again realized this was truly like living in purgatory and she couldn't help wondering – as his words echoed through her brain – if her mother had felt the same way.

---

28

*J*ess was not in a good mood. It had now been six weeks since she'd stopped taking the pill and still she hadn't managed to talk Brian round.

To top it all off, she'd got her period that morning, which for some reason had put her in dire form. OK, so she knew the chance of her conceiving so soon had been slim, but now that she'd set off down the path of letting nature take its course, nothing happening almost felt like a personal affront, and she was offended by the thought that she hadn't succeeded on the first go. After all, she usually succeeded at anything she put her mind to and had hoped that becoming a mother would be the same.

Still, maybe it was a blessing in disguise. Who knew what kind of a reaction Brian would have if he discovered she'd gone ahead and stopped taking the pill without consulting him? And in truth, Jess felt kind of guilty about that, but she'd been so sure she would be able to talk him round in the meantime that it didn't feel like she was doing anything wrong. She'd tried to convince herself that her husband would only thank her once they had a beautiful little daughter or son to play with.

She winced as she was hit with yet another menstrual cramp.

It didn't help that Brian still wouldn't really talk about it, and while they'd skirted around the subject a few times since she'd first broached it, some kind of problem at work had surfaced in the meantime, which meant that much of his concentration had been on that.

'Sweetheart, I know what you're like when you get an idea into your head. But the more I hear about it, the more convinced I am that this sudden maternal urge is all about feeling left out by the girls,' he'd said, when Jess had stupidly mentioned something about a recent outing with Deirdre and Emer. 'And as I said, that's no basis for a decision.' Thankfully, he still had no idea that as far as the girls were concerned a decision had already been made.

But no matter how much Jess tried to draw him away from that excuse and more towards the matter of her age, he wouldn't hear of it.

'You can be like a dog with a bone sometimes,' he said exasperated. 'But this isn't one of your work projects Jess; it's a lifetime commitment, and it's not one we should enter until both of us are sure we want it right now. And to be honest, I know I'm not certain we're ready just yet.'

'But why not?' Jess demanded. 'We love each other loads, have a great life, good jobs – we are ideally positioned to start a family now.'

'Exactly. We have a great life. I'm not so sure I'm willing to give up all the fun and freedom for late night feeds and dirty nappies. And I don't think you are either, but you just won't admit it.'

She hated that he was being so pessimistic about it all and especially hated that he usually tried to distract her from the subject with talk of parties and trips, when she'd made a point of the fact that she wasn't necessarily interested in any of those things anymore. She was an adult and there was more to life than shopping and holidays.

Oddly, though, when he did manage to get her to a party, she tended to forget all about babies and was easily able to throw herself into the thick of the revelry. She wondered what that said about her, was she really that vacuous that she could be so easily dissuaded?

With this new set of issues on her brain, Jess set out on the drive to Lakeview for yet another visit to Emer. Thanks to their newly shared interest in all things baby-related, the friendship was now fully restored and in truth, Jess relished spending time not only with Emer but her little daughter too. It was good practice and Emer was only too happy to fill her in and help her learn all the things there was to know about raising a child.

Some time later, she arrived at her friend's house, her thoughts so preoccupied she hardly remembered the drive there. Getting out of the car, she headed to the front porch. She was a little earlier than their agreed time – hopefully Emer wouldn't mind.

But as she was about to ring the doorbell, she thought she heard raised voices from within.

Jess looked around to see if anyone was observing her standing there. She wondered if she should just get back in the car and drive around for a while as the last thing she wanted to was to interrupt any awkward situation. From the inside of the house, she heard Emer say, 'That's just the thing Dave, you are never here! I never get any help!'

'What are you talking about? You're the one who wanted a house full of kids, a huge house in the country. Didn't you realize that it would come with a price?'

'Yes, but all those extra hours? I'm starting to feel like a single parent!'

'Well, how the hell do you expect us to pay for all this?' he retorted and Jess blanched, suddenly understanding the real reason behind Emer's barbed comments about her clothes and spending of late. It wasn't that she begrudged her; but more that cash was obviously scarce in her own household, and this was starting to affect her marriage.

Now Jess felt guiltier than ever for being so flash with her spending recently. To Emer it surely would have looked as though she was rubbing her nose in it. Yet until now, Jess had had no real idea …

'Look, I told you from the start that I didn't necessarily want …' Dave's voice continued, and again, Jess's interest was piqued. What didn't Dave want? The move to Lakeview? Or perhaps a baby?

But she was unable to think about it for much longer as on the other side of the door, she heard loud footsteps approach. Yikes!

If she didn't do something soon, whoever was on the other side would open it up and see her standing there. Fumbling for the doorbell, she accidentally pushed it twice.

'Bloody hell – where's the fire?' The door swung open and there Dave stood in his work suit. His face was flushed and angry, and at that moment, Jess felt about two feet tall, terrified he and Emer would realize she had heard every word.

'Oh, hello Dave. Didn't expect to see you home,' she said with an affected smile.

He snorted derisively. 'Yeah, I'm sure my lovely wife talks your ear off about it.'

'What?'

'Don't mind him,' Emer said, coming into view and Jess could tell her friend was trying her utmost to compose herself. 'Dave is just a bit ... stressed out with work at the moment, aren't you, love?'

'Yes *love* – that's what it is, stress,' Dave answered, ice in his voice. 'Anyway, I'll leave you two to chat and shop or whatever it is housewives do,' he added nastily, especially given that one of them wasn't a housewife.

He picked up his briefcase and walked out of the house, loudly rattling the doorframe as he left.

'Um, is this a bad time?' Jess asked. 'I know I'm early, but we could do this another time if ... you know ... you're not up for it.'

Emer stared at her blankly. 'What are you on about? Everything's fine. Come on in. Amy's having a nap so with any luck we've just enough time for a cuppa before she wakes up.'

Jess followed her into the kitchen. 'Are you sure you're all right? Dave seemed a bit ... stressed out.'

Emer flushed so brightly Jess was instantly sorry she'd said anything. 'Not at all, it's fine.'

But Jess barely heard her; she was too busy staring at the broken glass on the kitchen floor, curiously close to the wall.

'Oh, don't mind that; I knocked it off the counter as I was doing the washing up,' Emer stuttered making Jess even more suspicious. Despite her friend's protests something was seriously wrong here. But she wasn't going to push her to talk about it – if Emer wanted to reach out, she would do it in her own time.

Emer quickly cleaned up the mess and kept up a steady chatter as she readied herself with making a pot of tea.

'So, how have you been?' she asked. 'Any news?'

'Oh, fine, fine. I finally finished that blasted G-Force project, which I was really glad about, I can tell you ...' Jess said, happy to talk to someone who understood her work.

'No, I mean, any *news*?' Emer smiled, raising an eyebrow, and Jess reddened realizing what she was getting at.

'Oh, nothing yet, but here's hoping!' she grinned, raising crossed fingers into the air.

'I'm sure it won't take too much longer. Especially when you're so dedicated to the idea.'

Jess wondered privately how long it would take when she was the *only* one dedicated to this idea, but she couldn't share this with Emer.

'I suppose we'll just have to wait and see,' she said diplomatically, this time hoping her friend wouldn't push the subject.

'That's the right attitude. At least you're not like I was when we started. I was like a woman possessed! I don't know how poor Dave put up with me, but of course when Amy arrived, it was all worth it.'

'I can imagine.'

But considering the argument she'd heard not five minutes before, Jess wondered if this were actually true.

29

*L*ater that same evening, Jess sat in front of the TV with a glass of wine, feeling dejected. Despite that awkward situation with Dave, she and Emer had had a great day in Lakeview, having lots of fun with Amy, and discussing how much Jess's life would change once she had one of her own.

'You won't be able to remember what you did with your time,' Emer assured her, but Jess figured she'd remember all right, as much of her time was spent alone in this house while Brian was either working late or abroad.

Yet another good reason for starting a family; she'd be so busy with their child, it might help chase away the loneliness that she'd been feeling lately.

Jess realized she was slightly tipsy as she grabbed the TV remote and flicked through the TV stations. She channel-hopped for a while, unable to find anything of interest, until finally she stopped at one of those True Lives channels that was showing a program called: *My Surprise Baby*. It was a documentary about women who gave birth, not having the foggiest idea they were pregnant beforehand. She watched the show; entranced by the notion that a woman could go an entire nine months without knowing she was knocked up.

How could you *not* know? Jess thought to herself, feeling slightly put-out that these women could so easily achieve what she herself wanted.

Then she heard the front door open and immediately changed the channel.

Brian walked in, cheerful and smiling. 'Hello love,' he said, popping his head around the living room door. 'What are you doing sitting there in the dark?'

'Hey,' Jess managed a smile. 'I was watching TV, but there's nothing on.'

'There never is,' Brian wasn't a big fan of television, and Jess always joked that this was because he could never sit still long enough. 'Have you eaten?'

'Yes, I had something earlier. You?'

Brian patted his stomach. 'Just back from a very long lunch at my favorite restaurant.' He grinned satisfactorily. 'So I won't be hungry for a while.'

'You were at L'Ecrivain again?' Although she shouldn't have been surprised. The Travel Company always liked to wine and dine their clients in style.

'Yep – and we managed to get that Murray account situation resolved over a nice bottle of Sancerre. So a good day all round I'd say. How was yours? Did you enjoy your day off?'

'It was great.'

'Buy anything nice?'

Jess stared at him. Why did he automatically assume she would use her day off to go shopping? Maybe because that was what she usually did? she reminded herself quickly. More often than not she'd spend the day in town, getting her makeup done at BTs before dropping a fortune on shoes and beauty products. She really was a silly, one-dimensional person, and Jess was only sorry it had taken her so long to realize it.

'I didn't go shopping Brian, I spent the afternoon at Emer's.'

Her husband raised an eyebrow. 'Again?'

'Yes, again – why?'

'It's just that you seem to be spending all your free time in Lakeview lately. You'll be talking about us moving down there next.' The words sounded jokey, but Jess knew the sentiment behind them wasn't.

'Well, maybe that wouldn't be such a bad idea. It's a nice place, very friendly and peaceful.'

'Peaceful?' he chortled derisively. 'Since when did you like peaceful?'

Jess folded her arms across her chest. 'Maybe since I decided that it's time for you and I to grow up and start behaving like adults.'

Brian sighed. 'Oh, I get it. Here we go again.'

'Yes, here we go again. Although it seems there is no "we" these days. It's all about you and what you want.'

'For crying out loud Jess ...' Brian loosened his tie. 'Do we need to do this now? I've just got home from a very hard day and –'

'A hard day wining and dining in a Michelin star restaurant? Wow, sounds tough.' Jess couldn't believe how bitter she was sounding, but she couldn't help it. She felt bitter and frustrated and confused and a whole lot of other emotions that were alien to her. 'My heart goes out to you.'

'What the hell is wrong with you, Jess?' Brian said, sounding hurt. 'OK, so it might have been a nice restaurant, but trying to hold on to clients these days sure isn't fun. You know the company's been struggling lately so why are you laying this on me now?'

'You're right, I'm sorry. It's just that ... well, it seems that for us, life is all about work, and has been for years.'

'You've got to be kidding me,' Brian sighed heavily and rolled his eyes. 'I really can't believe you want to start this whole baby thing up *again*.'

'Start it up again? Brian, I haven't been able to start it up at all, because you won't even talk about it. You won't even let the subject be open for discussion.'

His mouth pursed. 'I thought I told you that we would talk about it when you give up the ridiculous notion of needing a baby to keep up with your friends. You're a grown woman Jess, so why are you behaving like some high-school teenager?'

'Exactly, I am a grown woman – well grown up actually and soon to be over the hill.'

'This is unbelievable ...'

'What is unbelievable Brian? The notion that I'm getting older, or that I'm growing up?'

'Don't talk nonsense, everything was fine before all this rubbish with Emer and Deirdre started, and now suddenly our life is pointless and immature! What the hell is wrong with you, love?'

'What's wrong with *me*? Actually, I think we need to ask what's wrong with you!'

'Oh, I can assure you I am perfectly sane. You won't come home to find me sulking and meeting you at the door with crazy talk.'

'Crazy talk? What's so crazy about wanting a baby, Brian?'

'Absolutely nothing, when you want one for the right reasons; however, there is something totally wrong with it, when you only want one to keep up with your friends who have turned suburban.'

She decided to ignore this, preferring instead to turn the spotlight on him. 'No, don't pretend to think that this has anything to do with me, when it has everything to do with you. You're a commitment-phobe Brian.'

He looked shocked. 'Commitment-phobe? In the middle of all this craziness have you also somehow forgotten I'm married to you?'

But Jess wouldn't hear of it. 'It's true; you're not willing to commit to fatherhood because you're too busy traveling the world and going to fancy restaurants and cocktail parties, and you're completely focused on your career –'

'Jess, are you talking about me or yourself? Because traveling the world and going to restaurants and cocktail parties and focused on a career sounds a hell of a lot like you too. So if those things make me shallow, what do they make you?'

Jess knocked back the remainder of her wine in one go. 'I'm a woman who wants a child, but has a husband who is too selfish to give her one,' she said self-righteously.

Brian stared at her as if unsure what to say or do next. 'Actually, I think you're drunk and I'm already tired of this subject.'

'Yes, yes, always tired ... always running away.'

'Spare me the raving shrew act Jess, and please just go to bed.'

With that Brian walked out of the room, and Jess sat there, staring into her empty wine glass. Her selfish? How could he say that when *she* was the one willing to commit everything to the idea of starting a family?

Her head was spinning as she slowly got up off the couch and went upstairs to the bedroom. Well, maybe he was right about one thing; she was a little tipsy.

Should she go into the kitchen and apologize to him? No, she thought determinedly; let him apologize to her. She had nothing to be sorry about. After all, he was the one depriving her; it wasn't the other way around.

Eventually, she collapsed into bed and fell into a fitful sleep and a night full of dreams in which she continued a heated argument with Brian.

The dreams were so intense and seemed so real that Jess woke up the following morning still completely exhausted. Her head pounded with a ferocious wine headache and she felt groggy and hung-over.

She sat up slowly in the bed, realizing that Brian was already gone. Or had he slept here at all?

Snippets of last night's conversation came rushing back, and she felt terrible.

In all honesty, she wouldn't blame him if he hadn't come up to bed last night; she *had* behaved like a nagging old shrew and Brian never reacted well to that – what man did? As it was they rarely argued, and had always had a blissful and untroubled marriage up to now.

But there was no denying that a rift was starting to develop between them. She was absolutely convinced she wanted a baby, yet Brian seemed equally convinced he didn't. Or more to the point, convinced that her reasoning was based only on some random fixation.

A sliver of unease surged through her; what if they couldn't resolve this?

If Brian couldn't come round to her point of view, and wouldn't agree to even discuss having children, what would that mean for them as a couple?

It would mean that they would be forever on the outside looking in at their friends sharing the different happy stages of family life; christenings, birthday parties, even college graduations. It would mean that they would of course end up losing touch with those friends, as soon they would have practically nothing in common.

And then as the years went by she and Brian would continue to work, go on holidays, eat out in nice places and wear nice clothes, but then what?

How long could they realistically continue to do the same things without getting bored, not only of life, but of one another?

Jess felt a shudder as she imagined her future, and from this vantage point, it looked very, very lonely.

*T*he bus pulled up outside Clery's on O'Connell Street and Nina got out. As she did, she eyed the other passengers cautiously, hoping that none of them would recognize her or worse, start chatting about where she was going. She could have taken the commuter train from Lakeview either, but it was much more expensive and money was tight. Not to mention that the bus took her right to where she wanted to go.

Still, she didn't want anyone from Lakeview to know that she'd come to Dublin today to pick up maternity wear.

As the weeks went on, it had become harder and harder to fit into her old clothes – or worse to hide her bump beneath them, and it had got to the stage where she knew she had no choice but to get something more suitable.

She couldn't do this in the village of course; despite the lovely boutiques, someone would be sure to ask questions and Nina still wasn't ready to let the whole world know her business.

As it was she had been keeping a low profile since the blow up with her father. She tried to avoid meeting him and usually tried to leave or return to the house during times when she knew he would be out and about. She knew she was being a coward about it, but she still felt guilty about what she had said to him.

She had been spending lots of time at the library with Trish, rummaging through the archives and on occasion interviewing some of the older Lakeview residents for interesting stories that might suit the project.

Thankfully, since their argument, Patrick hadn't said anything more about her pregnancy, although he hadn't said much to Nina about anything at all really. It was as if there was an unspoken truce between them; he seemed content to let her stay until Cathy's return in September, but until then she was on her own.

This suited her in any case; the last thing she wanted was to be answerable to her father, but in truth, she was grateful that he hadn't pushed the subject any further.

Now, as she made her way across O'Connell Bridge towards Grafton Street, she shook her head. Never in a million years did she think she'd be searching for maternity clothes like this – all furtive and cautious.

She spent a little bit of time browsing in Mothercare and marveling at all the pretty little baby clothes and toys before moving on to M&S, where she hoped to pick up some nice clothes for herself. It was weird, but seeing all the tiny garments and para-phernalia in the shops somehow made it all seem real. Not that she hadn't known full well that it was real (there was no denying the changes in her body or the dreaded morning sickness!) but the sight of all these things made her think more about the end result, about what it would be like to physically hold this tiny person in her arms.

It was a scary thought certainly, but she had to admit, an incred-ible one too. Or at least it would have been if things had worked out the way she'd hoped; the way she'd assumed. She knew she'd have to think about going for another scan soon, and perhaps thinking about what hospital she'd attend when the time came. She'd sort of been putting that off until now, content in the knowledge from her first scan that all was well. And in truth, she'd sort of hoped that Steve might have in the meantime got in touch, maybe asked her to come back to Galway. But of course that was just her being silly... Why would Steve ask her to come back? And if he did, what would be the point in her doing so?

Flicking through a rail of maternity tops, Nina bit her lip, trying hard to contain the tears that were threatening. Damn it, she shouldn't be thinking of Steve, and certainly shouldn't be feeling maudlin about it.

'Nina, is that you?' she heard a voice from nearby say. She looked up to see a face that was familiar, but which she couldn't immediately place. Her confusion must have been evident because the woman continued. 'It's me, Jess. I've been into the café in Lakeview a few times – I'm a friend of Emer and Deirdre's?'

'Oh yes, of course!' Nina smiled politely, but inside she was annoyed. So typical that she would bump into someone she knew, and although this woman wasn't from Lakeview, she might as well have been. Nina had soon learned that the two women she'd mentioned could be quite gossipy, although in fairness, Jess had always come across as very kind and sweet. 'Sorry, I didn't recognize you there for a moment.'

'Just in the city for the day, are you?' the other woman enquired pleasantly.

'Yes. I was um ...' She followed Jess's gaze towards the clothes she'd been looking at. Damn, had she been rumbled? The maternity wear was right next to the office wear section in which Jess was browsing. Could Nina pretend she'd just wandered into the wrong department by mistake? 'Oh gosh, silly me. Here I was looking for some new shirts.' But she had never been a good liar and she suspected that Jess could see right through her.

'Yes, the office wear is fantastic here. I'm sure the maternity wear is too, if you need that kind of thing,' she laughed lightly, and luckily it did indeed seem as though she hadn't noticed anything untoward.

Then Nina remembered a recent conversation she and her friends had been having at the café. Jess was pregnant too, wasn't she?

'I guess you'll need this stuff yourself soon,' she joked, but one look at the woman's pained expression suggested that she'd got it all wrong. Oh no, Nina thought immediately realizing that she'd put her foot right in it. What a thing to say, especially when she wasn't sure if ... oh hell.

'Well, maybe someday.' Jess's smile was tight.

'I'm sorry, I ...' Nina decided the best option was to come clean. 'I just remember your friends mentioning something about it in the café, but I must have got it wrong, I really hope I haven't offended –'

'Please don't apologize. It's not your fault and I can completely understand why you'd assume that. The girls can be a bit ... full on about all this. Yes, I would like to have a baby – sometime,' she added gently, 'but it's not quite an option at the moment.'

'Oh.' Nina's heart went out to her and she understood completely what Jess meant about her friends. Despite her own initial misgivings about Trish's reaction to them, she'd got to know Emer and Deirdre quite well from the café; and they could perhaps be described as 'mumzillas'.

'I think the girls would love it if we could all be mums together, but of course it doesn't always happen like that and ...' she paused, as if suddenly realizing she was speaking out of turn and to a complete stranger. 'Anyway, it's nice to see you Nina, and enjoy your shopping.'

Jess went to turn and leave, but before she did Nina found herself asking; 'Um, do you want to catch a cup of coffee or something? I was just about to, so if you fancy it ...' She wasn't sure why she'd asked, but there was just something about Jess, something vulnerable, that made her want to chat to her for a little bit longer. 'I owe you one after shooting my mouth off like that.'

Jess looked genuinely delighted. 'Thank you; that would be lovely.'

The two went upstairs to the store's in-house café and chatted for a little while over cappuccinos. Nina discovered some more about Jess's work at the drinks business which sounded fascinating, and she in turn told her all about Cathy and her travels abroad.

'Six months is a long time, you must miss her a lot,' Jess said and Nina nodded.

'You have no idea. Staying with Dad is OK, but it's just not the same.'

'I can imagine. So were you living with your Mum before she took the trip or –'

'Oh no, I've lived in Galway for years, but I moved back when I broke up with my boyfriend,' she said, fiddling with a small packet of sugar. She smiled tightly. 'Things didn't end so well.'

'Sorry to hear that,' Jess said, and again Nina was amazed at how easy she was to talk to, and what a relief it was to have a conversation with someone who wasn't full of questions all the time. Trish was forever asking her about Steve and what had gone wrong, and Ella regularly tried to draw her out as to how long she'd be staying or what she'd do next. It was almost liberating to be with someone who wasn't constantly in her ear.

'So what other drinks do you do that I would know?' she asked Jess, referring to her work at Piccolo.

'Well, there's our newest one G-Force – it's an energy drink,' she told her. 'Of course Porters is the big one, and the one we hope will eventually hold its own with Guinness. Then there's Stingray, our main cider drink, aimed at the student market really – have you heard of that one?'

'Of course, although I can't touch a drop these days, unfortunately,' she laughed, momentarily forgetting herself.

'For the same reason you were shopping in the maternity section downstairs?' Jess said levelly and at first, Nina wasn't sure she'd heard right.

'What ...?'

Now it was Jess's turn to be dismayed. 'My mistake, it's absolutely none of my business, and I shouldn't have said anything, but I just assumed when you mentioned not drinking ...'

'You're right,' Nina said, with a resigned sigh. She was going to have to admit it to someone sooner or later and she didn't think she had anything to fear from Jess knowing the truth. 'It's not exactly public knowledge yet though. Hell, I haven't really told anyone else yet, what with Mum being away and everything ...'

'Well, I won't breathe a word,' Jess said, and was Nina mistaken or was there a slight catch in her voice? 'And believe me, I truly didn't mean to put you on the spot like that either – there's nothing worse than some old busybody –'

'It's fine honestly. And as you can probably guess, it's part of the reason I needed to get away from Galway.' To her dismay, tears came to her eyes yet again. Damned hormones.

'Oh, Nina sweetheart, are you OK?' Jess fished in her handbag for a tissue.

'Thanks,' Nina sniffled, feeling like an idiot. Why had she landed this poor woman, practically a stranger, in the middle of all of this? 'I'm sorry.'

'Hey, don't be sorry, I'm sure you have to deal with a lot of new emotions right now, never mind the usual ones.'

'Exactly.' Somehow Jess had managed to nail it all right on the head. From day to day, Nina hadn't a clue how to feel ... about Steve, her father, the baby – anything and it was liberating to be able to talk about it all out loud. 'I don't usually dump my problems on someone else.'

'You're not dumping anything, you're simply sharing them and that's always a good thing.'

Nina felt so comfortable in her presence, she couldn't believe it. Jess seemed like the only person she knew who wouldn't judge her; wouldn't ask questions or start making assumptions.

And perhaps for that reason alone, she decided to confess all.

'It's just all been so crazy,' she said, wiping at her nose. 'You see, I don't want Steve, the father to know anything about it and ...' she took a deep breath, deciding for once to be honest with someone or more importantly, honest with herself. She looked away, unable to meet the other woman's eyes. 'Jess, honestly, I'm not even sure I want this myself.'

31

A few days later, Nina was at the café helping Ella and trying, albeit unsuccessfully, to get her mind off her meeting with Jess.

What had gotten into her to tell all those things to a stranger?

Not that Jess was a stranger *per se*, and she had been especially lovely, but really Nina should have known better than to let her guard down like that. Jess probably thought she was a heartless cow talking about how she wasn't sure she wanted to keep the baby, especially when she herself was trying for one.

But in fairness, Jess hadn't batted an eyelid at Nina's confession and had instead nodded sagely and told her that yes, of course she would have mixed feelings about it all, given the break-up of her relationship and the part the pregnancy had played in it.

'Are you OK Nina?' Ella inquired now as she added cream cheese icing to freshly baked carrot cake. 'You look distracted.'

Nina looked down and realized that it was taking her ages to do something as simple as prepare a pot of tea.

'Oh. Sorry, I was miles away.'

'Are you sure you're all right? You look a bit pale today. Here, have some cake.'

Nina had to smile. The older woman was forever trying to fatten her up with cakes, muffins and the like – almost as if she were another one of what her mum referred to as Ella's 'sad rescue cases'. Well, perhaps she was.

'Honestly, Ella, I'm fine. I'm just thinking – that's all.'

'Well, you seem to be doing a lot of that lately,' her boss joked, but there was truth in her words. 'Anything I can help you with?'

'No, no, nothing at all.' But Ella stayed watching her, as if waiting for her to change her mind. Nina figured she'd better think of something, otherwise Ella would be on at her all day. 'Well, actually, did you know my mum and dad back when they were together?'

Ella's face changed a little, as if this was completely different to what she'd been expecting. 'Of course I remember. Why do you ask?'

'Well, I just wonder sometimes about ... well ... *why*, they got together. As you know, Trish and I keep finding all of these snippets and articles about mum, and it just seems that dad was her polar opposite. There's nothing about him, or at least nothing we could find.'

'Well, I don't think old newspaper clippings will tell you much about your parents' relationship,' Ella pointed out.

'Oh, I know that, but I suppose it just makes me even more aware of the differences between them. They've always seemed to me like such an odd couple, the last two people you'd put together.'

'I think that's a little bit unfair. Your dad might be a bit set in his ways, but I know he absolutely worshipped the ground your mother walked on.'

'Yeah, but it seemed like most of the men in this town did,' Nina laughed proudly. 'Which makes it even harder to understand why she chose him.'

Ella began folding a tea towel. 'I suppose your dad had certain qualities that appealed to your mother. Compared to most of the men in this town, he was mature and intelligent, quiet and restful, and from what I can remember treated her like a princess. Not to mention that he was quite handsome back in the day.'

Nina decided to bite the bullet. It had of course been bothering her since the day of the argument and she'd been waiting for the opportunity to ask. Now seemed as good a time as any. 'Was it a shotgun wedding Ella?' she asked bluntly.

The older woman looked flustered. 'Nina, such a question!'

'Hey, it doesn't bother me one way or the other – they're not together now so why should it make a difference? Seriously.'

'Well,' Ella sighed, 'I believe there was some effort to make things … legitimate, but truthfully I think they would have married regardless. She was like a queen to him, he loved her very much and she loved him too. Don't ever let anyone convince you otherwise.'

Nina felt guilty for being so harsh to her father. 'So why did they split up then?'

'Look, I really don't think it's my place to talk to you about this stuff, it is private after all. Maybe you should ask your mum?' Ella looked hopeful that Nina wouldn't press her.

She sighed. 'I've asked her, but she never gets into specifics. I just feel I have a right to know – they are my parents after all.'

'I suppose sometimes people just can't work things out. Anyway, what does it matter, they both love you very much, don't they?'

If you could call Patrick's behavior 'love', Nina thought uncharitably.

'I suppose so, but it still doesn't explain why they split up and –' but before she could continue the door opened and their first customer of the day arrived.

'Ah hello there, good morning!' Ella called out in greeting.

A blush automatically rose on Nina's face.

It was Dave.

'Hey there,' he said, grinning flirtatiously at her, as Ella went out back to get something. 'Told you I'd call in for a doughnut one day.'

'Well, you've definitely come to the right place,' Nina said smiling right back.

32

'So we're renting a huge villa with its own pool, and plan to have barbecues every night ...' Jess smiled, as on the other end of the phone Deirdre was explaining about the family's upcoming holiday in Tenerife. 'Oh, I really can't wait Jess, it'll be great fun and of course we won't have to worry about babysitters because all the kids will be together and –'

'What you mean "all the kids"?' Jess asked, puzzled.

'Oh, didn't I mention that Emer and Dave are coming too? And little Amy of course. We have it all planned out and it'll be great. As I said, barbecues and wine every night – it'll be bliss.'

'Oh.' Jess's heart sank, imagining the two couples sharing wine and food al fresco and enjoying each other's company while the kids were in bed.

It would be just like old times, the way the six of them used to get together here in Dublin back in the days before the others had families. 'That sounds lovely.'

'It does, doesn't it? Of course Amy is still a bit young for flying, but I'm sure she'll be fine and if all goes well, we'll probably do it every year, it'll be great for the kids and of course no better than Emer and Dave for the fun ...'

And Jess was faced once again with the prospect of her and Brian being left out of all this 'fun'.

'I mean, we'd have asked you and Brian, but I know he's always off to fancy places so he probably wouldn't be interested in boring old Tenerife ...' It was as if Deirdre had suddenly become conscious of the fact that Jess might be feeling left out.

'No, no, it's fine, and actually we've already booked something for later this year, remember I was telling you we were thinking about Borneo?'

They hadn't actually done anything other than talk about it, but Jess didn't want Deirdre to feel obliged to invite them. Best to let her think they wouldn't be interested anyway.

'Exactly, that's what I thought. And I'm sure you'd much rather see real orangutans that have to put up with Amy's carry-on! Seriously though, did you notice how brazen she is these days?' she went on, her voice low and conspiratorial. 'Always looking for attention and Emer *never* disciplines her, but I'll tell you one thing, if she starts throwing those tantrums in our villa then I'll be sure to say something.' Again, there was that competitive streak – as in *my* child is developing faster or is better behaved, and Jess wondered if the holiday in Tenerife would in reality be as heavenly as she was imagining.

'I can't say I have, although I'm sure it must be a struggle to keep up with her now that she's started crawling,' she replied diplomatically.

'Yes,' Deirdre sounded disappointed that Jess hadn't taken the bait for a bit of mummy-bashing. 'Anyway, I'd better go, Kevin will be home soon and the place is in a state and he hates that. Honestly, you'd swear I had nothing better to do all day than dust and clean, but I suppose I'd better make the effort,' she groaned. 'Men have it easy I reckon.'

Jess smiled. 'They sure do. Anyway, thanks for phoning and I'll see you soon.'

'Yes, come down and meet us for coffee next week if you can? Would be great to have a proper catch-up to see how things are with you – find out if anything's stirring,' she giggled, and Jess rolled her eyes, now beginning to regret she'd ever said anything to Deirdre about trying for a baby.

Hanging up the phone she checked her watch. It was six-thirty on a Friday evening. Might as well have a glass of wine while waiting for Brian to get home from work. While these days she and her husband were getting on reasonably well, there was still this unspoken rift between them, and the subject of children hadn't been touched on since their last discussion.

If only he could understand that this 'sudden obsession' as he called it, wasn't about the girls, but more about Jess holding up a mirror to her life, to *their* lives and finding something wanting. While she was prepared to admit, as she had to Nina recently, that the girls' opinion did have something to do it, it wasn't all about that. It was more about Jess and Brian and where their lives were headed, and she really felt that if Brian could see how fun and wonderful family life could be he would understand exactly where she was coming from.

Pouring herself a glass of Merlot, Jess went outside to her small patio, thinking about her recent encounter with Nina. She'd enjoyed their little chat over coffee last week; Nina was a nice girl, very approachable and as soon as Jess had spotted her in M&S the penny had dropped. Granted, finding her in the maternity wear department was probably a bit of a giveaway, but in truth there was no mistaking the burgeoning tummy, and slightly puffy face, not to mention her immense embarrassment at being recognized.

Seeing Nina's obvious discomfort, Jess wasn't going to say anything until she'd mentioned something about not being able to drink, which suggested the pregnancy wasn't a secret. Perhaps she shouldn't have been so forthright, but for some reason Jess really wanted to find out if her suspicions were correct.

And there it was; a woman with no partner, and no desire to have children was pregnant, while she, who had a loving husband and the ideal life in which to raise a child, wasn't. Although perhaps the loving husband part was possibly stretching that a bit these days.

Jess looked around at her and Brian's beautifully manicured

garden thinking that it would be ideal for children to run around in. As it was they rarely used it, except on the odd sunny day like today, and even then they only used the patio for drinks or barbecues and whenever Brian felt like making his 'world famous pina coladas'.

She thought about Emer and Deirdre and the fun the families would all have together at the villa in Tenerife. Just like they'd all had fun at Emer's house that time on her birthday. She recalled the way the couples used to get together for big barbecues in summers gone by; it had been ages since she and Brian had done something like that, that wasn't work related.

Then suddenly the thought struck her. Why shouldn't they hold a barbecue or a garden party and invite all their friends, including or perhaps *especially* those with kids?

She could invite Deirdre and Kevin, and Emer and Dave along with their children here for a party, and then Brian would be able to see first-hand all the fun and joy that the kids brought to their parents' lives. He would realize how proud Kevin was of his boys and how much enjoyment they had together, and you only had to take one look at Dave with Amy to realize that she was a daddy's girl through and through.

Yes, that's what she would do, Jess thought, feeling almost light-headed at this truly inspired idea. She was convinced that once Brian saw things the way she'd been seeing them that he would change his mind, and begin thinking seriously about starting a family. Especially given the fact that Brian wasn't sold on the idea because he could so far only think about the negatives.

Feeling energized, she stood up and went back into the kitchen to grab her BlackBerry. She scrolled through her calendar, wondering what would be the perfect date. She'd have to consult with Brian and the others, but she was sure a couple of Saturdays from now would be good. She smiled to herself and started to go through her address book, trying to find enough people to invite to the party; the only prerequisite for receiving an invitation was to have a child to bring along, Jess decided.

Now she couldn't wait for Brian to get home from work. She

topped up her wine and took another glass out of the cupboard, ready for her husband upon his return.

She was sure Brian would agree it was about time they took control of their social life and made more of an effort with their friendships.

A garden party – how perfect? Jess couldn't wait to fill him in on all the details.

33

*W*eeks passed in the blink of an eye for Ruth, and she seemed to be falling into step with the routine she had established in Lakeview. After finding out about her pregnancy, she had eventually managed to pull herself out of her self-imposed isolation at her parents' and started getting out of the house and occasionally meeting up for a chat with Nina at the café, or going power-walking with her mother.

'It's good to see you coming out of yourself a bit,' Breda commented and Ruth knew her parents had been very worried about her in the aftermath of the media scrum that accompanied her arrival.

'Good to see you putting on a few pounds too,' her dad said, which was somewhat more worrying as it meant that there was little chance of her pregnancy remaining unnoticed for too much longer. 'You were nothing but skin and bone when you came here first. Lollipop heads – isn't that what they call them in *heat*?' he said to her mother and Ruth had to laugh at the idea of Ollie reading celebrity magazines.

Then again, her parents had always tried to keep an eye on her; even it was just through the glossy pages. Goodness knows she hadn't really given them the opportunity to do so in person. She was enjoying spending quality time with them too, reading quietly in the garden with her father, or going shopping and watching TV with her mother. It was a peaceful existence and a massive contrast to the life she'd lived in LA up to now.

Ruth had been keeping that life at arm's length too. The cruel treatment she'd experienced from the paparazzi upon her return had stopped when they discovered her going about her days and quietly leading a suburban existence, and in the meantime they'd lost all interest in her and left to chase the antics of Paris Hilton in the Med. What surprised Ruth the most about this was she was certain she'd be somewhat peeved about their lack of interest, but instead she was appreciating the peace and quiet. There had been a couple of polite emails from Erik asking how she was, and a few brief and unimportant messages from Chloe, but other than that nothing. And more to the point, nothing at all from Troy.

She hadn't yet mentioned a thing to anyone other than Charlie about the baby. She had accidentally come close to it once or twice with Nina, but had checked herself just in time.

As far as Charlie went, well, she had seen him a few times around town and while something in his eyes changed when he looked at her, he generally kept his distance. She wasn't sure if she should be hurt by this – in that he had obviously thought about her situation and chosen not to get close to her – or if she should be relieved by the fact that she wouldn't have to complicate her life further.

As far as the father of her child went, she couldn't help but laugh with distaste. Barely a week after she'd told Troy she was pregnant, he was photographed sucking face in public with some new starlet who was being called the next Scarlett Johansson. All Ruth could do was shake her head at the absurdity of it all and again she was surprised by how distanced she felt from LA and her old crazy lifestyle.

In the meantime, she'd thought it prudent to see a doctor, and discovered she was in perfect health and her pregnancy was so far totally normal. Although the GP Jim Kelly was local, he was old school, and Ruth trusted that he would honor doctor-patient confidentiality and respect her privacy.

Actually she prayed he would.

Tonight she was meeting Nina and Trish for dinner locally, and was looking forward to going out and having some fun. She wouldn't be able to drink of course, and hoped the girls wouldn't notice anything, but she'd already thought of a cover story – namely a new diet she was trying.

She'd agreed to meet the girls at The Steakhouse, and as she was still rather self-conscious of being out and about on her own, her dad had agreed to give her a lift as far as Main Street. She knew she looked good though; she wore her hair up and was wearing a tulip dress from Gwen Stefani's line, which looked modern and funky, but was cleverly designed to hide her now-burgeoning figure. Her frame was so tiny that now, barely ten weeks in, she could already see herself beginning to show.

The girls were already at the restaurant when she arrived and they waved as she approached the table. While Ruth still hadn't quite forgiven Trish for some of the remarks she'd made in that article for the paper, she knew Trish probably couldn't help ramping up the drama for the benefit of her readers. It was how the media worked after all. And Ruth knew better than to let anyone think she'd hit any nerves. First and foremost, she was a professional.

'Hey there,' she said, enthusiastically greeting them both with air kisses. To her satisfaction she noticed Trish gazing enviously at her clothes. Her former classmate hadn't an ounce of style, and tonight she looked boring and ordinary in generic black trousers and a drab lime green top that did nothing for her. Nina by contrast looked beautiful; dressed in a gorgeous pattered shift that highlighted her dark coloring and her hair fanned out prettily around her shoulders.

'I love your dress,' she said, sitting down beside Nina.

'Thanks, it's new actually.'

'Where did you get it?' Trish asked. 'I haven't seen anything like that in Connolly's or Kramer's lately,' she said, referring to the town's main clothing stores.

Nina reddened a bit. 'Oh, I got it in Dublin actually,' she said almost as if she'd spoken out of turn, Ruth noticed.

'Really? I didn't know you'd gone to Dublin. When were you

there?' As usual the questions from Trish came thick and fast, and Ruth wondered if it was just force of habit from the journalism, or was she always that inquisitive?

'Um, a couple of weeks ago. I had a few things to do there.'

'You should have told me, we could have gone together and I could do with some new stuff.'

'Ah, it was only a last minute thing, and I knew you were busy with work.'

'How come it was last minute?'

'What?'

'You said it was a last minute thing. Was there some kind of emergency or problem or something?'

'Trish really,' Ruth interjected with a light laugh. 'Talk about the Inquisition!'

'Oh sorry,' she replied, with what seemed like genuine chagrin, and Nina gave Ruth a grateful look.

'Truthfully, I had a day off and I needed a couple of things so I decided to take the bus. I couldn't really find anything I liked here.'

'I know what you mean,' Ruth said groaning. 'I'll have to go on a shopping expedition myself soon, as the stuff I have won't fit ... *in* – around here I mean.' She paused, horrified by her inadvertent slip of the tongue and hoped she'd rescued it in time.

'I can imagine,' Trish said grinning. 'I suppose designer dresses and fancy shoes are wasted on Lakeview.'

'No, that's not what I meant. More the fact that all my LA stuff is much more suited to warmer weather.' She gave a meek smile. 'It's been so long since I was home, I'd almost forgotten we don't really do summers here.'

'You can say that again,' Nina laughed and the waiter came to take their drink orders.

'Are we all having wine?' Trish asked and to Ruth's surprise Nina shook her head. 'I'm on duty at Ella's tomorrow,' she said.

'Ah go on – one glass won't kill you,' the other woman replied and Nina shrugged. 'OK then, maybe just the one, but that's it.'

'Great, a bottle of the house plonk sound OK to you Ruth?'

'Actually ...' Ruth looked at the waitress. 'Could you just bring me a glass of water with lemon? And at room temperature please, not chilled.'

The waitress didn't bat an eyelid and if anything looked delighted with this bona fide LA-style request. 'No problem,' she grinned, moving away.

Trish and Nina were staring at her. 'What?' she asked. 'I don't drink usually. Way too many calories and I need to keep an eye on my weight.'

'Yes, I noticed you'd filled out a bit since you got back,' Trish commented in typical forthright fashion, but Ruth was pleased; it merely meant that her diet cover story would work all the better.

'Ruth, she's joking!' Nina said hastily, looking sideways at Trish. 'You're still only tiny.'

'No, no she's right. I've gone up to a size two since I got here as Mum keeps force-feeding me carbs – and she keeps forgetting that I'm lactose-intolerant,' she trilled, feeling almost as if she was back playing a part, and she noticed Nina and Trish exchange amused glances.

'So how is everything, Ruth?' Nina asked, after the drinks were brought to the table. 'Are you missing the LA lifestyle?'

'Not really,' she replied automatically, but just in time, figured she'd better keep up appearances, especially in front of Trish. 'Of course I miss having my assistant and the parties and the premieres, but honestly? The reason I came here was to spend time with my folks and that's what I'm doing.'

'Hmm, a little bird told me you've been spending some time with Charlie Mellon too,' Trish said coyly and Ruth looked at her.

'What? Where did you hear that?'

She smiled. 'I told you, a little bird told me.'

'Well, the little bird was wrong. I did see Charlie ages ago, yes, when he called to drop off something for Dad at the house, but other than that ...'

'Right. Whatever you say,' Trish replied in a tone that suggested she didn't believe a word of it. It was times like this when Ruth really *did* miss LA – even though Hollywood was a small town and the rumor mill moved fast, it surely wasn't as fast as the one in this place!

And once again she hoped against hope that her doctor wasn't in cahoots with Trish Brogan, or soon her little secret would be everywhere. As it was, one only had to count back the weeks to figure out exactly when it happened and worse, who the father was, and Ruth didn't need that kind of melodrama, not again. She didn't think she would be able to cope with it this time, not when she'd just about got over the last round.

She decided she'd better change the subject. 'Tell me, do you think they'd de sauce the meat here? My stomach *really* can't handle anything made with starch.'

THE FOLLOWING DAY, Nina was working the afternoon shift at the café – much to her relief as after last night's ginormous steak portion, she'd had a severe case of indigestion that had kept her up most of the night. Thankfully she'd got away with sipping slowly at the wine, and once Trish had made inroads into the bottle, she'd failed to notice that Nina had drunk hardly any at all.

She'd really enjoyed herself though; Ruth was good company and could be quite hilarious once you broke through her sometimes rather guarded persona. It was funny too how, despite her protests, she still hadn't quite left her LA life behind, and Nina knew the chef at the restaurant must have been scratching his head at her various requests.

They'd had great fun last night, especially when Ruth decided to fill them in on all of Hollywood's celeb secrets, like which massive male heartthrob was secretly gay and which long-time married 'power couple' couldn't stand the sight of each other. It was priceless stuff and Nina knew that Trish sorely wished she worked for a newspaper that would be interested in such juicy gossip. But then again, nobody would probably believe her, and in truth, it was hard to tell if Ruth was being serious or just ramping up the scandal for fun.

In the end, it had been well after midnight by the time they'd left the restaurant and by then Nina's sides were sore from laughing.

Half way through the afternoon, Emer, Deirdre and their respective broods came into the café, followed closely by Jess.

Nina's stomach knotted; she hoped that Jess wouldn't mention anything about their meeting in Dublin that time.

'How are you all?' she greeted, coming over to their table immediately. Meeting her gaze and obviously sensing her concern, Jess gave her a surreptitious wink.

'Hi there ... Nina, isn't it?' she said, purposely pretending she didn't know Nina all that well, and she felt relieved.

'I'm good, thanks. How are you all today?'

Once her customers were seated and the children settled in, Nina took their orders and dropped them into the kitchen. On her return out front she overheard part of the three women's conversation.

'Are you sure Brian won't mind the kids running amok on those gorgeous walnut floors?' Deirdre was asking Jess.

'Well ... I'm sure it will be fine seeing as it's a garden party, so everyone should be outside mostly ...' she replied, her tone hesitant.

'We'd better pray for good weather so!' Emer laughed, and Deirdre shot her a look.

Her interest piqued by their chat, Nina hovered around a nearby table, taking much longer than normal to clear it. She knew she shouldn't listen in, but she was eager to find out if they were still bending Jess's ear about getting pregnant.

'It should be fine,' Jess said. 'And Brian is really looking forward to it. It's been ages since we had you guys round.'

'Jess is having us all over for a party next Saturday,' Emer said, addressing Nina, who jumped guiltily.

'Oh ... that sounds nice,' she replied, smiling.

Jess caught her eye. 'Yes, I thought it would be good for all of us to get together, the kids too, so that no one will have to worry about babysitters.' Deirdre and Emer were smiling and nodding in agreement.

Nina looked at the children, secretly wondering if Jess knew what she was getting herself and her furniture, into. Little Amy was in the process of smearing yogurt on to her clothes and Deirdre's boys were in the middle of painting each other's faces with colored marker.

She swallowed hard. 'That's very nice of you.'

'Yes, and one we really appreciate,' Deirdre said. 'And I think it'll be good for Jess to see what her house will look like when it's full of little ones, since it won't be long until she has her own.'

Nina couldn't help but think that the woman sounded like an over-aggressive mother-in-law, and one look at Jess's face suggested she felt the same. The poor thing looked like she wanted to cry.

'Yes well, everything in its time, I suppose,' Nina said, trying to help get her new friend off the hook, and Jess gave her a grateful smile. 'Do you need any help with catering, or anything? Ella does a great line in finger food, although I suppose with it being in Dublin and everything, you've already made your own arrangements.'

'No, I would actually love that,' Jess said brightly. 'Saves me the headache of worrying about what to get, or how to cook it.' She grimaced. 'Brian is great on the barbecue, but I'd burn toast.'

'That's a really great idea, Nina,' Deirdre said, 'I would totally offer to give Jess a hand, but I'm afraid I might be more trouble than I'm worth with these two. Don't worry about tidying up too much beforehand though,' she said to Jess, 'Because the place will get torn up in no time.'

Judging by the barely masked glee on Deirdre's face, it was almost like she was relishing the prospect of letting her children loose on Jess's nice house. What sort of friends were these?

'Well, let me know if you want to talk to Ella about nibbles,' she said to Jess. 'I know she'd be delighted to help out, and we can organize someone to drop them up to you that morning.'

'I'd really appreciate that,' Jess smiled. Then she paused, as if something had just occurred to her. 'Actually Nina, I was wondering if you'd like to come along too? If you're free, that is.'

'To the party?'

'Sure.' She could tell that Jess was almost enjoying the surprised looks on the other girls' faces.

'You could get a lift with whoever's dropping off the food.'

'Oh, to *help* with the party, you mean,' Emer said in a patronizing tone that got right up Nina's nose.

Jess reddened. 'Of course not! No, Nina please don't misunderstand, I mean absolutely as a guest. It would be lovely to have you,' she assured her and Nina could tell from her tone that she genuinely would like her to come – perhaps as some form of ally? In which case she'd only be happy to accept, especially if it browned off the other two.

'I'd be delighted,' she said with a smile. 'Thank you for asking.'

34

*I*t was the following Friday morning and Ruth was getting ready to go to a hospital appointment. She looked in the mirror and realized that these days she had a glow about her; her face had filled out a little (as had her body) but she didn't mind.

Today, she was having her first ultrasound at a private maternity hospital in Dublin. As her parents still knew nothing about her pregnancy, she was taking a train to the city so as not to arouse suspicion. She was walking toward the station, deep in thought and thinking about what it would be like to see living proof of her baby's existence, when a car slowed alongside her and she heard her name being called.

'Ruth.'

She looked up and to her surprise found that the driver of the car was none other than Charlie.

'Oh, hello there.' She smiled and waved, trying her utmost to appear relaxed and unaffected. Still, she couldn't ignore the way her heart skipped a beat when she saw him and she quickly resolved to put those thoughts away.

'Where are you off to? Can I give you a lift?'

'Just into town, and no I'm fine walking.'

'Are you sure? It looks like it's about to rain and you don't want to get caught out in it.'

Ruth looked up. The skies did look formidably dark and no; she didn't want to get soaked – not in the circumstances. 'Well, if you don't mind ...'

'Not at all. Get in,' Leaning forward, he opened the passenger door and Ruth slid in alongside him.

'Nice car,' she said, taking in the top-end Mercedes's plush leather interior.

'Yeah, well, there are some benefits to being in this business,' he said smiling. 'But, it's not mine, it's actually a display model.'

'Oh. Well it's very nice in any case.'

He pulled away from the curb and they sat in a somewhat uncomfortable silence as he drove.

'So how are you these days?' Charlie asked eventually, his gaze surreptitiously moving to her stomach.

'I'm great thanks.'

'Are you feeling OK? Any morning sickness or anything?'

She looked sideways at him. 'No, just a little at the beginning, but nothing for a few weeks now.'

'You're lucky. My sister, Kelly – do you remember her? She suffered with it for the full nine months.'

'The poor thing. I guess I am lucky. How is she now and what did she have?'

'She's great and she had a little boy, Lenny. He's almost two now – a mad fellow altogether.' Charlie smiled fondly and shook his head. 'You couldn't keep up with him.'

'I can imagine,' Ruth said, finding it hard to picture herself running around after an energetic toddler. It still didn't quite seem real, although she supposed it would after today.

'So all's going well then ... with everything?' Charlie continued and Ruth wondered why he was so interested now when he'd reacted so badly to the news initially.

'Pretty much, but I'll find out more today.'

'How so?'

'I'm actually on my way for an ultrasound.'

'Really? Where?'

'Mount Carmel.'

He looked surprised. 'I didn't realize you were seeing someone here. I thought you'd wait until you got back to LA, you know just in case ...'

'I know what you're thinking, but honestly there's a much greater chance of me keeping it under wraps here than in LA. One phone call from a dodgy nurse and the *stalkerazzi* would be down on top of me in no time.'

'I suppose you're right. Well, I hope it goes well ... although, wait a second – how are you getting there – to the hospital I mean?'

'I'M TAKING THE TRAIN – my folks still don't know, so I thought it would be safer.'

'Don't be stupid, I'll drive you.'

'Charlie no. It's good enough of you to drop me into town ...'

'Forget it, I'm driving you. The last thing you want is the likes of Maeve McGrath or Molly Brogan spotting you on the train, following you to the hospital and working things out,' he argued, referring to the town's best known gossips, one of whom was Trish's mum. 'Then it would definitely be all over town.'

Ruth thought about it. It certainly would be safer having someone who knew her situation drive her there, and certainly less chance of her getting caught out on the way.

'Thank you for the offer, but I'm sure you must have lots of other things to do –'

'Ruth, shut up.' Charlie's tone was gentle, but firm. 'I'm driving you – and I'll drop you back afterwards too. As I said, you don't want to take any chances.'

She looked at him, touched by his concern. 'Thank you Charlie. I really appreciate it.'

'No problem.' At the bottom of the road, before they reached the center of Lakeview, Charlie took a left and drove along the main road out of town.

As they drove towards Dublin, Ruth sat alongside him in a comfortable silence, faintly relieved that she didn't have to take the trip on her own.

'So it looks as if Lakeview is growing on you,' Charlie stated eventually.

She smiled. 'I know, I'm sort of surprising myself actually. I have a routine and some friends and well, it's all just so easy, I guess.'

'When do you suppose you will go back to La-La Land?' he asked his features darkening somewhat.

'I'm not entirely sure yet. The plan was to stay until the end of September, but of course I hadn't bargained on this,' she said motioning to her tiny bump. 'Still, the break is nice and I'm starting to question some things.'

'Like what?'

'Oh, just things,' she said, being intentionally vague. 'I'm finding myself more relaxed than I've been in quite some time, and I'm wondering if it's me who has changed or this place. You know?'

Charlie smiled at her, but said nothing.

Less than an hour later they reached the hospital, and Charlie pulled into the car park outside. Stopping the car, he got out and came around to Ruth's side to open her door.

'Thanks,' she said gratefully reaching for his hand as he helped her out.

'No problem. What time is your appointment?'

'We're a little early actually, but I'm sure it'll be fine.'

'Right. So do you want me to ...' he trailed off and Ruth looked at him.

'What?' she asked, rifling around in her handbag for her referral letter.

'Never mind, it doesn't matter.'

She frowned, wondering what was up with him. 'Are you sure you don't just want to head back? I shouldn't be too long in there, but then again, I don't know what to expect from these places, there could be a line a mile long and I really don't want you waiting around.'

'I'm in no rush honestly. And I was just going to ask if you wanted me to wait with you.'

Her head jerked up. 'In the hospital ... with me ... really?'

'I'm sorry if it's inappropriate, it's none of my business after all and _'

Ruth was touched. 'Actually no, please do come, that would be nice, honestly.'

'I'm not intruding?'

'Not in the least, I would welcome the company.'

'Well, ok, if you're sure. I thought it would be easier than having you wait on your own – and at least then I'll have some idea of when you'll be out.'

'Makes sense.' Ruth smiled, but still couldn't help but feel taken aback at his request. It was a strange man indeed that offered to wait at a prenatal clinic amongst other women in various degrees of pregnancy, but if he insisted ...

It was only a half hour before Ruth's name was called and in the meantime she and Charlie sat awkwardly amongst the other women, some with partners, others without and a few with children in tow. It was a weird experience, but one that Ruth figured she'd have to get used to.

It was a private maternity hospital – the most exclusive one in Dublin – and luckily none of the other mums seemed to recognize or have any idea that the woman with her hair in a ponytail and whose skin was free of makeup was the famous TV star of *Glamazons*. And again, Ruth found she didn't mind. She was tired of being stared at and assessed and it sort of felt nice to just be normal, the same as everyone else.

Finally, the nurse came out and called her name. 'Thanks.' She picked up her bag and stood up, and for some reason saw Charlie do the same. 'I think I can take it from here,' she said grinning and he blushed.

'No, you should come along too,' the nurse insisted.

Ruth laughed, and Charlie looked mortified. 'Oh no, no he's not the father,' Ruth clarified. 'We're actually old friends; and he's just here for moral support.'

'Well, he can give you moral support in there too, if you'd like.' The nurse walked off leaving Charlie and Ruth staring at one another.

'If you want me ...'

'Do you want to?'

Conscious that they now had an audience, the two quickly followed the nurse out of the waiting room and down the hallway towards the examination room.

'I'll wait out here instead,' he said and Ruth sighed.

'Oh, for goodness sake – I won't have you standing out here in the hallway. Come in with me if you like.'

'Ruth, honestly ...'

The sonographer popped her head round the door. 'Ah, it's nice to see the dads involved in the appointments; so many men can get squeamish here. Better get used to it though; you'll be standing right there when the little one pops out!'

'Actually, I'm not ...' Charlie began, but the woman had already disappeared back inside. Ruth shrugged and beckoned him to follow her in.

'Sorry,' she mouthed and he shook his head and smiled, fully aware of the ridiculousness of it all.

When they came inside the sonographer smiled at them both. 'Before you ask, he's not the father,' Ruth blurted out, suddenly nervous at the sight of the exam chair with its stirrups and the formidable looking medical machinery.

'Well, that's allowed. And I think it's always nice to have someone else here for this,' she said. 'It is a big moment after all.'

Ruth popped up on to the examination table. 'I have to admit; I'm kinda nervous about it.' Her lip trembled a little as she spoke and she looked in Charlie's direction, noticing that he was watching her intently.

'Perfectly normal, but there's really no need,' the woman smiled. 'Alright, then, let's get started.' Charlie stood back as the sonographer started to get set up for the ultrasound. She pulled up Ruth's top and spread the cold jelly all over her stomach. Charlie stared at her tiny baby bump and she met his eyes and smiled.

'Okay, so there we go... see there you can just about make out the heart beating?'

Ruth nodded, trying to make sense of the image that was on the screen. Gosh, could that little blob really be a baby, her baby? 'I think so,' she replied, tears in her eyes. Staring at the screen she was suddenly overcome with emotion. 'Look, that's my baby!' she cried to Charlie, who reached across and took her hand.

'It's wonderful Ruth,' he said softly. He scanned the length of her body, allowing them to rest on her belly for a moment. He didn't say anything else, but he didn't have to. Ruth knew that of course he was thinking about what this would have been like if things had been different and the baby they were now looking at was his.

35

*R*uth and Charlie said little as they left the hospital and drove back to Lakeview. As they approached her parents' house, he slowed the car and pulled into the side of the road.

She looked at him, wondering what was happening. He'd been quiet for most of the journey back and she knew that what had happened at the hospital was bothering him.

'Charlie, I'm sorry that you got roped into all of that, it wasn't fair and –'

'No, don't apologize. I thought it was amazing actually.'

She nodded. 'Wasn't it? I must admit, I never thought I'd be that excited; after all, it's just a couple of white blobs, but ... wow,' she shook her head. 'Talk about a hell of a screen debut.'

He laughed. 'Do you think he or she will follow in their mother's footsteps?'

'What – you mean be a complete disaster? I certainly hope not.'

'That's not what I meant – and really you shouldn't say that in front of it,' he admonished almost like an over-protective father.

Ruth's eyes widened in shock as at this she felt some movement in her stomach. It couldn't be a kick, not at this early stage, but it was definitely something. 'Oh, my goodness!' she cried, grasping his hand. 'Feel that.'

'Feel what?' Charlie replied and sure enough, the baby seemed to move again. 'Oh.'

They both looked at one another in amazement and Ruth laughed. 'It's kind of cool, isn't it? I'm thinking baby must like you.'

She saw something in his eyes that she couldn't read. 'Yes, it is very cool. And I very much hope this baby likes me,' he went on. 'Because I think I'm already crazy about it, almost as much as I am about its mother.'

Ruth stared at him, not sure if she'd heard right. 'What ...?'

'You heard me.'

'Oh Charlie.' She turned to look at him, not sure what to think. 'I ... don't know what to say.'

'You don't have to say anything really. Except, of course, whether or not you feel the same way,' he said with a nervous laugh.

'But what about ... all of this?' she asked, her gaze flickering again to her stomach.

He shrugged. 'It is what it is. The little blob already has me, so who knows what it'll be like when it's born.'

Ruth stared at him, flabbergasted. Was he actually saying that he didn't mind that she was carrying another man's child? That he could still love them regardless? 'So where do we go from here? I must say ... this is a little strange – great, but strange ...'

'Me too, so why not just try and figure it out as we go? After all, neither one of us has ever experienced anything this before, so I suppose it's perfectly fine to be scared.'

'You really want to be involved in this?'

He looked hesitant. 'As long as you're OK with it.'

'Oh, yeah, I'm fine with it.'

Charlie reached across and kissed her on the lips, this time slow and gentle with none of the urgency of last time. Ruth kissed him back, amazed that after all these years and all that had happened; here they were sitting together in the car on the same laneway in Lakeview. Had they learned anything in between? Ruth certainly hoped so. Because this time it wasn't all about her; this time it was all about the new life she had growing inside her; one that today

Charlie had clearly fallen for just as fast, and just as hard as she had.

36

'Hello there. I'm delighted you could come,' Jess smiled as she escorted Nina into her house.

'Thank you for inviting me.' She looked around the uber-stylish South Dublin townhouse, thinking it suited Jess to a tee. 'Do you need a hand with the food?'

'Not at all, I think everything's pretty much under control and anyway, you're a guest!'

She smiled self-consciously not entirely sure why she'd agreed to come to this party, but she liked Jess and sensed that she needed a friend. Anyway, it was another excuse to get out of the house and all too easy to get a lift to Dublin with Ella's son Dan, who'd dropped off the party nibbles. 'Well, if you do need help with anything, don't hesitate to ask.'

'Honestly no.' Jess insisted. 'Come inside and meet my husband. Are you feeling OK? Can I get you a glass of water or anything?' She seemed especially solicitous, probably because she knew about the pregnancy, and while Nina wasn't used to such a to-do, she suspected Jess's friends must have demanded it in the past, which was why she was fussing over her now.

'Well, lemonade would be nice if you have it, thanks.'

'Of course. And how is ... everything?' Jess asked gently, referring no doubt to their conversation of before.

'Still a bit all over the place really, but I'm sure I'll be fine.' She gave a tight smile, hoping that Jess wouldn't push it too much. It was strange talking to someone who actually knew the truth, and Nina knew it wouldn't be much longer until she would have to go public with it all, exposing the real reason she was in Lakeview and not what she had been telling people.

'Of course you will.' Jess led the way to the kitchen where a man, presumably her husband was standing at the countertop cutting up vegetables. 'Brian honey, come and meet Nina Hughes, a friend from Lakeview.'

Brian looked up and smiled. He was tall, very handsome and had a kind face.

'Ah, nice to meet you.' He wiped his hands on a dishtowel, and extended one to shake hers.

'You too,' she replied. 'Great to get the weather, isn't it?' She nodded towards the open patio doors and the beautiful summer's day.

'I know – it rarely happens when you plan something like this,' he laughed, his brown eyes twinkling and Nina decided immediately that Jess was a very lucky girl. Brian was lovely.

Then his eyes rested on her stomach and something in his face changed.

'I'd better get these on to the barbecue,' he said, turning to look at Jess, and was Nina imagining it or was there a slight edge to his tone now?

'Yes, better not keep the hungry hordes waiting.' Jess trilled, but her smile looked forced.

Nina looked outside to the garden where the other guests were gathered. Wow, there were a lot of kids out there. She immediately recognized Deirdre's two, and Emer's Amy, but there were a few others she didn't know.

'Jess I'll say it again; it's really brave of you to open up your house to so many children,' she joked.

Brian brushed past them with an uncooked tray of chicken

kebabs. 'Yes, well, when Jess gets an idea into her head, she tends to run and run with it,' he said and again Nina detected some bitterness in his voice. She realized that Jess was making herself busy in another area of the kitchen and no longer taking part in the conversation.

'I suppose there's something to be said for spontaneity,' Nina replied cheerfully.

There was clearly some kind of atmosphere here, and despite their gracious welcome she was starting to feel awkward being in the company of her new friend and her husband.

'Well, it's a party, and there's always a mess after a party, isn't there?' Jess piped up brightly.

Soon more guests started to arrive and Jess welcomed each one (as well as their children) with open arms. Nina noticed that Brian and Jess were having little contact with each other and there was obvious discomfort.

For her part, she felt herself tense up every time a child spilled something or caused a mess in her host's beautiful house, and continuously found herself helping Brian clean up carpet stains, or running to pull a valuable looking ornament out of reach of little hands. Jess seemed oblivious to it all – as did the mums of the little ones in question.

'Nina, honestly, you really don't have to help me clean this stuff up,' Brian said scrubbing a fruit juice stain from the oatmeal colored carpet. 'Frankly, I have no idea what's got into my wife for encouraging these kids to run amok.'

'Oh, it's no bother honestly, and I know Jess is up to her eyes being the hostess.'

In truth, Nina didn't mind keeping an eye on the mischievous children; it was better than having to spend time with the adults some of whom – namely Deirdre and Emer – were downright rude.

'Can you take this into the kitchen for me?' Emer had said earlier, handing Nina a plate of her leftovers. Because she was used to Nina being at her beck and call at Ella's, she seemed to expect the same treatment here, and despite Jess's kind invitation Nina was beginning to regret coming to this party.

Not that Jess was behaving like anything other than the perfect hostess, and Nina knew would be horrified to learn that shortly after her arrival, Deirdre had come up and asked Nina if she could 'use her' for an upcoming get-together she was planning at her house.

'I'm not actually here as a caterer,' Nina pointed out, but knew her words had fallen on deaf ears when another of the mothers later asked if she could fetch some fruit juice for her daughter.

'Something unsweetened preferably, Saffy can get a bit hyper on sugar,' and Nina couldn't help but wonder what the already manic little girl was on now – speed perhaps?

She found it hard to believe that these fussy indulgent women had anything in common with Jess, but at the same time it was easy to see why she was feeling browbeaten by their child-centric obsessiveness.

Which was why Nina almost welcomed the opportunity to stay in the background, keeping an eye on the kids and cleaning up after their exploits. Hell, it would be good practice for her, wouldn't it?

Once again she felt a knot in her chest at the notion of having a child of her own to look after. She just couldn't see it; and the truth was it would never be like this, like these other mothers who all had partners and husbands to share the workload. She looked around at Jess and Brian's wonderful house, considered their steady marriage, good jobs and great lifestyle. They were the kind of people who should be bringing children into the world; not penniless singletons who had nowhere to live, and little to offer. But as Jess herself had admitted before, sadly this often wasn't the way life worked.

Just then Brian walked into the kitchen to find her at the sink washing out some glasses. 'Nina, what are you doing? Come outside and have a drink and enjoy the sunshine.'

'Oh, I don't mind. It's warm out there today, so really, I'm enjoying being out of the sun.'

'Well, come and sit under the parasol then. Can I get you a glass of wine, or some champagne maybe?'

She smiled. 'Thanks, you're very kind, but I'm sort of ... not drinking at the moment.'

'I see.' Again, a quick glance towards her middle.

'I'm not sure if Jess told you, but –'

'Ah I understand,' he said uncomfortably. 'Well, in any case, you really shouldn't be doing our washing up. You're a guest, and more to the point we have a dishwasher.' He chuckled and Nina smiled.

Just then, a noise sounded from outside, soon followed by almighty toddler screams. Brian grimaced. 'Then again, maybe you have the right idea hiding away in here.'

'They are a bit ... feisty, aren't they?' she ventured delicately.

'Feisty? Brazen is the word I'd use. I don't know what the hell is wrong with Deirdre and Kevin, but if any child of mine behaved like those two boys they'd get a swift kick up the backside for themselves. But of course, these days it's all about letting them "express themselves", isn't it?' He shook his head, and Nina was finally able to put her finger on why things seemed so strained between Jess and her husband; clearly *she* and she alone was the one driving the children thing.

And she wondered now if this party had also been solely Jess's idea. It would certainly explain Brian's reaction to the playfulness of the kids and his weariness about having to clean up after them.

'I guess you guys weren't quite sure what you were letting yourselves in for,' she said trying to be diplomatic.

'You can say that again. Anyway, please do come outside,' he insisted, gesturing towards the garden. 'I think the noise has stopped, so it looks like the coast is clear, for a while at least,' he added with a wink.

Nina duly followed Brian outside to where the other guests were either sitting at the patio table, or standing around in small groups on the lawn.

Looking around to try and find Jess, she saw that she was sitting on the bench at the bottom of the garden in conversation with Emer and Deirdre. The girls looked to be in deep discussion, but while Emer and Deirdre looked animated, Jess's face was pale.

Then all of a sudden Deirdre stood up and threw her arms around Emer, hugging her fiercely.

'Oh wow! Oh my goodness! Everyone ... great news!' she

exclaimed, and all conversation stopped as everyone else turned to see what was going on. She nudged her friend. 'Emer ... tell them.'

Emer stood up too. 'Well, I know my husband will kill me for saying this when he's not here today, but ...' She grinned proudly. 'I'm kind of ... expecting again.'

There was a huge commotion as various people shouted good wishes and even some applause as other guests swarmed to congratulate the new mum-to-be.

Brian approached Emer to wish her well and give her a hug, and Nina immediately noticed how Jess was sitting stock-still, watching the celebrations play out around her. There was a peculiar expression on her face as she watched her friend receive hugs and good tidings from everyone at the party, and knowing how badly Jess wanted a child, she could only imagine the disappointment she was feeling just then.

But then suddenly, out of the blue, Jess too stood up and cleared her throat.

'Everyone...' she said, calling people loudly to attention. 'I ... I actually have an announcement too.'

The party guests paused and turned expectantly towards their hostess.

With a brief glance towards her husband, Jess took a deep breath and smiled. 'Well, I hope my darling hubby doesn't mind either, but ...' she grinned sheepishly, her face reddening, 'we might as well make it a two for one today ... because well, I'm pregnant too!' A brief hush descended until suddenly, praise and congratulations echoed once more.

'Oh wow Jess, that is amazing news!' Emer hugged Jess fiercely and people once again flocked forward, this time to hug Jess.

Nina heard Deirdre tell her that she 'just *knew* there was something different about her lately!' and Jess nodded, obviously thrilled with her friend's joyful reaction. The men duly moved to shake Brian's hand, and pat him on the back

But for some reason, the whole thing seemed a little ... forced to Nina and she couldn't help but be surprised that Jess hadn't said anything about it before. It didn't seem all that long since that discussion in M&S but of course she clearly hadn't known then. She'd probably just found out she figured, and hadn't intended on telling anyone yet, but of course then Emer's news had pushed the issue.

Or perhaps the announcement was the true purpose of this party? If so, then why had Brian seemed so put-out about it? Unless ...

She looked over at Jess's husband, who contrary to the exuberance of his wife, was behaving almost like a robot. He was accepting handshakes and congratulations, but his face was ashen and the expression of his face was one of ... bewilderment?

Nina gasped involuntarily. If she didn't know better, she could have sworn that Brian had just learned – at the same time as everyone else at this party – that his wife was pregnant.

37

*J*ess's nerves were on edge. She couldn't wait for the party to clear.

What on earth had *possessed* her to blurt out such a thing right in front of everyone like that?

Granted, she'd got a bit carried away and at the time just wasn't able to resist – not when everyone had been so excited about Emer ...

But now in retrospect, and especially having seen the shocked and very hurt look on Brian's face, she was having major second thoughts.

Poor Brian, how would she have felt if he'd done something like that to her?

But unfortunately the damage was done, and while she knew her actions would have huge ramifications, she had no choice but to face them.

Hopefully he would understand why she'd felt the need to do it – although in truth Jess couldn't quite understand it herself. It had been a moment of madness, a rush of blood to the head, and of course if Emer hadn't made her announcement, the subject matter would probably have never even been raised.

She just hoped Brian would be able to forgive her. It was bad enough that they hadn't been getting on all that well up to now, and she thought back to the discussion that had ensued when she'd first proposed the idea of the get-together.

Suffice to say, he was less than pleased.

'Do you think that inviting a load of children around here will help the scales fall from my eyes or something?' he'd laughed, as if the very idea was completely preposterous. 'Jess, I'm not an idiot, so please don't treat me as such.'

'What's wrong with wanting to spend some time with the others and their families?' she'd retorted. 'We haven't done anything like that in ages and having some fun will do us good.'

'I wasn't aware our lives had got so boring. What about our impromptu afternoon down by the docks last weekend?' he asked referring to a lovely lazy Sunday afternoon they'd had enjoying mojitos outside in the sunshine at a café bar.

And when Jess couldn't argue with that, he just shook his head in exasperation. 'All right then – I'll go along with your little Happy Families party. You're right about one thing; maybe we don't see enough of the others at the moment. But honey, please don't expect me to have an epiphany just by having them here. I've been around little people before you know.'

So while Jess's grand plan had very quickly been rumbled, she was still looking forward to spending time with her friends, and pleased that at least Brian was willing to be sociable.

But of course, she hadn't anticipated Emer's announcement ...

Eventually, the last of the party guests departed and she and Brian were left alone.

'So, when were you going to tell me?' he asked and rather than the outrage that Jess had expected, instead his voice sounded strange, almost guarded.

Guiltily, she met his gaze. 'I know, and before you say it, yes of course I should have said something, and believe me it wasn't my intention to just come out with –'

'A bit of an understatement don't you think? For goodness sake Jess, I'm your husband, or have you somehow forgotten that?'

'Of course not,' She moved towards him, but immediately he stepped back.

'How long have you known?' he asked, again in that odd, faraway voice.

'Erm ... not long.'

'Really? And you didn't think it was important to let me in on such a monumental occurrence, before making a huge announcement to all and sundry?'

Now she understood the undertone – Brian wasn't just angry; he was incensed, and Jess couldn't blame him.

Deeply ashamed of herself, she bit her lip. 'I'm so sorry, I know I should have said something first ... but of course, it's all still very early days and ... I suppose I wanted to be sure. But then today with Emer ... well, I just sort of got carried away.'

'Right, maybe I can understand that,' he replied, looking thoughtful and Jess was faintly relieved that he seemed to accept this (admittedly weak) explanation. 'But how do you think it happened? I thought we were fully covered that way.' He was referring to the pill and by the tight set of his jaw, Jess figured that now wasn't the best time to reveal that she'd stopped taking it a couple of months ago.

'I suppose sometimes these things happen ...'

'Strange that it didn't happen in all the years we've been together up to now,' he said dubiously. 'Have you scheduled a doctor's appointment yet – just to be sure?'

She shook her head, her heart hammering. 'Not yet.'

'Well, I suppose you should get on to that then, shouldn't you?'

'Yes, I will, just as soon as I have time.' She paused and again went to move closer to him. 'Brian, I know what I did today was awful and I don't blame you for being upset about that. But how do you feel about ... this?'

There was a pause. 'Well, I suppose I'm happy if you're happy,' he sighed, which to Jess sounded like a complete non-answer. Then to her surprise, he reached across and gave her a light peck on the cheek. 'Why don't you go and lie down for a while. I'm sure you're tired after today, and I'll finish clearing up here.'

'No, honestly I can do it.'

'Really Jess, you should be taking it easy. Seeing as you're so ... into the idea, I'm sure you've read all about how pregnant women shouldn't inhale cleaning supplies and we wouldn't want anything to go wrong, would we?' he added, studying her intently.

She found herself eager to avoid his penetrating gaze.

'OK then,' she agreed, thinking perhaps it might be a good thing to give him some space, help him to calm down a little. 'It was a pretty crazy afternoon, so I suppose I might take it easy for an hour or two.'

'A crazy afternoon is right,' she heard him mutter under his breath, as he bent down and picked up an empty juice carton.

Jess left the room and headed upstairs as quickly as her legs could carry her. Once she was inside her bedroom, she leaned against the closed door and took a deep breath.

What on earth had she just got herself into?

38

*N*ina was on her way to meet Trish and Ruth. They were getting together at the library today to go over in detail the information Trish had so far collected for the charity book. Nina knew Trish was in a state; she'd not been getting as much work done as she'd hoped over the last few months, and the deadline with her publisher was fast approaching.

Of course she also knew why Trish was running behind, as she'd been spending an awful lot of time with this new man of hers. Nina remembered when she and Steve had started seeing one another at first, and knew how all too easy it was to get wrapped up in one another. Of course, now she knew why he'd come on so hot and heavy at first. She shook her head, thinking again about what a fool she'd been.

Just then her mobile phone rang, and seeing the number displayed realized it was her mother. 'Hi Mum,' she said cheerfully, putting the phone to her ear.

'Hello darling; just checking in to say hello. How are you?'

'I'm good, where are you?' Nina asked, sort of hoping that her mother would say she was on her way home. It was stupid of course, as Cathy and Tony weren't due back until late September, but there was a side of her that hoped they would be getting homesick by now. Some chance.

'We're in Moscow actually. Nina, you should see the place - absolutely incredible, but really, I think I've drunk enough vodka for the rest of my life.'

Nina rolled her eyes and smiled. Typical, the party always followed her mother.

'Any idea on when you're heading home?' she asked, trying to disguise the hope in her voice. Things hadn't got any better with Patrick; he still barely acknowledged her and tended to just eye her warily whenever he saw her. Which Nina ensured wasn't often.

'We were thinking of staying on just a bit longer, actually,' Cathy said.

Nina shut her eyes, almost willing her mother to understand how much she needed her. 'Oh really? How much longer?'

'Well, we didn't expect this part of the world to be so interesting really, so we might extend it by a week or two ... are you OK with that?'

'Of course, why do you ask?'

'It's just you seem a little surprised ...' Cathy sounded hesitant and again Nina could have kicked herself for making her worry. 'Is everything all right with you, love? How are things with your dad?'

'Everything's great Mum and Patrick's fine too. How's Tony?'

'Slightly hung-over,' her mother said, a smile in her voice. 'But he sends his love as usual.'

Nina laughed and stopped outside the library.

'Well I'm delighted that the two of you are having such a great time. Keep in touch, won't you?'

'Of course. We're going to start heading back towards that direction soon – we might take in Germany or maybe France?'

'Sounds great – at least you'll be closer to the right time zone.'

'Exactly – it'll help us with the jetlag. I promise I'll let you know where we end up anyway.'

'Thanks Mum, great talking to you.'

Having said goodbye to her mother, Nina entered the library, going immediately to the back room where she found Trish already hard at work. Ruth was sitting off to the side near a pile of boxes and looking rather bored.

Trish looked up. 'Hey there,' she said, her eyes narrowing slightly as her line of sight trailed to Nina's middle, and feeling self-conscious, she quickly sat down.

'So, where are we at?'

'Oh, running behind, as usual. I don't know why I agreed to this project in the first place.'

'Well, maybe you shouldn't be wasting so much time on other more ... energetic pursuits,' Ruth teased

Trish snorted. 'Ha! You should be the one to talk.'

'What?' Perplexed, Nina turned to look at Ruth, who blushed.

Trish filled in the blanks. 'High-school sweethearts reunite,' she said grinning.

'Really? That's wonderful!'

'I think so,' Ruth said, looking about ready to burst with excitement.

'I'm really pleased for you, Ruth,' Nina said, meaning it. 'So will Charlie be moving back to LA with you then?'

'Well, we're not entirely sure yet ... there's a lot to sort out before-hand really ...'

'OH?' As usual Trish's news antenna was ready and waiting. 'Like what? Do tell.'

'Well ...' Ruth took a deep breath. 'I suppose it's going to be public knowledge soon, and we've been debating about telling anyone, but we're just about to tell my parents so ...' she looked from one to the other. 'I'm pregnant.' Trish's mouth dropped open, as did Nina's. 'Of course, I'm already as big as a whale, so I really didn't think anyone would be all that surprised.'

'Oh wow, Charlie sure moves fast, doesn't he?' Trish chuckled, and Ruth looked sheepish. 'Wait ... are you saying ... holy crap! Is it Troy Valentine's?'

Ruth, who'd evidently forgotten herself, went immediately into full-on PR mode.

'Well, that's really neither here nor there,' she said uncomfortably. 'All anyone needs to know is that Charlie and I are back together.'

'Ruth, it's really lovely news,' Nina was quick to congratulate her, but was secretly shocked that she hadn't noticed anything, considering. And despite Ruth's protests at being as big as a whale, she was actually no larger than a goldfish!

'Yes, congratulations.' Trish looked thoughtful. 'So how far along are you?'

'Not far,' Ruth said evasively.

'Well, you must be twelve weeks at least, otherwise you wouldn't be telling people,' she insisted and Ruth blanched.

'Oh, what does it matter how far along she is? The main thing is she's happy, and you are, aren't you, Ruth?'

'Very much,' she nodded, beaming. 'I still can't believe that after all this time, Charlie and I worked everything out.'

'Well, I really think it's fabulous news,' she said, giving Ruth a hug. 'And you deserve it after everything that's happened.'

'Thank you. It's all pretty nerve-wracking to say the least, as I really don't know anything about babies, you know?'

'I know how you feel,' Nina said without thinking. Then she reddened. 'I mean, I can only imagine –'

'Oh, for crying out loud!' Trish groaned, throwing up her arms, 'Would you just go ahead and say it?' she said with a wide grin.

'What?' Nina said innocently.

'Well, to be honest, it's looked to me for some time that Ruth's not the only one heading for the maternity ward this year.'

'Is it that obvious?' she said, mortified.

'I'll say.'

'No, not at all,' Ruth said kindly. 'I mean, yes, you have put on some weight since I first met you, but in a lovely baby sort of way,' she went on. 'We must be only a few months apart?'

'Well, I'm actually a lot further down the road ...' she confessed, already feeling as if a large weight had lifted. It was sort of nice to be able to talk openly about this, instead of keeping it all bottled up. And especially nice to share it with Ruth.

'So I guess this is the real reason you've been sticking around so long,' Trish stated and Nina nodded. 'I'd kind of guessed it wasn't for the love of your dear old dad.'

'I didn't really have anywhere else to go – especially with Mum away ...'

'And what about the father?' Trish asked gently. 'The guy you were seeing in Galway – is that all finished with?'

'No, he and I aren't together anymore – and he won't be involved in any of it,' she admitted and Ruth leaned forward and patted her on the hand.

'Men are shits.'

'Oh no, it's fine really. It's just ... well I haven't said anything before now because I still haven't quite decided what to do about it.'

'I think it might be a little late for a termination or anything,' Ruth said worriedly, and Nina shook her head.

'No, that's not what I meant. More that I'm not sure what to do once it's born. I'm not exactly cut out for motherhood and ...' Feeling her eyes begin to water, she decided to change the subject, not wanting to be the center of attention anymore. 'Anyway, seeing as we're all confessing our secrets,' she continued, turning to Trish, 'are we ever going to meet your mystery man?'

'Well, he's not really that much of a mystery,' she said in a decidedly cryptic tone and Nina frowned.

She laughed. 'You know him, in fact I think you would have both met him at some stage.'

'Really? Where?'

'Remember Ruth's homecoming party – the one where you ended up hiding in the broom cupboard?'

Both girls nodded.

'He was there. Actually Ruth, his company sponsored the whole night.'

Suddenly it clicked with Nina. 'Dave?' she said, blood rushing to her cheeks as stupidly, she realized she'd thought the same guy had been flirting with *her*.

Ruth seemed lost in thought. 'Wait a second ... are you talking about that guy from the brewery?'

Trish nodded. 'Yep.'

'But doesn't he have a little girl?' she continued. 'I'm almost positive he lives in one of the newer houses out my direction, and I've seen him around a few times with a little girl.'

'Oh,' Nina said, feeling even more foolish, 'I didn't realize he was divorced.'

Trish said nothing, and Ruth and Nina both eyed her. 'Trish, Dave is divorced, isn't he?' Ruth pressed, her eyes widening.

In one fluid motion, Trish pushed away the articles and pictures she was fussing over. She bit her lip. 'OK fine, as long as we're all confessing something. No he's not divorced, he's still married, actually.'

Nina felt the blood rush from her face.

'You're kidding!' Ruth gasped.

Trish now looked as if she had just been caught stealing, as in a way, she had. 'I know, I know, but I didn't know at first ... he never said anything and it sort of just happened, OK? The marriage is pretty much over anyway.'

'But it is a marriage, nonetheless, and you are interfering.'

Trish looked wounded. 'Don't lay the saint act on me Nina; you only just told us about your little secret – talk about the pot calling the kettle black.' The words stung more than Trish could have imagined and she couldn't believe how her friend could knowingly carry on with another woman's husband. 'Anyway, it's my business not yours, and I don't know why I even told you.'

'No, and now I wish I didn't know.'

'Nina, try not to judge me until you've walked in my shoes and please don't sit there and presume to act like you're holding the moral high ground. You know his wife, and she's a pain; you said it yourself.'

Don't judge me until you've walked in my shoes. Nina looked at her. 'What? How on earth would I know this guy's wife?'

'She comes into the café, her and that friend of hers and their gaggle of kids.'

'Oh ... you don't mean ...' Realizing she meant Emer and Deirdre,

Nina's head spun as she tried to put this together. She'd met Deirdre's husband at Jess's party and was sure his name was Kevin, which meant that ... 'He told you the marriage is already over?' she asked Trish.

She gave a defiant shake of her head. 'Absolutely. Yes, they have a child, but that's partly the reason. The kid is all the wife cares about, and she just sits at home doing nothing while he's out trying to keep the payments on that big house going.'

'Trish,' Nina wasn't sure if it was her place to tell her, but she felt her friend should know that she was deluding herself. 'I'm not saying this to hurt you, but if you're talking about Emer, I heard only recently that she's pregnant again.'

Trish's face crumpled. 'What? What are you talking about ...?'

'Honestly. I was there when it was announced,' she continued gently. 'So if he's telling you the marriage is over ...'

'Oh no,' Trish said, putting her head in her hands. 'The stupid ... I swear I'll ...' Nina moved across to put a comforting arm around her shoulders, but Trish shrugged her off. 'Leave me alone,' she said tearfully, gathering up her papers and shoving them into her briefcase. 'And forget I ever said anything!' And with that Trish rushed out of the room, banging the door as she went.

Nina looked at Ruth, who'd stayed silent throughout the entire exchange.

'Wow, interesting day, huh?' she said, eyes wide.

Nina nodded her head glumly. 'I'll say.'

Trish was right, this wasn't any of her business and she knew she'd gone over the top with her accusations and for the wrong reasons. But her friend didn't know that, and as far as Trish was concerned she *was* trying to take the moral high ground and she, of all people, had no right to do that. All of a sudden Nina felt scared, about this baby and what the future held; scared that because of her actions, she had just lost another important person in her life.

Ruth stood up and picked up her handbag. 'Let's get out of here,' she said. 'I think now might be a good time for a carb-fest at the Heartbreak Café.'

39

*J*ess lay in bed and patted her stomach, yet again thinking about being pregnant. She so wished that Brian could be happier about the prospect and had been sure that once he'd got over the initial surprise would be over the moon about it.

But instead, since the day of the party, he'd been keeping her at a distance – as if she was breakable or worse as if she'd done something really terrible. Which in a way Jess admitted shamefully, she had.

As a result, everything seemed anti-climatic. After all this time she'd expected that it would all feel really gratifying and exciting, but it was far from it.

By contrast, Emer was getting along famously and had already set up a room for the new baby and started buying lots of clothes and toys. She'd urged Jess to join in, but her heart wasn't in it, not when Brian was so far refusing to participate.

She'd wished for so long that things could be different and now they were – but not in a good way.

Since the day of the party, she felt draped in loneliness and knew it was because the fun that had been a huge part of her marriage had disappeared almost overnight. She missed Brian and she wished she could get back the spirit of the man that she knew. Ultimately, she wondered now if all of the early baby mania she'd laid on him had been a big mistake.

What's more she was also figuring out that her friend's lives might not be that perfect after all, and the more time she spent with them, the clearer this became.

For instance, despite her baby news, Emer and Dave seemed to be experiencing some major tension in their marriage, and Jess wondered if her friend's surprise pregnancy was an attempt at a Band-Aid baby. If so, what did that make hers; a banana-skin baby?

Because it sure as hell wasn't mending her marriage; if anything, it was killing it.

Thinking back, she realized that her life had been altogether fine with Brian before she'd become obsessed about starting a family. But of course, now she'd gone too far and was wondering how she could attempt to fix it, when the bedroom door opened quietly.

Brian entered and Jess sat straight up in bed, hoping against hope that he would show some sign of wanting to be close to her.

'Hey,' she said, smiling softly.

'Don't let me disturb you, I just need to change my clothes and then I'll leave you alone.'

'No, you don't have to leave me alone. I don't mind the company.'

Brian barely looked at her. 'But you must be tired.'

'No, really – stay, please.' Jess heard his barely imperceptible sigh, and felt as if her heart was ripping in two. 'So, how was work?' she asked, wondering why this felt so hard. Before this, their conversation had always been so effortless whereas these days it was stilted and hard to come by.

'It was fine.'

'Anything interesting happening?'

'Same old, same old for the most part.'

Jess bit her lip, realizing she wasn't really getting anywhere. 'Well, I'm glad you're home.'

'So, have you made that appointment with the doctor yet?' he asked quietly. 'You know – about the … situation.'

She reddened. 'Not yet – I haven't really had the time, what with work and everything ...'

Brian looked at her and slowly shook his head. 'Jess, what do you want from me?'

'What?'

'Again, what do you want from me?'

Did he mean he didn't want to accompany her to the doctor's? Well, that was fine by her. 'I don't want anything from you as such ... obviously I just want us both to be happy.'

'And do I get a say at all in the matter? Do I get a say in *anything*?'

'What do you mean?'

'You should know exactly what I mean, Jess. These days, I feel like I don't know you anymore. Our whole marriage has been built on trust and mutual respect, but lately you have been crazy, absolutely crazy. The whole obsession with this baby thing, and now...' he threw his hands up in frustration. 'I mean, announcing such 'news' the way you did in front of the whole world.'

'Look, I know that was out of order and I said I was sorry...'

'Don't you understand? A while ago you were calling *me* self-centered and superficial! You just want it every way, don't you?'

'Brian please ...'

'No Jess, seriously!' He held a hand up to stop her. 'I don't know what to do for you, I really don't.'

'But I don't know what you mean! All I want is for you to love me –'

'I'm trying, but I have to be frank, you are making it very hard at the moment,' he interjected his tone hard, and Jess's breath caught in her throat.

'I'm sorry Brian, really I am. I love you and I just wanted what was best for us.'

'Best for us? You think all this was best for us?' Brian now echoed what she'd just been thinking. 'You know I wanted children too, but I truly felt we should do it on our terms, instead of on your stupid friend's terms. Why the competition?'

Now Jess felt tears run down her face. 'I honestly can't explain it. I just felt so ... left out, like *we* were being left out ...'

'Well, you should be proud of yourself then, because now we're just like everyone else, with the same problems the rest of them have. Have you ever even opened your eyes to Dave and Emer? The two of them are always sniping at each other these days. Or are you just seeing the bull that Emer wants you to see?'

Jess wanted to agree with everything that he was saying, because it was exactly the same thing she'd been thinking, but she found herself unable to speak.

'Look Jess, I don't want to upset you, not while you are ... pregnant.' He seemed to struggle with the word. 'You should rest and ... I have some work to do.' He collected his clothes and left the room.

Jess could do nothing but remain motionless on the bed, listening to his footsteps echo down the stairs and away from her.

40

When much later at around 3 am, she woke up in the darkness and reached her arm out to Brian's side of the bed, hoping he would pull her close and welcome her into an embrace. Exploring the area, she opened her eyes tentatively, allowing them a moment to adjust. He wasn't there.

Jess felt her chest tighten. He hadn't come to bed last night? Why not? And more to the point, where had he slept instead?

Slowly getting out of bed, she went out of the bedroom and tiptoed downstairs. The house was in full darkness and she felt her heart sink as she realized that Brian didn't simply doze off at his desk while working or something.

She passed the study. All the lights were off and the computer was shut down.

Jess headed for the next door down the hallway and opened it silently. The room was dark, but she could hear him breathing heavily, the way he did when he was sleeping. She stood back, unable to believe that he had purposely slept in the guest room. She tried to tell herself that perhaps he had done it out of consideration, so that he wouldn't wake her when he came upstairs, but she couldn't force herself to believe the lie.

She knew better and what's more he had never done that before.

He never hesitated to come up after working late and slide into bed next to her, giving her a goodnight kiss whether she was fast asleep or awake.

This was something different. Since her big announcement, he didn't want to be around her.

Jess shook her head as she remembered her behavior of the past few months; it was almost as if she had been possessed, that someone else had been controlling her mind, someone with a crazy baby obsession.

She wished she could have seen things the same way Brian had; that they should wait until the time was right, wait for them to both be on the same page. But instead she'd just ploughed ahead; and in the process had purposely driven a wedge between them. And for what? Just so she could have something in common with her friends?

Overcome by so much emotion and regret at that moment, she almost collapsed on to the floor. She couldn't believe that this was all her doing, that everything had been fine until that day at Emer's house, the day after her birthday.

Who had she become? This wasn't like her.

Jess shook her head as if trying to throw off the fog that she'd been living under for the last few months. Why hadn't she seen it before? Did she really think that she was cut out for motherhood? What had she done?

She quickly went through her options, trying her utmost to stay calm and focused, as if this was just another project that had gone awry.

How could she fix this? How could she set things right with Brian and their marriage? How could she repair what she had done?

After all, she had a variety of mistakes to clean up and really, the question was what should she start fixing first, the current problems in her marriage or the ensuing problems with the whole 'baby situation'?

A million different thoughts raced through her mind all at once. Jess really didn't know what to do, but glancing down at her flat belly, she realized she would have no choice but to do something soon.

harlie and Ruth wandered aimlessly through the shops in Lakeview.

Over the last few weeks they'd really enjoyed easing back into their relationship, and taking the time to get used to one another all over again.

Her parents had been over the moon upon hearing of their rekindled romance. 'Oh, my goodness, it's almost like something from a movie!' her mother declared, and Ruth and Charlie exchanged an amused glance.

'If so, it's possibly my best role to date,' she joked, laughing happily.

'So does this mean Charlie's going back to LA with you?' she asked.

Ollie shook Charlie's hand. 'I hope you know what you're letting yourself in for, mate,' he said to him.

'Well, there's kind of something else to consider before we decide that ...' Ruth began, tentatively breaking the other piece of news.

Ollie stared at Charlie, faintly impressed. 'Boy, you're a fast mover,' he declared, and they looked so pleased that Ruth almost didn't want to ruin the jovial mood by telling them the truth. But she had no choice.

'That idiot?' her mother said, referring to Troy.

'I never knew you felt like that,' Ruth said, faintly shocked, 'but yes, now that you say it, he is an idiot.'

Charlie grinned and put an arm around her. 'He's even more of an idiot to let this one slip through his fingers,' he said gently, and by the beaming smiles coming from both parents, Ruth suspected that although they were taken aback by this unconventional arrangement, they weren't unduly concerned. Their only daughter had been surprising them for most of her life, so this was really nothing new.

However, up to this point, regardless of all the other plans they'd been making, very little had been said about her return to LA. She'd talked to Chloe and her agent in the meantime and had been purposely vague about what her plans were.

As much as she wanted to put down roots with Charlie, she knew she still had commitments in LA and would have to return soon, especially when the show started filming again in a few weeks time. It was now September, the plan had been to return to LA at the end of the month, and she hadn't yet made arrangements to do so, so she knew Erik would be getting antsy. There were already a couple of missed calls from Chloe on her mobile, and she'd been avoiding checking her emails on purpose, for fear that they'd start putting pressure on her to return.

Ruth was living in denial and she knew it. Here she was practically playing house with her old (and now new) boyfriend, almost four months pregnant and still undecided about her future. These days Lakeview was feeling very much like home, which for Ruth was a surprising feeling, and she was shocked and ultimately panicked by this notion, especially when she remembered the career she'd worked so hard for.

Today, she was doing a very good job of keeping those thoughts at bay, as that afternoon, she and Charlie wandered around town, picking up various bits and pieces in the shops. She had to admit; she was really looking forward to going shopping for cute little things for her baby, and knew she'd really enjoy dressing her son or daughter up when it was born.

They were leaving a shop hand in hand, chatting merrily and enjoying the day, when suddenly, out of nowhere, a flashbulb went off in Ruth's face. It hadn't happened in what felt like so long that she was stunned, almost forgetting that just a few short months ago she'd had photographers chasing her like she was Lindsay Lohan.

'Hey!' Charlie yelled, shielding Ruth from the photographer who was becoming increasingly aggressive. 'Back off!'

The photographer ignored him, instead, shouting in Ruth's face. 'Is it true you're knocked up?' he said, pointing a lens at her middle.

'No comment. Leave me alone,' Ruth snapped, shielding her face and throwing a protective hand over her bump. This guy clearly wasn't local, as no one from the *Lakeview News* would have the nerve, or indeed the lack of manners to speak to her like that.

'Whose kid is it? This guy's or Troy Valentine's?'

'Get away from her!' Charlie grabbed Ruth's hand and pulled her into a nearby restaurant, shutting the photographer out.

He ushered her inside and sat her down at a table, asking a waitress to please get her a glass of water. 'Are you ok, love?'

'Oh no.' She put her face in her hands. 'It's going to be all over the place now. Oh no. We have to leave, we have to get out of here!'

Charlie clasped both of her hands in his. 'We can go wherever you want. But do you really think they're going to swarm you again? It's been ages, maybe that's just a random guy.'

'Charlie – you don't understand, they're going to be all over this – especially if they think it's Troy's.'

He looked pained; obviously this was something he was foreign to. 'I'm sorry, I ... ah ... I'm not sure what I should do.'

'Well we need to get out of here anyway. Let's go to your house ... although no, I don't want them knowing where you live, if they haven't figured it out already ...'

In the end, they managed to arrange for a taxi to pick them up, and drive them to Ruth's house via one of the back routes, in the hope of avoiding being followed by the photographer.

She'd phoned her mum to give her an advance warning, and her parents, who'd had some experience of this type of thing over the years, knew exactly what to do. The sight of Ollie with his hunting gun at the end of the driveway was usually enough to put off even the most enthusiastic newshound.

When they got back to her place, Ruth paced the floors; she knew it was only a matter of time before someone started calling her to confirm the story, and asking for her comments.

She sighed, she supposed she'd been lucky that it had taken them this long to sniff it out. She wondered how that photographer had known, though? He obviously worked for one of the Dublin tabloids.

She tried to avoid thinking about it, but her thoughts kept coming back to Trish and her reaction to the news in the library that time. She really didn't want to think that way and truly hoped that her friend wouldn't have sold her out, not when she was just now realizing what she wanted out of life.

The rest of the day passed slowly as Ruth, Charlie and her parents sat on the sofa watching TV, while Ollie kept a close eye out for any unwanted visitors. Ruth was trying her best to relax, but she could almost feel the anxiety radiating through her body. She kept staring at the clock, trying to figure out what time it was in LA and realizing that every second that passed was one second closer to when the news broke out on some gossip blog like TMZ or Perez Hilton.

Finally, she could take the suspense no more. Getting up from the sofa, she went upstairs to the small room beside her bedroom that Ollie used as a study. Sitting down at the desk, she flipped open a laptop and powered it up.

Charlie appeared in the doorway. 'What are you doing?'

'Just checking something.'

'Checking what?'

Ruth's mouth set in a hard line. 'Something I haven't looked at in months.'

It was true, since she'd become more comfortable back in Ireland; she hadn't attempted to look at any of the celebrity gossip sites or blogs because somehow the distance made them less relevant.

Charlie was looking over her shoulder. 'I can't believe people read this stuff,' he said, his tone full of disdain.

'This is big business, darling.' She waited impatiently for the site to load, and at that moment her cell-phone rang. She fished it out of her pocket, feeling nervous as she recognized the ring-tone that belonged to Chloe.

Taking a deep breath as she looked at the display, she accepted the call. 'Hello?'

'For the love of all things holy, why didn't you tell me?'

Ruth's heart sank. So the news *had* broken then. 'I'm fine Chloe how are you?' Ruth said wryly. 'And because it is no one's business but my own, that's why.'

'Well, you could have mentioned something, so that when someone calls me at least I could be prepared, instead of letting them catch me off guard.'

'I'm sorry,' Ruth said glumly. 'Surprise!'

'So it is true then? Jeez, I can't believe it! What the hell are you still doing over there anyway? And whose baby is it? That new boyfriend of yours?'

Ruth knew just how easily she could say yes and get all of this off her back – the LA press wouldn't be interested in an unknown like Charlie, the story would soon fizzle out and she could have a normal life.

But there was only one problem – well two actually. Chloe was the one who'd bought her the morning after pill, and she'd already told Troy the baby was his. She couldn't bear getting into a case of he said/she said, not about the paternity of her child. That would only make the story hotter.

'His name is Charlie by the way; we used to date way back when I lived here.'

'How wonderful,' Chloe said dreamily, although Ruth couldn't be sure if this was said with a hint of sarcasm. 'But still, it is Troy's isn't it?'

'Yes,' Ruth said swallowing. 'He knows and he isn't interested, so –'

'Have you checked out TMZ? He sure as hell seems to be interested now!'

'What? What are you talking about?' Ruth turned back to the

computer where Charlie was sitting stonily reading the headlines. The breaking news TMZ feed was all about her. There in full glory for the whole world to see was the picture of her and Charlie on the main street of Lakeview, her hand placed protectively over her stomach. Then further down, a screenshot and video clip of Troy, confirming that yes, he and Ruth Seymour were having a baby together and he couldn't wait for her to come back to LA. The video couldn't have been more than a few hours old, as it was now morning in Hollywood and he looked as if he was leaving a nightclub. He was also very obviously drunk.

'Oh no,' Ruth cried. 'You've got to be kidding me.'

'Ruth, when are you coming back?' Chloe demanded.

'I ... I'm not sure yet, there are no immediate plans,' she said, slightly shell-shocked by what she was seeing. Charlie was patting her back reassuringly. 'I'm just...happy here.'

'Are you on medication or something?

'What?'

'Sorry, it's just you sound weird, you know? And you haven't been taking my calls – I hardly hear from you now.'

'You don't understand,' Ruth said, starting to babble. 'I'm not really sure about Hollywood anymore ... I'm not sure if I was happy.'

'What's not to be happy about? The press are loving this! Seriously, come back and have this baby with Troy – you guys can be the new Brad and Angie.'

Ruth couldn't believe what Chloe was saying, it all sounded so sleazy and jaded.

Did she truly expect her to go back to LA and have a baby with a man she didn't love and who'd already rejected this child ... all because it would be good PR? Had *she* really been that jaded? Ruth wondered now.

'Chloe, it's not that easy. I don't love Troy and I refuse to bring the baby into some kind of media circus.'

'You know, you're missing out on an incredible opportunity here,' Chloe scolded. 'The phone's been ringing off the hook all morning. I've had *Variety*, *Newsweek* and *People* ...'

'I don't care about the damn press, Chloe.'

'Well OK, fine, forget the press then, but what about the offers?'

'Offers …' Ruth's ears pricked up. 'What kind of offers – what are you talking about?'

A loud groan. 'Don't tell me you haven't been taking Erik's calls either.'

Well, yes she had missed a couple of calls from him in the last week or so, but she'd assumed he was just phoning to tell her to get her ass back to LA. She'd been putting off talking to him, Chloe or anyone else from her old life that might interrupt her current blissful existence. She knew she'd have to face them eventually, but for the time being was happy to put things on hold. Until today.

'Hell, it's been crazy … like I said, the press has been calling. Today mostly about the baby thing. But they've also been ringing about some offer, something about you being in line for something Peter Jackson's doing?'

Ruth felt faint. 'What …?'

'You don't know about this – seriously? Ruth, call Erik, would you? This is *freakin' huge*!'

42

'*W*hatcha' looking at?' Nina jumped and quickly closed the web page she'd been browsing on the computer while waiting for Trish to arrive at the library.

Her friend had phoned earlier wanting to apologize for her behavior the last time they'd seen one another. 'I'm so sorry for going off on you like that. You were right about Dave; and I know I shouldn't be messing around with a guy who has a family, but it sort of just happened.'

Nina, who, at any other time, would have questioned how such a thing could 'just happen' had come to realize that life wasn't always black and white. And she too had felt bad about lecturing Trish; it was none of her business and her friend was a big girl after all. Not to mention that this Dave seemed to be a bit of a player, given that despite having both a wife and mistress on the go, if she wasn't mistaken had been flirting with *her* not too long ago.

'Do you love him?' she asked.

Trish let out a little sigh. 'I think I do. It's been hard, and I didn't want to feel that way, because you know, I figured it was just a fling, and that it would end eventually, but yes, I actually do love him. That's why I reacted so badly when you told me about this new baby.'

'I'm sorry – it really wasn't my intention to hurt you. It's just when you said he'd told you the marriage was over –'

'I know, the old cliché, huh?' But there was no mistaking the hurt in her friend's tone. 'Anyway, you'll be pleased to know I've decided to end it.'

'Oh.' Nina was surprised. For some reason she'd just assumed that Trish might continue regardless.

Trish smiled as if reading her mind. 'I might have been taken in before, but I'm not completely stupid. Anyway, you were right – and it's not nice to be thought of as a home-wrecker.'

The air cleared, they'd arranged to meet up at the library for another round of research before later heading to Ella's for something to eat.

Now, Nina turned away from the screen to face Trish, who she hadn't noticed creeping up behind her. She tried to look nonchalant. 'Oh, nothing really, just trying to use an internet connection that has some speed. The one at my dad's place moves slower than a turtle.'

Trish smiled. 'I can imagine. So are you ready?'

'Sure,' Nina smiled, relieved that her friend didn't press further. The truth was, when Trish walked up, she had been on a crisis pregnancy page, researching some of her options.

When she thought seriously about what she was considering she felt guilty, but still she couldn't help it. With all that had happened over the last while, what with her father's reaction, her mother's absence and not to mention Steve, she was seriously confused over what to do about this baby.

Some of it went back to the conversation that she'd had recently with Ruth. A fellow mum-to-be, she'd found herself almost envious of the other girl who by contrast didn't have any worries when it came to her pregnancy. And why should she? She was confident and capable and would get on great with or without Charlie, Troy or whoever. Here she had loving supportive parents, and in LA a gaggle of assistants as well as plenty of money. In Ruth's world, there would be no shortage of anything for her baby, be it support, care or finance.

Nina on the other hand, had none of those things. As it was she could barely look after herself sometimes, and being completely responsible for another life scared the hell out of her.

Yes, her mother was wonderful and she was sure Cathy would help out as much as she could if it came to it, but hadn't she taken up enough of her mum's life already? Cathy had raised her practically single-handedly, and despite her protests that Patrick had let them want for nothing, she knew it had been for the most part a solitary feat.

So, just when she was really enjoying life with Tony and getting back her freedom, how could Nina seriously expect her to help raise her mistake?

No, the more she thought about it, the more Nina realized it was her burden to shoulder and she couldn't – shouldn't – put it on anybody else.

But what to do?

The idea of adoption had popped into her head a few times, but she wasn't sure what it entailed and how she would even go about it. After all, thanks to improved state support, few people in Ireland seemed to do that kind of thing anymore, but surely they could if they wanted to?

Then, after Trish's phone call and their subsequent arrangement to meet at the library, Nina decided to head down there early and do a little checking on the computer.

Although she was confused, she also knew she had limited time to figure out what to do about this.

But one thing was for sure; Nina knew she wasn't the right person to bring up this baby. And seeing as she'd got herself into this situation, she now had little choice but to find some way out of it – and soon.

43

'What's going on?' Charlie inquired after Ruth got off the phone with Chloe.

Her heart rate was going a mile a minute. 'I need to talk to my agent,' she said, her tone of voice suddenly business-like. She found Erik's number on her cell phone speed dial and put the phone to her ear.

He answered on the first ring.

'Ah, finally! It's the lady of the hour.'

'What's going on Erik?' Ruth said without preamble. 'I just talked to Chloe.'

'So is it true, are you knocked up?'

'So what if I am? What's up? ' At this point she didn't particularly care if she sounded rude; he was a Hollywood power suit and well able to take whatever she dished out.

'Well, it seems everyone loves a mommy-to-be these days,' Erik boomed in his usual loud-mouthed way. 'Please tell me this baby is Troy Valentine's though, and not some unknown Irish nobody's?'

Ruth was immediately on the defensive about Charlie being called an 'unknown Irish nobody' and when she turned to see if he had heard, she saw him staring at her opened-mouthed. Great. She thought about what he'd said that first day outside the café; how he'd wanted no part in this sort of nastiness.

'That's really none of your concern.'

'Oh, but you see babe, it is. Your stock is hot enough at the moment so we don't need you messing it up with something provincial.'

'My stock is hot ... how?'

'Well ... like I said on those thirty or so messages I left you, Peter Jackson has you in mind for the part of Clara in *The Soldier's Daughter*.'

'The S ... Soldier's Daughter?' Ruth felt the wind go out of her. *The Soldier's Daughter* was the movie adaptation of one of the best-selling books of the decade, and Clara was the female heroine who had captured hearts the world over. 'Oh ... my...'

'Exactly. Seems he's a fan of *Glamazons* and he thinks you'd be perfect for the role of leading lady. You've still got to do a screen test for it, for the studio of course, but I reckon it's a sure-fire thing. Jackson knows what he likes.'

The room was spinning. Sure-fire thing ... Peter Jackson ... leading lady ...

It was everything Ruth had ever dreamed of.

After all these years, all the struggling, finally Ruth Seymour was being offered the part of a lifetime.

'Course, the way he does things, it's probably got Oscar written all over it, too,' Erik was still talking. 'This whole baby thing shouldn't be a problem either – as long as you lose the pounds of course. Actually no, forget I said that, 'cause you won't be gaining any.' There was a smile in his voice, but Ruth knew he meant every word of it. She looked down at her bottom half, realizing she'd already gained quite a few pounds.

But she would watch her weight from now on, of course she would. After all, she'd have to get in shape for *The Soldier's Daughter*.

And oh my goodness, wasn't it just wonderful that the baby didn't seem to be affecting any of this? Granted, she'd have to reschedule some of the filming for *Glamazons* so it wouldn't clash with the feature film, but she knew Erik probably already had all of that under control.

It was incredible – all of a sudden it seemed like she really could have it all – the movie-star career and the baby! How lucky was she?

'I just can't believe this, Erik,' she cried, yelping enthusiastically. All those stupid ideas she'd been having about giving up on Hollywood to stay in Lakeview had suddenly vanished, and as she got more and more details from Erik, she noticed Charlie stand up and begin to pace the room. She looked away, trying to ignore him.

'Hey, I'm dead serious babe. They want you, so hurry up and get your ass back to LA. And what the hell have you been doing in some stupid Irish backwater all this time anyway? We could have had you rolling in it a long time ago if you'd told us about Valentine's baby. The press are going crazy over this – what the hell were you thinking leaving us out of the loop?'

She chose to ignore the faint warning signals at the mention of her pregnancy as a PR coup and immediately pushed them to the back of her mind. 'I'm sorry ... I should have taken your calls ... and yes, I'll be back as soon as I can ... thanks Erik – you're amazing!'

'Yep, that's what they all say,' he chuckled, before disconnecting.

Ruth hung up, completely elated and a million miles away from the state of mind she'd been in just moments before Chloe's phone call.

She threw the phone on the desk and looked at Charlie. 'Oh my goodness, you are not going to believe this!'

'Actually, I think I heard most of it,' he said flatly.

'I mean, can you imagine? Me, the leading lady in a major Hollywood feature? Maybe even in with the chance for an Oscar?' she felt slightly crazed; as all the glamour and promise of the Hollywood lifestyle came rushing right back to her. 'Oh this is just amazing.'

'Amazing ... yeah.'

'I just can't wait to get back there now. Shove all their stupid comments in their faces and let them know exactly who they're dealing with!'

'What are you talking about? Shove what in whose faces?'

'Well the media, of course. And all the other smug assholes who dismissed me as a talentless slut.'

Charlie stared at her, dumbfounded. 'I don't believe this. You're really going back there – for good?'

'Of course. How can I not? You heard what Erik said –'

'But what about us? What about making the right choices?'

'Charlie ...'

'No, answer me, what about us?'

She bit her lip. 'Honey, I know it might seem confusing, but I don't think you understand. This kind of thing doesn't happen that often, a call out of the blue with an offer of a lifetime. It's what I've been working for my entire life.'

'Oh, I understand all right. But you're the one who's confused. Don't you realize what they're doing? Where was their interest in you before they knew there was a story around you? Until you started sleeping with someone "interesting"?' His voice was a sneer, and Ruth looked away, not wanting to hear this now. It wasn't fair of him to make her sound like that; she was a good actress, a dedicated, hard-working actress, and this wasn't because of whom she was sleeping with.

Was it?

'See,' she cried, stung, 'this is exactly what I was afraid of last time – you, holding me back.'

'A couple of hours ago we were talking about how we should raise this baby!' he yelled.

She felt a pain in her heart. 'I know.'

'Are you really going to do this to me again?' The disappointment in his eyes was almost unbearable.

'Charlie ...' she moved to embrace him. 'I really don't know what to do. This is everything I've ever wanted.'

He looked down at her. '*This* is everything I've ever wanted.'

She felt as if he had plunged a knife directly into her heart. 'But ... you said you would have done all this with me before, gone with me to LA, if I'd asked.'

He shook his head. 'All I want is you and the baby – *our* baby.

Although,' he gave a short laugh, 'I know I have no claim on either one of you 'cause I'm just an unknown Irish nobody, yeah?' He pulled away from her. 'Ruth, I don't know if I can stand by and watch you trade on your pregnancy.'

'That's not what it's about, and of course that's not what I want.'

'I know it's not what you want, but the only person that needs to be convinced of that is you.'

In her mind, Ruth skimmed back through the last few months. She'd been the one who'd been hiding, so of course there would have been offers if she'd only gone back to LA soon after. Granted, the publicity from the thing with Troy might have helped bring her to a lot of important people's attention, but that was often the way Hollywood worked.

And Peter Jackson ... wow...

'Look, I really think that I should at least go back and talk to them, see what they have to say. It's not totally in the bag yet and I need to talk things over with Erik to see what's involved. I could go tomorrow and be back within days, it's no big deal.'

Charlie threw his hands up in the air. 'Come on, Ruth!'

'Just let me talk to them at least,' she pleaded. 'Nothing has changed between us, I promise and nothing will. But if I don't go, I'll wonder about this forever.'

He nodded, but his eyes were sad. Ruth's heart swelled. She loved Charlie, and up to recently had loved her career and wanted to prove to him that she could do both. *Or that she could* have *both*? The little voice inside her ventured.

Ruth ignored it. She was silly to even consider settling down in Lakeview and throwing away long, hard years of a career because of one stupid mistake.

A mistake that, with the way things were going, could well turn out to be the making of her.

44

*I*t was Friday afternoon and Jess sat in the living room of Emer's house, playing with Amy.

Her friend had invited her to stay over for the night, and Jess complied, happy to have something to do. While she wasn't yet sure if she was ready to confide in her friend about the problems she was having with Brian, she felt it was better than sitting around at home, staring at the walls of her bedroom. Her husband was again away at a work event and at this point Jess had started to wonder if he was volunteering for any trip that came up, so that he wouldn't have to spend time with her. It was a horrible thought, but she knew her husband well – or at least she thought she had, before all this baby stuff had started.

Emer was doing something in the kitchen, and for once Dave was home. According to her friend, he was supposed to have been working late, but had obviously finished whatever he was doing earlier than expected.

But almost as soon as Jess arrived at the house shortly after six, she started wishing she was somewhere else, because neither one of them seemed to be in the best mood.

Frankly, considering the circumstances, she didn't understand why Emer had invited her over today, especially since she was always complaining about how Dave was never home, so you'd think she would want to spend time alone with her family.

"Emer, are you sure there's nothing I can help with?" Jess called out to the kitchen.

"No everything is fine," Emer said, overly cheerfully, but Jess could hear sharp whispers coming from the kitchen, as if the couple were trying to have an argument but didn't want her to feel uncomfortable.

So much for that Jess thought, wondering if people really thought they were being quiet when they did that?

Then she heard the sound of a mobile phone ringing on the chair beside her and thinking it was Emer's, she picked it up and brought it through to the kitchen.

'Here you go,' she said absentmindedly handing it to Emer, 'someone called Trish?' She couldn't help but catch sight of the caller display on the way out, but by the look on her friend's face, immediately wished she hadn't said anything.

Emer grabbed the phone from her, all the while staring furiously at Dave, whose face had gone white.

'Why are you calling my husband?' Emer barked into the phone, and Jess winced, all at once realizing she'd done something she really shouldn't have.

'Give me that,' Dave said through clenched teeth, and Jess wanted the ground to open up and swallow her. *Oh no.*

'I'm asking you – why are you calling my husband?' Emer demanded. 'Oh, don't give me that claptrap, why would the *Lakeview News* be interested in the sales manager of a stupid brewery? You must think I came down in the last shower.'

'Emer, I swear ...' Dave reached again for the phone, but his wife sidestepped him, while Jess stood there watching, aghast. Then all of a sudden, Emer disconnected the call and flung the handset across the room.

'What the hell is going on here, Dave? Why is that silly cow phoning you on a Friday night? Is this the change of plan you were talking about earlier? Was it that *she* let you down, and wasn't able to meet you for one of your trysts?'

Emer was practically screaming now, and Jess was mortified. She'd heard the name before and tried to recall who Trish was – one of Nina's friends, wasn't it? Hell, was Dave sneaking around?

'Oh for goodness sake – you're completely overreacting, probably your hormones.'

'Don't you dare blame my hormones, I *know* something's going on. I called the office on Monday, and they told me there was no client dinner that night. You must think I'm an idiot, Dave – I *knew* you were with someone. And thanks to Jess, now I also know who with.'

There was a heavy tension-filled silence, and not sure what else to do – Jess backed out of the room silently and made her way back into the living room to check on Amy, who despite all the noise was now sleeping soundly in her playpen.

Jess couldn't believe it. Of all the stupid ... clueless things to do. She should have at least made sure it was actually Emer's phone before gullibly handing it to her. But then again, why should she assist Dave in his cover-up if in fact that was what it was?

Because that was certainly what it sounded like. She picked up her handbag and tiptoed out into the hallway, on the way to the front door.

She shouldn't be here for this; she'd already done enough damage as it was and she knew Emer would hate her later on for witnessing what was happening.

She opened the front door and began to make her escape, just as Dave started to bellow. 'OK, yes, I admit it! I have been seeing Trish, but what the hell do you care anyway? The only time you have any interest in me is when you want to get pregnant, and clearly you don't care what I do as long as I keep paying the bills!'

Oh no, poor Emer, Jess thought, shaking her head, and forgetting about being quiet, she scurried out the door, letting it close behind her.

Dave was having an affair. She couldn't believe it. Yes, it had been evident lately that there was some tension between the two of them, but ultimately, she never believed that it was anything more than money worries, or the adjustments involved with the new baby, and the move away from the city ...

She certainly hadn't anticipated anything like this. To think that Dave would be so heartless as to cheat on Emer when she was doing her best to bring up their child... Not to mention sleeping with her as well as his mistress.

Once again, the reality of the last few months came rushing back to Jess. All this time, she'd been operating under the illusion that her friends had the perfect lives, and ironically now it seemed like the more time she'd spent with them, wanting to be like them, she realized their lives weren't perfect at all.

She felt so sorry for Emer though – regardless of how full-on her friend had been about motherhood towards her, Jess's heart went out to her. No one deserved to be cheated on, betrayed on the grandest level. And to think that only a couple of weeks ago, she'd been so overjoyed about her new pregnancy.

In the same way that she herself had been about her big announcement, Jess realized worriedly.

Now, thinking of Brian's recent withdrawal, and Dave's obvious betrayal of Emer, she began to draw some very uncomfortable parallels.

All this time, she'd wanted to be like Emer, to share in her life and the choices she'd made.

Had she made an even bigger mistake than she'd thought?

45

The following morning, Nina was preparing to take the bus for another errand in Dublin.

Going downstairs, this time she couldn't avoid her father, as it was eight o'clock and he was in the kitchen making his usual eggs and bacon.

'Morning,' she greeted tentatively.

'Good morning, Nina,' he murmured in return.

She went to the cupboard to take out the toaster, in two minds whether to have breakfast here or just pick up something in town to eat on the bus on the way.

'Er ... I'm just putting on some toast, would you like some?'

Patrick looked at the clock. 'In a few minutes, when everything else is ready.'

Nina nodded impassively. Of course. 'Well, I'll just have a quick slice. I'm going to Dublin this morning.'

'Permanently?' he asked, and despite herself, Nina felt a twinge of hurt. Was he really that eager to be rid of her? She knew he didn't approve of what was going on, but did he have to make it that obvious?

'No, not permanently, just for the day.'

'Hmmph,' he grunted, his typical response.

'I promise you I'll be out of your hair when Mum gets back. Hopefully it'll be soon – last time I talked to her, she was in Russia, but I think she's in France now,' she said, in an attempt at friendly conversation.

But as usual this was wasted on Patrick.

'Hmmph.'

'Anyway, I'm going to Dublin, just for the day. Can I get you anything there?'

'From Dublin?'

No, from bleedin' Mars, Nina wanted to say, but there was no point. She'd been around long enough now not to let her father get to her, and today she had enough to worry about as it was.

Taking that as the end of the conversation, she ate her breakfast in silence, and soon after, left the house and headed to the bus stop.

The journey to the center of the city wasn't long; only about an hour, but to Nina it felt like ten.

She was jaded and exhausted from thinking of what her options were with regard to this baby. She knew she had few at this stage and the thought of being solely responsible for a little baby terrified her. She was sure she couldn't do it, but as she was getting so far along in her pregnancy she couldn't continue to sit on these feelings of indecision. She had to make a plan.

Which was why she'd made an appointment with a health board agency today, to see if this was perhaps something she could consider. She'd chosen this particular one because their offices opened on Saturdays until lunchtime, and when the bus stopped in the city center, she caught a cab in the direction of the agency which was on the south side. The driver regarded her skeptically when she gave him the name of the clinic and she met his knowing gaze with a defiant stare. Old goat, probably thinking she was some kind of shamed, pregnant disaster.

Well, Nina shrugged, thinking about that description – a single mother with no man, no real job and no permanent home – in a way she *was* a disaster.

Reaching the agency, she walked slowly up the steps, realizing the significance of what she was planning. It would be all too easy to just turn around and go back, and not to think about any of this. But instead, she took a deep breath and pushed open the door to be greeted by a pleasant waiting room decorated in neutral, calming colors.

'Hi,' she said as she approached the receptionist. 'Nina Hughes. I have an appointment at ten.'

'No problem. Maura will be with you soon if you would like to take a seat.'

Nina did as she was told, picking up a newspaper from a selection of papers and magazines on a nearby table. She idly flipped through the nearest one, not really concentrating on it, but hoping that she wouldn't have to wait too long and Maura would call her in soon. Then suddenly she paused, catching sight of a picture of Ruth.

She flipped back to the front of the newspaper to check the date, thinking that it must be a very recent one, as the photo was of Ruth with Charlie. He was standing on one side of her, and reaching out towards the lens of the camera, it looked like.

Ruth was carrying a shopping bag and holding it up halfway between her face and her stomach, as if she didn't know which one to shield.

Underneath, the caption read: 'Breaking News: Ruth Seymour Pregnant! Celeb-spawn of Troy Valentine?'

Oh no, Nina thought, just when everything was going so well for Ruth. It was such a shame as not too long ago she was talking about how everything had been so quiet for her lately, and how much she was enjoying the peace and quiet.

She must be really upset by this. Taking her mobile out of her bag, she dialed Ruth's number, hoping her friend was holding up OK. However, it went straight to voicemail.

She wondered how the photographer had known to find Ruth and Charlie, right there, outside that shop in Lakeview. It seemed so *convenient*, didn't it? Against her will, her thoughts drifted to Trish, and given her over-interested reaction to Ruth's news, she wondered if she had anything to do with this. Oh, no she wouldn't, would she?

Nina didn't want to think about it too much. While she was grateful for her friendship, particularly over the last few months, she suspected that they each had rather different ideas about what was acceptable. Nina prided herself on her ethics and carried with her a great sense of responsibility. Which was why Steve's behavior had hurt a million times more once she'd learned the truth about him.

'Nina?' She looked up as a woman standing beside a nearby door called her name. She looked to be in her sixties, had a kind face and was wearing a sharp looking suit.

'Yes, that's me.'

'I'm Maura Lowry. Come inside.'

Nina walked forward and shook the woman's outstretched hand. 'Nice to meet you. Thanks for meeting me on such short notice.'

'Not at all, we completely understand that we sometimes need to work on deadlines,' Maura smiled. She led Nina inside to her office and invited her to take a seat. 'So, I hear you're considering adoption?'

Nina filled Maura in on the details, making a vow to herself that she wouldn't cry in the process. She didn't want to look like a crazy, emotional pregnant woman who doubted every decision she made. Instead, she tried to come across as business-like as possible.

'Well, all of your reasoning is quite valid, I assure you,' Maura smiled. 'The majority of mothers who go down this route generally choose closed adoption.'

'Closed adoption?' Nina questioned. 'I'm not sure if I know what that is.'

'Well that's when the baby is given to the new parents right after it's born.'

'So I would never see him or her, I would never even lay eyes on it?'

Maura agreed, nodding. 'Exactly.'

'The baby would never know about me, never know I ever existed.' For some reason this bothered Nina more than she'd anticipated.

'Correct. Unless the new parents decide to tell their child about you one day.'

'Their child?' Nina repeated, feeling somewhat stung by the idea that her child, the one she was sharing food and life with right now, would never know her. She would never even lay eyes on her son or daughter and it would be hustled away as soon as it was born, off to its new life and new parents. She felt a sob forming in her chest and tried to keep it in.

'Yes around here we like to try to use such terminology to prepare both you, as the donor, and the new parents for the transition. After all, most parents start to think of the fetus as 'their child' as soon as they become pregnant and sometimes it is easiest for birth mothers to start thinking that way as soon as we have a donor available for them. It also helps them create some distance.' She smiled pleasantly.

Create some distance ... Nina thought, the words Maura was speaking echoing in her brain. She sighed unevenly. 'I don't know ... I'm not really sure if I can do this.'

'Nina, you are having a very normal reaction. But you did just state several good reasons for wanting to give this baby up for adoption. Wouldn't you feel better if the baby went to a family who had a mother and a father? Parents who would love and take good care of him or her?' Nina bit her lip. 'I suppose.'

'Dear, how far along are you?'

She shifted in her seat. 'Almost thirty-two weeks.'

'Now, the last thing we'd want is for you to feel any pressure, but the fact remains that we don't have that much time and this is something that needs serious consideration, for both yours and the child's sake.'

'I know.'

But all of a sudden, Nina stood up, realizing that coming here was a big mistake. She offered Maura her hand. 'Thanks so much for your time and the information. I have a lot to think about and I'll be in touch with you.'

'I really hope our conversation helped.'

'Yes, it did.' *But not in the way you think*, Nina added silently. Now that she'd ventured down this path, the thought of giving her baby away to strangers, and never being able to see it again just seemed too difficult to get her head around.

Thanking Maura again, she left the agency and made her way outside, her thoughts all over the place. She couldn't explain it, but as soon as Maura had started talking about her never being able to see the baby again, she couldn't bear hearing any more. She didn't know what the hell the alternative was going to be, but ...

The agency was located on a side street, so Nina had a way to walk to the main road, hoping to hail a cab back to the center of the city. Then she realized that she didn't really want to go straight back to Lakeview; what was she going to do, spend the rest of the day pondering over this?

She looked around, wondering if there was a café or something nearby – somewhere she could sit for a while and gather her thoughts. Although ideally it would be nice to talk to someone about this, someone with whom to thrash out what she'd learned from her visit to the agency, so that she might be able to see things more clearly and in a less emotional way. All of a sudden she thought of Jess, who lived around this area, didn't she? She fished in her handbag for her mobile, deciding that she would give Jess a call and ask if she might be free for a coffee this morning or maybe an early lunch?

Disappointingly, Jess's phone went straight to voicemail and Nina's heart sank. Oh well ... she trundled along the road, deciding to head for the nearest bus stop that would take her back into town. Maybe she could go shopping or something, not that she had much money for that ...

She was halfway down the street when she heard her mobile ring.

'Nina – hi.' Jess said. 'I saw your number come up – sorry I was at the gym and have just come out of the changing room. What's up?'

'Listen, I know you're probably busy, but it's just I'm in Dublin this morning and I wondered if you might like to meet for coffee or something? No problem if not –'

'You're in Dublin? Fantastic! Yes, that would be lovely. I'm just finishing up here so let me know where you are and I'll come and meet you.'

'That would be great. I'm around your neck of the woods actually – in Blackrock?'

'Really? What are you doing around these parts?'

'I was ... I just had a couple of errands to run,' Nina replied quickly.

'Well that's even better, as my gym is only a few minutes from there. Tell you what, why don't I meet you in the village – there's a nice café on the corner by the seafront – not as good as Ella's mind, but a great place for a catch-up.'

'Sounds lovely.' Nina was delighted Jess could meet her and felt immediately calmed by her kindness and enthusiasm.

'Perfect. Give me a couple of minutes to finish up here, and then I'll be with you in a jiffy, OK?'

Jess was as good as her word, and as it turned out, had reached the little café she'd mentioned even before Nina had made her own way there.

'So how are things?' Jess asked when they were settled over a couple of coffees. 'I haven't seen you since the party at my place; your bump is so much bigger now.'

'I know.' Nina automatically looked towards Jess's stomach, but of course it was way too early for her to be showing any signs. 'How are you feeling yourself? Any morning sickness? I'm pretty much over it now, but I had a terrible time at the beginning.'

Jess looked away. 'Nope, nothing at all. I guess I must be one of the lucky ones!'

'You sure must be. And speaking of lucky, how's Brian? I really liked him you know, he was so lovely to me at the party.'

'He's fine.' Her tone changed unmistakably at the mention of her husband and Nina's radar went up. 'So were you able to finish your errands?' Jess went on, smoothly changing the subject.

Nina nodded and now it was her turn to feel uncomfortable about the topic of conversation. 'Pretty much.'

'So did you have a doctor's appointment or something?'

'Um no ... I was just ... shopping actually.'

'Really?' Jess said and Nina realized the stupidity of this excuse, in that of course Jess would have noticed that she wasn't carrying any shopping bags.

Both women were silent for a moment, until finally Nina sighed. 'Actually I wasn't shopping.'

'I kind of figured that,' Jess said with a grin. 'But look, don't mind me, I was only making conversation, not trying to pry into your business or anything.'

'No, it's fine, actually, it's sort of the reason I phoned you. I wouldn't mind talking to somebody about this. I did have an appointment, but not with a doctor.'

'OK.'

Nina sighed again. 'You're going to think I'm a horrible person, but honestly, I don't think I was thinking straight.'

'I doubt that,' Jess snorted. 'Goodness knows we've all done regrettable things on the spur of the moment,' she added cryptically.

As she began outlining her experience at the agency, Nina relaxed a little, relieved to have someone to open up to about this. Maybe that was partly the problem; she had been shouldering so much lately, stress over the situation with Steve, guilt in keeping secrets from her mother, and then what to do about it all – that some kind of mental distance might be exactly what she needed.

She recalled how relieved she'd felt after confiding to Jess her doubts about the pregnancy a while back. She was such a good listener and completely non-judgmental and from the sound of it, seemed to be having some personal problems of her own.

Jess looked thoughtful. 'So what's bothering you the most is that if you give the baby up, you're worried that you'll never see it again – never be part of its life?' she asked, when Nina had finished telling all.

She nodded. 'That's it in a nutshell.'

Jess took a deep breath. 'Well, I think I might just be the person to talk to about that, but before we go any further ...' She looked at Nina, her expression solemn, 'I have a little something of my own to confide ...'

46

*W*hen Ruth touched down at LAX she was mentally spent. She had been juggling too many thoughts for too many hours and was eager to get off the flight so she could focus on something else.

While she was of course eager to get back to LA and find out from Erik and the producers about all the wonderful things in store, there was also something eating at her, an internal voice nagging that perhaps she was making the wrong choice again.

Determined to silence that voice, she focused on other things. Namely that she wouldn't make the same mistake as last time when arriving at Dublin airport. This time she had brought all the essentials – plenty of makeup and a change of clothes, and most importantly she hadn't touched a drop of alcohol in ages so there would be no hangover. No, this time she would look perfectly fabulous when she got off the flight.

Feeling a stirring in her stomach, she put her hands on her bump. Imagine, she thought, no doubt her son or daughter would someday see the pictures of this very moment, Mom strolling triumphantly out of the airport on her way to meet her agent to talk about a career-changing movie role. She smiled and patted her belly, feeling more movement from inside.

'Ouch,' she said out loud, attracting looks from other passengers. 'Oops, I don't think Junior likes flying,' she laughed.

Her thoughts immediately went to Charlie. He would have loved to hear about what just happened; what she'd just felt and she wished again that she'd managed to persuade him to come with her.

'Ruth I have the dealership to run. I can't just hop on a plane and fly half-way across the world whenever it suits me,' he'd insisted.

But even if he had been able to, Ruth suspected he wouldn't have come. While he'd (reluctantly) gone along with her decision to fly back and see what was on the table, he would have been just as happy if she'd ignored the offer and given up Hollywood altogether. But Charlie hadn't fought as hard as Ruth had; in fact Charlie didn't really understand having to fight for anything. He'd walked into a ready-made family business and had nothing to prove to himself or anyone else.

Whereas Ruth felt she still did.

She got off the plane and having collected her baggage, went through to the arrivals area. Almost as soon as she appeared through the doors, Chloe rushed forward to greet her.

'Oh my goodness, you're *huge*!'

Ruth grimaced, that was the last thing she needed to hear. 'Thanks, that's awfully nice of you.'

'No, no, I mean it's adorable! It's not like you have double chins or anything like some actresses when they're knocked up. That's not what I meant.' Ruth thought she spotted her assistant give a brief eye roll before she looked away. It was strange because Chloe was always so enthusiastic and complimentary towards her. Or Ruth wondered, had she just wanted to see it like that?

'Anyway, there are loads of press outside waiting for you and ... well, there's another surprise too.'

'Oh. What kind of surprise?' Ruth couldn't help but picture Peter Jackson waiting for her with a glass of champagne, ready to whisk her away in his limo.

'Well, he mentioned it to Erik, and he thought it would be great for publicity, so we arranged to have Troy here for your reunion.' She grinned as if this was the best idea ever.

Ruth blanched. 'What? Oh no!'

'But I thought you would like that?' Chloe pouted as they walked outside into the LA sunshine.

'No, I want absolutely nothing to do with Troy, and I certainly don't want to be photographed with him.'

'Uh, I think it might be kinda too late for that ...'

Before Ruth could react, Troy stepped forward and caught her in his arms, completely blindsiding her. He must have been aiming for a dramatic, passionate reunion, purely for the benefit of the swarms of photographers flashing away right behind him. Ruth went to push him away and he moved expertly out of their embrace and ran his hand over her stomach, before finally kneeling down to kiss it.

What the heck ...? Ruth was still too shocked to say or do anything, before Troy suddenly jumped up and grabbed her face, kissing her passionately. The photographers ate it up and then in a final flourish, he flung Ruth backwards, holding her in his arms and halfway to the floor, like some scene he'd stolen from a movie. Come to think of it, the idiot probably had.

Finally Ruth went from shocked to helpless to completely outraged. She pried her mouth away from his and brought her hands to his chest, pressing away from him. 'What the hell do you think you're doing?' she hissed and he looked at her, surprised.

'I'm welcoming home the mother of my child of course. Babe, what's up? I thought you'd be happy to see me.'

Finally managing to get some distance from him, Ruth straightened her clothes. 'Chloe, get me the hell out of here now. NOW.' Her assistant duly started pushing their way through the photographers and Ruth hoped Troy would be swallowed up in the throng. But no, apparently he was determined to play a role, and he took Ruth's arm gallantly leading her through. He then put the other arm across her stomach, as if now protecting her from the greedy lenses of the paparazzi.

No doubt it made a good picture and Ruth knew that was all he was after – press. Charlie's words echoed in her brain. '*Would they still want you if you didn't have a story?*' And she knew that the man who'd rejected her so completely only wanted her now because her star was on the rise, and by association his would go even higher.

As Chloe and Troy rushed her into a waiting car, Ruth started to realize that Charlie was right and this whole thing could very well be a runaway train. When the doors closed and the limo pulled away from the curb, she rounded on Troy.

'What the hell are you doing here?'

'What babe? Come on – that was great! You know you loved it. We're going to be on the cover of every magazine in the world! Our kid is already famous and it's not even done cooking.'

'How dare you! How dare you!' Ruth raged. '*My* baby is not a marketing opportunity for you. You wanted nothing to do with me a few months ago and yet now because you've suddenly clicked it'll help raise your profile even higher, you're all over me!' Ruth huffed and puffed, furious about what had just happened.

'Like you aren't loving this,' Troy sneered. 'You're just like me, you want your name in lights too – fame, money, the whole lot – I know you do. Don't act like the Virgin Mary now babe, cause I know better. If I remember correctly, the very night we made the kid I had you howling at the top of your lungs. "We're celebrities! We can do whatever the hell we want!"' he mimicked with a wolf-like grin, and Ruth cringed. 'You may not remember that sweetheart, but I sure do.'

Through new eyes, she studied the people she was traveling with – her co-star, minders and so-called 'protectors'. Chloe was sitting directly across from her and possibly for the first time ever, Ruth took a closer look at her appearance.

She was bleached blonde and her skin was tanned to the point of resembling shoe leather. Her breasts were surgically enhanced, larger than they should be on such a tiny frame, and her gaze kept flipping from her BlackBerry to the scene that was taking place between Troy and Ruth. Ruth thought morosely that she was probably recording all of it and would sell it to TMZ at the first opportunity.

Troy was sitting next to her, looking unaccountably smug. She studied the face she used to think was so handsome, but could now see just how tired he looked, how worn and jaded. How many women had he been with, she wondered? And how many had he used, or indeed impregnated? Was she the first one that he'd decided to use as a merchandising opportunity?

He kept rubbing his nose, which looked red and irritated. He'd probably been doing cocaine last night; or maybe even on the way to the airport, Ruth thought disgustedly.

Looking away, she stared out the blackened windows of the limo as they made their way to the studio offices in Santa Monica. The city which had always looked so vibrant and glossy to Ruth, today looked smog-filled and grim. And instead of focusing on the thirty-foot-high movie posters hanging on the buildings, her gaze shifted to the wandering beggars on the streets beneath; some of them even younger than she was. Just like her, they had come to Hollywood searching for the dream, but eventually found out that they were as disposable as the coffee cups they picked up off the ground.

She looked away, wondering if returning to LA after all that time spent in Lakeview was forcing her into some kind of epiphany. But no, she wasn't like those dreamers – never had been – she had a successful TV career and was here today to talk about an incredible movie offer. She would never have to pick empty cans and coffee cups off the street – she, Ruth Seymour, had made it.

In Santa Monica, the limo eventually came to a stop outside the studio entrance and Ruth and her entourage stepped outside.

'Where do you think you're going?' she asked Troy, who was making no move to leave.

'Erik is my agent too, babe. In fact, if I remember correctly, didn't I give you the recommendation?'

'So? I'm here for a private meeting with the studio people and you're not part of it.'

'But Ruth, you and me – we're a team!'

'The hell we are,' Ruth said, turning her back on him. As she headed into the building she thought she heard Chloe mutter some-thing about waiting in the car. 'What is it with him?' she commented to her assistant on the elevator up. 'Ugh, talk about a leech.'

The other girl shrugged. 'Well, you are shit-hot right now. Like I said, people haven't stopped calling since the whole *Soldier's Daughter* thing broke.'

Ruth smiled, feeling undeniably smug that an A-lister like Troy Valentine was now trying to get kudos from *her*. My, how the tables had turned!

She checked her appearance in the mirror, making sure that she looked every inch the leading lady. Her hair was held back by her D&G sunglasses and the silk Matthew Williamson maxi-dress she'd changed into upon arrival looked suitably glamorous, but more importantly she thought somewhat guiltily, was especially effective in hiding her bump.

'Ruth ... darling!' Erik was all smiles and hugs when she entered the boardroom. The studio suits hadn't yet arrived; typically, they were taking the power-play to the max by making everyone wait. Ruth didn't care; if anything she welcomed the opportunity to talk to her agent beforehand.

'So what's on the table?' she asked, having banished Chloe outside to the waiting area.

Erik's beady eyes shone. 'I won't kid you sweetheart – it's big, real big.'

'How big?' Ruth's heart pounded. 'And do I have the part or what? You said something about a screen-test?'

'Personally, I think it's just a play by the studio guys. I know for sure Jackson wants you, and a guy like him always gets exactly what he wants.'

She wanted to hug herself. 'When's filming? And what about *Glamazons*? Won't this interfere with scheduling?'

'I already spoke to them, and they can work around it. One of their stars in a movie this big is only going to help the show's profile.'

It was really all happening! Ruth couldn't believe that the movers and shakers of Hollywood were rescheduling around her. She wished Charlie were here so he could see what she meant. This *was* a big deal, and by the numbers Erik was throwing out, in more ways than one.

Erik was staring at her stomach. 'So sweets, what's the deal with this kid? Jackson wants you in December, so I guess it'll need to come out soon, so you'll have enough time to bounce back.'

Ruth looked at him. 'Sorry ...what?'

'You know, get it ... born or whatever, I don't know.'

'Erik the baby isn't due until January,' she chuckled. 'This isn't like TV; you can't do these things on cue.'

Erik was dismissive. 'Of course you can.' He made a slicing motion across his own stomach. 'The hospitals do it all the time.'

Ruth stared at him. Was he seriously expecting her to intentionally deliver a premature baby by C-section? 'Are you crazy? That's way too early; there could be all sorts of problems...'

'Nothing compared to the problems we have if the shoot's delayed.'

'Erik, please tell me you are not serious. Surely Peter Jackson wouldn't expect me to –'

'The studio sets the terms sweetheart. As far as I know Jackson doesn't know jack-shit about you being knocked up. And I don't think he cares either. Hell – who does? The important thing is we get it born and then we get you down on set – to some outback Australian hell-hole, I heard.'

'Hold on – and I'm supposed to bring my premature baby down there too?'

Erik looked at her. 'Are you crazy? They have people for that sort of thing. Nah, you just do the *Vanity Fair* shoot with Troy and then get your ass down –'

'What? What *Vanity Fair* shoot?'

Erik grinned. 'The one I nailed just yesterday – one *million* dollars for first world pictures. Honey you have no idea how hot this kid is – the whole world wants to see Troy Valentine's ...'

Ruth stood up, red-faced. 'You arranged a photo shoot for pictures of *my* child, a child that you expect me to put in danger by delivering prematurely to meet a ... goddamn *scheduling* commitment? And if that wasn't bad enough, *then* you want me to leave it in the care of complete strangers?'

Erik looked at her as if she was crazy. 'Of course.'

Ruth's brain pounded. She just couldn't believe this, and instead of wishing that Charlie could hear this, she was delighted he was thousands of miles away. This was disgusting, depraved, immoral ...

And suddenly Ruth realized that to get what she wanted – what she'd always dreamed of – this was the deal she needed to do with the devil.

Well to hell with that ...

These people ... Erik, the studio, Troy, Chloe ... the whole lot of them were corrupt and nasty – this *life* was corrupt and nasty. And while she'd always known that life at the top was supposed to be tough, there was always just enough gloss, just enough glamour to hide the truth and keep idiots like her striving to get there. These people weren't her friends and they didn't care about her.

Ruth felt sick. And clearly they didn't care about her baby.

Despite her realization of the sickening truth, suddenly Ruth felt a surge of relief.

These last few months she'd been lucky enough to discover what was real, and who *did* care about her and her baby. Her parents, whom she'd shut out of her life for far too long, her friends like Nina and Trish and her trustworthy GP, Jim Kelly, back in Lakeview.

And Charlie. Always Charlie. There really had never been anyone to take his place, and why it took her so long to realize that she didn't know.

But what she did know was that she couldn't spend another minute away from him. She didn't want to separate her child from the man that would love the two of them for the rest of their lives.

Ruth smiled. If Peter Jackson wanted her that badly, then he and his crew would just have to talk to her from Lakeview.

Without another word to Erik she stood up and headed for the door.

'Hey, where are you going? Now's not the time to go powdering your nose – the suits will be here soon and –'

'I don't care.'

He looked at her, incredulous. 'What do you mean you don't care?'

'I'm leaving,' she said, going outside and coming face to face with Chloe.

'Um, you just got here?' her assistant said, smacking her gum. 'You have a meeting, like … right now.'

'No I don't. Tell them I had to cancel.'

Her assistant eyeballed her, as if she was some kind of crazy woman. 'Like … why?'

'Because I'm getting the hell out of here, getting a flight back to Dublin.'

'The hell you're not …'

Her gaze shifted to Erik, who had followed her out to the hallway. 'Actually Erik, I am.'

Chloe and the agent locked eyes and an understanding seemed to pass between them.

'OK then, I'll get the car brought round,' Chloe said sweetly, as if addressing a small child, and she nodded at Erik before the elevator doors closed.

Inside, Ruth took a deep breath. 'Thanks Chloe, I owe you one.'

'No problem,' she replied, distractedly keying something into her BlackBerry.

Outside, the car was waiting, and Ruth quickly got inside, relieved to be out of there.

Then she saw none other than Troy sitting opposite her. He was drinking bourbon from the limo's bar.

'Not you again,' she groaned. 'Well, get out – you'll need to hitch a ride from someone else.'

'Why?' There was a smile in his voice.

Ruth purposely ignored him. 'Driver, take me back to LAX please. Troy, out of the car – now.'

'I'm not going anywhere sweetheart and neither are you. That's my child and you're staying here.'

Chloe spoke firmly. 'Driver, do *not* drive to LAX. Ms Seymour is confused.'

She glanced sharply at her assistant who averted her gaze. 'I don't believe this! Are you two trying to *trap* me? You treacherous little ...' In the rear-view mirror, Ruth met the driver's hesitant gaze. 'Please sir, if you can help get me out of this hell-hole, you'll be doing me the biggest favor of my life.'

'Like I said, you're not going anywhere,' Troy repeated, before the car started up and quickly pulled off.

'What the ...?' Chloe cried, trying to twist around her twig-like neck. "Where the hell are you going?'

'LAX like the lady asked.'

'You goddamn idiot – you stop this car right now or you're fired, you hear me!'

'I'll give you a thousand dollars ...' Ruth pleaded and the driver gave her a small nod.

'This is kidnapping!' Troy piped up. 'If you think you can take away my child...'

Ruth had a sudden thought. If this ... ass thought he could get away with playing the loving daddy with her baby he had another think coming. 'It's not your child,' she said blithely, waiting for his reaction.

Troy leered at her. 'Come on, you're peeing up a rope if you think I'm going to believe that. You *called* me, after you took the test and told me it was *mine*, remember?'

'I was wrong.'

'Yeah? So whose is it then?'

Ruth smiled, 'Just some Irish nobody's,' she said, recalling Erik's words and Troy frowned, thinking hard. 'After all *babe*,' she continued, 'when I called you, didn't you yourself accuse me of being a whore? Oh, and I also remember you saying something else – like how you wanted nothing to do with it?' She eyed him steadily. 'Back then while you were urging me to get rid of it, it didn't seem like you had any interest in being a father, so why the sudden change of heart?'

He shrugged. 'So what? It's your word against mine, and if you try and pretend the kid's someone else's, I'll just demand a paternity test.'

Ruth flicked an imaginary piece of lint off her dress. 'Well I guess you *could* go down that route, but then *somehow* the press might get their hands on the transcript of our conversation that day, mightn't they?'

'What transcript?' Then his face changed. 'Oh man. You *recorded* us?'

'Of course.' Ruth tried to keep a straight face, knowing she had played an ace. That would be the last thing Troy wanted; it would be bad for his doting daddy act if there were proof of him implying she was a whore and saying he didn't want anything to do with it. Of course, there was no such recording, but Troy didn't have to know that.

Anyway the lie was all too easy to believe; they all knew the way this town worked, and this was just the sort of thing a lesser person would do.

He glared at her, but remained silent. 'I thought so,' Ruth smirked. 'Like I said, we're going to the airport.'

It didn't take long for them to get back to LAX, but for Ruth it felt like the longest journey of her life.

'Please, don't do this,' Chloe pleaded, and Ruth knew that such pleas weren't out of love for her; but more about her pay check and the removal of her Hollywood meal-ticket. Being assistant to a potentially Oscar-nominated actress was about as good as it got in PA-world. Still, Ruth recalled how, whatever her intentions, Chloe had often been there for her when she needed her over the years.

'I'm sorry Chloe, but I've made up my mind. It's over; I'm done with all of this.'

'You are making such a huge mistake,' Troy hissed, looking at her with pure venom when the car pulled up outside the departures area.

The driver got out and came round to open her door. 'Actually, for once in my life, I know without a doubt that I am *not* making a mistake.' Getting out of the car, Ruth smiled and shook her head. Then, taking huge satisfaction from slamming the door in Troy Valentine's face, she looked at the driver who was wearing a half smile.

She opened her bag and reached inside, privately hoping that he wouldn't mind taking a check, but the man stopped her.

'Please, there's no need.'

'But you might be fired –'

He grinned. 'Ma'am, if I had a dollar for every time somebody in this town threatened to fire me, I wouldn't need a job at all. I'm not worried.'

'Well as long as you're sure –'

'I'm sure.' He handed Ruth her bags. 'Now you take care of yourself – and good luck to you and that little kid of yours.'

'Thank you. Good luck to you too,' she replied, meaning it.

Entering the airport building, she marched straight to the ticket counter, a spring in her step. 'Could I get a ticket for the next flight to JFK please?'

The wide-eyed clerk put a hand to her mouth. 'Oh my gosh, Ruth Seymour! I just *love* you in *Glamazons*, you're the whole reason I watch that show!'

Ruth smiled. 'Thanks honey, but I guess you'll just have to watch me in syndication.' When the girl frowned, she explained further, a smile in her voice. 'From now on, I'm going off the air.'

47

After a cozy lunch in Blackrock, during which time Jess heard all about Nina's 'errand' that morning, she dropped her friend into the center of the city.

She felt a great camaraderie with Nina – much more than she'd felt with her own friends recently, and was especially glad that she'd decided to take her into her confidence. She got the sense that with her mother abroad, Nina didn't have all that many people to talk to about this – and from what she'd heard about her father, he seemed the kind of old-fashioned country type that wouldn't give her much support. No wonder the poor thing was considering adoption.

Well hopefully Jess had given her something to think about.

As Nina had pointed out, her and Brian's circumstances were completely different; they had security, a (mostly) solid marriage and were mature enough to deal with whatever parenthood might throw at them, whereas she was faced with being a single mother of a child who would most likely never even know its father.

They'd had a very enlightening conversation, and as Nina outlined the extent of her problems and her confusion over what was to come, Jess hoped that their chat would help her see things more clearly – might even offer her a solution.

But now she needed to talk to Brian, *really* talk to him. The news of Dave's affair had shocked her, and if such a thing could happen to their friends, then it could very well happen to them too. Jess figured that the time had come for them to be frank and completely open with one another about what was going on.

She'd spoken to Emer on the phone that morning; her poor friend understandably distraught about the situation and Jess, in return distraught that her actions had brought it to a head.

'I had my suspicions, though,' Emer had sniffed. 'Things have been tough this last year, with the new baby and all, but I can't believe he would do something like this.'

'But are you absolutely sure he has done something?' Jess asked, wanting to play devil's advocate. 'It could very well have been an innocent phone call.'

But apparently in the end, Dave had admitted everything. 'He said I was too wrapped up in Amy to even notice. He said he feels like I don't need him anymore, that I don't even notice him most of the time, and it's like he's just there to put food on the table and money in the bank.'

'That's no excuse Emer, and don't even *think* about blaming yourself for this.'

But Jess realized that Dave's words were dangerously close to the ones Brian had used in a recent conversation. 'Jess what do you want from me?'

She realized now that she couldn't fall into the same trap Emer had, of making babies and motherhood her first priority, and sidelining her marriage in the process.

She knew that work-wise things had since calmed down a bit for Brian; he'd sorted out the problems with the errant clients and seemed, while not exactly in good form, at least more positive about where the business was headed. She bit her lip. She just wished he could be as positive about where they were headed. Well, she'd work on that when he came home tonight.

Now that Jess had stopped feeling guilty about the repercussions of what she'd done, she was certain she could bring Brian around to her way of thinking.

48

*B*rian was already at home when Jess returned. After dropping Nina off in town, she'd had a couple of errands of her own to run and it was late in the afternoon by the time she got back to the house.

'Well this is a surprise,' she said cheerily, coming into the kitchen where he looked to be preparing dinner. 'I thought your flight wasn't in until six.'

He looked at her, his face impassive. 'I decided to get an earlier one.'

She reached forward and put her arms around him, but he returned her hug with none of his usual enthusiasm, handling her as if she were something fragile. He was being so careful around her these days, which she'd interpreted as distant, but wasn't it just as possible that he was worried about her health? It was only natural that he'd be concerned about the physical side of things, given her own worries about her age.

So perhaps she'd been fretting for nothing?

'Well, you deserve it!' she said, determined to be upbeat. 'You've been working so hard lately. And there was no need to make dinner, I could have done it.'

'No problem.' He shrugged and went back to the hob, where he looked to be making pasta. 'We're almost good to go here – do you want to get the cutlery organized?'

'Of course.' Jess moved to the drawer, pleased that he seemed to be on the same wavelength as she was. Clearly Brian too had got tired of their tiptoeing around one another for the last few weeks. He was home early, being convivial if not exactly friendly *and* he was making dinner.

'Should I open a bottle of wine too?' she said, going to the fridge. 'I know it's early, but what the hell, it's the weekend and I think we both deserve it.'

He paused and looked at her with furrowed brows and too late Jess realized what he was thinking.

'Oh I'm sure one glass won't be a problem,' she said quickly, cursing herself. 'I know Deirdre used to have one now and again with the boys.'

'Right.' Again his expression was unreadable. 'Whatever you think is best.'

Worried about what he might think of her slugging back wine, she decided to backtrack. 'Actually you're right. If you fancy one go ahead and I'll just stick with fruit juice.'

Brian dished up the food and they sat across from one another at the table; Jess chatting away about the latest at work, and about bumping into Nina. She didn't say anything about Dave, having promised Emer she wouldn't, but there was a side of her that wondered if Brian already knew.

'Oh, how is Nina?'

'Great, she was in Dublin for the day so we went for lunch.'

'That's nice,' Brian said, idly stirring through his pasta.

'Yes, she had some errands to run, things she couldn't do in Lakeview.'

'I'd imagine you can't do too much in Lakeview actually,' he commented.

Jess tried to continue steering the conversation in the direction she wanted it to go; namely about their own situation. 'Yes, there are limited options there, I suppose. That's why she was here, with the baby coming and all.'

'Oh, is she thinking of moving closer to the city or something?' he asked. He still seemed distracted, Jess noted, but at least the discussion was moving along the right track.

'Possibly.' Jess didn't want to break Nina's confidence about the adoption idea so she came at it from another direction. 'I feel so sorry for her actually, having to bring up a baby on her own – you know how I told you about her breaking up with the father and all that?'

He gave a vague nod.

'We're so lucky by comparison. I mean, we won't have to face any of those problems. We're very comfortable money-wise and have plenty of room here and –'

'Jess,' he said, sighing softly. 'We've known each other for a long time now haven't we?'

She stared at him, confused. 'What?'

'You and me – we've known each other for a long time and I'd like to think we know each other inside out too.'

She liked the gentle and faintly teasing way he said that; it was the kind of way the old Brian used to talk. 'Yes of course we do.'

'And you know that I've always loved your drive and determination – it's what makes you so successful in everything you do.'

'OK.' She seriously wondered where this was going.

'You've also always had an amazing imagination, again which I love. But you also have this crazy side that gets you into some incredible fixes.' He smiled. 'Remember that time you tried to get out of spending time with that couple we met in Thailand by telling them we were going to the zoo?'

She grinned. 'Yes.'

'And the time you pretended to those politicians who called here that you were French and couldn't speak English?'

'Of course,' Jess laughed.

'So we both know that that imagination of yours can sometimes run away with itself,' he went on and Jess looked at him, mystified.

'And like I said we know each other well and have always been one hundred percent honest with one another, haven't we?'

'Well, yes of course.' What on earth was he getting at with all this?

'So can't you just tell me the truth?' he said gently.

'About what?'

'About this ... the whole baby thing.' Brian put down his knife and fork. 'I know what's going on.'

'What do you mean "you know what's going on?"' she repeated, her heart thumping.

He sighed, as if disappointed. 'I know what you're doing, and why you did what you did that day at the party. I really don't know where you think this is going to end, but don't you think it's about time you came clean with me?'

'I ... I really don't know what you mean.'

'Jess, I know that you told everyone we were trying to get pregnant,' he said then and her heart almost stopped. *Oh no.* 'Kevin was joking one day about how me and Dave must have been in competition to strike first or something,' he wrinkled his nose in distaste. 'At first, I didn't have a clue what he was on about, but soon enough, the penny dropped.'

'Well I didn't actually say that, Brian, they just assumed –'

'Did they also just assume that you'd stopped taking the pill without telling me?' he said and her face flushed. 'Because it's all a little coincidental, don't you think? Jess, honestly –' Now he sounded not only frustrated, but disappointed, and Jess hung her head.

'I'm sorry, but I had no choice,' she interjected. 'You wouldn't talk to me about it and I knew it could take ages for my body to get back to normal, and in the meantime time was moving on so –'

'OK fine. I'm not happy about being lied to, because as far as I was concerned we didn't do that to one another. But what about the rest?'

She looked up. 'The rest?'

'What exactly is my role here, Jess? Am I just supposed to play sidekick to you and all of your crazy notions?'

Crazy notions ... was he talking about the baby? 'Of course not – it's something we'll be doing together and –'

'Jess, I'm going to ask you one more time. Tell me the truth.'

She felt tears in her eyes. 'But I really don't know what you mean.'

Brian stood up and now she saw a combination of hurt and anger in his eyes. 'Wow, you've really lost it, haven't you? This whole thing has driven you crazy. I must admit I never expected it, least of all from you.'

'Expected what?'

'This! All these lies and so much subterfuge. What the hell has happened to you Jess? Where is my lovely, fun-loving, *sane* wife?' He pushed his chair away from the table. 'I came back early today in the hope that we could have a nice dinner and a good long chat and that maybe, just maybe, you would open up to me, confess to me how silly you've been and that it had all gone too far. But you're determined to push ahead with this, aren't you? What's going to happen in a few months time, Jess? When this ... baby is supposed to arrive?'

The disdain in his tone was almost too much to bear. 'I ... I don't know ...'

Jess wasn't sure what to say, she was so terrified. He was going to leave her, wasn't he? He was going to give up on their marriage like Dave had given up on Emer.

It was too late, and despite her hopes of making things better, instead she'd blown it.

She should have told him the truth, should have confessed about giving up the pill, but he'd been so weird since the announcement she didn't want to run the risk of letting him know she'd deceived him. But now it seemed he'd given her an opportunity to tell the truth and she'd blown it.

Brian's eyes were sad. 'I don't know what to do with you anymore, Jess, really I don't. I feel completely irrelevant.'

'But you're not. Of course you're not. We're both in this together and I want us to be happy. I thought ... I thought this would make us happy.'

'Jess, we were happy before. And did it ever occur to you that I would have been fine with children if you hadn't jumped the gun and made the choice for us? I thought we were an equal partnership.'

Recalling how close they'd always been, Jess couldn't blame him for being upset about how she had gone about it. But at the time she just couldn't see any other way.

'I don't even know why I come home anymore,' he said wearily.

'What?'

'You heard me. I don't even know what I am doing here. I'm a fixture.'

'No,' she said, terrified now. 'I need you. I love you.'

'I think you've made it perfectly clear that you need your mummy friends a lot more than you need me. And that's why we're in this situation.'

'Brian ...'

'No,' he interjected, refusing to let her speak. 'So if it means that much to you, I think you should go ahead with your little plan.'

She frowned. What was all this 'you' business? Wasn't this something they had to do together?

'You mean the baby?' she asked and he nodded. She stared at him, relieved. 'I'm so glad to hear it ... I mean, I –'

'I'm not finished.'

'OK.' She would agree to any of his stipulations, whatever he wanted if it meant that they could get back on track.

He took a deep breath. 'As I said, I think that you should go ahead with your ... baby.' Did he hate the idea that much that he could barely say the word? 'Yes go ahead and make all the crazy plans you want,' Brian continued. 'Just don't expect me to be around for the fallout.'

And with that, Jess's beloved husband turned on his heel, and walked quietly out the door.

49

*N*ina spent the rest of the afternoon wandering around the Dublin shops. The bus back to Lakeview wasn't due to leave until five-thirty so she had plenty of time to take it easy and think about the day's events.

After her conversation with Jess, she felt as though a huge weight had been lifted from her shoulders. Her friend was right; there *were* many different ways of looking at all of this, and she just needed the courage to go for it.

Having promised Jess, she'd think about everything and examine all the options, she'd spent much of the afternoon doing so. She was lost in thought and still thinking about the possibilities when she realized that she was dead center in the middle of a very busy O'Connell Street.

Having battled through the busy Saturday crowds for a couple of hours, she figured it was time for a break. Not to mention that it was an all-Ireland hurling semi-final replay day and the streets were beginning to fill up with revellers and fans on their way back from the game at Croke Park. Although she hadn't yet heard the result, Nina really hoped it was Galway who had been victorious – after all, the place had been her home for the last few years and she had no such allegiance to their Tipperary rivals.

Walking a little further, she spotted the Kylemore café on the corner, and figured it would be as good a place as any to stop for a cuppa. And maybe a slice of cake or something. Almost as soon as she'd had that thought, her stomach growled and the baby kicked approvingly.

'I get it, I get it. Don't worry, we're going to feed ourselves now,' she laughed.

Going into the restaurant, she bought a coffee and a pastry and sought out a quiet spot near the back.

Catching sight of a recently vacated table by the wall, she scooted over, eager to nab it before someone else did. The place was busy with sports fans from the participating counties scattered throughout the restaurant, and as Nina ate her pastry, she idly surveyed the tables around her, trying to figure out which team had been victorious.

Then suddenly, she heard a voice from behind that made her heart stop.

'I told you Steven. If you don't eat something, you'll be starving by the time we get home,' the male voice scolded.

As if in a trance, Nina turned and her gaze zeroed in to where the voice was coming from. At the table a couple of feet away from her was a family – two parents and three young children whose ages looked to range from about two to seven. All were dressed in Galway sports jerseys.

Nina was frozen to the spot. She couldn't believe it; couldn't comprehend what she was seeing. She attempted to look away, but try as she might, she couldn't take her eyes off them. It was like some invisible entity had a hold on her body, not allowing her to move.

'Daddy, why is that woman staring at us?' the little boy at the table asked.

The father looked up and his gaze briefly met Nina's, before immediately dropping to her very obviously protruding stomach.

She snapped her mouth shut and heat automatically rushed to her face.

'Oh ...' she whispered, turning away, still rooted to the chair for a couple of moments, unsure what to do.

Then finally, she somehow found her feet and stood up, moving quickly towards the door, trying to go as fast as her legs would carry her.

Going outside, she was conscious of the rivulets of sweat running down her back, and her heart felt like it was going to explode.

She was only a little way down the street, when she heard someone calling her. 'Nina, Nina wait, please.'

She turned to see Steve behind, trying to catch up with her.

'Leave me alone,' she cried. She didn't care if she was attracting the curious stares of people on the street, she didn't care about anything except escaping from him just then.

'Nina hold on a second,' he yelled. 'Please.' He reached out and grabbed her arm and spun her around.

'Don't touch me!' she exclaimed. 'You've done enough.'

'Stop please. Um ... you forgot your handbag.' Only then did she notice he was holding something in his hand, and she realized that in her haste, she'd neglected to take her bag with her.

She quickly grabbed the bag and went to walk away.

'Please Nina, stop for a minute. Just listen to me.'

She felt the tears springing to her eyes. 'What do you want Steve?'

'Just, please.' His gaze was fixated on her stomach and she realized sadly that there was no hiding from this anymore. 'Hell.' He said, running a hand through his hair.

Nina wouldn't meet his eyes. 'Well I guess now you know,' she said with a shrug.

'So this is why you ... why you reacted so badly when ...'

'When I found out you were married?' she spat. 'Yes.'

'But why didn't you say something about ... this?'

'What did you expect me to say, Steve? That I was perfectly fine about having a baby with you when I'd just found out you had another family tucked away somewhere? Give me a break.'

He shook his head. 'I just didn't expect ...'

'What? Expect me to get pregnant? I didn't *expect* you to be married!'

'I know, I'm sorry Nina, I made a mistake.'

'You're damn right you did.'

He seemed to be at a loss. 'Look ... is there anything I can do for you?'

'Except stay the hell out of my life? No.' She knew her tone was harsh, but she wanted to hurt him, in the same way he had hurt her.

The way he had devastated her all those months before when she'd learned that the man she was in love with was not only married, but a father of three. Nina had never suspected a thing and could hardly comprehend that someone she'd fallen so deeply and utterly in love with had been living a lie all the time they were together.

Although they'd both worked in the same company for some time, she hadn't got to know Steve until she'd been moved to the IT department where he worked. Back then, right from the beginning something had clicked between them and Nina had fallen hook, line and sinker for the attractive, but rather quiet guy who worked on the same floor. He didn't wear a wedding ring and at work there had been no mention of a wife or anyone else. They'd gone out a couple of times and got on so well that Nina had never thought to question his personal circumstances, why would she?

She'd only learned the truth shortly after discovering she was pregnant, and while she hadn't yet worked up the courage to share the news with Steve, she had begun dropping little hints about them perhaps moving in together.

'Love, that can't happen at the moment, not for a while anyway,' Steve told her, and when Nina looked blankly at him, he sat her down and took both of her hands in his. 'Nina, I'm sorry, I haven't been completely honest with you,' he said, before going on to calmly tell her that he couldn't move in with her because he was married to someone else. 'I'm sorry, I know I should have said something about it from the outset, but there was never a right time, and by then I'd already fallen for you,' he continued sheepishly, while Nina tried to pick her jaw up off the floor.

'You're ... married?'

'Yes, but it's over – it's been over for a long time, you must know that and we're only still going through the motions for the sake of the kids. I would never have got involved with you otherwise. I wanted to tell you from the beginning, but I was afraid you'd react badly –'

'Damn right I'd react badly! We've been seeing one another since the end of last year, Steve – how could you *not* tell me something like this?'

And how could she not have known, Nina wondered, feeling unbelievably stupid. Looking back, perhaps the signs were there, how they always stayed at her place instead of his, how on certain weekends he wasn't able to see her ... but at the time, he'd given what Nina had thought were reasonable explanations, namely that his place was too far out of town, or that he was visiting an elderly mother who lived down the country.

It was all such a cliché, and she'd been such a fool. And to think that she was just about to share what she'd thought was wonderful news ... Not only that, but Nina was horrified to think that she'd played a part in taking another woman's husband, albeit obliviously ...

Suddenly, everything had become a nightmare.

But unlike Trish, once Nina had discovered the truth about his marriage, she wanted nothing more to do with Steve, baby or no baby. Which was why – without saying a word about her newly discovered pregnancy – she'd that night ended the relationship, and soon after got out of Galway as fast as possible.

Now, standing on O'Connell Street, she tried to summon all the anger and betrayal and this time, use it as a defense mechanism.

'Steve, it's absolutely none of your business.'

'Well of course it's my business ... I mean ... it's mine too, isn't it?'

Nina rounded on him. 'You have no right – no right to even ask about me, or this baby. Anyway, you needn't worry about this messing up your happy family if that's what you're concerned about. I'm giving the baby up ... so I won't have to be reminded of your face, won't have to be reminded of you. Ever. It will be as if you didn't exist.' He winced a little and she realized her words had hit the mark. 'I only hope that the poor thing hasn't inherited too much of your DNA, so it doesn't grow up to be a liar and a cheat.'

She looked over his shoulder then and saw his wife and kids walking slowly towards them. Hah, let him explain this one, she thought sarcastically, although of course the forgotten handbag had conveniently given him an excuse.

'Go back to your wife, Steve. She's waiting for you.' With that, she turned on her heel and walked away. She didn't look back and she knew at that moment, she wouldn't have to. She didn't regret what she had said to him, in fact, it merely helped her come to a decision. She hoped her little son or daughter would forgive her, but the words were necessary.

It was as if she was supposed to meet her baby's father today – and seeing him again had given her a completely new perspective.

Nina knew now that Jess's solution was the answer, maybe even the one she had been searching for all along.

*a*t the airport, the time seemed to be creeping by.

Ruth had tried to call Charlie several times, but kept getting his voicemail. Then again, she thought, it would be very late in Ireland now. She didn't want to worry him, and was sure that he would be happy to see her. All she wanted to do was get on the plane and get back to Ireland, back to Charlie and her family. She felt elated that reality had finally dawned on her and she now knew her future.

She'd caught a quick flight to JFK so she didn't have to wait too long to get out of LA, but the waiting game that she was playing now in New York was absolutely killing her.

As soon as her overnight flight to Dublin was called, she raced to the gate and as she waited for the other passengers to board, she practically bounced in her seat she was so anxious. When the plane took off, she couldn't concentrate on anything – the movie that was playing or the paperback novel that she had picked up at the airport, nor could she sleep. Instead, she stared out of the window, into the blackness of the Atlantic Ocean, thirty thousand feet below.

She knew she was giving it all up, everything she had worked for, all she had fought for, just to be with the man that she should have chosen from day one. Of course, she was also giving it all up for her son or daughter.

But maybe her acting career didn't have to be completely over? Maybe she could do something closer to home ... the stage in London or perhaps she could even fly back to the States for stuff, depending on the role. After all, some US actresses were able to do it from London, so as long as you were mobile, you could do anything, right?

Regardless, it didn't matter. She knew her priorities had changed, and ultimately she just wanted a happy life, both for herself and the baby.

Hours later when she finally landed in Dublin, she flipped open her phone, certain that Charlie would have left a message by now. He would have definitely heard hers as he was an early riser and had probably already been up for a couple of hours. She frowned, surprised to find she had no messages, no texts, no emails from anyone back home, let alone from Charlie.

That troubled her somewhat, but Ruth didn't have time to dwell on it for long when she saw the other messages that had accumulated while she was airborne.

One was from Erik, informing her that he was not impressed with her behavior and that she was treading very close to being in breach of contract with the TV studio if she didn't get 'her ass back to the States pronto'.

Warning bells went off in her head as she knew there would be repercussions, most likely legally, with the decision that she made. After all, there were shooting commitments and contracts she would be held to for *Glamazons* as well as other promotional-related stuff. She figured she would deal with all of that later, but now it looked like she might have to deal with it sooner than she thought. Ruth cringed at the idea of being sued.

The next message was from Troy blasting her for being such a 'dumbass bitch.'

She shook her head at his stupidity. The idiot really didn't learn anything, did he? She thought for sure after she'd threatened him with a recording of the phone call he'd be more careful with his communications to her. This message certainly didn't make him come across like an adoring father. She smiled and marked it 'saved' on her phone.

Just in case.

Finally, she scrolled to Charlie's name in her contacts to phone him directly. This time the call went straight to voicemail without even ringing. A niggling worry bubbled up inside her. Something was wrong.

She rushed from the plane, and this time didn't give a second glance at herself in any mirror, she was so intent on getting back to Lakeview as quickly as possible. Going through to the arrivals area, she rented a car and drove as fast as possible down the M50 towards Lakeview, her mind racing as she imagined her reunion with Charlie. She was sure he'd be over the moon at her decision.

In the end, she made it there much faster than normal, and was impressed with her driving ability and the fact that she didn't get pulled over for speeding on the way there. She drove through the center and finally turned off on the street that led to Charlie's house. Her heart was racing and the baby must have picked up on her mood because it was moving around like mad.

Ruth rubbed her stomach and got out of the car. 'Shh, baby,' she whispered to her stomach, 'I know, I'm excited to see him too.'

She took slow steps up to the front door, feeling as nervous as a bride. For once in her life, the rest of her life was right in front of her, her happiness there for the taking, and she couldn't wait for it to start.

She had a key and could have just let herself in, but she really wanted Charlie to come to the door, so she could see his face as he welcomed her into his arms. She rang the doorbell and waited to hear footsteps. Nothing.

She turned around and looked at the car in the driveway; he must be inside. Ruth knocked a little louder this time; maybe he hadn't heard her the first time. She realized she was holding her breath as she waited to hear something, some kind of activity from inside, but still there was nothing.

Finally she reached into her bag and dug around until she found her keys.

Stepping gingerly into the hallway, she called out his name, but heard nothing in return. Then she walked through to the living room and straight away noticed that something was different.

Her gaze zeroed in on the pile of baby things; a rocker and crib that was still in the box waiting to be assembled, and some bags from various baby stores – all the things they had bought together over the past few weeks. They had all been stowed in Charlie's spare bedroom upstairs, which they'd planned to use as the nursery when the baby was born. Ruth's heart thudded nervously. Why were these things now neatly arranged in a pile in the living room?

A tight knot rose in her chest and again, she went back out to the hallway and started to mount the stairs. 'Charlie? Hon ...are you here?'

As she reached the top of the stairs, finally she heard some sign of activity; a low noise that sounded like the TV on with the volume turned very low. Moving down the landing she saw a strip of light under the bottom of the door to Charlie's room. 'Charlie?' she whispered, gently opening the door.

He was sitting on the bed and staring blankly at the TV, the sound barely audible, with a selection of newspapers splayed out in front of him. When she saw his expression, so blank and devoid of animation, she knew something was seriously wrong. She knocked on the door-frame, trying to alert him to her presence.

'Hey, I'm back,' she said, attempting a smile, but as he turned to face her, that smile quickly faded.

'So?' he replied coldly and Ruth's heart sank. She supposed she couldn't blame him for still being upset with her for taking off so quickly, but ...

'I mean I'm back. I'm finished with LA.'

'Yeah. For how long?'

'For good.' Ruth smiled; it actually felt good to say the words out loud. 'I told them all to shove it, the studio, my agent, even Chloe. I'm probably going to get sued by every lawyer in Hollywood, but what the hell.' She shrugged, trying to make light of the situation, but found it was impossible when faced with such a wall of indifference.

She was desperate for him to say something encouraging, something to show her he was happy to see her. Yet his expression still didn't change. 'Aren't you happy to see me?'

'How can I be happy?' he grunted. 'It's only a matter of time before you change your mind again, isn't it?'

'What? No, you don't understand. This time, I'm here to stay. I told everyone that I was finished, that I didn't want any of it, that I –'

'Really. Then what the *hell* is this?' He grabbed one of the newspapers and threw it in her direction. The pages flitted to the floor and Ruth reached down to pick it up, realizing that yet again she was in trouble, although for what she didn't know.

Opening out the page she was confronted with a huge picture of her and Troy kissing at the airport. The headline above it read 'Celebrity Reunion! Ruth and Troy's Love-Fest with Their New Baby!'

She sighed loudly. 'Oh, come on honey, this is nothing. You know by now how these things work.'

'How can you say that?' he cried, his voice shaking. 'How can you just ... dismiss it like that?'

Ruth was genuinely shocked at his reaction. Surely he knew that this was just the paparazzi and their usual garbage, a dressed-up photo-op designed to sell copies.

'No, really Charlie, he ambushed me,' she said, trying to explain. 'I was walking along in the airport with Chloe and all of a sudden I turn around and Troy was there. He was doing it for the cameras. He practically knocked me over. I was so shocked.'

'Yes, you look very... *shocked* all right.'

She looked at the picture again, trying to see it from his point of view. Troy had an arm wrapped around her and his other hand was resting on her belly. His mouth was on hers and her eyes were closed, her hand on Troy's chest. The picture reflected passion and contentment, when Ruth knew that in reality they were squeezed shut out of distaste, and her hand was on his chest in an attempt to push him off of her. But without knowing that, Charlie was right; this picture did look like two lovers being reunited after a long and painful separation.

She groaned internally, unable to believe this was happening. 'No sweetheart, you have this all wrong. If you could have only seen ...'

'Oh, I see, is that what you want me to do? Follow you around like a good little nobody playing second fiddle to this idiot? That sounds like a great life.'

'Charlie honestly, please. I pushed him away, I didn't kiss him back; he wasn't even supposed to be there! He was just using it to get press.'

'You see, that's the difference between you and me Ruth, what you use to market yourself and to grab some time with cameras is something I see as a non-negotiable piece of life.' His eyes rested on her stomach. 'You can use whatever you want to further your career, but don't expect me to be a part of it.'

'No!' Ruth cried, stung at the implication. 'I would *never* use the baby like that! Look, I know what it looks like, but if you would just believe me when I tell you that I realized all that, I realized I didn't want to be a part of that, and didn't want the baby to be a part of it either. I'd barely set foot in LA when I told the driver to turn around and take me back to the airport – back to you. I thought you'd be proud of me, that you'd be happy I'm giving it all up, for us, for the baby. Don't you see?' She felt the sob building in her throat, almost as if she was choking.

Charlie looked at her dully. 'I don't believe you.'

'You don't believe me? Well, do you want me to call a witness, Charlie? Because I told them all to get stuffed! There was a driver there, he can tell you ...'

'I'm not talking about what you said to who, when you had this sudden epiphany or whatever the hell it was,' he said nastily. 'I'm talking about the fact that I don't believe you've made such a choice. It will be only a matter of time before you change your mind again, resent me, resent the baby, and frankly Ruth, I can't take it. You've walked out on me twice now, I can't do it a third time.'

'I didn't walk out on you this time! I said I would be back, and now I am like I told you I would.'

'Yes, but it's always your interests, it's always about you and what you want, what you decide. You just trample the people who love you because you feel like you can, but Ruth, you can't with me – not anymore. I can't be another sideshow for you until something better comes along.'

'No, no Charlie, you have to listen to me ... I want this life. I want what we have ...' She was crying now, full on crying. She was one step away from throwing herself at his feet and begging, and would do it too, if it meant that he would listen to her.

'Maybe you do think you want this life, at least for the moment, but Ruth, you're fickle, you know that. The moment you get bored, the moment that life seems too steady, too normal, is the moment I'm going to wake up and find myself alone again. We're too different, this can't work and I'm trying to save us both the misery by putting an end to it right now. Can't you accept that?' His voice had softened just a touch and Ruth realized that he truly did believe what he was saying. 'I just wish that ... oh, I don't know ... I wish when that phone call had come through the other day from your assistant that you could have let it ring. That you could have seen through it all. That you could have seen how they were manipulating you. I saw it and I told you and you still went. But you didn't even consider what I thought because it was all about you.'

'That's not fair, I had to see for myself, and now I know I made the right choice –'

'You made it too late, Ruth. As I said, I can't live like this, can't live not knowing how your mood is going to change from one day to the next.'

Ruth didn't know what else to say. She didn't know how she could convince him. It seemed as if his mind was made up. He didn't want her.

'What about the baby?' she asked feebly, her voice barely audible.

Charlie looked at her for a long moment before finally uttering words that cut her like a knife.

'Ruth it's not even mine.'

 *M*uch later that day, she stood looking out the window of her bedroom, tears streaming down her cheeks. Sleep had evaded her and a low level of panic made every nerve in her body stand on end. It was over. Charlie didn't want her. He didn't want the baby either.

She had cut herself off from her career, had smashed her life in LA into a million pieces, all for a life here that rejected her. She had nothing, she was starting from scratch again and now she was going to be saddled with a baby on top of it.

So she was selfish. A fickle person, always changing her mind.

Sudden bitterness towards Charlie and his words flooded her heart. She loved him, had given up everything for him. She had only considered him and her baby and had done everything for *them*. And where had it got her?

She gritted her teeth. Maybe Charlie was right; maybe she was just like the rest of them. Her thoughts drifted through the faces that she knew in LA, Chloe, Troy, Erik. Maybe her mistake wasn't just giving up everything for Charlie, but actually thinking that she could have a normal life, be a normal person when she'd spent most of her life pretending to be someone else.

It was ironic. To think that Ruth Seymour had spent five years in

Hollywood trying to get to the top and now she was willing to throw it all away to become Mrs Nobody Single Mom.

Ruth's heart raced. Charlie was right – what had she been thinking?

At that moment, her BlackBerry buzzed and she picked up the device and looked at the screen, seeing that it was an email from Erik.

Maybe there was hope, Ruth thought, maybe she wasn't entirely cut off and more importantly, maybe it wasn't too late to make amends. Now that she knew for certain that things were over with Charlie, she might as well go back to LA and try and get things settled with her contracts. She could meet with the studio and see if they could work something out about the scheduling for *The Soldier's Daughter*, something that would work around the baby.

The baby ...

While juggling all of that stuff sounded fine and doable when she had Charlie behind her, Ruth knew deep down that LA was no place for a single mother.

Erik's email was brief and to the point.

I don't know what the hell is going on with you, but for everyone's sake I hope it's just hormones. We have forty-eight hours until the TV studio hits us hard with a lawsuit so I suggest you get your ass back here pronto. Oh, and Peter Jackson just called and he's still interested – for now.

Ruth stared down at her stomach, realizing she had a very big choice to make.

Movies or motherhood?

52

_N_ina's due date was getting closer by the day and she knew she needed to solidify her plans before things were out of her control.

After bumping into Steve in Dublin, she was even more convinced that Jess was right; maybe there was a better solution – one that would work for everyone.

She followed Trish into the room that she felt they'd been living in for months. Trish was nearing the end of her research and Nina was glad, she was tired of spending most of the summer sitting in a windowless room for hours on end.

'I tell you, I'll be happy to get this out of the way once and for all,' Trish said with a roll of her eyes. 'Problem is, I think it's all a bit well ... boring.'

Nina looked at her. 'Well how interesting can a photographic history of Lakeview actually be after all?'

'I know, but with the old timers' stories and the stuff from the archives, I really thought we could come up with something fresh and interesting. Instead it's reading like an old fashioned tourist brochure.'

'Yes, but everyone will buy it to help the charity in any case. Especially if there are photos of themselves in it.'

'Hmm, there are still only so many black and white photos of old buildings I can use. I need something to hang it all together, a theme as such, but at the moment the theme might as well be "Lakeview – a place where nothing much happens".'

'I thought history was the theme,' Nina ventured, not really understanding what her friend was hoping for. And at the end of the day it was a charity book for the locals, not a potential Pulitzer winner. 'What about the Ruth bit? That'll be interesting, won't it?' she asked, referring to the section on 'local heroes' in which Ruth was the only person featured.

'Yes, but I'd hoped to interview her properly for that. Fat chance now that she's gone back to LA.'

'No, she's back.'

Trish's head snapped up. 'What?'

'She's back – for Charlie, I suppose. I saw her yesterday. Why?' Nina's brow furrowed at Trish's troubled expression.

'Oh, no reason. Did you see the pictures?'

'Yes, I felt so sorry for her. Everything's been so quiet for her here lately it was horrible that they tracked her down like that.'

'I'm not talking about the ones of her and Charlie outside the shops,' Trish said. She reached into her handbag and pulled out a newspaper. 'I mean *these*.'

Unfolding the newspaper, Nina was horrified to see a snap of Ruth and Troy Valentine locked in a passionate embrace. 'What? When did this happen?' she asked wide-eyed.

'A couple of days ago I think – while she was in LA'

'But why would she be kissing Troy Valentine? What about Charlie?'

'Who knows?' Trish shrugged. 'All I heard was she flew back to LA to talk about some big movie role. Did she say anything when you met her yesterday?'

'I didn't meet her. I was heading home from the café when I saw her pass by in her dad's car. So what's all this about a movie role? Is she going back to LA then? And how come you know so much about all this?'

'Oh, just something I heard on the grapevine. But I'll tell you one thing, when she's accepting that Oscar, I hope she gives us some credit for putting her back on the Hollywood map.'

'Trish, what on earth are you talking about?'

She smiled. 'Well ... as a true journalist, I couldn't exactly let a good story go to waste, could I?'

Nina looked at her. 'Oh no. What did you do?' But already she understood. Trish had leaked the story about Ruth's pregnancy. 'Ah, Trish, how could you? She trusts you, she told us about that in confidence and you betrayed her.'

'Oh come on, she's a Hollywood actress, there's no such thing as "in confidence". Besides, she loves the press!'

Nina shook her head, not understanding her friend. Irrespective of the fact that she was a journalist and it was part of her job this just seemed so unscrupulous. 'I think that was really mean of you. Think of how she must have felt when she was ambushed by that photographer here in her home town. And think of how Charlie must feel.'

'Come on, it's not like she's dying! Hollywood are going crazy over the story of her and Valentine's baby, and my help may well have led to her being offered a part that could win her a bloody Oscar. She'll be delighted.'

'I'm going to phone her,' Nina said, reaching into her handbag for her mobile.

'What? Why?'

'To see how she is, of course. Those pictures must have really upset her. She can't stand Troy Valentine now, and goodness knows what Charlie thought when he saw them.'

'Ah Nina, leave it be ...'

'Why? Unlike you, I actually consider her a friend, and I'm worried about her.'

'I suppose I didn't really think of that ...' Trish sat there, a serious look on her face.

'Ruth? Hi, it's Nina. Look, I just saw those photos and I was wondering if you were ... what? Sure ... I'm just at the library with Trish – where else?' She smiled. 'Yes, if you want to, that would be great. OK ... see you soon.' She snapped the phone shut and turned to Trish. 'She's coming here.'

'What – today?' her friend replied, white-faced.

'Yep. I was right – she does sound upset.'

'Nina ... maybe we won't mention anything about ...'

'You leaking her personal life to the press?'

'Ah Nina, come on. I was only doing what any decent journalist would –'

'No you weren't, you were betraying a confidence and I think you need to come clean and apologize.'

'But she'll go through me!'

'Well, you should have thought of that before, shouldn't you?' Nina knew she was being sanctimonious, but she couldn't help it. Trish, it seemed had made a habit of hurting other people for her own ends, and needed to be made aware of the consequences of her actions. While she couldn't do anything about poor Dave's wife, at least she should ensure Trish was confronted by the fallout of her actions concerning Ruth.

The two worked silently for a while, Trish idly flicking through some of the older newspapers, until about a half hour later, Ruth arrived.

She seemed the worse for wear and looked very tired. All the usual glamour was today absent. 'Hi,' she said glumly.

'How are you?' Nina smiled, her gaze automatically going to Ruth's growing bump. 'Wow, you've got even bigger since the last time I saw you.'

'Unfortunately,' Ruth huffed and sat down in a chair.

'Are you OK?' Nina asked gently. 'You sounded a bit down on the phone.'

Ruth shook her head and bit her bottom lip. 'No, I'm not. Not at all.'

'What happened? Did something go wrong at your meeting with Peter Jackson?' Trish blurted out.

Ruth's eyes narrowed. 'What are you talking about? How do you know that?'

Trish said nothing, just nervously looked around the room and Ruth's gaze quickly rested on the newspaper photo sitting in front of her. Nina could see that all the chips were starting to line up. 'You? You were responsible for bringing them here?'

'Look, Ruth, I thought you would be happy about it, OK?' Trish said guiltily. 'I mean, everything was so quiet for you here, whereas now the media are all over you.'

'Did it ever occur to you Trish that maybe I don't care about that? That maybe I was liking the quiet and that I wanted to be left the hell alone?' Ruth raged, ripping the newspaper page in two.

'But why would you want that?'

'Because of Charlie – why else? But then that didn't work out either.' She went on to tell them about Charlie's reaction to Troy's staged photos and how he was still refusing to talk to her. 'So congratulations Trish. You've ruined my life.'

Trish looked shell-shocked. 'I'm so sorry ... I just didn't think ... I really thought you would be happy,' she whispered.

'No, I'm not happy. I'm miserable. My life is ruined and I want to go back to Los Angeles. I want to forget everything about this stupid place.'

Nina put a comforting hand on her arm. 'Ruth, it will be OK. Things will work out, with Charlie, I know they will – and with the baby and all.'

'No they won't. He doesn't want me or the baby. He made that perfectly clear.'

Trish sighed heavily. 'Ruth, I'm truly sorry, I really am.'

Ruth turned her face away, it was clear she wasn't finding any of it easy.

'Tell you what,' Nina said, hoping to make peace, 'why don't we pop down to Ella's and get a coffee? It's been a rough day already, and I'm not sure I can take much more of all this.' She indicated the surrounding papers and boxes.

'You guys go ahead,' Trish said in an absent tone. 'I've got a bit more to do here.'

'Oh you can come if you like,' Ruth muttered, realizing it was up to her to make amends.

'No seriously,' Trish continued frowning, looking with interest at a newspaper clipping she held in her hand. She turned to Nina. 'Remember I said that nothing interesting ever happens in this town?' She held up the paper and pointed to the headline. 'Well, take a look at this ...'

53

*J*ess felt lost as she looked at Brian's side of the wardrobe. Since his decision to leave, most of his clothes had in the meantime been transferred to a nearby hotel where he was currently staying.

Staring at the empty rails, Jess still couldn't quite believe that this was happening. Her husband, her soul mate and best friend was leaving her. This was not supposed to be happening; and not what she'd pictured when it came to their future.

All that had happened over the last few months had shattered their lovely life, and now she had no idea how to start picking up the pieces. Even worse, it was all her own doing.

In truth Brian had every right to feel betrayed and hurt by her actions. What had she been thinking giving up the pill without telling him? Or informing all their friends that they were trying for a baby? What on earth had possessed her? Had she really been that desperate to hold on to her friends that she was prepared to risk losing her husband in the process?

She'd tried in the meantime to talk to him about it, to try and explain the reasons behind her behavior, but he wouldn't listen. It seemed that this time, she'd pushed him too far.

And the worst part of it all was that she didn't really have anyone to talk to about it. She couldn't realistically call up Deirdre or Emer to discuss it; notwithstanding that Emer had her own problems, it would mean coming clean about how Brian had all along been clueless about their so-called decision, which would only lead to more egg on Jess's face.

It was such a difficult situation to explain, and she was sure most people would think she was barmy. As it was, she couldn't quite explain her behavior to herself. The other day she'd been sorely tempted to talk to Nina about it ...

Nina, Jess thought, perking up ... she could confide in her about this, couldn't she? After all, she'd already revealed so much to her, especially after their chat the other day.

She picked up the phone and scrolled through it, trying to find the number.

'Jess, hi,' Nina said answering the phone, but Jess could immediately tell that she was distracted.

'Hi – is this a bad time?'

'No, no, it's fine. I'm just at the library with Trish and Ruth. I've been meaning to call you actually to say thanks for the other day. You know – for the lift and the advice and everything.'

'Actually, speaking of advice ...' Despite, herself Jess felt her voice waver.

'Are you OK?' Nina asked. 'You sound a bit ... sad.'

The kindness in her voice was enough to set Jess off, and before she knew it she was in floods of tears. 'I'm sorry,' she sobbed, giving Nina the short version of what had happened. 'I shouldn't be boring you with all this, but I really have nobody else to talk to –'

'Oh you poor thing – don't be silly. Of course you need to talk to someone.' Her voice lowered. 'Hold on a second, and I'll just go into the other room.' After a brief wait – one that Jess used to try and calm herself, Nina came back on the line. 'Look, are you sure it's not just an argument?' she asked gently. 'Maybe it'll blow over and you and Brian will be back on track before you know it.'

'I don't think so Nina. This time, I really think I blew it. He kept going on about how deceitful I was and how I was deluding myself ...

you should have seen the look in his eyes.' The pain of the memory was almost too much to bear; and strangely Jess realized, it really did feel like physical pain – a sharp, acute dart in her abdomen. Overcome, she sat down on the bed, just as another sudden pain shot through her and she doubled over. '*Ow.*'

'Jess?' Nina's concern was audible. 'What is it? What's wrong?'

'I'm OK,' she replied breathlessly, although she really wasn't. And when another cramp assaulted her, she realized that this wasn't some physical manifestation of her sadness, it was real, actual pain. 'Oh hell,' she uttered, gritting her teeth.

'Jess ... you're scaring me now. What's happening?' Nina enquired, urgency in her voice.

'I'm not sure. I've just started having really bad stomach pains ...' she managed, her breath short.

'What ... just now? Keep an eye on it. After all, something like that when you're pregnant is not good.'

'OK.' Jess felt panicked all over again. This was turning into the worst week of her life. 'Oh...!' she squealed, as another painful wave rushed through her and she dropped the phone on the floor.

'Jess? Jess!' she heard Nina call out, but she had no choice but to wait for the pain to subside before she could reach down and retrieve it.

'I'm here,' she said, trying to stand up. She leaned against the dressing table, realizing then she'd broken out in a cold sweat. 'I'm OK.'

'That didn't sound OK to me.'

She shook her head, ready to insist to Nina that everything really was fine when she turned back to the bed she had been sitting on. 'Oh my goodness ...' she said softly, her heart racing.

'Tell me what's happening.'

'I'm bleeding,' she told Nina breathlessly, before stumbling into the en-suite bathroom. She checked her trousers and found them coated in blood. 'Nina, I'm bleeding a lot. What do I do? What do I do?'

'Oh, no ... look, OK, try and stay calm.'

Trying to control her panic, Jess doubled over yet again as a fresh cramp seized her abdomen and this time she physically felt something moist rush through her.

'Jess try and stay calm, OK? What you need to do now is call the hospital and get them to send out an ambulance. But before you do that, can you give me Brian's number?'

'No – I don't want to involve Brian. He doesn't want to be involved and –'

'Jess, he's your husband and you need help. Unfortunately, at the moment I'm too far away to help you. Now give me the number,' she asked, her calm, controlled voice convincing Jess that there really was no other option. She rattled off Brian's mobile number, all the while afraid to stir, fearful that the tiniest movement would make it worse.

'Right, now hang up and call the hospital. And Jess, again, try to stay calm. It could be nothing sweetheart, but it needs to be checked out, OK?'

'OK,' Jess nodded, grimacing afresh as she hung up on Nina and called the hospital, all the while trying to fight her mounting terror.

54

*I*t seemed like it was taking the ambulance forever to get there and Jess was growing more nervous and exhausted by the minute. On the advice of the hospital, she'd spent the last fifteen minutes on the downstairs bathroom floor with her feet elevated, and had left the front door on the latch for the paramedics. By now she was breathless and damp with sweat, her fair hair plastered to her face, as each new cramp felt like it was tearing her body in two. Finally, she heard movement at the front door. Thank heavens, thank heavens ...

'In here!' she called out, hearing frantic footsteps from down the hallway. However, it wasn't the paramedics, but Brian, who looked just as terrified as she felt.

'Oh Jess, honey, what's happened?' He flung off his coat, casting it to the floor and got on his knees next to where she lay.

She burst into tears, partly out of relief of not being alone any longer, but mostly because it was Brian who'd come to her rescue. 'I'm not ... I'm not sure, I've been having cramps and then I started bleeding and well, all this blood ...'

'Ssh, ssh, let's get you to the hospital.' His hands were shaking as he grabbed a towel and soaked it in water, before gently cleaning up some of the blood on her legs. 'But what's going on ... I mean ... are you hurting?'

Jess wasn't concentrating on the pain any longer; she was much more focused on his presence. 'Nina called you?'

'Yes, love she did.'

'And you came,' she said tearfully.

'Of course I came, of course I did.'

'But after everything ...' It would be too much to bear if he was just here out of duty, and then took off again after all of this was over. Way too much.

'Let's not talk about that just now, OK?' he said, his voice catching, and Jess noticed that he too had tears in his eyes. Then, they both heard some commotion outside, followed by a knock on the door, and Brian quickly got to his feet. 'That'll be the ambulance.'

She couldn't remember the last time she had seen him cry – if ever – and it made her worry all over again. 'Brian this is all my fault. I should never have –'

'Oh honey, it will be fine, we are going to get you to the hospital and everything will be fine. We'll be fine ... the baby will be fine.'

'But you don't even want ...'

'Of course I do. I promise I do,' he mumbled, his voice choking. 'Everything will be fine.'

*a*n hour later, the doctor left Jess's hospital room and she sobbed into a pillow. Brian was half-sitting on the bed next to her, trying awkwardly to hold her while also avoiding the surrounding tubes and IV.

She had lost a lot of blood.

'I can't believe it,' she cried, turning to look at her husband, relief flooding through her. 'I can't believe everything's OK.'

'Told you it would be,' he replied with a lopsided grin, but his face was still pale and there was something in his expression that Jess couldn't quite read.

Well, maybe he might be having mixed feelings about it all, but the one thing that had come out of this momentous scare was that she now knew for sure that she wanted this baby, wanted it with all her heart.

And if it meant that as a result she couldn't have Brian, well she would just have to live with that.

'You don't have to stay, you know,' she said tentatively. 'You heard the doctor; I can go home. I'll be right as rain.'

'Of course I'm going to stay. Where else would I be?'

'Well, where you've been for the last few days I suppose.'

'Jess, I ...' he ran a hand through his hair and she waited for him to tell her that he couldn't deal with being a father, didn't plan for this, all the words she knew he wanted to say.

'It's OK, honestly. I understand. You never wanted this. It was all my doing, and you were right to be angry.'

'It's not that ... yes, of course I was upset that you didn't include me in all of this, but ...'

'But what?'

'Jess, I have to tell you. Until today, I was convinced that you were ... well that day at the party ... I'll be honest, I truly thought you were making it up.'

'Making what up?' she asked, frowning.

He looked at her stomach. 'Well ... the baby ... the whole pregnancy thing.'

She stared at him, flabbergasted. 'You thought I was *pretending* to be pregnant?'

He nodded.

'Oh, my goodness Brian, what kind of psycho would do something like ... I just can't believe that you would –'

'Calm down ... I know –I know it was stupid, but I figured you got carried away and then didn't know how to fix it.' Brian now looked like he was sorry he'd said anything, but Jess was dumbfounded. All this time he'd been thinking she was making it up? So *that* was why he'd been going on about her 'coming clean' and 'telling the truth'.

'But why would you think I would ever do something so ...?' She shook her head. 'OK, so I know I have an active imagination, but ... I just can't believe you would *think* such a thing.'

'I don't know I'm sorry ... it was a combination of things. I'll be honest, I was mad. I was mad about how stubborn you were, how you seemed to have a one-track mind. I was mad how you announced you were pregnant. I mean, Jess, I didn't even know. There was nothing private, nothing special about that moment. That should have been something you and I learned about together.'

She nodded, once again ashamed of that.

'So you have to understand that I was hurt, and yet you were more worried about your friends, about what they thought of you rather than our life together.'

Jess couldn't believe it. No wonder he hadn't engaged with her throughout it all and no wonder he'd been so distant and weird about everything. And although she couldn't immediately forgive him for thinking so badly of her, in a way Jess was glad there was *some* kind of explanation. 'But what did you think I'd do when the baby was supposed to be born – steal one or something?'

He shrugged. 'Honestly, I wasn't sure. But then for a while there you were talking a lot about Nina and how she might not be able to cope when her baby was born and I wondered if …'

Jess's mouth dropped open as she tried to follow his line of thinking. 'You seriously thought I was considering taking in Nina's baby? And you say *I* have a vivid imagination?'

Now Brian looked shamefaced. 'I know, it was stupid and then when I found you earlier in the middle of all that blood, I felt so guilty,' he added, shaking his head. Then he took a deep breath and reached for her hand. 'But now that I know you weren't making it up, and that everything is … OK, I suppose now I'm trying to get my head around the idea that we're going to be parents.' He smiled. 'Can you imagine me – a dad?'

Jess's heart flooded with relief. 'You'll be an amazing dad,' she said, taking his hand and squeezing it. 'That is, if you still want to be.'

'Of course I do, and I promise you that I will never walk out that door again – never let another misunderstanding come between us. I just need you to promise me that whatever happens, you'll talk to me about it – the way you used to.'

'I promise.' He reached across to kiss her and Jess realized she had been hungering for him, needing him and his support. She ran her fingers along his face.

They sat together in silence for a moment until the peace was broken by the sound of Brian's mobile. He looked at the display. 'Oh no, it's Nina. I promised I'd let her know how you were and I forgot.'

'The poor thing, she must have been frantic. She was very good with me when it was all happening – despite you thinking we were in some form of cahoots together,' she added wryly. 'I really don't know what I would have done without her.'

She took the phone from Brian and explained to a relieved and delighted Nina that everything was fine. 'Thankfully it was just a scare and I'm going home this evening.'

When they'd finished talking Brian smiled.

'I thought from the start that she was a good person, a good friend,' he said. 'She's been there for you more in the short time you've known her than people like Emer and Deirdre, I hope you know that.'

Jess nodded sadly. She wasn't sure what the future held for her friendship with the girls, but whatever happened she was going to be there for Emer, the same way she always had. That was what real friendship was about, being there when people needed you, not about making them feel left out and vulnerable. But, Jess thought, perhaps in that regard, she herself had been her own worst enemy?

'It'll be nice though, our baby growing up at the same time as Nina's won't it?' Brian said smiling.

But Jess didn't reply. Because from the recent conversations she'd had with Nina, she knew that such a thing still wasn't guaranteed.

56

'*S*he's going to be fine.' Nina declared, hanging up the phone to Jess.

She, Ruth and Trish were in the café pondering over the newspaper article they'd found that morning.

'Oh, that's good news,' Ruth said, her hand moving to her stomach in a subconsciously protective gesture. 'The poor thing; she must have been terrified.'

'Yes, all's well that ends well,' Trish said impatiently. She eyed Ella, who was serving a table nearby. 'So. Which one of us is going to ask her?'

Ruth sat back in her chair. 'Well it's your project, so I guess you should.'

Their conversation was cut short when at that moment Ella came over to greet them.

'Hello girls, how are you all today?'

Ruth smiled. 'We're good Ella, how are you?'

'Oh busy, busy as always,' she trilled. 'Nina pet, don't think twice about throwing on an apron, sure you won't?'

Nina laughed. 'Actually,' she glanced at Trish, who nodded. 'We were just helping Trish with the material for the charity book and well ... we found something we wanted to ask you about.'

'Well of course I'll help if I can,' Ella replied easily. 'Heaven knows I've been around this town forever. So what can I get you girls? Coffee and pastries, maybe? Or I've just taken a fresh batch of muffins out of the oven ...'

'Well actually, we wanted to talk to you about something that happened here – in the café, I mean.'

'Oh?' Ella looked puzzled as Trish reached into her bag and took out the photocopy they'd made of the article in question. 'That's odd, I can't remember anything of interest ever happening –'

But immediately upon catching sight of the headline, and the accompanying photograph of the café, Ella's memory was well and truly jogged. Her face went white and she stood frozen to the spot.

'Ella, are you OK?' Ruth asked.

She shook her head, 'Yes ... I'm fine.'

Trish turned to her and immediately went into journalist mode, 'Ella what can you tell us about this? What happened that day? Who was responsible?'

'Well, really, it was all such a long time ago I'd almost forgotten about it,' she said with a tight smile, and Nina noticed her hands were clasped tightly together. 'So coffee for everyone, yes?'

'Really? Seems like something like that would be difficult to forget. I mean, it's not every day that –'

'I'm sorry love, but I really don't have time to stay and chat. Maybe come back later when things aren't so busy?'

'But –'

Ella scuttled off, and although the café was pretty full there was nothing pressing that Nina could see, which could only mean that the woman was reluctant – no that was the wrong word – she was *afraid* to talk about the article.

But why? Had she done something wrong herself? Despite their best efforts back at the library they hadn't been able to find any follow-up articles in the microfiche. It was as Trish had pointed out, 'almost as if the entire thing had never happened'.

Nina wondered now if they'd been too hasty in probing Ella about it. After all, as she was directly involved, then chances were she was also involved in the eventual resolution, whatever that was.

'Well that was weird,' Trish said, staring at Ella's retreating back. 'Did you see her reaction when I showed her the photocopy? There's a lot more here than meets the eye, I'm sure of it. Why else would she be so reluctant to tell us anything?'

'I don't know Trish, maybe it's something personal – something she doesn't want made public knowledge,' Ruth suggested, echoing Nina's own thoughts.

'Well, I thought it was a good story back in the library, but now I *know* it is. And I'm not going to rest until I find out more.'

'Man, do you ever learn?' Ruth said pointedly, and Trish flushed. 'You have no idea what you're dealing with here. You're talking about poking into other people's lives, maybe opening up old wounds.'

'Ruth's right, Trish. Clearly, it's none of our business, and there's nothing to be gained from pursuing this.'

'What makes you so sure?' Trish replied, looking from one to the other. She smoothed the paper out on the table. 'Look at the date.'

Ruth shrugged. 'Exactly it was something that happened ages ago.'

'No, I mean the *actual* date.'

'I'm not sure what you're getting at, Trish.'

'Girls, it happened over thirty years ago, the same age we all are now – well apart from Ruth who's twenty five of course,' she added jokingly.

But neither Ruth nor Nina was laughing. Instead, they stared at the article, both finally understanding what Trish was getting at.

'I don't believe it,' Nina whispered, re-reading the headline: *Abandoned newborn found on café steps*. 'That baby could be someone we know.'

57

'*D*on't be silly,' Ella said, when shortly afterwards they accosted her again. But her face was flushed and her eyes kept darting from left to right as if trying to find an escape route. Had she taken the baby in herself, maybe raised it as her own? Or perhaps there was some temporary arrangement ...

Whatever it was, there was no denying that her boss was seriously thrown by the appearance of the article, and their accompanying questions.

'As I said, it's a long time ago – really, it's so long ago I'd almost forgotten about it myself.'

'What about the mum?' Ruth asked, referring to the police appeal mentioned in the piece. 'Did she ever come forward?'

'Yes, yes of course. There was no problem ... it was all sorted out within a day or two. Really, I don't know why the three of you are so interested. It's a nothing story, really.'

'A nothing story?' Trish chortled. 'Ella, it's probably the most interesting thing that's ever happened in this town – well apart from Ruth's big success, of course,' she added quickly and Ruth smiled. 'Look, we just want to know who was involved, you know, just for interest's sake. I mean, the baby is about the same age as us, so chances are we know the person –'

'And if you did know all the details, how do you think the people involved would feel?' Ella snapped. 'Look Trish, for once just mind your own business. Nothing good will come from you snooping around in things that you have no business with. You need to stop this immediately.'

There was a brief silence as the three were confronted with a side of Ella they had never seen before. Clearly this was something very personal to her.

'Ah, come on Ella, really, it's no big deal, we're just curious –'

'Trish, leave it.' Nina interjected softly, deciding they should leave the older woman alone. 'Ella's right, it is none of our business. Let's just forget about it.'

Trish was about to say something else, but seeing Nina's exasperated look, seemed to think better of it. 'Oh all right then,' she said wearily. 'I just thought it might be interesting for my book, that's all.'

But it was a pitiful excuse and they all knew it.

'Well pet, some things are just better left undisturbed, trust me on that.' Ella said, sounding somewhat calmer now. 'Now, I'm sorry, but I'd better get back to work.'

'Would you like me to stay on and help out for a while?' Nina asked, feeling somewhat guilty. 'Things seem to have calmed down a little since, but –'

'Not at all, Alice and I will be grand.' Ella headed back towards the kitchen. 'See you tomorrow morning?'

'Sure. You know how much I love the early shift,' Nina joked, thinking that early mornings would no doubt be par for the course once the baby arrived in a few weeks time.

The three girls exited the café and drifted down towards the lake.

'Bloody hell,' Trish said. 'The way she acted you'd swear it was Prince William that was left on the front step.'

'Yes, she was pretty reluctant,' Ruth said thoughtfully as they walked along.

'You know, we could still figure this out,' Trish went on. 'All we have to do is ask someone else, someone who was around at the time.'

Nina rolled her eyes. 'Trish, didn't you hear anything Ella said back there?'

'Oh come on! We can't just forget all about it and surely I'm not the only one who's curious.' She looked at Ruth. 'What do you think?'

'Well ... when Ella was talking back there, something struck me. What if ... well, what if she was so adamant that we leave this alone because ... because it was one of us?'

Trish's eyes widened. 'You mean the baby? Oh my goodness – I never even thought of that!'

'You cannot be serious.' Nina said. 'Sure we all know that none of our mums would have done that. Abandoned us on a doorstep? Come on?' Nina certainly knew that Cathy would never in a million years have done something like that. She adored her, always had.

Ruth's eyes were downcast and she looked vulnerable. 'The date on the article – it was only a few days after I was born, whereas you two are a little older. It could be me.'

'Ruth no –'

'Seriously Nina, it wouldn't be that much of a surprise. I know I was ... an accident.' She looked ashamed. 'It's why I'm an only child.'

And perhaps also why you've spent most of your life striving to be accepted, Nina thought silently.

'Oh.' For once Trish had little to say on the subject. 'Well look, if you're seriously worried it might be that Ruth, it's your call. We won't go any further with this. As Ella said, maybe there's nothing to be gained from pursuing it.'

'No, I think I'd like to know actually. I mean, it would hurt of course, but at least then I wouldn't always be wondering, like I am now.'

Nina put an arm around her shoulders. 'Are you sure? It was a long time ago, remember? And if something like that did happen, it's really nobody's business but yours and your family's.'

Ruth looked out over the large expanse of water, which looked almost black in this light. 'No really. I think I would like to know.'

The three were silent for a while as they digested the implications of what they'd found, and what else they might eventually discover.

'So where do we go from here?' Ruth asked finally.

'I suppose we just keep asking around,' Nina ventured. 'Trish, maybe we could try some of the older people you spoke to before, the ones who were around at the time. Lakeview was tiny back then, surely everyone would have heard about it.'

Trish was looking into the distance, towards the direction of Nina's house. She seemed to be thinking hard. 'What about your dad?' she asked, turning to look at her.

'Patrick? What would he know?' Nina looked dubious.

'You're the one who's always complaining that he's never put his nose outside of Lakeview, so it's likely he was around at the time.' Trish looked from one girl to the other. 'So maybe he's the one we should have been talking to from the beginning.'

58

'Do you think he'll know anything?' Ruth asked as the three made their way across the stone bridge to Patrick's house.

'Well, if he does, there's no guarantee he'd tell us anyway,' Nina replied in an odd tone and saw both girls look questioningly at her. 'Let's just say we haven't been on the best of terms over the last couple of months – especially since he realized it wasn't a beach ball I was hiding under here,' she said wryly. 'These days we sort of just stay out of each other's way.'

Ruth sucked air through her teeth. 'I'm not sure if this is such a good idea then. I mean, he barely even knows me ...'

Nina gave a short laugh. 'Don't worry, he barely knows me either and I'm his daughter. I'm sure it'll be fine.'

Soon they reached the house and with Nina leading the way, the three climbed up the steps and into the house. As they entered, she called out. 'Dad? Are you home?'

A sound that resembled something like a grunt came from the direction of the kitchen and the girls exchanged looks. Nina just shook her head and smiled as if to say 'See what I mean?'

'Dad? It's me, and I have some friends with me,' she said.

It was only then that Patrick peered out of the kitchen, obviously curious.

'Oh hello,' he mumbled, and Nina noticed his gaze rest ever so briefly on not only her bump, but Ruth's too.

Obviously noticing this too, Ruth stepped forward and flashed her best Hollywood smile. 'Hi Mr Hughes,' she said amiably. 'You probably don't remember me, but you fixed up a lot of stuff for my parents over the years. I'm Ruth, Ollie Seymour's daughter?'

'Right,' Patrick mumbled, staring at Ruth's outstretched arm as if he wasn't sure what to do with it and Nina was surprised to see some form of recognition dawn in his eyes all the same.

Could her old man be a fan of *Glamazons*? Nah, she couldn't see it really – Patrick wasn't really into TV (apart from his obsession with their insides). But more to the point, could it be that Trish was right – and that he recognized Ruth because she was indeed the abandoned baby from all those years ago?

No, no, she was stretching it now – of course her father would have seen Ruth before, if not in recent newspaper articles, then almost certainly when she was growing up in the town. Hadn't she just said herself that he used to fix things for her family?

'And of course you know Trish,' Nina supplied, and Trish in turn waved hello.

No one could say that her dad was a beacon of hospitality, that was for sure, Nina thought, embarrassed that he hadn't the manners to even say hello, to say nothing of shaking hands. But she reminded herself, they were here for a reason and it wasn't hospitality.

Patrick looked at her. 'I'm making dinner, but I don't have enough for everyone,' he said pointedly.

Nina groaned, mortified. Could he be any more unsociable? 'That's OK, we're not here for that. We actually just wondered if maybe you could help us out with something.'

'Oh?' Patrick looked past them, almost instinctively seeking out a TV or electronic appliance of some sort, Nina figured. 'No, no, we don't want you to fix anything, we just hoped we could pick your brains really.'

He frowned, although it was more a look of confusion than irritation.

'Seeing as you've lived in Lakeview your whole life,' Trish interjected. 'Remember last time I was here I was telling you about that book I'm doing?'

There was a short grunt and Nina was sure he wouldn't have the foggiest idea what her friend was on about, much less a recollection of it, but to her surprise he said: 'I told you I didn't have any photographs.'

'No it's not that. We actually just came across something in the news archives, something that happened here a long time ago and we were hoping you might remember it.'

Another grunt.

Trish reached into her bag. 'Do you mind taking a look at this article?'

'I'd really rather have my dinner.'

'Look we're just asking for a quick favor Dad – if you don't know anything about it, then you don't know anything about it. If you could just take a look –'

'Your mother would be a much better source of information. Yes, you should ask her Nina; she would know.'

'But Mum isn't here now is she?' Nina replied through gritted teeth.

'You should ask her,' he repeated, as if his daughter hadn't spoken and she looked to her friends, as if to convey that this was a complete waste of time. Clearly he had no interest whatsoever in helping them and as usual, couldn't be more brusque and obstinate if he tried.

'I'm sorry guys,' she sighed, as Patrick retreated into the kitchen. 'There's no point, we might as well just go.'

'Oh for heaven's sake,' Trish exclaimed following him. 'Mr Hughes, really, if you could just take a quick look at this for us, we'll be out of your hair in no time.' She offered the piece of paper to Patrick. 'We were just hoping to find out more about what happened.'

Nina's father glanced at the piece of paper and he skimmed through it a little before his gaze dropped to the floor.

'Why did you come to me with this?' he asked flatly.

Ruth stepped forward. 'Like we said Mr Hughes, we thought you might remember something about it,' she replied, her tone eager.

'*Do* you know something about it Dad?'

'Yes, I know something about it.'

Ruth stared at him, as if the strength of her gaze could urge more information out of him. *Welcome to my world*, Nina thought.

'What do you know Dad? What happened?' Almost instinctively, Nina knew that they needed to tread softly with this. You could never coerce anything out of Patrick and if they pushed too hard he would simply clam up and walk out.

'Please, Mr Hughes, we're just curious, none of us have heard anything about this before,' Trish pleaded.

Patrick exhaled heavily and shook his head. His gaze roamed around the room, as if he was looking for something. But upon closer inspection, Nina realized that there was something in his expression, almost like some kind of internal struggle. She didn't understand.

'Mr Hughes, really, it's not a big deal –'

'It is a big deal!' he bellowed and all three girls jumped back in unison, shocked by his ferocity.

Nina's heart began to beat very fast. Something was going on here; something very important, but she couldn't quite put her finger on what it was. Was ... he somehow ... involved in this?

'Maybe we should go ...' Ruth ventured quietly. She looked at Patrick. 'I'm sorry we upset you sir, but we just wanted to find out if you knew anything about this. We thought it could be important, but it doesn't matter, sorry.'

She and Trish turned to leave and looked at Nina, who was standing rooted to the spot, her gaze boring into her father. It was like every room in the house had suddenly begun to shrink, the walls closing in on her. And Nina knew she needed to ask the question, even though she already knew the answer.

'That baby ...' she began breathlessly, 'the one that was left on the steps of the café all those years ago. It was me, wasn't it?'

Patrick looked at her, and as always, his face was expressionless.

'Yes Nina,' he replied simply, 'it was you.'

59

*N*ina stood there, hurt beyond her wildest dreams. She was unable to speak, unable to move, barely able to breathe. Trish stood frozen next to Patrick, looking at him in horror. Ruth too was rooted to the spot, as if afraid to move.

Meanwhile, after dropping his bombshell, Nina's father simply turned around and resumed making his dinner.

She'd been abandoned as a baby, cast aside by her parents, by Cathy – but why? What had she done wrong? What was wrong with her – or more to the point what was wrong with her father? How could he just drop a bombshell like that on her and then go back to his business as if nothing at all had happened?

'Nina ...' Finally she felt Ruth touch her arm, which broke through her reverie.

'I don't believe you!' she cried, addressing the back of Patrick's head. 'Mum would never do something like that. She loves me! She's always done everything for me – you're the one who was –' Then she stopped short, realizing something. 'Oh wait...' she whispered, talking to herself more than anyone else. 'It wasn't Mum who left me there, was it? It was you.'

Patrick stiffened then and Nina was briefly aware of Ruth and

Trish retreating slowly from the room, evidently deciding it was best to give them some space.

But Nina didn't want time alone with her father; if anything she wanted to get as far away from him as possible. But first she needed to know the truth.

'It's the reason she left you, isn't it? The reason she took me away from this place. And she was right – because now I know why you never made the effort to see me, never tried to spend time with me; hell even now you barely give me the time of day. What's so bad about me that you hated me enough to throw me away, even at such a young age? What the hell did I ever do to you?' Eyes flashing with anger, she waited for Patrick to turn and face her, but instead he opened a drawer and started to fidget with the utensils.

Nina gave a short, humorless laugh. 'Wow,' she said, 'What kind of cold, heartless bastard are you that you can't even give me an explanation? Don't I deserve that much, at least?'

'I'm sorry Nina,' he said simply, but his voice was so low she had to strain to hear it.

'That's it – that's all I get? You throw me out in a cardboard box and all I get is *sorry!*'

Meanwhile Ruth had returned to the room. 'Nina, maybe you should go outside for a couple of minutes. It'll help clear your head.'

'Oh I'm going outside alright,' she answered sharply. 'But it'll be for good, because I am never, ever setting foot in this house again!'

But Patrick remained unmoved and still shaking, Nina was barely aware of Ruth taking her by the arm and leading her out of the kitchen and then out the front door of the house.

'He gave me away ...' she mumbled slowly. 'He gave me away, he didn't want me.'

'Sssh, it's OK,' Trish said, coming forward to put an arm around her.

'I don't have anywhere to go ...' Nina started to cry.

'Don't worry about that honey, we'll take care of you, and you can stay with me,' Ruth told her gently.

'I never want to see him again ...'

'And you don't have to if you don't want to,' Trish cooed, 'Try not to worry.'

They walked further away from the house, Trish and Ruth gently guiding Nina along the path towards the other side of town.

'I need to talk to Mum,' she wailed, rooting in her handbag for her mobile, but Ruth put a hand on her shoulder.

'I think that's a very good idea, but maybe wait a little until you've calmed down. I know you said she's away so I'm sure she'll be doubly frantic if you call her in the state you're in now. Best to wait until you've had a chance to get over the initial shock.'

Nina knew that Ruth was probably right, but still how could she not try and contact her mother? She was the only one who could shed some light on what had happened, as clearly Patrick wasn't going to tell her anything and there was no one else who would –

'Ella,' she cried, stopping dead in her tracks.

Trish looked at her. 'What about her?'

'I need to talk to her again. I need to ask her what happened that morning – the day she found ... me.' She looked at her friends. 'Now we know why she was so determined not to talk about it earlier.' Nina's mouth set in a thin line. 'But she has no such excuse now.'

'Sweetheart, you've had a shock ... it really might not be the best idea ...'

Nina marched forward. 'I don't care; I need to know what happened – everything that happened.'

Conscious that they really didn't have any say in the matter, Trish and Ruth went quiet and didn't challenge her any further.

And when a few minutes later, they reached the door of the café, all three stopped outside it and stared down at the steps, the same thought going through each of their minds.

Then having issued instructions to the others that she needed to do this alone, Nina stepped gingerly over the top step of the Heartbreak Café, the same one upon which she had been found thirty years before.

60

*I*nside, she scanned the area, searching for Ella.

The older woman was at the end of the counter, talking to a customer, but as Nina approached, she looked up and met her gaze. Immediately her expression changed and Nina knew that something in her own face had signaled to Ella that she'd uncovered the truth.

Her boss said something briefly to the person she had been talking to, before walking forward to approach her, her manner tentative and gentle. When she was within a few feet of Nina, she stopped and nodded her head in resignation.

'So you know,' she said quietly.

Anger rushed through her, so intense that Nina wanted to pound her fists on something just to get the frustration out.

'Yes, I know and more to the point, so did you. You knew about this, knew for all these years that it was *me* – and yet you didn't say anything.' Tears were running down Nina's cheeks and she had to gulp for air.

'Oh love,' Ella rushed forward and gathered Nina into an embrace. 'Let's go out back and we can talk about this.' She nodded at the waitress to take over, and swiftly guided Nina through the kitchen and out towards the food storage area.

'My own parents didn't want me, they don't love me ...' Because even though Nina was sure Cathy had no part in this, she couldn't be absolutely certain. After what she'd just learned, how could she be certain of anything?

'Your parents love you very much Nina Hughes, you must know that.'

'But then why would they try to ... get rid of me?'

'Oh honey, no. That's not what happened at all.'

'But it is! My dad ... Patrick – he told me himself.'

Ella took a deep breath. 'Yes, you're right, he did do that, but I believe there was actually a reason for it.' She rubbed her hand up and down Nina's back in an attempt to soothe her.

'Exactly. He did it because he didn't want me ... he doesn't love me ... never has, and what's worse, Mum let him.' At this thought, which had just occurred to her, Nina cried as if her heart would break and as she did, she felt the baby stirring inside her.

'No she didn't. Please Nina ... let me explain. Perhaps it's best if I start at the very beginning, let you know exactly what happened that night.'

Nina gulped, not sure now whether or not she wanted to hear it. 'Fine.'

Ella cleared her throat. 'To be honest, the first thing that crossed my mind was that it must be my doughnut delivery,' she began. 'Or a delivery of some kind – it isn't unusual to find fresh stock on the doorstep of the café so early in the morning ...'

61

*N*ina sat for a moment in silence after Ella had finished recounting step by step the events of that morning thirty years before, how she'd found the cardboard box on the step and had initially thought that someone local had left her yet another sad case to take care of – to the subsequent arrival of the doctor, and investigations from Frank, who Nina recognized from the café, when he popped in now and again for coffee and a sausage roll. She'd served the older policeman a number of times and he'd never let on a thing.

She shook her head at Ella; hardly able to take it all in. 'I still can't believe you thought I was a box of doughnuts.'

The older woman hugged her. 'I know – but you soon let me know I was barking up the wrong tree.'

'But to think that my own father would just ... throw me away like that,' she continued, fresh tears in her eyes. "Like a piece of rubbish.'

'Like I said, it's all too easy to play judge and jury until you know the whole story,' Ella repeated pointedly. 'And there's a little more to it.' She sighed. 'Here's the thing. Patrick ... your dad ... he's not quite the same as everybody else you know.'

Nina snorted. 'That's an understatement.'

'Now I know what you're thinking and it's not like that. How can I put this ...?' She paused for a moment before speaking again. 'For instance, think about what you're going through right now. You're hurt, deeply emotional, and feeling terrible. Well, your dad ... he doesn't process things in quite the same way.'

'Because he's a heartless bastard.'

'Actually you're wrong. Your father does indeed have a heart. He's just not very good at showing it.' Nina was silent as she tried to decipher what Ella was telling her. 'Patrick looks at the world somewhat ... differently from most of us – in truth, a lot differently.' She struggled to explain. 'For instance, you know how he works on his TVs and all that? Takes things apart and puts them back together in perfect working order?'

Nina nodded, not understanding where this was going. 'Exactly, he's weird; he pays more attention to those damn TVs than he does to his own flesh and blood. If I even am that,' she added then, another thought suddenly occurring to her. 'Was that it?' she asked Ella. 'Is that why Mum married him? Was she pregnant with somebody else's child and that's why he hates me?'

'No, no, no – your imagination is working overtime now. It's nothing at all like that. As I told you before, your father adored your mother and of course you're his daughter.'

'Pity,' she spat.

'Try and concentrate on what I'm telling you. Patrick is your father, but he's not the same as most people. He struggles to form bonds or emotional relationships with lots of different people in the way you or I do. Usually, people like him can only concentrate on one thing at a time – first Cathy and then you, although that did take time.'

'What do you mean, people like him?'

'Okay, let me try and explain this. Have you ever heard of Asperger's Syndrome?'

Nina frowned. 'You mean like autism?'

'Yes, it's considered a version of autism, but a more behavioral form, as opposed to the more dramatic version most of us imagine when we think of that description. Of course, I'm no expert on any of this, but there is a good chance that your father has what's described as Adult Asperger's.'

Nina looked at her, dumbfounded.

Ella continued. 'As I said I'm no expert, but remember I told you that my older daughter Carly works as a special needs assistant? Well, she told me a few years ago that when learning about adult neurodivergent characteristics that your dad kept popping into her mind – his awkwardness amongst other people, inability to read social cues, repetitive routines, fixed interests ... that kind of thing. I mentioned it to your mother and she read up on it and agreed that yes it was indeed a possibility.'

'My father is autistic and nobody ever told me?'

'No, no – it's completely different from the kind of thing you're thinking. It's more of a behavioral ... *difference*. He struggles more with the kind of easygoing social communication most of us enjoy without thinking about it. Many neurodivergent minds tend to process stuff in more black and white terms. And if there is a problem take a logical approach towards fixing it.'

'So I was a *problem*?' Nina said icily, not sure what to think. How could she not have realised this about her dad before now?

'Of course you weren't, not to someone who has some prior understanding of what life with a newborn is like and certainly not to someone who understands that some woman can be differently affected by motherhood.'

'I don't follow ...'

'Well, as you know this was a very small village back then and it was no secret that your mother ... struggled a little after you were born. Perhaps she might have explained this to you before?' When Nina shook her head, Ella went on. 'Baby blues or postnatal depression as it's termed now, usually sorts itself out after a time or with the right medication. But your dad – he didn't understand. You must remember that while Patrick always marched to his own beat as such, the one thing he was truly passionate about was your mother. He adored her when they were younger and I'd imagine he still does. So when you came along ... well as I said, Cathy was finding things a bit tougher than expected and this troubled him.'

'She had postnatal depression?'

Ella nodded. 'Completely natural, completely normal, but your dad didn't see it that way, all he saw was that your mum was tearful and sad, and this conincided with your arrival. So in his own logical way, he decided to take it upon himself to solve the problem – his thinking I suppose being that Cathy didn't know how to deal with a baby. So he decided to take you to someone he knew who did.'

'Which is why he left me here – at the café.'

'My lot running around the place were a common sight back then.' Ella smiled sadly. 'And of course, everyone knows the way I am about children and animals and all the rest of it, so as far as your dad was concerned, who better? If you think about it and maybe try and see things through his eyes, he thought what he was doing was for the best – for both you and Cathy.'

Nina stared into the distance, still not quite sure how to process this. From that perspective yes, it certainly did seem less hurtful, but still ...

'Really, it didn't take too much investigating; the place was small and it didn't take long for Frank to figure out who you belonged to. Besides, your mother was frantic.'

'But why wasn't my dad arrested?'

'Because most of us already knew he was that little bit ... different, I suppose.' She smiled. 'Frank figured it out faster than the rest of us and went to have a quiet chat with your dad. He was a good friend of your grandfather's when he was alive and thus aware of Patrick's ... quirkier way of seeing things from a very young age. Of course, there was no label for it back then, but people knew his motives were honest. So realistically why would anyone arrest him? Especially when your dad was only doing what he thought was right. In any case, your mother wouldn't hear of it.'

'She defended him?' Nina gasped, amazed. 'Why?'

'I suppose you're going to have to ask her about that.'

Nina was silent for a moment. 'So the whole town knew he had this ... Asperger's thing?'

'Of course not – in adults there are no hard and fast rules, and even now one can't say for sure. Neurodivergence is a tough one to identify even now, whereas back then it was almost impossible and most people like that would just have been considered as oddballs and whatnot. As it is, if it wasn't for Carly's knowledge we might not have even considered the notion.'

Nina nodded, something in her own brain clicking into place when she thought about her father's mannerisms. The highly regimented timekeeping, habitual behaviors and of course, his apparent lack of empathy. It was hard to comprehend, yet it did in a way fit. Yet, at the same time she couldn't help but feel bad for her dad. Who knew what what was really going on beneath his supposedly offhand persona?

'You should understand Nina, that your dad does try, but I'm sure it's hard. I bump into him on the street occasionally and I sense he tries to jumpstart his brain into asking the right questions – socially appropriate or caring questions. It's so tricky for him.'

'Funny, he's never tried that with me.'

'Well, perhaps there is some guilt there too and when he sees you he gets flustered.'

'So this is why he's freaked about my being pregnant?'

'Is he?' Ella nodded, as if it was all very reasonable. 'I guess to Patrick, tiny babies equal trouble.'

Nina gave a short laugh. 'I suppose he might have a point there.' Then she shook her head. 'I just don't know how I'm supposed to face him now. How do I even ... deal with all this?'

'Just be understanding. You have great friends, close relationships and a good heart. Your dad has the greatest intentions, but he's never been able to achieve what you have. Show some kindness and most importantly, some empathy. Think of it this way. You know the way non-verbal autistic children are said to be living in their own world?' Nina nodded. 'Actually, they do live in our world, but in their own way.'

Nina thought for a moment. 'I need to think about all this, try and digest it somehow plus I also really need to talk to Mum.'

'You'll do the right thing by Patrick, I know you will. And of course your mother will be better able to explain and - '

But Ella wasn't able to finish the sentence because at that moment, Nina reached out and roughly grabbed her arm. Then a little while later there was a splashing sound and startled, both women stared at the wetness on her legs and feet.

'Oh no,' Nina said, unable to believe it. 'I think my waters just broke.'

'This is silly,' Trish whispered. 'Why are we waiting out here?' She and Ruth were both leaning against the wall of the café.

'Because obviously this is something Nina needs to do on her own. The poor thing. Can you imagine the shock? I hope Ella is able to give her a good explanation.'

'Yeah, the explanation is that her father is a messed-up ...' Her words trailed off. 'Oh hell ...'

Ruth's head turned at Trish's obvious change in tone and following her gaze, she saw a trim, smartly-dressed woman walking down the street towards them.

'What's wrong?' she asked, but there wasn't time for an explanation as suddenly the woman was standing right in front of them, a scornful expression on her face.

'You,' she said, addressing Trish. 'How dare you?'

'Emer, I really don't think this is the time or the place –'

'But of course, there was a time and place for sleeping with my husband, wasn't there?' the woman raged, and Ruth gulped. Oh dear...

Trish's face flushed and for once Ruth noticed she seemed lost for words. 'I ... I'm sorry,' she uttered finally. 'Believe me, I had no idea that you ... I mean, I thought that you were –'

'No idea that he was sleeping with me too? Oh please, spare me the wronged mistress thing, and don't tell me you fell for "the wife doesn't understand me" act? I thought you were supposed to be smarter than that.'

'Honestly Emer, I didn't know. But either way, it doesn't matter. It was wrong and I'm sorry, but it's over now, I told him that.'

Hearing this, Ruth looked at her friend with interest. Somehow she'd presumed that even after finding out that Emer was pregnant, Trish would have carried on the affair irrespective of his wife's feelings. But perhaps she did have a heart after all.

'Oh, how nice of you!' Emer trilled, her voice a high falsetto. 'So tell me this, how am I supposed to pick up the pieces? How do I tell my daughter and my unborn child that their father is a cad who pretends to be working for their future, but is really out with the town whore?'

'Now hold on a second ...' For some reason, Ruth felt duty bound to defend Trish, even though there was nothing to defend. But she had never seen her friend like this before, looking so small and ashamed and very obviously affected by it all. It was clear that despite her bravado, Trish really did have feelings for this Dave, married and all that he was. And learning of his wife's pregnancy had clearly hurt her a lot more than she'd let on.

'It's OK Ruth,' Trish said softly, before turning again to Emer. 'You're right and I'm sorry. I really don't know. I guess I never stopped to think ... about you or the children. Please believe me, I'm really sorry.'

Emer seemed taken aback, and somewhat disappointed that Trish wasn't putting up more of a fight – any kind of fight in fact. Actually, the poor woman looked defeated and who could blame her? Ruth thought. To find that her so-called perfect life in the country hadn't worked out after all? She recalled Nina telling them that this particular woman spent a lot of time lording it over her friends, and she thought not for the first time, that you never really had any clue what went on behind closed doors.

Up until recently, this Emer woman thought she had it sorted, but how wrong she was. It almost put Ruth's own problems into perspective. At least there was a chance she could go back to LA and pick up the pieces. It would be difficult, especially with a baby in tow, but she was willing to give it a shot. The problem was that she wasn't sure if her heart would be in acting now, but what else could she do? That life was all she'd ever known.

Just then there was some kind of commotion from inside the café and Ruth turned to see one of the waitresses rush to the doorway. 'Please, please come inside!' Alice called to Ruth and Trish who exchanged a concerned glance. What on earth was happening in there?

Trish turned to Emer. 'I'm sorry, but I need to go – maybe we can discuss this another time.'

'Oh forget it,' the other woman said, huffily walking away. 'There's nothing to discuss.'

Ruth and Trish went inside and followed the girl out back to the storage room where they found Nina sitting on boxes and breathing heavily.

'What's happening?' Ruth gasped.

Nina looked up helplessly. 'My waters broke.'

'You're kidding!' Trish exclaimed. 'I thought you had a few more weeks to go?'

'So did I,' she said panicking, 'but it must be coming early.'

Just then a contraction ripped through Nina's body and she let out a howl.

'We need to get her to the hospital,' Ruth beseeched.

Ella looked at Nina with growing trepidation. 'I know. A lot of things might have happened in this café, but I'm not about to open it up as a maternity ward.

Trish headed for the door. 'I'll go out front – see if I can find someone to give us a lift.'

Good luck with that, Ruth thought silently. What person in their right mind would risk giving a woman in the middle of labor a lift?

Poor Nina was writhing uncomfortably on the chair, panting heavily, while Ella held a cold towel to her forehead. Wanting to help, but completely unsure how, Ruth simply held her friend's hand.

'We're in luck!' Trish said, bursting back into the room with none other than ...

'Charlie,' Ruth gasped, the words almost catching in her throat.

He stared at her. 'Everyone was talking about it outside. I thought ... I was worried that ...'

Immediately she understood. 'No, no, I'm fine,' she reassured him. 'I've still a long way to go – unlike some,' she nodded in Nina's direction. 'Do you mind?'

'Of course I don't mind. What can I do?'

'Seriously no,' Nina protested. 'I can't risk messing up your car –'

'It's not mine – it's a display model, and I know a good valet service,' he said, winking at Nina and Ruth noticed, immediately putting her at ease.

'Are you sure?' she said helplessly. 'Because I really don't know how long this will ... oww!' Yet another contraction went through her and she blanched.

'Ella, get whatever we might need, blankets, towels, etc. together.' Charlie quickly took charge and Ruth watched him, impressed by his decisiveness. 'I'll bring the car round, so she doesn't have to go through the café. There's rear access from here, isn't there?'

'Yes.' Ella too was spurred into action and all the activity seemed to have the effect of calming Nina.

All too soon, she was being helped into the back of Charlie's car – or one of the garage's fleet at least.

'Sweetheart, do you want me to call your father?' Ella asked rather stupidly, Ruth thought.

This suggestion seemed to bring a fresh wave of discomfort. 'No,' Nina replied, 'I don't think I could handle all that just yet.'

'Of course.'

'Will you guys stay with me?' Nina pleaded from inside the car, and although she wasn't keen, Ruth couldn't ignore the terrified look on the poor girl's face.

'Of course I will,' she replied.

'Good idea,' Trish interjected brightly. 'But I'll pass if you don't mind – this is more Ruth's kind of thing really. I'll keep an eye on your stuff though!'

Cursing Trish, Ruth duly got in the car beside Nina and soon after, Charlie pulled away and headed straight for Dublin.

63

'That's it Nina, that's it,' Ruth said, as she held on tightly to Nina's hand in the delivery suite of the maternity hospital. Actually, it was more like Nina holding tightly to her hand, and Ruth was sure she would have broken bones when this was finished. When they'd reached the hospital, and the midwife had immediately confirmed that she was about to deliver, Nina hadn't wanted to let Ruth go.

'I don't have anybody else,' she'd said tearfully and how could Ruth refuse? And if anything, it was no doubt good practice for her.

'That's it, keep breathing, keep breathing,' she reassured her, patting her forehead with a cool washcloth.

'Owww!' Nina yelled.

The midwife stood at the base of the bed. 'We're almost there Nina, not much longer, one or two more good pushes ...'

'Ughhhh,' Nina moaned, red in the face.

'That's it. Here it comes!' the woman encouraged and Nina's eyes went wide. 'Good girl, the head is out now, so all we need now is to push out the shoulders, OK?'

Nina nodded helplessly and then pushed, struggling for breath. Then all of a sudden, the baby came out and after a brief moment, they heard a cry erupt.

'You did it! You did it Nina!' Ruth cheered.

'I did it, I did it,' Nina breathed, tears coming down her cheeks.

'Congratulations love,' the midwife smiled. 'You have a son.'

She lay her head back on the pillows, as if in disbelief. 'I have a son.'

Ruth leaned forward for a closer look when, after all the necessary medical checks were done, the midwife placed a tiny baby boy in Nina's waiting arms. He had a shock of dark hair.

'He looks just like you. He's beautiful Nina; you did such a good job.' Ruth said smiling.

'Thank you,' Nina whispered, staring in awe at her baby.

_a_ few minutes later, once Nina and the baby were settled, Ruth exited the delivery room and pulled off her hospital scrubs. To her surprise, she saw that Charlie was still waiting in the hallway.

'Everything going OK?' he asked, standing up.

'Everything's already gone actually,' she said, telling him all that happened over the last hour. 'A little boy – he's beautiful.'

'That's great news – I'm glad we got here in time.'

'Yes, nice driving Schumacher,' Ruth teased.

There was a brief silence, until Charlie sighed and turned to look at her. 'So you're still here,' he said.

'Why wouldn't I be?'

'I guess I thought you'd get the next flight back to LA.'

'I told you – I'm finished with that life.' Well, at least she would be if there was perhaps a life in Lakeview waiting for her. And thinking about the look on his face back in Ella's when he appeared in the stockroom, she wondered if there might just be a chance. But she figured that this time, she really should put all of her cards on the table. 'Actually, I can't go back because I'm getting sued by the network,' she added wryly.

'Ahh, I see, so that's the reason,' Charlie said, in a wry tone. 'You're only still here because you're stuck here.'

'Come on Charlie, do you think Ireland or LA are my *only* options? If I hated it so much here, why wouldn't I just hop on a plane and go to London or Paris, and do something there? Being so shallow and all ...' she added, deliberately goading him. 'Of course, the baby wouldn't exactly make any of that very easy, but I'm sure I could manage. I always do.'

'So you are leaving then?' he said, staring straight ahead.

'I don't know yet,' she said honestly. 'There's a lot to sort out.'

He shook his head. 'When I saw those pictures ... of you and that asshole, I wanted to put my fist through the wall.'

'I know and I can only imagine how it looked to you, but surely you must know by now that that's the way the media works. Everything is spun and slanted and ... skewed. It was a set-up Charlie, and maybe you don't believe me, but I'm telling you the truth. And the truth is that Troy Valentine is a brain-dead moron who is never, ever going to be involved in this baby's life.'

'You really mean that.'

'Of course I do. Come on, you know how I feel about all that, why would you just assume that I'd go back to LA and take up with him again. It's insulting.'

'I know, but then again, when it comes to La-La Land I've never really understood the spell it holds over you.'

'*Held*, Charlie, held. I'm finished with LA. Period.' They both laughed at her unintentional Americanism and then to Ruth's disbelief, he reached for her hand.

She stared at him, her breath frozen in her chest.

'And what about Peter Jackson – and that Oscar?' he asked, rubbing his finger lightly over her skin.

'They can give it to Scarlett – she needs it more than I do,' she said haughtily and he laughed again.

'You'd really consider giving up all that for a boring old life in the country?' he asked then and her heart almost stopped.

'I know that life with you could never be boring.'

Charlie leaned forward and pulled her into a passionate kiss. She threw her arms around his neck as he kissed every inch of her face, her eyes, her mouth, her neck.

'I love you. Never do that to me again,' she said in between kisses. 'I need you, *we* need you.'

'I won't, I swear. I promise I'll –'

'Oh for crying out loud!' Ruth and Charlie broke apart at the sound of the voice and turned to see Trish striding down the hallway, a bunch of flowers in her hand. 'Don't you two ever stop with the melodrama? Hepburn and Tracy eat your hearts out.'

65

The following morning, after a surprisingly good night's sleep, Nina was in the maternity ward welcoming the first of her visitors. She was sitting up in bed, wearing a pale pink nightgown with her dark hair tied up in a small ponytail.

She felt great and couldn't stop smiling, still unable to believe that the tiny baby lying in the crib beside her bed was truly hers. And she especially couldn't believe that she'd actually considered giving him up. How could she when he was so beautiful?

She immediately thought back to her and Jess's conversation in Dublin, whereupon Jess had confessed that she herself was adopted, but had been reunited with her birth mother a few years before.

'Giving your baby up doesn't necessarily mean you'll never see it again,' she had told Nina kindly. 'And doing so definitely doesn't make you a bad person. My birth mum had her own reasons for giving me up and in her shoes, I'd probably have done the same thing.' She smiled, but didn't elaborate and Nina didn't like to ask. 'My adoptive parents are wonderful and gave me a wonderful life, the kind of upbringing my mother wanted for me. I wanted for absolutely nothing and while I might have liked a brother and sister, it wasn't an option for them. So speaking from experience, if you really feel you can't give this child the life you think it deserves, then yes, you should consider adoption, but at the same time are you absolutely sure you couldn't raise it on your own?'

Today Nina realized Jess was right; millions of women over the years had managed it without partners and she was sure she could too – especially when there were so many people willing to help. Yes, it would be hard, but she would make it work.

Now Jess herself took a couple of tentative steps towards the baby's crib. 'Little thing like that sure required a lot of work, eh?' she said, and Nina caught Brian's eye and laughed.

The two looked relaxed and happy in one another's company and Nina suspected that Jess's scare had given them both a fright and concentrated their energies on what was most important, their love for each other.

'Well, he's lovely, but you can keep him,' Trish commented. 'As it is, there's no chance of me going down that road any time soon,' she said, and although there was bravado in her tone (as always) Nina knew that she was still hurting over the situation with Dave. A couple of minutes before, she'd looked terrified at Jess's appearance, obviously worried that Emer's friend would deck her, but of course Jess did no such thing. Nina wondered how things were between the two women these days.

'Trish, I really can't wait to see you when you have a baby,' Nina said.

Her friend's eyes widened. 'So does that mean you're sticking around?'

She turned her attention back to her son. 'Yeah, I'm sticking around,' she said softly.

'Knock, knock, Mummy,' Ruth trilled coming into the room, closely followed by Charlie.

'Congratulations Nina,' he said softly.

'Thank you – we might not have got here in time if it wasn't for you.'

'My pleasure.'

'Pleasure?' Trish repeated disbelievingly and they all laughed.

'Seriously, thank you both. Now come and meet my son,' she said to Charlie, who stared in amazement at the little person fast asleep alongside her.

'What are you going to call him?' Ruth asked.

'I'm not sure yet, actually.'

'You didn't have anything in mind?'

'Not really,' she said and Jess knowingly met her gaze, understanding that she hadn't picked out any names because she was trying to distance herself from the baby in case she went ahead and gave it up.

Ruth smiled and looked lovingly at Charlie, who seemed transfixed by the tiny baby. 'Do you want to hold him?' Nina asked

'No, no, he's so tiny I'm afraid I'd hurt him.'

'Better learn fast honey!' Ruth quipped and the others laughed. She smiled at Nina. 'Won't it be brilliant, our kids growing up together?'

'Does that mean that you're sticking around too?' Trish asked and Ruth nodded and smiled at Charlie.

'Well, if I could just give you mums one piece of advice,' Jess piped up, a grin on her face. 'Try and give poor Trish a bit of a break on the baby talk if you can.'

'Thank you! Clearly, a woman after my own heart,' Trish said, not realizing that this was far from the truth and that Jess herself was already on the road to motherhood. 'But what about *Glamazons* and the Peter Jackson movie?' she asked Ruth then. 'Surely you're not giving up your chance of Oscar glory for life as a boring old housewife?'

Charlie and Ruth exchanged smiles. 'Well, actually Charlie thought a little gold statue might be a nice addition to the baby's room, so I'm going to try and do the movie after all,' she grinned and Nina smiled, pleased that the couple had come to some form of compromise about Ruth's career.

Just then, another figure appeared in the doorway and she looked up, expecting to see Ella, who hadn't yet been in to visit her. But to her surprise (and considerable confusion) stood her mother.

Cathy paused on the threshold, taking in the scene around her, before her gaze finally focused in on the tiny baby lying alongside her daughter.

'Mum ...' Nina whispered. 'What are you doing here? How did you ...?'

'Hello darling.'

Charlie put an arm around Ruth's shoulders and with a brief nod at Nina the two of them left the room. Jess and Brian followed them out, Jess offering Nina's mother a small smile. Trish got up from the chair next to the bed and walked towards the door. 'Hey Mrs Hughes,' she said, glancing sideways at Nina, who recalled that Trish didn't know Cathy's current married name.

'Hello ... Trish is it?' the older woman replied. 'Forgive me, I'm still trying to catch up with recent events.'

'Join the club,' Trish said as she left.

There was silence as Cathy – who with her dark hair and petite frame looked like an older version of Nina – approached her daughter. She took a small step forward. 'You could have told me,' she said quietly.

'Funny, I was just about to say the same thing to you.'

Cathy inhaled deeply. 'You mustn't be angry.'

'Funny, I was just about to say the same thing to you,' Nina repeated. She turned her head away and towards the baby. 'All this time ... you lied.'

'I never once lied. Yes, perhaps I'm guilty of omitting a few details, as you are,' she replied, her gaze too resting upon the baby. 'I spoke to Ella just now,' she added quietly. 'And I gather you've filled in some of those blanks.'

Nina looked up. 'How could you have let him do that to me? Leave me out in the open on the steps of a café? How could you?'

'Honey, I'm sorry, but you know it wasn't like that.' She sighed. 'Look, I have always tried to be a good mother to you and regrettably, I didn't take to motherhood the way you appear to have already. I was a mess, I could barely look at you – I couldn't even hold you. Your father thought he was helping – doing me a favor even.'

'A favor? And once you found out what he did, how could you have forgiven him?'

Cathy looked pained. 'Nina, in my defense, I went absolutely crazy when I found that you weren't in your crib. From that day on, I've tried to never let you out of my sight and I always kept you close, didn't I?'

Nina had to admit, that was true. For all her life, Cathy had always doted on her.

'This was the reason that you two split up? The reason that I could never get out of you?'

Cathy nodded. 'There was no other choice. I loved Patrick, but after all of that happened, I realized I wanted you more than anything and I knew that a future with your dad would be too difficult. He was finding it all so hard and it wouldn't be fair on either of you. After all, a crying baby is only the start of the trouble and upheavals involved in raising a child. I knew Patrick wouldn't be able for it, and so I couldn't risk it.'

'Why didn't you tell me he was ... different?'

Cathy sighed. 'How do you even start to explain something like that? Hell, back then *I* didn't know what it was, or that it even *was* a thing. I just knew that Patrick had his ways and despite them, or perhaps even because of them, I loved him.' She sat on the side of Nina's bed. 'Back then, when we first started going out, he was so different to all the other lads our age, so gentle and restful and ... mature I suppose. There was always something almost ... brooding and mysterious about him and I guess I was drawn to that. Not to mention that he's deeply intelligent and as you know, has always had a unique way of looking at life.' She shook her head. 'So when we discovered you were on the way, the natural thing to do was make things official and we got married. But right from the outset, once we started living together, things became difficult. Patrick ... he's such a creature of habit.'

Nina nodded. 'Don't I know it.'

'Still, as I've told you all your life, your father is a good man and he's always been wonderful to us.'

'I still don't understand how he could just throw me away ...'

'It wasn't like that pet. He loved you back then, same as he loves you now, but you must remember that he struggles so much with change. Imagine how it would feel just now if you baby's arrival mystifed or even terrified you. Can you imagine that?'

Nina looked at the sleeping face of her son and felt her heart twist. 'No ... I really can't.'Nina paused for a moment, musing over what Cathy was telling her. 'Does ... does he love me at all?

Cathy nodded. 'Of course he does and I can say that without an absolute doubt. Who do you think called me and asked me to come back?'

Nina's eyes went wide. 'He did?'

'Yes. I guess after what happened yesterday ... he knew you needed me. And here I am.'

Nina tried to take it all in. Given his impassive reaction the day before, she couldn't believe that Patrick had even realized that anything was amiss, let alone taken the initiative to contact Cathy because Nina 'needed her'.'

'Tony must have been pleased,' she said jokingly. 'Where were you?'

'Paris and he was fine about it. Actually I think he was delighted; Paris really isn't his cup of tea,' she added wryly and Nina smiled.

'Then Ella called me and filled me in on the rest. Look, I've told you before how your father never let us want for anything, even after we split up,' Cathy went on. 'He conceded that maybe it was best not to stay together yet he never hesitated to do anything for you, provide you with anything and everything you needed. That was his way of showing he cared, his way of showing he loved you. He might not be able to do it with hugs and kisses, but he had his own ways. I have all the respect in the world for your father Nina and I would ask that you try to have the same. It would mean a lot.'

Nina nodded and seeing her son stir in the crib, she reached across and lifted him into her arms. 'I really wish you would have told the truth sooner.'

'About being left at the café? I didn't see the point. After all, there was nothing to be gained from telling you about that as it was all sorted within a day or two. As for the truth about your dad, well I thought about broaching it many times over the years, but the timing just never seemed right. And I suppose I was worried that the notion might change your opinion of him, and I didn't want that.'

'I always thought he was just ... odd.'

'Exactly, so I didn't see any reason to rock the boat. It wouldn't have done either of you any good. But now that you do know, how do you feel? About what happened I mean.'

Nina kissed her baby's forehead. 'Well, it was a long time ago, there was no real harm done and I suppose, knowing what I know now, I guess I can forgive him,' she said.

Cathy exhaled. 'Thank you. And speaking of keeping secrets, darling daughter,' she went on her tone changing, 'when exactly were you planning on telling me you were pregnant?'

Nina smiled sheepishly. 'You know now.'

'Indeed I do. So do I get to hold my grandson?'

'Sure.' She handed the baby to her mother.

'He really is perfect, sweetheart and he looks just like you.' Cathy paused for a moment. 'I'm assuming Steve is the father.'

'Yes, but he's not going to be in the picture.' She shrugged. 'His loss.'

Cathy nodded, apparently realizing that now wasn't the time to ask questions. 'Well, if anyone can do this, you can and you know of course that I'll do as much as I can to help you. When will they release you? I can get your clothes and everything sent back to our place.'

Nina shook her head. 'I'm not going back to Dublin, Mum, I've decided to stay in Lakeview.'

'In Lakeview? But you don't even like it there – and I thought considering ...'

'No, I have friends there and sort of a job. I can get a place of my own, maybe a little flat on Main Street or something. Besides, you've done enough for me over the years and you deserve to be able to live your own life now, without having to be roped in for more child-minding.'

This had been Jess's idea, and she was right. All along Nina had been worrying about disappointing her mother and the baby being an additional burden on her – so much so that she'd never really conceived bringing up the child without Cathy's support.

'Well, what's to stop you bringing it up in Lakeview?' Jess had suggested. 'You said yourself you're happy there, you'd have a job and lots of friends who I'm sure would only be too happy to help you out.'

'You're serious about staying there?' Cathy asked now. 'Even after all that's happened?'

Nina nodded, feeling more and more certain by the minute. 'I think it might be a good place to raise a child, better than a big city.' She smiled gently at the baby. 'And of course little Patrick will have a playmate soon too, when Ruth has hers ...'

'Little Patrick?' Cathy interrupted, her voice catching a little.

Nina nodded. 'Yes, Patrick,' she repeated smiling. 'I think it suits him.'

Cathy had tears in her eyes. 'I think it's wonderful.'

Just then there was a quiet, muffled knock on the door. 'Come in,' Nina called out and the door opened slowly to reveal a very nervous looking Patrick.

'Dad!' she exclaimed, taken aback. In his arms he carried a bunch of pink roses, and as always glanced around wary and unsure of himself. 'Please come in,' she greeted warmly.

He walked forward, taking in his surroundings, his gaze resting first on Nina and then turning to Cathy and the small bundle she held in her arms.

'It seems we're grandparents now, Patrick,' Cathy smiled happily, encouraging him to share in the joy of the moment.

'Oh.' He hesitated a little. 'I suppose we are.' His gaze moved to

Nina and it looked as though he was searching for some kind of reaction from her – as if worried that she'd exhibit the same postnatal symptoms that Cathy had.

'Dad, it's OK. I'm OK, I promise.'

He nodded, still seeming unsure of himself.

'Would you like to meet your grandson?' Cathy asked brightly.

'Yes please.' He looked at the baby and then abruptly held out his arms which Nina noticed were shaking.

'It's OK Dad, he won't break.'

Patrick gently cradled the tiny baby in his arms. 'He looks like you, Nina.'

She beamed. 'Thank you. His name is Patrick too – after you.'

There was a long silence and eventually her father bit his lip and for the first time in what felt like forever, looked directly at her. 'Oh. I hope he likes fixing things too.'

And as her parents gathered around the newborn, Nina smiled tearfully, realizing that already, her little baby son had fixed everything.

THANKS FOR READING **The Truth About You. Continue for an excerpt of *The Getaway*, another unputdownable novel from Melissa Hill, out now in print and kindle.**

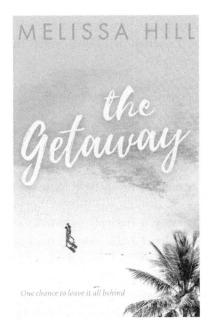

Also available via Kindle Unlimited.

THE GETAWAY

EXCERPT

Another unputdownable book club read from the Irish Times #1 best-selling author.

Careful what you wish for...

Three women routinely take the same coastal train service to the city. All they have in common is that each is desperate for an escape.

Newly-wed Dara would give anything to go back in time and make a different choice. But she's married now and nothing can change that. Can it?

Louise always wanted to be slim, pretty, and popular. So she can't believe it when her luck seems to be changing. But is it all too good to be true?

Widow Rosie has always tried her best to make her children happy. Even though they're both grown adults, they seem to expect more from her than ever.

But one summer morning, a shock incident on the train allows each woman an opportunity to alter life's trajectory. Will they have the courage to grasp it?

1

*S*he couldn't miss this. And come hell or high water, she was *not* going to miss it.

But the rumbling was getting louder by the second, so despite her stilettos and pencil skirt she had no choice but to make a run for it. If she failed to make the train today she was in big trouble. Big. *Huge.*

She wasn't the only one running late this morning either she noted, seeing another harried commuter rush to the ticket booth. Tapping her travel pass, she scurried through the barrier and breathed a sigh of relief to see that the train was still at the platform.

Just in time.

Breathing heavily, she nipped inside the double doors seconds before they shut – nearly catching the hem of her trench in the process. But the person behind hadn't been fast enough, and as the train pulled off she felt bad for the unlucky straggler.

The coastal commuter service to Dublin was a busy route with usually only standing room in the carriages. Though today there was a precious seat a little way down that no one else seemed to have noticed.

She hurried to nab it, but as she pushed through the standing crowd her handbag slipped off her shoulder, falling awkwardly onto the ground.

Typical. She inelegantly bent down to try and pick it up – forward momentum plus the weight of the briefcase in her other hand, jerking her off balance.

"Here you go." A girl sitting nearest the aisle retrieved the bag, giving it a blatantly appreciative glance while handing it back. "Orla Kiely?"

"Yes it is, and thanks," she replied a little breathless. Sinking gratefully onto the seat, she put her briefcase on the floor and her prized handbag on her lap. The fashion label had since closed and thus these bags were rare as hen's teeth.

Dusting off her skirt, she shuffled exaggeratedly, trying to give a not-so-subtle hint to the guy beside her to move over. She'd noticed some extra padding on her ass lately, but his manspreading was ridiculous.

Catching the eye of an older lady sitting across the way, she flashed a conspiratorial smile. The woman was reading one of those fluffy romance novels and certainly didn't look to be on a work commute. Then again, she thought, catching sight of some guy in a tracksuit and briefcase pushing his way through the crowds, who knew what people might be up to?

Lucky thing, she thought eyeing the older woman's book and trying to remember the last time she had been able to lose herself in a cosy read.

Speaking of which . . . She reached for her briefcase and withdrew the documents for this morning's meeting. Cosy reading it wasn't.

Her idle musing was cut off by an overpowering, ear-splitting screech. *What the hell?* Heart leaping, she instinctively put her hands to her ears.

Then the carriage began to shudder, her body tensed and the hairs on the back of her neck stood up. She looked wildly around, wondering if everyone else was experiencing the same thing.

Yes, the older woman across from her looked terrified, confused . . . everyone looked bewildered . . . and then there was an almighty roar, a sound so deafening it was unlike anything she'd ever witnessed.

Her heart hammered and her brain flooded with even more

excruciating noise . . . then her seat jerked. . . and time slowed to a crawl. Until surreally, the entire carriage lifted and the vehicle seemed to be travelling in thin air.

But that couldn't possibly be, she reassured herself, before a tremendous force winched her out of her seat.

Trains couldn't fly. Could they?

---

he typically self-assured and flawlessly composed journalist was ragged and white-faced as she looked unseeingly into the camera. In her earpiece, she heard a voice from the news studio.

"Our correspondent, Clare Rogers is now live at the scene of this morning's tragedy. Clare, can you tell us anything concrete at this point?"

"Emergency services have just arrived at the location, so details are sketchy at this time." Clare's voice trembled as she spoke. "All I can confirm is that a train on the morning coastal commuter route to Dublin City has derailed and crashed at Sandymount Beach."

"Any indication as to what might have caused this horrific incident?" the news anchor prompted.

"Again we can't confirm any details at present. Rail Ireland will be making an official statement soon. But I spoke to some witnesses earlier – motorists stopped at the level crossing – who helped me reconstruct the scene. They saw or rather heard, the train braking from some distance, suggesting that the driver may have identified a problem with the signal. The locomotive derailed a few yards from the gates, careered across the tracks and crashed through a stone wall before ending up on the beach here behind us." Clare swallowed hard. "Luckily, there was no southbound train passing at the time," she added solemnly.

"So the driver tried to avoid crashing?"

"Again, we're just not sure. No doubt there will be a full investigation in time, but at the moment the emphasis is of course on the rescue effort."

"Signal failure, something that's unusual for our rail network, isn't it?" Richard went on – intent on getting to the bottom of the situation.

"Correct. Derailments are sadly more common for our neighbours in the UK, given that multiple rail companies operate there. The system is fine-tuned but signals can occasionally be confused. Which," she added, struggling to keep her voice even, "can lead to incidents like this."

"But we have only one rail carrier in Ireland, thus such mistakes are rare."

"Usually. But in recent months, Rail Ireland has been carrying out upgrades throughout the network. Although it is only speculation at this stage – and again, the company will issue a statement soon – it would appear that the signalling system on this particular crossing failed."

"Which would have serious implications for all involved," Richard finished.

"Very serious implications indeed," Clare agreed, her voice grim. "At this time of the morning, the train is packed with commuters, regular users of this busy city route, and – as I'm sure viewers can tell from our footage – there's likely a high incidence of serious injury and undoubtedly some fatality too."

"Thank you, Clare – we'll come back to you later for the Rail Ireland press conference."

Live footage of the wreck disappeared, and the feed cut back to the newsroom, where the anchor looked somberly into the camera.

"Our thoughts and prayers go out to any viewers at home with loved ones onboard the coastal service this morning. Stay tuned for further updates."

3

---

*R*osie Mitchell waited patiently at the platform. The train was a little bit late this morning, she noted, checking her watch. Not that it mattered to her. A mid-sixties retiree, she was long past the morning rush.

Thank goodness for the train all the same, otherwise she'd be stuck. Her late husband Martin had always been the one to do the driving and often encouraged her to learn, but she never had any interest.

Luckily her home town of Lakeview was the first stop on the commuter route to Dublin. She and her family had lived for decades in the popular tourist village, centred around the broad oxbow lake from which it took its name. The fact that it had direct train access to the capital made it even more popular with visitors and relocating city families.

Rosie liked the train and enjoyed being able to sit back on the journey and admire the picturesque coastal view, gaze at the birds weaving in and out over the cliffs at Greystones, or stare in awe at the crystal clear waters of beautiful Killiney Bay.

Or if the day was cloudy and the scenery not so spectacular, she would read a book. Sometimes she'd be so stuck in the story that she didn't notice the hour or so journey.

So she wouldn't dream of getting a car. What was the point? The station was a short walk from her house, and with the service running multiple times a day, she had plenty of options. She could nip into the city whenever she fancied and her friend Sheila's new place was close to the rail line, as was her daughter Sophie's house.

For the moment anyway.

The train finally pulled in, and Rosie stood back, patiently waiting until the cluster of younger commuters were seated before she boarded. The upside of this was that she wouldn't get pushed and shoved. Since putting her back out in a badminton match a few months ago, her balance wasn't as sure as it used to be, and she liked to take her time. Course, the downside of waiting was that she was often left without a seat. But Rosie didn't mind. These people all had a hard slog ahead of them, whereas she didn't have a care in the world.

In fact, wasn't she the lucky one – a lady of leisure meeting with her daughter? She'd hate to have to face into work now like her fellow passengers. You could see the stress and strain in their expressions – all preoccupied with whatever awaited them. It was a shame really; the lengths people had to go to these days just to keep their heads above water.

It had been a lot different when she and Martin were starting out. Neither of them had to spend hours commuting and they were the better for it.

Her husband had worked in his father's gardening business in Lakeview since he was old enough to use a trowel, and Rosie had worked in the tourist office. They'd bought a house close to town so she could walk to work, while Martin went off in his van to wherever he happened to be working that day.

She smiled sadly as she thought of her beloved husband. There wasn't a day that she didn't think of him, or miss him, but she couldn't complain. They'd had a wonderful marriage, two healthy children, and in all their years together rarely a cross word had passed between them.

They'd both known that the day would come when she would be left on her own. High blood pressure was in Martin's family and when he suffered two near-fatal heart attacks in his latter years, it became clear that a simple change in lifestyle or medication wasn't going to save him. But it was lovely that he'd died doing what he loved, tending the roses out in the back garden – the evening sun just beginning to fade when Rosie found him.

Eighteen months ago she had buried the one great love of her life, having made him a promise that she would keep going, keep laughing and smiling and enjoying life, so that it wouldn't seem all that long until she saw him again. At times it was hard but Rosie was doing her best to keep that promise.

Anyway, she was very lucky. Her two adult children were happily married and with good jobs, David to a lovely Liverpool girl named Kelly (there was no sign of kids yet, and Rosie wouldn't dream of asking) and working as a builder in the UK.

Sophie and her husband Robert had toddler Claudia and good jobs too, but were still on the hunt for a house. That was another hardship for the younger generation. House prices in Dublin were obscene.

Today her daughter was taking Rosie to view a house she had her eye on.

"Mum, it's just ... perfect," she'd gushed on the phone the day before. "You've simply *got* to see it."

While she was delighted with her daughter's enthusiasm Rosie couldn't help feeling a little disappointed that Sophie would want to live so far away on the other side of the capital.

Still, it would be nice to see the three of them settled somewhere other than the city centre rental they were in now. There wasn't much space in an apartment, and with Claudia hitting the terrible twos, it couldn't be good for them all to live in what was basically one big room. With luck, this house Sophie wanted her to see today was a tidy semi-d like Rosie's own, with a small garden for Claudia to run around in.

The train emptied some of its passengers at the first city stop, and Rosie sank gratefully onto a recently-vacated seat.

Her back had been giving her a bit of trouble lately, and as much as she tried to tell herself otherwise, there was no denying that she was starting to feel the effects of advancing age.

Despite how energetic and cheerful she might want to feel, she *wasn't* getting any younger, was she? Rosie smiled. She definitely wasn't one of those glamorous granny types. With their coloured hair, perfect make-up and up-to-the-minute fashion, these women looked for all the world like they were still in the first flush of youth.

Sophie had injections into her face to keep the wrinkles at bay, which sounded horrific, but that wasn't Rosie's way. No, she was going to let her auburn hair go as grey as it liked, and her skin as wrinkly as it wanted – weren't these marks of a life lived? Getting older was nothing to be ashamed of and as much as you might like to, you couldn't outrun time.

But today Rosie wasn't running anywhere, she chuckled, getting off the train at Connolly Station and heading to the nearest bus stop. Shame that Sophie's car was in for a service today, otherwise her daughter could've collected her. Because today's train had been late, Rosie had missed the usual bus connection, but such was life.

She reached into her bag and took out the novel she was reading to pass the time.

The bus duly arrived, and forty or so minutes later, Rosie finally reached her daughter's apartment building.

She took extra care selecting the right buzzer, always afraid that she'd push the wrong one and wake up some poor misfortunate sleeping off night duty or something. Originally from County Clare, and despite living in Lakeview for all of her married life, she still couldn't shake off the 'small village inferiority complex' as her husband used to call it.

Rosie called it good manners and concern for a fellow human being, but outgoing and confident all his life, Martin didn't understand.

Nor it seemed, did Sophie.

"Mum, I'm just drying my hair – can you hold on for five minutes?" her daughter's voice blared tinnily through the speaker.

"No problem," Rosie replied agreeably, although the coastal chill was making her fingers numb.

"Hi!" It was a good ten minutes before Sophie appeared downstairs, dark hair sleek and shiny, and make-up beautifully applied. Her daughter always looked so stylish, and today she was dressed in a gorgeous fitted suit, something that even Rosie's inexperienced eye could see had cost an arm and a leg.

But it couldn't have cost that much because Sophie and Robert were mad saving for this house. Knowing her daughter's incredible talent for spotting a bargain, she had probably picked up the outfit for next to nothing.

"Sorry about keeping you waiting, but I think you were a little early – I said ten thirty, didn't I?"

Sophie could be a little bit scatty sometimes.

"No, the train was late actually – where's Claudia?" Rosie stepped into the hallway, eager to get out of this cold. Although it was supposed to be summer, the Irish seasons generally set their own agenda.

Sophie linked her mother's arm and steered her back outside. "With the childminder of course. I couldn't bring her with us – we'd have no peace with her wailing and whinging and *touching* everything."

"Oh." Rosie was disappointed. She had been looking forward to spending time with her only granddaughter. "Maybe we could pick her up after?"

"Ah Tracy offered to take her for the day – she knows I need the break," Sophie answered dismissively. "And of course, she won't say no to the money either." Rosie nodded reluctantly as her daughter chattered on. "Oh, Mum, I am just *dying* for you to see this place – it is truly incredible!"

"I'm sure it is, pet, but don't get your hopes up too much either, OK? You know yourself there's a lot of competition out there and – "

"Mum, this is ours – I just know it is!"

As they ambled towards the residents' carpark, Rosie had to smile at her daughter's enthusiasm. She had been the very same as a young-ster, always full of excitement and mischief.

The kids had been quite the handful growing up, and while Martin always insisted that Rosie spoiled and sheltered them too much, she was proud to say that they had both turned out well. 'A credit to them,' her own mother might have said, had she been alive today to see it.

"And I thought we might go for a nice lunch and a chat after – what do you think?"

Rosie was thrilled. A good old gossip with her daughter was long overdue. Although they spoke on the phone, she hadn't seen Sophie in a while, and she wanted to tell her all her news and she wouldn't mind confiding in someone about how her back was starting to give her a bit more trouble and . . .

She was startled when the flashy yellow sports car in front of them beeped noisily.

"What do you think?" Sophie grinned, proudly waving keys.

"Is this yours?" Rosie gasped in confusion. A brand new car? Despite herself, she couldn't help feeling a bit hurt. If her car was no longer giving trouble, why hadn't Sophie collected her from the station instead of having her wait twenty minutes in the cold and then another twenty on the bus? And how on earth would they get a child seat into that tiny thing?

"Yep," Sophie confirmed happily.

"But what about the old one? The one that was giving you trouble."

"I told you it was having a service because I wanted this to be a surprise." Sophie looked a bit crestfallen. "Don't you like it?"

"Of course I do." Now Rosie felt guilty. "It's lovely, pet – I can't wait to get a spin in it."

"Well, you won't have long to wait!" Her good humour restored, Sophie opened the driver-side door and sat princess-like at the steering wheel, while her mother eased herself into the passenger seat. She tilted the rear-view mirror and applied a fresh coat of lipstick. "Ready?" she asked, turning the key in the ignition.

Rosie's back ached from trying to manoeuvre herself into what amounted to little more than a biscuit tin. Sophie's swerving and quick lane-changing all the way to Malahide didn't help much.

About fifteen minutes later, they pulled onto a quiet tree-lined avenue.

Rosie was certain that behind all those expensive wrought-iron gates, intercoms and granite stonework were equally expensive houses – houses way beyond the reach of a part-time insurance clerk and her department store manager husband. There was a For Sale sign outside the one at the end, but surely they couldn't even *dream* of . . .

But Sophie slowed the car in front of the gates, rolled down the window and pushed the intercom button.

"Sophie Morris," she announced in a haughty voice that Rosie had never heard her use before.

"Love, surely you couldn't be thinking of buying a house like this? It must cost an absolute fortune."

"Well, in the scheme of things, it isn't that expensive," she replied airily. "Anyway, I just want you to take a look at it first and see what you think. We'll discuss the rest later."

The rest? What rest? Rosie wanted to ask.

But then it hit her. Just then she realised why Sophie was so eager to show her this house today, why her daughter had been so cheerful and attentive these last few weeks.

She had to give her credit, to be fair. Sophie had bided her time and had waited until well after her father's death before she once again raised The Question.

Now, she felt sad and more than a little used. She supposed she should have known better than to think that her daughter had brought her all the way out here just to get her opinion. Sophie didn't need an opinion – her mind was already made up.

And deep down Rosie knew that this time she probably *would* give in. In truth, she would have that first time too, only Martin wouldn't hear of it. Her husband had been dead set against the idea and that had been the end of the matter.

Until now.

As they approached the admittedly beautiful, but eyewateringly expensive house, Rosie sighed inwardly. Martin would not be happy with her – not happy at *all*.

END OF EXCERPT.

Continue reading THE GETAWAY, out now in print and kindle.

ABOUT THE AUTHOR

International #1 and USA Today bestselling author Melissa Hill lives in County Wicklow, Ireland.

Her page-turning contemporary stories are published worldwide, translated into 25 different languages and are regular chart-toppers in Ireland and internationally.

A movie adaptation of SOMETHING FROM TIFFANY'S - a Reese Witherspoon x Hello Sunshine production - is due for worldwide release in Dec, 2022.

THE CHARM BRACELET and A GIFT TO REMEMBER (plus sequel) were also adapted for screen by Hallmark Channel, and multiple other projects are currently in development for film and TV.

www.melissahill.info

Made in United States
Orlando, FL
20 September 2024

51752014R10232